LOVE'S AWAKENING

"Leave the lamp lit, Harmony." It was a gentle command. She could feel his masculinity, knew by instinct what he wanted. She stood rigid, in love but afraid. "Take off your clothes. I want to look at you."

She swallowed, shaking. "I can't."

He reached out to her then, and her eyes teared. She made her legs take her around the table, and she grasped his hand. "Help me Buck. I'm so scared."

"Do you love me?"

Harmony nodded. Buck pulled her closer then, wrapping an arm around her waist and pulling her over him down onto the bed. His broad, strong shoulders hovered over her as he gently kissed her forehead, her eyes, her cheeks, her throat, her lips. The kiss on her lips lingered until he could tell her curiosity and love were overcoming her fear, and finally she began to return the kiss, suddenly eager with a passion that matched his own. . . .

RAPTURE'S GOLD

F. ROSANNE BITTNER

ZEBRA BOOKS
KENSINGTON PUBLISHING CORP.

ZEBRA BOOKS

are published by

Kensington Publishing Corp.
475 Park Avenue South
New York, NY 10016

First printing: September 1986

Printed in the United States of America

To the State of Colorado, rich in history, glorious in beauty; her mountains rising to meet the heavens, her valleys quiet and colorful, warmed by Colorado sunshine

"There's gold in her hills," came the call from Colorado.

And so I answered, coming to this golden land to find a dream.

But it was a different gold I found—not hard and cold . . . but soft and warm.

I no longer seek gold from beneath the earth,

For richer, more dependable, and more beautiful is passion's gold.

The major portion of this story takes place in Colorado, in the vicinity of Cripple Creek, Pike's Peak, and Colorado Springs. In 1893 there really was a gold rush to Cripple Creek, and within a few short years the town's population had grown to 25,000. Although this story is based on that historical fact, its plot and characters are fictitious and any resemblance to persons living or dead, or to events that may have occurred at that time but of which the author is unaware, is purely coincidental. Factual material on the period was derived from the Time-Life/Old West series, especially "The Miners," "The Townsmen," and "The Women," and from other resource books.

Chapter One

A mist began to roll in off the broad, muddy waters as night descended over the docks of St. Louis. Sounds—voices and laughter, bells and whistles of huge steamers—were carried, magnified, over the still waters, so that voices from far away could easily be heard by those on the docks now being quietly deserted. The din of the daytime crowd that swarmed noisily over the pier to board ships heading west had diminished, and now there was only the sound of water lazily lapping against dock posts and boat sides. Few people remained on the docks. At night all activity seemed to take place away from them, in town, where voices could be heard echoing through the mist, along with laughter, the piano music drifting from saloons, the clattering of horse-drawn carriages, and in the distance the rumble of a Kansas Pacific engine which was carrying even more passengers westward by faster but more expensive means. It was 1885, and the westward movement was in full swing.

Little Harmony Jones sat huddled against a barrel,

pulling her plain cotton dress over her bent knees in an attempt to keep warm. She clung to a rag doll and a worn carpetbag, its contents her only other possessions. Earlier, the bright May day had been very warm, and Harmony's mother had carried her cape for her. Now as the mist settled in, Harmony had nothing to put around her shoulders for protection from the damp, cool air. But she tried not to despair. Surely her parents would come for her soon, for they had promised that if she waited here and did not move from this spot, they would come and get her as soon as they had settled a few things with the captain of the steamship they intended to take west.

She had waited faithfully, for she was a good little girl, an obedient child who tried very hard not to make her parents angry. She loved them, even when her father drank too much whiskey and shoved her around, or when her mother pinched or hit her for getting on her nerves. They were Harmony's only security, and after all, what six-year-old child does not have faith in her parents? They would come, and her mother would put the cape around her shoulders and apologize for taking so long to come for her.

Her green eyes began to fill with unwanted tears, for if they came back and found her crying, they would be angry. She thought about going to look for them, but if she moved from this place, they might return and find her gone. No, she could not leave. Her rosy little lips puckered, and a tear slipped down her pudgy, still babyish cheek. Her naturally curly, golden hair, curlier in the damp air, was almost wet now from the mist. It clung to her pretty face in ringlets, enhancing the large green eyes and unusual beauty of this child.

The smell of fish and oil hung in the air, mixed with the pungent odor of seaweed and moss. All women had vanished, and the few men who walked the docks now were loud and usually drunk. Little Harmony huddled farther into the shadow of the barrel, not wanting anyone but her own parents to notice her. She was afraid of strangers, especially the kind who walked these docks at night. A gripping fear crept into her soul. What if one of them saw her! Perhaps he would take out a big knife and cut her into little pieces! Perhaps he would sell her to pirates! Even worse was her fear of that unknown thing she sensed despite her young age—something vile and horrible that wicked men did to little girls—yet she didn't really know just what it was, only that something awful awaited her in the night in this strange place.

Why, oh why, didn't her parents come? In the deep recesses of her mind a small voice gave her the answer: They were not coming. They had abandoned her. But she refused to listen to that voice, for it evoked such terror in her that she wanted to scream. Yet she dared not scream for fear someone would hear her and capture her. No! They would not abandon her! They were her mother and father. She loved them. She was a good girl—as good as she could possibly be. She seldom talked. She was not demanding. She did what they told her to do. Mothers and fathers might get mad at their children, but they did not abandon them!

She closed her eyes, and more tears ran quietly down her cheeks. She prayed to the God she had heard existed, a God she knew little about. Her lips puckered more, and she sniffed. They must come! They must! Yes, they would come soon, and never again would she feel this awful terror, this desperate loneliness. She did not know what to do. Her parents had always made the decisions for her. How could she make her own?

More laughter came to her ears, carried on the mist. Were her parents among those laughing? Were they having a good time on a steamship they had boarded without her? Of course not. They would not have done that. Perhaps something terrible had happened to them. Perhaps some of these evil men had attacked her parents and stolen their money, beaten them and left them for dead! Surely it was something like that, for there could be no other reason that they would not come for her. Perhaps she should sneak away from here and try to find the police, tell them they must search for her parents.

She squeezed the rag doll closer to her breast, her pudgy fingers digging into the cloth desperately. She shivered, fought back more tears, and dreamed about being in bed, with a nice warm comforter covering her, a warm fire nearby. Not that there had always been warm fires where they'd lived. It depended on what hotel they were in, in what city. Sometimes they had slept in a tent or a wagon, or someone's barn. Harmony Jones had never known any real home, for her parents were drifters who made their money by a variety of means—singing, dancing, gambling, and although Harmony did not know it, stealing. They never stayed in one place for long, and had often complained that soon they would have to light so Harmony could go to school. But their discussions of settling down always ended in drinking and arguments, so Harmony quietly stayed out of their way, trying to attract as little attention as possible and blaming herself for her parents' unhappiness and anger.

It was the same wherever they went, Harmony waiting in the shadows while her parents put on performances, gambled, or sometimes just left for a while and then came back with money in their hands. When they had money they drank and often fought. Finally, when they slept, Harmony would curl up under her quilt, hugging her doll, and sleep too, pretending a barren hotel room was a grand house—a home of her own that she did not have to leave.

Now she would give anything just to be in a hotel room, wherever it might be; to be with her parents, wherever they might be. There had been times when her mother held her, rare moments when the woman cried and told Harmony she was sorry for hitting her, when she asked the child to forgive her. And, of course, Harmony had always done so, for she loved her mother. She loved her father too. When he didn't drink, he was often jolly and joking. On occasion he played the banjo for Harmony and sang a funny song about dancing turkeys, making her laugh. Sometimes her parents were not kind to her and they didn't have a real home, but Harmony was sure that they loved her, just as she was sure she loved Patrick and Sadie Jones. They would never abandon her.

She could not hold back the tears then, for terror and indecision finally erupted in her. She squeezed as far back against the barrel and the wall behind her as she could. She would wait there until morning, she decided. When the sun came out, everything would be better. Then she could walk along the docks, unafraid, and find a policeman and tell him something must have happened to her parents. A policeman would find them; everything would be all right. However, another voice told her a different story, and tears kept welling up until they seemed to be emerging from her soul.

Moments later she saw four legs in front of her, two of them wearing shiny black boots, the other two wearing baggy pants that fell over old, worn shoes. She quickly wiped at her eyes and looked up into the faces of two men, both grinning, both holding whiskey bottles and wearing ugly black woolen jackets and worn caps.

"Well, looky here," one of them remarked, bending down and grasping her face in a rough, dirty hand. "A little golden treasure."

She jerked her face away, her heart filled with terror. She quickly pushed with her feet to get back even farther, but there was no place to go. The man put a hand on her knee.

"What are you doin' here, little angel?" he asked with a grin. "You lost?"

She stared at him with wide, frightened eyes, and he grabbed her arm then, jerking her up and shoving her over toward the second man, who grasped her about the waist and held her up.

"Say, I know somebody who'd pay a dear price for something like this," the second man said in a near growl.

"That's what I'm thinking," the first man answered, taking a slug of whiskey. "Only nothin' says we can't have our own fun first, Harry. I don't see nobody around claimin' the pretty little thing."

Harmony's terror erupted in a fit of screaming and kicking and punching. Unwittingly she landed a foot in the right spot, and the second man let go of her so quickly she fell backward. She tried to scramble away, but the first man grabbed her ankle and she screamed more, over and over, until her cries echoed in her ears and all she could feel was the helplessness of being a child in the hands of terrible men.

The train lurched and Harmony awoke with a start. She rubbed at her eyes, realizing she had been having the nightmare again. Had it really been eleven years ago when her parents had abandoned her on the docks? It still seemed like yesterday, and she wondered if the horror of that night would ever leave her. Yet it had all led to this moment. Here she was on a Kansas Pacific train, headed for a new and unknown land, preparing to do something practically unheard of for an inexperienced, single, seventeen-year-old girl. She was going to Colorado to take over a gold claim she had inherited.

She shifted, stretching weary, sore muscles; then she strained to visualize the Rocky Mountains from her window, certain she should be seeing them at any moment even though the train still rumbled through Kansas. To her disappointment she saw only more vast, rolling hills, fences and farmland, cattle and horses, and here and there a small dot of a farmhouse. Sometimes the hills disappeared, and the land was totally flat and seemingly endless, the horizon always the same. She began to wonder if there really were any mountains somewhere in the West. Perhaps she didn't even really own a gold claim.

It was difficult for her not to think the worst about everything, for the worst always seemed to be happening to her. She knew she must be on guard almost constantly now, for she was young and alone. She had purchased a small pistol, which she carried in her handbag but didn't really know how to use. Now she wondered if she was actually capable of shooting anyone should the need arise.

Her predicament was both frightening and exciting. She felt brave and grown-up at one moment, at another terrified, six years old again and abandoned on the docks. Could she really do what she intended—go to a wild town like Cripple Creek and take over what was rightfully hers? How on earth would she even find the claim? Someone would have to lead her there. How would she know who to trust?

She swallowed her doubts. She would find a way, no matter what. She had money and property, and she would make good on what Brian O'Toole had left to her. She looked out the window again. A few buffalo, perhaps only ten or twenty, could be seen in the distance. She stared. She'd never seen the shaggy beasts before and had heard that they were virtually extinct. Apparently that wasn't true. She watched, fascinated, hoping that the Plains Indians were really extinct or safely tucked away on reservations. Yet in watching the buffalo, now disappearing around a bend, and in looking over at the rolling green hills in the distance, she felt a little pang of pity for the Indians she knew nothing about. This had once been their land. It must have been wonderful, being free and having all this land and its game to themselves. Now, though they were on reservations and supposedly well housed and fed, perhaps they felt as abandoned as she had when her parents had left her. Weren't they in the same position in a sense—their lives suddenly and drastically changed, all familiar things removed, suddenly dependent on others for help?

It was confusing to think about how some peoples' lives were determined by fate or chance. What if her parents had not deserted her? Where would she be today? And what if Brian had not found her on the docks, had not left her a gold claim? How much control did people really have over their lives?

Yet if fate had brought Brian O'Toole to her rescue that night, then thank God for fate—and for Brian. She rested her head against the cushioned seat again, remembering that night and all the events that had led to this moment, events that had made her what she was today, determined to be independently wealthy, secure in her own property, dependent on no one. That childhood experience on the docks had left its mark on her emotionally, as had that terrible night not long ago when she'd almost been raped. Maybe in Colorado she could forget those things, could come to terms with the fact that her parents had not loved her and had left her to whatever fate awaited her on the docks. The docks . . . Yes, she had endured things and had had to assume responsibilities no child should have to handle. But Brian probably had thought he'd done his best. At least he'd left her his claim.

Brian. Poor dead Brian. She would miss him. She was indebted to him, for if it were not for Brian O'Toole, where would she be today? Brian . . . Her mind floated back again . . . back to that awful night. . . . She could still feel the grip on her ankle, the terror of tugging to get away. . . .

"Let go of her!" she'd heard a man's voice demand.

19

"Let go or I'll cut you from one earlobe to the other!"

The hand grasping her ankle suddenly released its hold, and Little Harmony turned to look up at a third man, who held a knife to the throat of the man who'd grasped her ankle. Her mind whirled. If she ran, she might run into more men like the first ones, with no one to help the next time. This third man obviously had come to her aid. She could only hope she was right. She backed away, moving toward her doll and carpetbag, while the man with the knife shoved the second man toward the first, waving the knife at both of them.

"You filthy scum!" he snarled at them. They both backed away. "Let's see how well fully clothed men swim when they're stinking drunk!" He charged at Harmony's abductors and they started to run. One tripped on a rope and fell, and the man with the knife shoved the blade into its sheath and tackled the second ruffian, spinning him round and landing a sound punch that sent him flying into the water. He turned then and ran after the first man, who had gotten up to flee. He dived, grabbing the man's ankle and making him fall again; then he scrambled up and began to kick him and roll him over until, with a yell and a splash, the man fell off the dock into the water.

The child's apparent savior then stood there, staring after her persecutors for a moment, breathing heavily, watching to make sure they either swam away or drowned. Harmony could not see what happened, but neither of the men reappeared, and the man who had thrown them into the water did not seem to care. He turned, the rage in his brown eyes changing to gentle concern. Harmony watched carefully as he approached, her natural instincts telling her she need not fear this man. His hair was so red it intrigued her, and his eyes were full of a sparkling kindness. In spite of being shorter than the men he had attacked, he had exhibited a mighty fury in her defense, and she saw now that his arms and shoulders were husky and strong.

"Don't you go running off now," he told her gently. "I won't hurt you."

She clung to her doll and carpetbag, pressing her back against the wall of a warehouse as he came closer and knelt in front of her. "Who are you?" he asked. "What are you doing here?"

She swallowed, wiping at more tears. "I'm waiting . . . for my parents," she whimpered. "They'll be here . . . any minute."

The man looked around, unable to see up and down the docks because of the misty darkness. He frowned and turned back to her.

"Where did they go?"

She could not stop her breathing from being quick and desperate. She must believe they were coming! "They . . . went to talk to a man . . . a captain of one of the steamships. We're all going west . . . my mama and daddy . . . and me."

The man sighed and rubbed at his eyes. "How long ago did they leave you here?" he asked, sounding almost angry again.

"I don't know, mister. The sun was still out. We'd just ate lunch. They told me to sit here and wait . . . and they'd come back. They'll be here pretty soon. I know they will!"

She started to cry harder and he grasped her arms gently. "All right. All right. Don't get excited, honey. Did those men hurt you?"

When she sniffed and shook her head, he felt rage in his heart at seeing such a beautiful child abandoned in such a place. If the two men had carried her off . . .

"What is your name? And your parents' names?" he asked.

Her little chest heaved in frightened gasps. "Harmony. My name is Harmony Jones. My daddy . . . is Patrick Jones, but everybody calls him Patty. My mother is Sadie Jones. Daddy plays the banjo . . . and they both sing and can dance. They . . . make people laugh. We travel all over, singing and dancing and making people laugh. Mama is very pretty, with gold hair, curly like mine. Daddy has brown hair and blue eyes . . . and he always wears a jacket with red and white stripes on it." Her tears flowed harder again. "Something terrible happened to them! I know it did, or they wouldn't have left me here alone!"

The man sighed and patted her shoulder. "Sure. That's probably the reason," he told her, not believing it himself. Many people had been abandoned here by westward-bound dreamers, often children. "But you know you can't stay here all night, don't you, Harmony? More men might come along like the two I threw in the river. Why don't you let me take you to a warm house, where a very nice young lady lives. She'll give you something to eat and tuck you into bed so you'll be safe from ruffians. In the morning, we'll go to the police and report your missing parents. They can search for them, and we can check the passenger rosters of the steamers tomorrow to see if their names were on any of the lists. Wouldn't that be better than staying here where it's cold and dangerous?"

She studied his kind brown eyes and warm smile. Did she have any choice but to trust this man?

"I . . . guess so," she replied. "But I don't know your name."

He gave her a wink. "My name is Brian O'Toole, and I own a warehouse on these docks. I was working late, lucky for you. I was just on my way home when I heard you screaming."

"A warehouse?"

"That's right. I own a big supply store in town, and I keep a warehouse down here for storing things that are coming in or going out—mostly things coming in from factories farther east, and going out to places in the West where supplies are often hard to come by."

She hugged her doll closer. "Who is the lady?"

"Where I am taking you?"

She nodded, and he picked up her carpetbag.

"Her name is Rebecca—Rebecca Peters—and she will soon be my bride. Becky's only eighteen, but she's a woman, for sure, and I love her. You will too. She'll take you under her wing like a mother hen."

Harmony studied him intently. Although he was only thirty, to her child's eyes he seemed much older. Her curiosity about this man who owned a big store and a warehouse, and about the girl called Rebecca, stirred enough interest in her to calm her a bit. She wiped at her eyes again and reached out trustingly to take the hand he held out to her. Her tiny hand was lost in his big palm as he slowly began to walk along with her.

"That's quite a name you have there," he told her. "Harmony. It's very different, and very pretty."

"Thank you, Mister O'Toole."

"You must call me Brian. How old are you, Harmony?"

"I'm six years old. Mama and Daddy were going to

23

start me in school soon. Is there a school here?"

"Oh, yes. We have lots of schools."

As they walked along quietly, Harmony looked back, but she could no longer see the barrel where she'd been sitting. An aching loneliness crept through her, for she suddenly feared that she was never going to see her parents again. Her mind was filled with confusion and despair. This man was helping her, yet she didn't even know him. What if the woman called Becky wasn't really kind? What if this man had some evil fate in mind for her? She kept staring up at him as they walked, intrigued by his red hair and the abundance of freckles on his face and arms. Surely he didn't mean to do her harm. He had risked his life to save her from the men who had attacked her. She wondered if he was one of the rich men her parents often talked about, a man who had everything. After all, he did own a big store and a warehouse, and he dressed nicely. Whatever he was, there was no doubt he was all she had at the moment, and with every passing second his valiant efforts in her defense became more magnified. She was quickly coming to the conclusion that perhaps he was the strongest man in the world.

He led her away from the docks and up a dark, cobblestoned alley to a wide street that was well lit. There he hailed a passing carriage and gave the driver some instructions; then he got in, plopping Harmony on the seat across from him. He had not said anything or done anything that indicated he meant her harm, and the genuine concern in his eyes continued to reassure her that everything would be all right. She clung tightly to the rag doll and stared at him.

"Sadie and Patty Jones, you say?"

24

She nodded.

"Do you know which ship they were to board?"

She shook her head.

"Are they young? Old? In between?"

She blinked, breathing with more regularity now, feeling calmer. "In between, I guess," she replied. "Mama always said she was too young when she had me."

He grinned and leaned back. "Yes. Well, I suppose to you even twenty would seem old. I'll bet she's no more than twenty-five, if that much. These drifting entertainers often get started young at everything in life." He studied her closely, his eyes running over her pudgy little frame, her angelic face, and her spell-binding green eyes. What things had this child been through, seen, heard? How many places had she been? It would do no good to ask if her parents had been cruel to her, for children usually defended their parents, no matter how bad they were. "I'll say one thing," he added aloud. "If I had a charming little girl like you, I'd not let her out of my sight for even one second, especially not on the docks of St. Louis."

"But they didn't mean to be gone so long," Harmony said. "They were going to come right back. They told me so."

He sighed and nodded. How could he tell her what he thought really had happened? There was little doubt in his mind that she had been left deliberately, and when he checked the steamship rosters the next day, he wagered he'd not find the names of Patrick and Sadie Jones on any of the lists. They wouldn't register under their own names. They were most likely on their way west to make their fortune, and the little girl was a bother to them. No. He would not tell this poor little girl that her parents were not coming, for she believed they were—and for now she had to believe it. As time passed, she would come to understand what had really happened without his having to explain it.

The carriage bounced over the streets, finally coming to a halt in front of a row of houses that all looked the same. The street was well lit and very neat, and all the houses had concrete steps leading up to double doors with frosted glass windows in the upper panels. Brian O'Toole climbed out and lifted Harmony down; then he paid the driver of the carriage and took Harmony's hand, leading her up the steps. Inside, he knocked on a polished oak door, one of many in the hallway where they stood. After several minutes a young woman's voice responded.

"Who is it?"

"It's me, Becky," Brian replied. "I know it's late, but I have a little problem here."

Harmony could hear locks being unhooked, and then the door opened slightly and a very pretty young woman peered out at them. Her face lit up when she looked at Brian O'Toole; then it reddened slightly. "I'm in my robe, Brian."

"Don't worry about that. I need your help. I found this little girl on the docks. Her parents have disappeared. Two men attacked her, and she's got to have a place to stay tonight. I thought maybe you could—"

Before he finished speaking the door was flung open, and the young lady took Harmony by the hand, leading her inside a cozy, nicely furnished apartment. Rebecca said, "How awful. You must be starving and cold, you poor thing." Harmony liked the young woman right away, and before long her stomach was full of warm oatmeal and, dressed in the flannel gown from her own carpetbag, she was put to bed on a sofa, under several warm quilts. All the while the young woman called Becky repeatedly told Brian O'Toole that he must do everything he could to find the "sweet child's" parents. She also fussed over Brian's bleeding knuckles and carried on about how he was going to be killed someday, walking those "awful docks" among those "scurvy men."

Harmony quickly fell asleep due to the strain of the day, a suddenly full stomach, and the wonderful warmth of the quilts. Her last thoughts were that her parents would be found, perhaps tomorrow. And as she fell asleep she vaguely remembered whispered words between Brian and Becky, some kisses, and light laughter just before Becky insisted Brian O'Toole leave before her reputation was ruined and the landlady had words with her.

"You will find her parents, won't you?" Becky asked as Brian went out the door. His only reply was a sigh, and Harmony did not see him shake his head doubtfully.

The days turned into weeks, and the weeks into months. The police found no trace of foul play, and no one named Sadie or Patty Jones had registered on any ship or wagon train. When Brian O'Toole married Rebecca Peters, the child moved with them to a large, fancy house, and she was enrolled in school. She was treated more like a little sister than a daughter by

27

Becky, for Becky was young herself. But Brian was somewhat fatherly, and Harmony found herself beginning to think of him as a father. He was her friend, her protector, her provider. In her loneliness she looked to Brian O'Toole more and more for security and comfort, praying every night that she would always be able to stay with him.

But the fact that someone had helped her and given her a home did little to ease the terror in Harmony's little soul at the memory of that night on the docks. Slowly but surely she admitted to herself that her parents had left her there on purpose, and the awful emptiness she experienced at being abandoned was a feeling she wanted to forget but could not. Somehow she knew, even at her young age, that she would never forget that feeling, and already her mind was building its defenses, determining that she would never again feel that afraid or that helpless. She decided she would never again trust anyone who went away and promised to return. She knew that Brian O'Toole would never go away, for he was rich. He owned a supply store and a warehouse in a big city. He didn't need to travel around like her parents. He had everything right here. And even if he did go away, he would not go alone. He would take his beloved Becky with him, and he would take Harmony—and his brother.

Harmony did not like Brian's brother, Jimmie, who at fifteen came to help Brian with the store shortly after Brian and Becky married. Jimmie was tall and gangly, also with red hair and brown eyes, but he was not nearly as good-looking as Brian. He was a spoiled boy, sent to St. Louis from New Orleans by Brian's grandparents, who had raised the lad after Brian's

28

parents had died. The older couple had hoped that working in Brian's business would give the boy some direction in life and help him settle down, for Jimmie had left school and did not last long at any work he tried. When he arrived at the O'Toole household, there were a few days of bedlam and arguing, during which Harmony kept a low profile, fearing that she would lose her happy home to Jimmie, whom she disliked right away. But it was not long before a stern Brian had the boy working long hours, so that Jimmie was almost never home, and when he was he soon fell into an exhausted sleep. Jimmie had been the only cloud in Harmony's new life in the O'Toole home. But Brian had quickly blown that cloud away.

Harmony spent her days helping Becky: cleaning, sewing, cooking, and doing everything she could to make herself worthy of being allowed to stay in that beautiful house with the people she was growing to love. Months turned into years, and Jimmie matured, although Harmony continued to dislike him. Poor Becky suffered three miscarriages, and her bright happiness began to fade, turning to self-pity and sorrow over not being able to give Brian O'Toole a child. Harmony's own devastation at the realization that her parents had abandoned her was relegated to the recesses of her mind, deliberately buried there to avoid terrible hurt, and she turned her thoughts and heart to the people who had given her a home. She helped Becky as much as she could, for the young woman so often seemed ill, and she put up with constant teasing and derisive remarks from Jimmie whenever the young man was around, for he resented her presence, knowing Brian liked the abandoned girl

29

better than he liked his blood brother. Jimmie called Harmony names whenever he could get away with doing so, and he constantly reminded her that she was living in a "borrowed" home and she'd better watch out or she'd be cast out into the street.

Harmony didn't believe his threats, yet they haunted her, dredging up old fears, making her work even harder to please Brian and Becky O'Toole. She was a bright girl, and Brian began taking her to the store with him, letting her help, much to Jimmie's resentment. By the age of thirteen, Harmony was helping to keep the books, filling out orders, and becoming more of a help than Jimmie had ever been. Brian bragged about her nightly to Becky, boasting about the clever mind and business instincts Harmony possessed even at her young age. Jimmie would glower at her when he did that, but Harmony paid no attention. She was pleasing Brian O'Toole, and that was all that mattered. She owed the man everything, and she would do whatever she could to earn her keep, trusting that the man had grown to love her and certain in her own heart that she loved Brian like a father.

Never had her own parents treated Harmony the way Brian and Becky treated her, and although she resented and now almost hated her parents for abandoning her, she realized that the life she'd ended up living with Brian and Becky O'Toole was much better than the kind of life she would have had with her wandering parents. Still, she could not forget what might have happened to her at the hands of the two men who had attacked her on the dock, or that she would have had her parents to thank for that. When she thought of that night of terror she could not help

30

but hate Patrick and Sadie more and more as she got older. They had left a helpless child on the docks to meet whatever fate might befall her, not even caring; the innocent, trusting love Harmony had once felt for them had vanished. The only thing that kept bitterness from overtaking her was the kindness she had found with the O'Tooles.

From a blond little girl Harmony grew into a young teen, her babyish looks melting into beauty which promised to increase when she became a woman. Golden hair hung in gentle waves nearly to her waist, and her green eyes were catlike and provocative. By the age of fourteen her firm young figure was rounding to enticing proportions, her waist was tiny, her breasts were blossoming, and her cheeks were a natural pink. But her heart and soul held the innocence of the six-year-old child found on the docks. She still did not know the intricacies of the relationship of a man and a woman, nor did she even care to know.

She was simply Harmony Jones, adopted daughter of Brian O'Toole. There were no legal papers. The situation was merely understood, for although Brian often talked of putting something on paper, he never got around to it because of his busy schedule. Harmony didn't care. She loved and trusted the man. He was her father, whether papers said so or not. They got along well, and she worked hard at the store, taking on more and more responsibility, as did Jimmie, who finally began to behave the way a mature young man should. He still was not nearly as business minded as Harmony was becoming, but proud that his younger brother was finally making something of himself, Brian made him a full partner.

It was in her fourteenth year that other changes began to take place in Harmony's life, for that was the year a new gold strike was made near a town called Cripple Creek, Colorado, in that faraway place called the West, the place to which her parents had fled so long ago. All over St. Louis there was talk of gold, and there was a surge of business at the supply store as thousands of men became wrapped up in the quest for gold, many of them coming to O'Toole's to stock up for their westward ventures. Harmony watched with growing fear as these men boasted to Brian about the riches lying in wait out west, telling him that he ought to leave the store to the care of Jimmie and Harmony and seek his fortune in the gold hills of Colorado. Until that time Brian O'Toole had resisted such talk, for he had heard it many times in this city that was a springboard for west-bound travelers. But something was different now. There'd been a sadness about Brian O'Toole since Becky had had another miscarriage that past winter. Even Becky had changed. The pair suddenly seemed to have given up on life; they were drifting apart. Somehow the latest miscarriage, and the depression Becky had fallen into, had affected Brian, and he often said that it might be best if he went away for a while. Harmony tried to ignore such talk. Surely it resulted from his disappointment over not having any children of his own. Surely it was a temporary thing. Becky would recover soon and be her bright, happy self again. Maybe she would even be pregnant soon. But on a rainy spring night in 1893 Brian O'Toole called Harmony into his study, after first talking to Jimmie for over two hours.

Harmony approached the door, looking up at a

grinning Jimmie, whose eyes ran over her voluptuous young shape with a strange hunger she had never seen in them before. She felt a chill run down her spine and she scowled at him as she turned to enter the study. Brian O'Toole sat at his desk, a whiskey bottle in front of him.

"Sit down, Harmony," he told her, his eyes red and tired. The girl obeyed, her heart pounding with dread at the look on his face. He sighed deeply and studied her quietly for a moment, then poured himself another drink. "You're fourteen now, Harmony. And you've got a good sense about the supply business. I'm . . . going away for a while, and I want you to promise to help Jimmie with the store as you've always helped me—and to watch after my darling Becky."

A terrible ache consumed Harmony. No! It was just like the day her parents had said they were going away "for just a few minutes" and that they would be back. But they had not come back!

"You . . . can't!" she gasped. "You can't go away!"

"I must, Harmony. I'm sorry, but things are . . . strained . . . between me and my Becky. With all this talk of gold, I've decided to head west. I need a change, Harmony. I've worked very hard the last several years. And Becky—she's not easy to live with right now. I think it would be good for me to be gone for a while."

Harmony's breathing quickened, and she stood up. "No!" she pleaded. "It will be . . . just like my parents! You won't come back!"

He rubbed his eyes, feeling weary and beaten. "I will, Harmony. It won't be like them. You know me better than that, child. I'll be back in a couple of years."

"A couple of years!" she exclaimed. "That's forever!

What will I do without you? I'll be afraid without you! You're my best friend! You're like a father! I love you!"

In her puckered lips and tear-filled eyes he saw the little girl on the docks again, and his heart ached for her. But he knew he must go. He wanted to go. Something was driving him—something beyond his troubles with Becky, beyond his boredom with the routine of his life. He was tired of watching other men go off to find their dreams, tired of supplying others who went on to find adventure and riches. He was a wealthy man by most standards, but his was hard-earned money. Now he was ready to become even richer in an easier way, and to leave St. Louis and his troubles behind. He knew deep inside what gripped him. It was gold fever, plain and simple, a foolish feeling that led men to do foolish things; yet he could not stop himself, not even when he watched poor Harmony's desperate fear.

"Harmony, it isn't the same as when your parents abandoned you. You have a home here, as long as you need one. Soon some young man will come along and sweep you off your feet and you'll be making a home of your own. You can work at the store as long as you like, and Jimmie and Becky will provide you with all your needs. You have Becky, who loves you as I do, and who needs your friendship. I'm not leaving you alone and helpless."

"Please! Please don't go!" she whimpered. "What have I done to make you want to go?" Again she experienced the feeling that it was her fault that her parents had left her. Why did people always leave her?

"You've done nothing, Harmony. You've been wonderful, and I love you like a daughter. I'm leaving

34

for reasons you could never understand, honey. How can a grown man explain to a fourteen-year-old girl his marital problems, his personal yearning for a one-time chance at adventure and easy riches? A man can't explain those feelings—how it is to be thirty-eight and never to have done one exciting thing in his life, to be thirty-eight and childless, to love a woman and to watch her waste away from self-pity and loneliness for a baby she can't have. I can't explain that, Harmony. I can only ask that you understand it just a little bit, enough to accept it. Love me enough to let me go without breaking my heart with your tears. I've been good to you, Harmony, and I'm not taking away any of your security. Nor am I even taking away my love, for I'll care about you wherever I go, just as I'll care about my Becky. The store is secure, doing a good business, and Jimmie and you both know how to run it. And when you're twenty-one, if you're still interested, I'll see that you get a share in the store. In the meantime you can help Jimmie keep it running well."

"Don't go!" she pleaded. "I never thought . . . you'd ever go away! This is where your store is! This is where the people you love are! Don't leave me! I'll be afraid without you!"

He rose from the desk, walking around and giving her a hug. She clung to him, weeping against his chest. This was the brave, strong man who had fought off two men to save her, the kind man who had opened his home to her and had made her feel important, who had given her an education and taught her about business. This was the father she never would have had if not for the night he'd rescued her. How she wished she could do something to help his own loneliness and despair, for she knew that was why he was going away.

"You needn't be afraid, Harmony," he reassured her. "You have a home. And you're a strong, independent girl. In fact, it will be good for you if I go. You depend on me too much. Perhaps I've let that happen because I've always felt so sorry for you. After your parents deserted you, you relied on me too much for security, Harmony. But it's time you found security inside yourself, time you learned to rely on your own strength, child."

"No! No!" She was a little girl again, huddled against the barrel, hugging her doll, afraid and alone. Would the memory of that night and the way it felt ever leave her? Brian grasped her arms then, gently pushing her away.

"I've got to do it, Harmony. And if you truly love me, you must let me go without making it so hard for me."

Tears streamed down her face and her body jerked in sobs. "Will you . . . write . . . often?"

"Every week. I promise. I'll tell you all about my adventures."

"And you'll come back? Promise? Promise?"

"I'll come back. Promise. I have my Becky to think about too, don't I? Maybe when I come back she'll be all better—happier. And us being apart, well, that will make us just that much happier to be together again." He forced a smile. "And maybe I'll strike gold, Harmony! If I do, I can send for all of you! We'll be rich—much richer than I'll ever be running that damned store."

She studied the sad brown eyes, the red hair now very gray about the temples. To her young mind he was an old man. Maybe he would die before he could come back! All kinds of things happened in that wild place called the West, where there was little law and where ruffians tramped the gold fields. He was no longer as strong and sturdy as he'd been the night he'd fought two men to save her. A little of his spirit had left him with each miscarriage Becky had had.

"Promise me again!" she pleaded, the old terror refusing to leave her. "Promise you'll come back!"

"I said I would, Harmony. You have to learn to trust people."

There was nothing more to do or say. He was right in asking her not to make it hard for him. She owed him that much. She owed him everything. She left him then, crying all night in her room, hugging her rag doll close. Another loved one was leaving her for that strange place called the West. Again that land had coaxed a loved one from his family and everything familiar to him. The same little voice that warned her her parents had abandoned her spoke again, declaring that Brian O'Toole would never come back. There was no comfort for her, no way to stop the torrent of terror and despair that overwhelmed her.

She fell asleep to the memory of bells clanging and water lapping against docks, of distant train whistles. She huddled under the quilts, but in her sleepy mind she was huddled against the barrel again, watching a mist roll in from great muddy waters to shroud her very heart and soul. She was abandoned, alone and helpless, left to face the world with nothing but her own will to survive. Perhaps that is all anyone has after all.

Chapter Two

Harmony bent her head down, stretching her neck which was sore from the monotonous train ride, and she sighed with reawakened grief. She had never seen Brian O'Toole again. Somehow she had known she would not from the day he left. Still she had hoped. Now that hope was gone, but she had one sign that he had thought about her, had loved her. He'd left her a gold claim. Perhaps it was worth nothing. Perhaps it was worth a fortune. She was not going to let anyone swindle her out of it. She would go there herself and make her own decision. At least it was something that was hers, all hers. No one could take it from her. Never before had she had that kind of security. Soon after Brian's departure, Jimmie had set in motion a plan to master her mind and body, using her own insecurity to do so. She now vowed that she would never be so insecure that anyone could ever take advantage of her the way Jimmie had tried to do.

She removed her gloves and pondered life. Surely one could have a hand in determining the course of one's own life, despite the uncontrollable events that fate brought about. Brian O'Toole had left her a gold claim. Now it was up to her to decide what she would do with it, whether she would make it work for her or lose it. Yes. One did have considerable control. The Indians had fought. Defeated, they were now controlled by someone else. She would not let that happen. She would fight and she would win. No one would ever control Harmony Jones. She would be her own master, and would make good use of the good fortune that had come her way. Being young and a woman would not stop her.

She leaned back and listened to the rhythmic clatter of the train wheels as they passed over the rail connections. She could have taken a less expensive means of getting to Colorado, but she knew nothing of wagons and driving a team, and she did not want to board a steamer. The thought of doing so repulsed her, bringing back the memory of that day her parents had boarded one and had never returned. The train was much more practical and much faster—and she could afford it. She had saved frugally. She was glad of that.

The sun fell and she slept, lulled by the motion of the train. When she awoke the terrain had changed. It was more golden now, a little more barren. The hills were steeper but still only hills, not the mountains that had been described to her by those who had been to the Rockies. The train stopped at a town whose name she didn't even know, and passengers disembarked to freshen up and eat breakfast. Harmony kept to herself, ignoring the stares of people who wondered why such a young girl was traveling alone, and of men who admired her beauty. She ate alone, listening to the talk about Denver and the mountains. "You can see them now if you look very hard," a tall man told a thin woman. "At first you think they're just dark clouds hanging on the horizon, but if you look again, you'll realize it's the mountains."

Harmony quickly swallowed her food and walked outside, shading her eyes and staring at the western horizon. Indeed, there was a long, dark line ahead, very distant, very misty. Was it truly the mountains? She boarded the train again, her heart pounding with anticipation and an almost pleasant fear. She wished she had just one friend with whom she could share this experience, just one person who cared and who would know it if something happened to her. What if she died in the mountains as Brian had? No one would even know or care. There would be no one to notify of her misfortune. She would be as oblivious and forgotten as yesterday's wind. It was a strange feeling, a sad feeling. But there was nothing she could do about it.

When the train started rolling, she settled back into her seat and gazed out the window. What big country this was! So different from anything she had ever set eyes on. What was it about this barren land that attracted people so? Perhaps most of them just wanted adventure, courted danger. Who could tell? The temptation of gold, as well as silver and other valuable ores, was also a lure. That temptation had taken her parents from her, then Brian. Now it was her own turn. Would she disappear into the mountains, never to be found or heard from again? It seemed that everyone who came to this land disappeared, as though they fell into a great bottomless abyss.

But she had good reason to come. If she wanted to

41

survive, she had to do this. She closed her eyes again, feeling weary and wishing she could bathe. Trains were so dirty.

It was then a man walked up the aisle, searching for a seat. He noticed a pretty hat ahead of him and grinned to himself. Stealing a glance as he walked past the hat, he decided he'd sit by the pretty girl who wore it so he could see her better. He lowered his tall, powerful body into the seat across the aisle from her, the one that faced her seat, and he noticed she had her eyes closed and was trying to sleep. That gave him the chance to look at her more closely, and he liked what he saw. Her hair reminded him of golden prairie grass gently rolling under the sun. He could only guess at the color of her eyes, but whatever color they were, he was certain they were beautiful. He'd not seen a woman this pretty in a long time, so he settled back, deciding he'd enjoy the short journey he was taking by rail.

As Harmony sighed and shifted in her seat, the man grinned even more, picturing her settling herself between soft sheets, trying to envision how her exquisite form would look with nothing on. It was an enjoyable thought, and one easy to conjure up, for Buck Hanner had had his share of women. But the one he was looking at now seemed so young—too young to be traveling alone by train into the places this train was headed. He had to wonder about her, although he knew he had no right to inquire. Besides, she looked tired. For some reason the circles under her eyes pulled at something inside him, making him feel guilty for thinking of her as just another of many. Instinct told him otherwise. This girl was different, special.

Well, it didn't much matter, he told himself. He'd be

off the train at the next stop and on his way by horseback to Cripple Creek.

Harmony remained oblivious to the man's presence, for she'd quickly fallen into deep thought again, her mind filled with memories of how she had ended up on the train. At the moment she was thinking about Jimmie. How she hated him! She would always hate him for what he had done! It was wonderful to be away from him, no matter what might happen to her.

After Brian had left, she had poured all her energy after school and on weekends into the O'Toole Supply Store. The only way she could avoid the terrible fear that Brian O'Toole would never return, the only way she could feel close to him while he was gone, was to be at the store, where so much of the man who was her whole world still lingered.

She remembered that she felt much older than her fourteen years then, and acted it. By fifteen her bright mind had earned her the equivalent of a high-school education, and she received a certificate signifying that accomplishment. From then on she worked full time in the store. Meanwhile she was blossoming into a young woman of unusual intelligence and she was displaying an uncanny knack for business, often coming up with ideas to make tens of dollars turn into hundreds. But her talents had both frustrated and fascinated Jimmie O'Toole. He did a decent job of managing the store, but he knew he would not have done nearly so well without Harmony's natural instinct for turning a profit.

She hadn't realized then the thoughts that were going through Jimmie's mind. But she could remember the way he'd looked at her. It had made her uneasy, as if she were naked under his gaze. Her sixteenth birthday came, and after that it seemed Jimmie always found an excuse to stand close to her, and to touch her in some way. His behavior unnerved and irritated her, for she'd never liked him.

Now she knew what he'd been thinking. Oh, yes, she knew! She still shuddered at the memory. She'd prayed every night for Brian to return. Her problems would have been solved if he had come back. She would have told him to make Jimmie stop staring at her all the time, to stop hanging around her. And he would have made Becky happier. Poor Becky! She had not gotten any better. If anything, she'd grown much worse after Brian had left, hardly ever speaking to anyone, never smiling.

Harmony remembered those lonely times. Jimmie had frightened her, and she hadn't been able to talk to Becky anymore. More and more she had begun to feel like the little girl on the docks. Brian's letters had been frequent at first, and exciting. But then they had come less often and had sounded somewhat discouraged. He'd had to move into the mountains around Pike's Peak, where there was less likelihood of finding anymore gold. So many men had surged into Cripple Creek that most good sections were already staked. Because of his distance from town, he could not write as often, and the letters were few and far between. After two years, Harmony had been sure he'd come home to St. Louis where he belonged, and that she would feel truly safe again. But he had not, and then on that terrible night Jimmie had attacked her. . . . Again the memory overwhelmed her. She wished she could rid her mind of it, but she was unable to do so. It was only last December—December 1895—that the final events which led her to board a train for Colorado had begun.

Becky O'Toole fell ill that cold December. Confined to her bed with a dangerous cough, she was so weak she was unable to rise from her pillow. Harmony, remembering her promise to care for Brian's wife, stayed home from the supply store to nurse and feed Becky. Although the woman had not been much company the last several months, for years she had been most kind to Harmony, a true friend. Indeed, she was a kind and sweet person who had not minded keeping little Harmony even when newly wed.

Now Harmony's old fear worsened. What if Becky died? Where did that leave Harmony if Brian did not come home? But surely he would return if something happened to Becky! Yes, he would come home and somehow legally assure Harmony of a permanent home. And of course once he got there, he would stay. He'd not found any gold, so why should he go back?

It was the only hope Harmony had. Soon! Brian would come soon! It had been two and a half years. Even if nothing happened to Becky, he would come. He'd promised, hadn't he? He'd said two years, and it had been more than that already. He wouldn't break his promise the way her parents had. Not Brian. He would take care of her as he always had in the past.

She nursed Becky faithfully, bathing her, changing her gown and bed, rubbing creams on her bed-sore skin, feeding her. The care was time consuming and tiring, and Becky did not get better. Harmony began sleeping outside the sick woman's room on a sofa,

45

wanting to be close by so she could hear the terrible coughing and go in to help Becky sit up. When the rocking cough tore at the poor woman's insides, she held her until the spasms subsided and Becky lay back moaning with pain, struggling to breathe.

It was on one such night, while Harmony lay nearly asleep on the sofa, that she was awakened by a hand on her breast. She gasped and sat up, staring wide-eyed at a grinning Jimmie, who had come home late from the store and had obviously been drinking. She yanked the blankets up to her neck.

"What do you think you're doing!" she hissed. "Get away from me!"

He laughed lightly, sitting on the edge of the sofa. She curled up toward the arm, clinging to the blankets. "We hardly ever see each other anymore, Harmony," he told her. "I miss you at the store."

"Why should I care! And get off this sofa!"

He reached out to touch the lustrous blond hair that cascaded over her shoulders, but she jerked her head back, eying him like a she-cat ready to strike.

"Come on, Harmony. You want me and you know it. We belong together, you and me. You can be my partner. We'll build another store, and another. We'll be rich, you and me. The biggest suppliers this side of the Mississippi."

"How dare you touch me!" she almost growled. "And how dare you think I'd want to join with the likes of you! Don't you know how much I've always hated you? You get away from me!"

He snickered. "Harmony. Harmony," he said chidingly. "You're such a little girl. You're just afraid, because you don't know anything about men. You've never had a chance to find out. What a pity—such a wonderful body going to waste. It's time you married and let a man use that body the way it's supposed to be used."

"And who would I marry? You?" Her eyes narrowed, became hard with hatred. "You get away from me!"

He sighed and pretended to get up, then suddenly turned and grabbed her hair, jerking her forward painfully and leaning down to kiss her, a hard, painful kiss that hurt her lips. She grasped his wrists, trying to make him let go of her hair, repulsed by his cold lips and rudely searching tongue, and horrified that someone she hated was touching her this way. He would not let go of her hair, so she reached up and scratched at his eyes, making him break the kiss and cry out.

He quickly grabbed her wrists then, pinning down her arms and burying his face in the fullness of her breasts, mumbling that if she relaxed and let herself enjoy it, it wouldn't be so bad. Horror engulfed her as she thought of the two men who had grabbed her on the docks. Where was Brian now? If he were here, he'd beat his brother for doing this. But there was no one to help her. Becky lay in the next room only half-conscious and too weak to help even if she were aware of the situation. Harmony recalled Brian's words—that she must rely on her own will to survive. He was right. She could not expect anyone to help her, to protect her. Even her parents had not done that.

Jimmie O'Toole, slobbering over her neck, begged her to marry him, telling her what married men and women did to get babies, telling her how badly he wanted to do that to her. His breath was foul from whiskey and smoking, his grip painfully tight on her wrists. His words revolted and terrified her. He moved on top of her, and she felt a hardness against her stomach, realizing it was that with which he intended to show her what he'd been describing. It was all ugly and confusing. She could not imagine doing what he was suggesting.

He finally released her wrists, sure he'd seduced her into submitting, and he tore away the blankets, one hand moving up under her gown. But she pulled his hair as hard as she could, and he cried out, sitting up slightly. She yanked a leg from under him and kicked out, landing her foot under his chin. In his drunken state he lost his balance and fell backward off the sofa, landing on a small table and flipping it.

Harmony jumped up from the couch and ran to the fireplace, picking up a poker and waving it at him.

"If you touch me again I'll kill you!" she hissed at him. "I wouldn't want the likes of you if you were the only man alive!" Tears began to fill her eyes—tears of humiliation and horror. Never had she felt more desperate and alone! "You get out of here!" she screamed. "Get out! Go sleep at the store . . . or with those bawdy women on the other side of town! Let them do whatever it is you want from me! You'll not get it here! I'll die first!"

He slowly rose, panting, rubbing at a sore shoulder. There were bloody scratches over his eyes, and his hair was sticking out oddly. He stood staring at her then, fists clenched, unsure what to do, in pain with the want of her. She was beautiful. He'd touched her voluptuous body and wanted more. But the way she stood there holding the poker . . . there was something about her—the look of a wild animal ready to kill. He had no doubt she'd swing the poker stick if he went near her, and in her state she'd probably manage to land it right into his skull. He'd been so sure that with a couple of kisses and a man's touch she'd submit. After all, she was just a stupid kid. Weren't all young girls curious about boys? Weren't they all for the taking if a man could get them excited? Not this one. Not the way she was looking at him now.

"You cold bitch!" he growled. "It's too bad those men didn't have at you on the docks when you were six years old."

She raised the poker more and he backed away. "All right. I'm leaving." He sneered. "But you remember one thing, Harmony Jones! You're not only living in a borrowed house but on borrowed time! When Becky dies, and she will, I'll be the only one left. Brian won't come back once she's dead! Why should he? What's left to come back to if not Becky? He sure won't come back for you! You don't really think he cares about you, do you? You were just somebody to help Becky and work with him at the store, that's all! Now he doesn't care about either one, and there are no legal papers saying you belong to him or have a right to anything that is his. If you want to stay on here and be taken care of, you'll have to come to my bed eventually!" He smoothed back his hair. "I can wait. Someday you'll have no place else to turn, Harmony Jones! And you'd better not take too long deciding, because when I get tired of waiting, I'll throw you out into the streets. Then see what happens to you! You'll be wishing it was me moving over that pretty body of yours instead of the scum waiting for you out there! They won't be half as

49

kind as I'd have been!"

His breathing was still rapid, and she moved closer, still waving the poker. "You get out of here!" she repeated, tears flowing fast now.

"I'm going!" He walked away and then stopped. "And one more thing! When you decide to come to my bed for security and a home, don't expect me to marry you! I would have, but not now. If you want to stay here, you'll have to start paying for it, and since you have no money, there is only one alternative! But I'll not marry you, bitch!"

He turned and stormed off, but she just stood for several seconds, still holding the poker, watching to be sure he wasn't coming back. Then she dropped the stick and fell to her knees, bending over and crying, sobbing with horror and humiliation. She did not doubt he'd meant every word he'd said, and her mind raced with indecision. Why didn't Brian come home? Perhaps he had abandoned her after all, just like her parents. Was there no one in this world who could be trusted? What was she to do at sixteen, with no family, no help, and nothing she could truly call her own?

She slowly got to her feet, getting a handkerchief and blowing her nose and wiping her eyes. She thought again about the fact that she really had no one but herself. Then she walked to a mirror and stared at her image. She was pretty. Of that there was no doubt. But she was small, only five feet, two inches, and barely a hundred pounds. She was only sixteen and had no family or property. She had nothing to start with, but she was certain she would not make her way through life by letting men use her body the way Jimmie O'Toole had suggested. In fact, after the horror of his touch and his remarks, she was even more convinced that no man would use her that way, no matter what. The only experience she had had with that side of men had been ugly and horrifying. She wanted nothing to do with it. Then a little voice told her that surely it was sometimes pleasurable. Brian and Becky had been blissfully happy when first married. But at the moment she could not imagine enjoying any man's touch.

That left her with only her instincts, her strength, and her determination to survive. A coldness crept into her soul. Yes. She would survive, in spite of parents who'd abandoned her, in spite of a guardian who had deserted her, in spite of men like Jimmie O'Toole, in spite of her age and sex. The keys were pride, cleverness, and determination, as well as property and money. She had the first things. Somehow she would get property and money, if she had to dig ditches or scratch the earth to get it! She would ensure that nothing—no one—could defeat her or make her helpless again! Men like Jimmie could never threaten her! She wouldn't need them, nor did she need him now!

Her lips were tight, her tears had dried. She would not cry again. She would not beg, and she would not be afraid. She picked up the poker stick and the blankets. She would sleep with Becky in the big bed. Jimmie O'Toole wouldn't dare come in there and attack her! It was a start—not much, but a start. At least she was thinking about survival. Her next step would be to confront Jimmie, to surprise him by showing no fear. She would go to the store in the morning and get to work. She'd hire a woman to care for Becky, for Becky was so far gone most of the time that Harmony's presence no longer seemed to matter to her. She'd march down to the store in the morning and go to work. She smiled.

And she intended to tell Jimmie that she would write to Brian about what he had done. That would bring Brian back, and Jimmie O'Toole would wish he'd never even looked at Harmony Jones!

The next day, Jimmie looked up in shock when Harmony did indeed walk into the supply store, slamming the door behind her and heading directly to the office in back. He stared at her, then followed, finding her already getting to work on the account books. His voice would not come when she looked up at him with cold green eyes.

"Why haven't you kept things up to date?" she asked sternly. "I've been away from here for three weeks and everything is a mess!"

He swallowed. "I . . . haven't had time."

"You have time to drink and attack innocent girls."

He reddened, putting a hand to his aching head. She was pleased to see scabbed scratch marks over his eyes. "I . . . I'm sorry, Harmony . . . about last night."

She turned away and picked up a quill pen. "Sorry isn't enough. Have you ordered the seeds as I asked you to do before I left?"

He sighed deeply. "I forgot. Look Harmony—"

"Forgot!" She favored him with a scathing look. "You're as worthless as a pig! You know we always order seeds early so there are plenty on hand for the farmers come spring. And we were nearly out of picks and tin plates and cups down at the warehouse a month ago. There are still plenty of men coming through here wanting mining supplies. Have you restocked those things?"

He was visibly shaken, and he rubbed at his neck. "I . . . I'm not sure. Harmony, I really am sorry. I didn't mean what I did . . . what I said."

"Of course you did. You've never liked me, any more than I like you. I'm smarter than you and you know it. Brian knew it too, and that irritated you. I don't blame you. He's your brother. But if it weren't for him, you'd be worthless today. You used him to make something of yourself, and you want to use me to keep this place in business. I'll not be used. I'll help you, Jimmie, but I want to be paid for it. And if you ever touch me again, I'll write Brian and tell him what you've been up to. No matter what you say, I know he loves me like a daughter, and if he knows you're threatening me, he'll make sure you have no part of this store. You know he'll do it. In the meantime, I made him a promise to care for Becky and for this store until he returns, and I intend to do just that. It's already obvious I have to be present here for things to be handled correctly, so I've hired a woman to stay with Becky. I'm going to write Brian and let him know she is ill, and I have no doubt he'll come home to see her. He wouldn't want Becky to die before he saw her again. And when he gets back, I won't tell him what you did to me if you don't touch me from here on and if you cease all talk of marriage. I'd slit my own throat before I'd marry you."

Her voice was cool and determined. She was changed, and Jimmie suddenly felt as though someone had punched him in the nose. It was he who felt like the child, like the one being threatened. She had a sureness

53

about her, and somehow he thought she just might be able to destroy him, as long as Brian was alive anyway. She was right about the favoritism, right that Brian would come back to see Becky. Jimmie was furious with himself. He had intended to woo her the right way, to be good to her and carefully talk her into marrying him, for he truly wanted to bed her and he needed her business knowledge. He had chased her away and would probably never get her back. Not that he loved her. But it would have been a wonderful revenge on his brother's favoritism if he could have made her his wife and taken her virginity . . . and then made her life miserable. Unfortunately she'd seen him for what he really was. She probably had all along.

The look she gave him now almost frightened him. She had not reacted the night before the way he'd thought she would, and she did not cower now. For the time being, he had no choice but to play the game her way.

"I'll order the seeds . . . and the mining supplies," he told her.

"Fine," she replied, turning back to the books. "I'll spend the day getting these figures in order."

He stood there for several more seconds, but she did not look up again and he left. As soon as he was gone Harmony breathed a deep sigh of relief. It had worked! Showing determination and authority had worked! He needed her help and he knew it, but by God, he'd not get his way! Inside she was shaking like a leaf, yet she had refused to show it. She had something on him now, and she'd not let him forget it. As long as Brian was alive, even far away, she had a hold over Jimmie. And once she wrote to tell Brian about Becky's health, he'd come home; then everything would be fine. She was almost glad now for Jimmie's behavior the night before. Dealing with it had given her courage and had cleared the air between them. Now each knew where the other stood. Jimmie needed the store—it was his security—but he was incapable of running it without her business sense. He needed her. She would work there for a salary and save her money, and if Brian did not return, she'd use that money to start a business of her own so that she wouldn't need anyone but herself!

Harmony was pleased with her new power, but before she could write to Brian about Becky's health, Becky died of pneumonia, just two days after Jimmie and Harmony's confrontation. The woman's death threw Harmony into despair. Again someone she loved had left her. If people did not deliberately leave her, death took them from her. It seemed she was determined never to keep those she loved. A letter was quickly dispatched to Brian, no one knowing how long it would be before he received it at his remote mining site, but immediately after the funeral Jimmie's attitude changed somewhat. Harmony could see her power slipping slightly, see the old haughty attitude coming back to him.

"Brian will never come back now," Jimmie told her the next day at the store. He seemed little affected by Becky's death, but because of her own sorrow Harmony went to work the very next day. She wanted to keep busy. She did not want to weep. She had promised herself she would not weep or be afraid or give in to her terrors ever again.

"He'll come back," she replied quietly, as she ran a feather duster over some dishes. "As soon as he finds out, reads my pleas to come back for a while, he'll come."

"Becky is the only reason he'd have come. He won't come for you. I'll bet he'll write and say the store is mine and I'm to let you work here and live in the house." He grinned. "I'll let you—if you're nice to me."

She cast him a dark look that wiped the smile from his face. "If that happens, I'll manage on my own. I don't need you or this store, but I'll remind you that you need me—and I come a lot cheaper than a professional accountant."

"So, you think you can make it on your own, do you? No woman makes it on her own, let alone a sixteen-year-old kid."

"I'll be seventeen soon. And a lot of women make it on their own."

"You need a man."

"I need no one but myself. And if you want this store to keep running at a profit, you're the one who'd better be nice to me, Jimmie O'Toole!" She abruptly turned and walked to the office, fully realizing that her position was now precarious but still one in which she could exert reasonable control. She would have to be on the alert now though, constantly on guard against his remarks. She must not falter.

It was five months later, in the spring of 1896, when the awful news came. Upon hearing of his wife's untimely death, full of grief because he had not seen her again and in ill health from a fever, Brian O'Toole collapsed when the messenger gave him the letter about Becky. The messenger loaded Brian onto a travois and

56

took him to the doctor in Cripple Creek. Shortly thereafter Brian O'Toole was dead. The doctor wrote a reply addressed to Harmony, who had sent the letter about Becky. In the letter he enclosed a separate envelope marked Harmony Jones—Personal. But once Harmony read the initial letter, she didn't bother to look at anything else.

Brian! Brian was dead! She sat alone in the big empty house when the news came—the house where she had spent those early, happy years with Brian and Becky O'Toole, who were so kind to her, who had been like parents. In that house Brian O'Toole had been happy with his beloved Becky, until constant miscarriages had destroyed pretty Becky's spirit and had driven a wedge between the pair. It had been devastating for Harmony to watch Brian O'Toole walk out of her life to go west. Now he was dead. Dead! No! It could not be! She loved him, needed him, had counted on his return. Again death had claimed a loved one. But would he have returned? Was Jimmie right in saying that he would not have come back? Was it true that he didn't love her like a daughter? After all, he hadn't returned in three years, and he'd promised it would be only two.

Brian O'Toole had abandoned her too, for there was not even a will stating she had any claim to anything he owned, despite how hard she'd worked for the man, despite all she thought she'd meant to him. Jimmie had already affirmed that. A will was something Brian had always meant to take care of but had never drawn up, and now all the property would surely go to Jimmie. Harmony had no right to any of it.

Her personal grief was only made worse by her

awareness of the predicament she was in and by wondering over whether Brian had really cared about her. Was she so unlovable? All she had ever done was try to please people, yet she kept losing them. Again the haunting memory of the night on the docks came to her—the terror, the loneliness, the indecision. As long as Brian was alive, she'd felt confident of his love, certain he would return to take care of any unfinished business. She grieved now, not only for his death but for all the things that meant to her—most of all the renewed abandonment. More than ever she was sure that she could never again trust another human being, that she should never again love for fear of losing, that she would never again rely on help from anyone. It must come from her, and she was right back to the fact that she must have money and property. In those things lay her only power, her only independence, her only strength.

How long she lay on the bed weeping she wasn't sure. When her tears finally subsided the sun was setting. She had not gone to the store that day, but had stayed home to clean. Because of her threats, Jimmie had stayed away from the house, taking an apartment of his own. But what would he do now? Brian's death would change everything. She realized then that she hadn't even told Jimmie of it yet. Perhaps she should wait. The longer she waited, the better it would be for her; for Jimmie would think Brian was still alive and might come home. That was her last hold on him, except that he needed her at the store, but he was becoming more self-confident, more sure he could handle things himself and didn't need her anymore.

She was torn by indecision. She didn't want to think.

She didn't even want to grieve. She hated crying. What good did it do? Crying made her feel like an abandoned little six-year-old again, and she didn't like that feeling. Besides, she was angry now—more angry than sorrowful. Hadn't Brian abandoned her after all, just like her parents?

She sniffed and straightened, walking out to the dining room, where the envelope marked personal still lay on the table. She stared at it, her heart beginning to pound. Personal! Why had she paid no attention to it before? It could be a will, or some kind of legal paper awarding her money! It could be . . .

She grabbed up the envelope and ripped it open.

"To the attention of Miss Harmony Jones, ward of Brian Howard O'Toole, St. Ann Street, St. Louis, Missouri:" the paper read. "Please be advised that upon the death of Brian Howard O'Toole a claim has been left in your name only, said claim being near Pike's Peak, a size of one hundred feet (100') by one hundred feet (100') and said claim yielding five ($5.00) in gold (roughly) daily from placer mining Wildcat Creek, which runs through said claim, and into Cripple Creek. Please be advised that said claim has never yielded more than the above-mentioned amounts in gold, that no shaft has been dug on this claim and no coyoting has been performed, nor has any mother lode been found to designate the source of the meager gold on this claim; and it is doubted that any mother load of any great value exists.

"Since you are the sole owner of this staked claim, as duly recorded in this assayer's office as of the fifth day of September, Eighteen Hundred and Ninety-Five, this assayer must be informed forthwith of your intent as pertains to the above-mentioned claim. Please be advised that if notice is not received by the thirtieth (30th) day of June, Eighteen Hundred and Ninety-Six, under the laws governing such claims, and giving you due time, considering distance and circumstances and the fact that you are a woman, said claim will no longer be considered your property and will be up for bids to anyone who wishes to stake it and duly records himself as owner of said claim.

"I await your prompt reply."

The letter was signed Jonathan C. Humes, assayer in the claims office of Cripple Creek, Colorado.

Harmony put down the letter with shaking hands. A gold claim! A gold claim all her own! So what if it only yielded five dollars a day! To her that was a fortune! She put a hand to her chest. Brian O'Toole had remembered her after all! He had left her his claim! There was no mention of Jimmie! None at all! She read the letter again—and again. She had no idea what placer mining was, or what was meant by digging a shaft or coyoting. And what was a mother lode? It made no sense to her, but that didn't matter. She had property! And that property yielded enough gold to live on. She had only to learn how to get the gold out, and woman or not, she would do it! For once in her life she had something that was all her own, even though it was over a thousand miles away in an unknown land. It was hers, and as long as she went there and claimed it, no one could take it from her. She had to rely on herself now, herself and no one else. The claim gave her the independence she needed, gave her property and money. Somehow she would work it. She would do whatever was necessary to hang on to it!

She immediately took out some paper, her eagerness

and determination overshadowing all grief, all fear, all reasoning that a young girl alone could not go into a wild land and work a gold claim. Never in her life had she had something that was just hers. She composed a letter, stating her intent to come to Cripple Creek and claim Brian O'Toole's property and declaring that she would work the claim herself. She sat back then and read the letter before folding it and putting it into an envelope. She would see that it got into the mail the very next morning.

She reread the assayer's letter. Yes. There was no doubt. The mine or claim or whatever it was belonged to her alone. Brian O'Toole had loved her after all. Perhaps the only reason he hadn't come home sooner was that he'd hoped to strike a richer claim before returning, wanting his Harmony to have all that he could give her. She had to believe that. She needed to believe it.

Rising, she threw on her cape, and picked up the letter from the doctor about Brian's death. She stuck the assayer's letter up under her dress into her undergarment. She did not want Jimmie O'Toole to get his hands on it. What if he destroyed it? Then she decided to do the same with the letter of reply until she could mail it in the morning. She had already cried herself out. Brian O'Toole was dead, and nothing would bring him back now. All those she loved had abandoned her or died, and she was left alone, to fend for herself however she could. With her Colorado property she would do just that. She went out the door and hailed a carriage to take her to the supply store, where she knew Jimmie would be working late. Her heart raced, her cheeks were flushed with victory.

Several minutes later the carriage pulled up in front

61

of the store, and she hurried inside to find Jimmie taking inventory. He cast her a scowl.

"Fine time to come to work," he told her. "I've worked my fingers to the bone today."

"Good," she replied. She watched him a moment, unable to be so cruel as to throw the news at him without feeling. "Jimmie, I have bad news," she said quietly. "You'd better sit down."

He frowned, setting down his tablet and pen. "Brian?" he asked.

She nodded. "A letter came to the house today, from a doctor in Cripple Creek. Brian . . . collapsed when he heard about Becky. He died a few hours later."

Jimmie just stared at her a moment, and to her surprise, he didn't look at all upset. His eyes scanned her rudely, and a faint grin swept across his mouth. "Well. I've had enough talks with our attorney to know what that means. I am now sole owner of this store and the warehouse and the house." He looked her over again. "And you."

She smiled right back at him. Whatever pity she had felt in telling him of his brother's death was gone. "No, Jimmie. You do not own me. I own myself—and a gold claim."

He paled to an alarming white, and his eyes narrowed. "What are you talking about?"

"Brian left me sole title to a gold claim. And I intend to go to Colorado and take it over. It's my property, and it yields five dollars daily. If I'm lucky, it will come to more than that."

He stepped closer, the little crimson dots on his white cheeks betraying his anger. "He wouldn't do that! If he struck gold he'd have left it to me!"

She smiled. "There was no mention of your name in the letter I received from the assayer." She reached into her handbag and held out a piece of paper. "Here. This is the assayer's address. If you doubt me, you are free to write to him and find out for yourself. I do not intend to show you his letter. It's mine. And I have already replied that I am coming to claim the strike. You can have the store and everything else. My savings will finance my trip to Colorado and pay for the supplies I will need when I get there. I need nothing more from you, Jimmie O'Toole." She turned to leave.

"Wait!" he called out. "What . . . what about the store? The books?"

She smiled haughtily. "If you don't know how to handle this business by now, Jimmie, you deserve to lose it. I have done all I can to keep it going, and I would have done more if you had been kinder to me. But I'll not forget the night you attacked me, nor the fact that you have not shown any remorse for Brian who gave you all that you have. I have no feeling for you; therefore, I do not care whether you keep this store or lose it. Do what you will. I am going to Colorado."

She turned again. "You can't go out there and pan for gold!" he yelled. "You're only seventeen! You're a girl! You don't know anything about panning for gold! You don't have anybody to help you. You'll never survive!"

She turned back again. "I've survived so far, haven't I? I'll manage." She opened the door.

"I hope you die on a mountain!" he growled at her. "I hope a grizzly attacks you, or claim jumpers rape and murder you! I hope there's no gold left when you get there! Bitch! You'll come crawling back to me, that's what you'll do, if you don't die out there!"

She grinned. "I would much prefer to die under a grizzly's claws. Good-bye, Jimmie. I'm going home to pack and I'll stay at a hotel tonight. The house is yours. Everything is yours, just as you wanted."

She walked through the door and closed it, reentering the carriage. Nothing mattered now—nothing but getting to Colorado and claiming what was hers. She was truly on her own from here on, and never again would Harmony Jones trust anyone, love anyone, depend on anyone but herself. Yes. That was truly all she had—herself . . . and a gold claim in Colorado.

Chapter Three

So . . . it was done. She was on her way to Colorado. Jimmie O'Toole could have his supply store! Someday she would be richer than Jimmie O'Toole, richer than most people. She didn't need a man pawing over her, she didn't need parents to take care of her. She could care for herself. She hated depending on anyone, and she hated men who thought all women should be available to them. No man would use Harmony Jones that way!

It was then she noticed someone new had boarded the train. He sat across from her, and his appearance fascinated her. Surely he was one of those cowboys she had read about—men who herded cattle, captured mustangs, and broke horses. They were wild, roamers, she'd always heard. This one must have got on board at the little town where the train had stopped for breakfast, or he had been in one of the other cars. At any rate, she had not noticed him before.

She stole quick glances at him out of purely childish curiosity, for he did not wear a suit and vest like the other men on the train. He wore high boots that were well worn and dark blue pants of a strong-looking material. The clean calico shirt that adorned his very broad shoulders was tucked into his waist which was encircled by a wide leather belt that held a beaded sheath in which a huge knife rested. A holster containing a gun with a polished mahogany handle also hung from his belt, and a wide-brimmed hat lay in his lap, held by very big hands that looked as though they had done hard work. His white shirt was decorated with blue designs, and at his neck he wore a bright blue scarf, which accented the very blue eyes that were suddenly looking back at her.

She reddened deeply, angry that she had bothered to look at him at all. Surely he thought she was a loose woman who was giving him the eye, when on the contrary she was not even looking at him as a man or even as a person, but rather as a curious object she had never seen before. But how would she ever explain that? She stared back out the window, determined not to look back for a long time so he would know she had only been curious. But the memory of his face, of that one quick look, stirred something in her she did not understand. She tried to ignore the odd, quick flutter she had felt when she'd met his eyes. His face was rugged and tanned, and from what she could remember in that quick glance, handsomer than that of any man she had ever set eyes on, if she would call any man handsome. She had long ago determined that no man would ever be attractive to her, and that she would never, ever, desire a man. It was not that she had such a feeling for this one. It was just that she had never seen one dressed as he was and wearing weapons, or one with eyes quite so blue set in a face quite so perfect. She wanted to look again, out of sheer curiosity, but could not bring herself to do it for she was sure his own eyes were still on her.

She felt suddenly overdressed for the country into which she was headed. She wore an expensive green velvet skirt and jacket, the jacket short and tight fitting flattered her lovely shape. Her blond hair was coiffed into sweeping curls that were set off by the elegant velvet hat she wore. At her neck the neat white ruffles of her silk blouse filled the space between the lapels of her jacket, and at her throat a lovely broach decorated the blouse. It had been a gift from Becky O'Toole long ago. Her high-button shoes were shiny and black. She suddenly wondered if people would laugh at her when she disembarked at Cripple Creek. Surely in such a wild town full of itinerant miners, a young, inexperienced, fancily dressed girl from St. Louis would be out of place.

She stared ahead although she still couldn't get a good view of the western horizon. Then she saw the dark shadow again against the western sky, and suddenly white peaks. The mountains! She leaned forward, her gaze intent now. They must be gigantic, for their tops were covered with snow and this was the first of June! Her heart pounded with anticipation, hope, fear, doubts. What was she doing coming to this land? What awaited her out there?

"Where you headed, cowboy?" a voice asked nearby. It startled her, and she looked up to see a conductor standing near the stranger with the gun and high boots, looking at a ticket.

"Cripple Creek," came the deep but gentle voice.

Harmony's heart raced harder. He was going to the same place she was! What a small world it was after all. She stared at her lap, pretending not to listen.

"Another gold-seeker?" the conductor asked with a laugh, punching the ticket.

Harmony dared to glance in the man's direction again, and he was flashing a wide, handsome grin, his teeth white and even, his blue eyes dancing. Thick, sandy hair was combed in neat waves away from his face, but a few little curls hung over his forehead.

"I'm not that crazy," the man replied to the conductor. "I wouldn't waste my time scratching the earth for something I might never find. I've seen plenty of men die or go home in broken despair after searching for gold. I make my money an easier way."

The conductor chuckled. "You a gambler?"

"No, sir. I work for a supply store, and the man I work for is thinking of raising good sturdy pack horses, sent me to Arriba where a man I know raises the best. I've got a valuable thoroughbred stud and a good sturdy roan broodmare on board. I'll be getting off at River Bend and will herd them straight west from there instead of going on into Denver."

The conductor nodded. "Well, sounds to me like you've got a more dependable means of income than panning for gold, I'll say that. Me, I'd just as soon have a good, steady job. You look more like a cowboy, than a man who'd work for a supply store."

The stranger shifted in his seat, and Harmony glanced at him again. He was a big man. She guessed that if he stood up he would be a good six feet tall. He looked uncomfortable in the seat, and he stretched one long leg out into the aisle so he could unbend it.

"Not so much use for trailherders anymore, thanks to the railroad," he answered. "Some ranchers still need cowboys. But it's hard for me to stay in one place. With this job I do a little traveling, supplying miners. I go up and down into the mountains and back to Cripple Creek. And I meet a lot of people."

"I'll bet." The conductor handed back the ticket, after first studying the name on it. "Raymond Hanner. Glad to meet you, Mister Hanner."

"Just call me Buck. That's the only name I go by."

The conductor grinned. "Well, you have a good trip, Buck. And I hope you get the horses safely to Cripple Creek."

Buck nodded. "Thank you."

As the conductor walked farther down the aisle, Harmony stole another glimpse of the stranger called Buck Hanner. What was it about him that attracted her? It wasn't just his rough, powerful frame and the different way he dressed, or the ruggedly handsome face and intriguing blue eyes. There was a sureness about him, a power, the air of a man who controlled his own life. She wished she could be a man, be one like Buck Hanner, a man who did what he pleased, went where he wanted, took orders from no one. If she were a man, life could be so different for her. She wouldn't have to be afraid of everything and pretend that she was not. Perhaps that was why most women thought they needed a man, to be all the things they could not be—to do the protecting, to be in control. But not her. She would be different. She needed no man. She would control her own life.

Buck Hanner glanced at her again, flashing that handsome smile and nodding. "Afternoon, ma'am," he said.

Her face went crimson again. She knew it would be polite to answer, but she must not do it! What would he think! She quickly looked away again, then moved to the seat opposite her so that her back would be to him and she would not accidentally meet his eyes again. Doing so meant she couldn't watch the mountains looming on the horizon, but that didn't matter. It was better than feeling his eyes on her, better than not being able to look up without seeing him. She was glad he was getting off at River Bend. That was the next stop. Buck Hanner would be gone then. She would go on by train to Denver, then come down to Cripple Creek on the Denver & Rio Grande, for there was no other easy way to get there, unless one was a horse-riding cowboy like Buck Hanner.

Horse riding! She just then realized she couldn't even ride a horse. Surely everyone at a place like Cripple Creek knew how to ride. How would she get around? She suddenly felt like crying. She didn't know anything about the place to which she was going, knew nothing about riding, nothing about mining. What had made her think she could do this? She breathed deeply. She must not falter now. She must not let negative thoughts overtake her. She owned property in Colorado—gold! She would go there and she would learn what she needed to know. Anyone could learn, and she was smarter than most people. She had learned other things. She would learn to ride, learn about panning for gold; and she would be all right.

She sighed deeply, imagining herself falling into that abyss that had swallowed others who had come to this land. How she wished she had one friend—just one!

And what about Buck Hanner? He was going to Cripple Creek too. What if she saw him there? What would she say or do, after so rudely turning her back on him? She'd had no reason in the world not to give him a nod or a good afternoon. He seemed nice enough, and what harm could any stranger do her on a train full of passengers? If she had answered him, she might have struck up a conversation and discovered some things about Cripple Creek. Surely he could have told her anything she needed to know.

But it was too late now. She had ruined her chance, but it was probably just as well. If she had conversed with him, he'd have thought less of her, and then if he saw her in Cripple Creek, he'd think he had a right to talk to her. Perhaps he would approach her rudely or try to attack her as Jimmie had done, just because she had spoken to him. No. It was better this way. This way he knew she was a proper lady.

The train rumbled on for two more hours, then came to a stop for lunch. Harmony did not get off. She couldn't eat. She was too nervous now, too excited. In a few more hours she would be in Denver, a city that was a mystery to her, although she'd heard many things about it. It was difficult to believe there could be such a thing as a big, thriving city in this desolate, endless land. She would not believe it until she saw it for herself.

Several minutes later she saw him—Buck Hanner. The wide-brimmed hat was on his head, and he led a saddled horse. A rifle rested in a boot at the side of the saddle. He tied the horse at a hitching post, then left, returning a few minutes later with two grand-looking horses, one a deep brown, the other a reddish color. He

71

mounted the saddled horse with such ease it was obvious that riding was as familiar to him as walking. Then picking up the lead ropes that were tied to the bridles of the other two horses, he took the reins of his own horse and turned it.

For a brief moment he glanced up and caught her at the window, watching him. He smiled and nodded again, and she turned away. Why, oh why, did she feel so drawn to him? Why was she so fascinated? Surely it was just that his rugged manliness was what she'd pictured men in these places to be like. And it was all the more reason for her to be alert. Such men were probably as rude and demanding as Jimmie—surely much worse! After all, they were men who took charge of their own lives, and she was going to a place where young ladies were a rare sight. She must be very, very careful.

After several minutes she dared to glance out the window again, but Buck Hanner was gone. Why did that disappoint her? Never had she felt so confused by her own feelings. She rose from her seat, walking out to the platform and leaning out to try to see him. Far in the distance she spied a little cloud of dust. She could see three horses and barely make out one rider. Surely it was him. Why did she have a ridiculous urge to call him back? Never in her whole life had she felt or acted so foolishly.

She went back to her seat. Soon the train would be off again, heading north toward Denver. Buck Hanner was heading directly west and would probably get to Cripple Creek before she did. It felt strange to think that when she got to that town, there would actually be one person there that she knew. Yet she didn't know him at all—had not even spoken to him. He did not even know her name. But she knew his. Buck. Buck Hanner. It had a nice ring to it, a solid sound.

She sighed disgustedly then, angry with herself. Solid? He'd said himself he didn't like being in one place for too long. He was a drifter, a loner, that was sure. He probably had a woman in every town. And what if he did? Why did she care? She didn't. She was simply curious about that strange creature called a cowboy. Until now she had only read about them. And she was fascinated by the fact that he, too, was on his way to Cripple Creek. But a character like Buck Hanner would probably already be gone by the time she got there. That was just as well. She totally ignored and denied the truth, for it was too ridiculous and inexcusable to be acknowledged. Nonetheless, it lay deep inside her, creating disturbing new feelings in her young body and mind. She'd been attracted to him, something that had never happened to her, something she did not want to happen. She determined that she would not let it happen again. She would remember her purpose—to go to Cripple Creek, get a map of Brian's claim, and get supplies. Then she would seek out the claim and pan for gold. She would become wealthy, and forever after she would be in charge of her own life.

She settled back as the train rumbled toward Denver. But every time she closed her eyes to rest, she saw a handsome, tanned face with unusually blue eyes. It angered her. She moved to the other side of the car, where the windows faced the mountains now. She watched the peaks, allowing her thoughts to be lost in the great Rockies so she would forget about a man she would probably never see again.

Denver was bigger than Harmony had thought it would be—a sprawling raw city, booming with growth, but lacking the quiet refinement of St. Louis. In the short time she was there, Harmony could tell that although Denver had its large buildings, its theaters and schools and museums, it did not have the flavor and warmth of a city that had aged. It reminded her of a child not yet fully wise and mature. But there was no doubt that Denver was well established, a city that would not die off as she'd heard many western towns had, especially the mining towns. Denver was the center of all mining activity. It had banks, investors, and mining company headquarters. Even though mining towns came and went with the rising and setting of the sun, this city would remain the central point for the mining business, for gold or silver or copper or any new mineral that might be found in the vast expanse of the Rocky Mountains.

She boarded a Denver & Rio Grande coach, proud of how well she had so far accomplished her journey. She had spoken to few people and had made her way by asking questions and keeping to herself. She had spent most of her journey reading the books on mining she had purchased, but reading explanations and studying diagrams couldn't possibly be as helpful as physically panning for gold. Much as she hated to admit it, someone would have to show her how, and she didn't like the idea of having to rely on anyone to do that. But she would worry about that when she got to Cripple Creek.

Steam hissed from the black engine of the narrow gauge railroad, and they were underway. Now she had a grand view of the blue and purple mountains, their snow-covered peaks fascinating her. She felt a little light-headed, and realized that was because she was not accustomed to the altitude. Or was it simply her excitement? She wondered how far the range of mountains stretched. And how had man managed to get across them? Now he not only crossed them, but railroads had been built over them. Men even lived among the peaks, mining for gold, silver, lead, copper, and all sorts of mineral wealth. And she was going to be a part of all this. It was a wonderful, exciting feeling. She would belong to a special place, own a little piece of land, be her own person. She was no longer dependent and helpless, no longer lost. She knew exactly where she was going, and so far she'd done a good job of getting there. She would ride the D&RG south to Colorado Springs, where she would board a stagecoach that would take her to Cripple Creek. There she would see the assayer and announce her arrival, after which she would buy the necessary supplies, find a trustworthy guide, and go to Brian's claim.

Brian. Her heart fell a little. She had been so busy and excited, she had not thought of him for a while. It hit her with sudden agony that she would never see him again. Her throat ached, her eyes filled with tears. The kind man with the red hair and brown eyes who had fought off the men at the pier was dead. His lovely Becky, whom he'd been so happy to marry, was dead.

Both had been kind to her, had given her a home. If only Brian hadn't left, if only Becky could have had a baby, things might have been so different. She'd be cozy and warm and safe in St. Louis. She wouldn't be out here in this wild, strange land, walking among strangers, depending on strangers to help her. She would miss Brian O'Toole, the only father she had ever had. She would even miss the store. She'd gladly have worked there forever if Brian had been there to run it.

But Brian O'Toole was dead—nothing could change that—and it felt good to be away from Jimmie's evil stares and the constant fear of another attack. She didn't care what happened to him; she even hoped his business went bankrupt. It would serve him right. Without Brian the store meant nothing to her; St. Louis meant nothing to her. She had learned not to trust others, not to depend too heavily on any one person. Her experiences there had hardened her, trained her for what was now to come, made her independent. She now had stamina and determination. She would rely on her own know-how and judgment. She had decided that she could do anything she set her mind to, and there was no more wonderful feeling than believing that she could, that she would be successful on her own terms, paying her way with good hard work and intelligence and no other way. She knew that she must never show fear in front of others. She must always appear determined, sure, stubborn. She must be proud and forward, demanding and fighting for what belonged to Harmony Jones.

It seemed only a short time until she disembarked from the D&RG and her luggage was being tied onto the top of a stagecoach into which she climbed, settling

76

into a creaky leather seat. Moments later a heavily painted woman climbed into the coach, feathers dancing in her hat, her large bosom billowing over the low neckline of her dress. Harmony could not help but stare wide-eyed at her, for judging by the woman's shadowed eyes, brightly painted lips, and her garish attire, she was certain this was one of the many prostitutes who came west to make a living off the cowboys and miners.

The painted woman met her stare with kind brown eyes, and she smiled. "Hi, honey. Where you headed?"

Harmony could not find her voice at first, and the woman frowned, looking outside.

"Where's your ma and pa?" she asked.

Harmony straightened. Was it proper to speak to such a woman? How could any woman take money to be with a man, doing the ugly things Jimmie had once described to her during his vicious attack? She shuddered, and her stomach felt uneasy. She had no choice but to answer the woman, who looked genuinely concerned, and she could not deny that her fellow passenger's eyes were truly kind.

"I . . . I have no parents," she replied. "I'm traveling alone." She held up her chin, feeling more grown-up with every word. It was time to start being strong and unafraid. "I'm traveling to Cripple Creek, to take over a gold claim my stepfather left me. He's dead, and—"

"Cripple Creek! You?" The woman laughed lightly, running knowing eyes over Harmony's prim attire, studying the youthful face and sensing the fear that lay beneath the proud eyes. "You're just a kid, and a female besides. How do you think you're going to fare in a place like Cripple Creek, and what do you know about mining for gold?"

Harmony held the woman's eyes steadily. "I can learn all I need to know, and I will do just fine. I do not intend to stay in town for long. I will leave for Pike's Peak right away. The claim is mine, and I intend to keep it that way."

The woman frowned. "Well, I gotta admire your courage, kid. But there's a lot more enjoyable way to get rich at Cripple Creek. I can attest to that. I've just been to Denver and made some big investments, all with . . . uh . . . hard-earned money, if you know what I mean."

Harmony reddened, and the woman chuckled.

"I guess that sounds pretty terrible to the likes of you, but out here it's considered quite a legitimate way of making a living. Why, one of my best customers is Wade Tillis, the richest man in Cripple Creek. Owns half the town. And he's a handsome cuss to boot. The only problem is, more and more wives are coming out every year, making a fuss about women like me, wanting to chase us out of town. But they haven't been able to yet. We have a right to be there. There's no law against it—yet." She grinned. "Say, honey, if you have problems or anybody gives you trouble, you come to me. I don't bite. I'd see that you was safe and sound and well took care of. I live with some other girls in rooms above the Mother Lode, one of the fanciest saloons in Cripple Creek. Wade owns it. If anybody gives you trouble, I'll send them hopping."

Harmony reddened, believing the woman was sincere, but she was too kind to tell her she wouldn't be caught dead running to a whore for help. Everyone might think that she was "one of the girls."

"Thank you," she said aloud. "You're very kind."

"That's okay. I was once an innocent thing like you, till my old man up and ran off to the gold fields, leaving me with big debts to pay. Me, I was never very smart, didn't have any skills. I did the only thing I knew would pay off the debts and keep me from going to prison. Then I came out here. Never heard from my old man again, but I swore I'd never be poor again either. By God, I haven't been. I'm good at what I do, and I don't care who knows it."

Harmony fingered the strings of her purse nervously. "Do you . . . do you know a man named Buck Hanner?"

"Buck? Sure. He's about the best-looking drifter that ever landed in Cripple Creek. I'd like to get that one between my sheets, but I've never had the honor. Far as I know, neither have the other girls. Buck's the quiet type, kind of mysterious, you know. He just sort of appeared one day, works at a supply store. He comes over and gambles once in a while, but he don't drink much, and he don't say much. He's well liked, far as I know, but nobody knows much about him. Say, you know Buck Hanner?"

Harmony shook her head. "No, I . . . I saw him on a train . . . overheard him tell a porter he was headed for Cripple Creek. I was just curious, since I know no one there."

The woman laughed lightly. "I don't suppose you're curious because he's the best-looking hunk of man in these parts, are you?"

Harmony frowned. "I don't think of men that way," she answered tartly. "He just seemed like an interesting person." She scowled and looked out the window of the coach at what someone had told her was Pike's Peak. It was difficult to tell how far away it was. She had learned already that in this land something that appeared to be twenty miles away could be a hundred miles off, and vice versa. This truly was a strange land, full of strange people.

"Well, maybe you don't look at men that way, but someday you will, honey; and you'll find out what you've been missing. I've got to say, you're sure pretty. You'd better be careful. 'Course, the men in mining towns have a lot of respect for us women, even the ones like me. Women are a rare sight, although, like I said, more and more wives are coming out now. But there's a certain code out here that says any man who'd violate or hurt a nice young girl, or even a favored prostitute, ought to be hung for a yellow-bellied coward. I've seen it happen. You just keep up that pride and properness, and you'll be all right. But you'd better be prepared for a lot of remarks and a hell of a lot of stares. You'll be a tempting sight, I'll say that."

Harmony held her chin proudly, folding her arms. "The last thing I care about is men. I just want to get to my claim and be left alone. I intend to be totally independent for the rest of my life."

A wry grin passed over the woman's face. "Sure. By the way, my name is Dora May Harper. What's yours?"

"Harmony. Harmony Jones."

The woman scrutinized her closely. "Sixteen?"

"Seventeen."

Her eyebrows arched. "Oh my! You're all grown-up then, aren't you?" She laughed lightly and a man boarded the coach, much to Harmony's consternation. She wished no one had boarded. She would much

80

rather have finished the trip alone, especially in the cramped quarters of the coach. It was obvious that Dora May Harper was going to babble all the way to Cripple Creek, and her attention turned immediately to the man, who was soon telling the woman all about himself, his eyes on her bosom more often than on her face. At least Dora May kept the man's attentions on herself and off of Harmony. She was glad of that much.

The coach lurched forward and Harmony grasped a hand grip to steady herself. They hadn't gone three miles before the man had practically told Dora May his life story, explaining that he was headed for Cripple Creek on behalf of a real-estate firm based in Colorado Springs, and that he hoped to see more of her when they arrived.

Dora May smiled and winked. "As much as you want, honey," she replied.

Harmony reddened deeply, feeling sick, from Dora May's attitude toward a complete stranger and from the motion of the coach, both of which mingled with her own excitement and fear so that her stomach actually ached. They rode for several hours, up hills, down hills, past rocky hills patched with sage and small cactus plants, around amazingly huge boulders, through canyons with walls hundreds of feet high.

Harmony soon forgot her concern over the prostitute and the realtor. She practically hung out of the window, gawking at scenery far surpassing what she had imagined. There were waterfalls and forests of pine. Always in the distance, disappearing and reappearing, were the mountains, always changing, seemingly moving, yet ever the same. To her right would be a certain snow-capped peak, then suddenly it would be

81

behind her, on the other side of her, then to her right again. Or was it a different one? How on earth did a person find his way in this maze of rocks and canyons and forests? Yes, she would most certainly need a guide. Had she gotten in over her head? Could she really do this? Had she come to this land to be forever lost, perhaps raped and murdered and thrown over a cliff to be crushed in the fall? Would someone shoot her for her claim? Would a bear eat her, a boulder fall on her? How was she, Harmony Jones, who knew nothing about this land, to survive in it?

Dora May laughed then, and when Harmony looked at her, the man was nuzzling the prostitute's neck, a small bottle of whiskey in his hand, which lay against her billowing bosom, partly touching the woman's breasts. Harmony thought of the night Jimmie had dared to touch her own breast, and a chill went down her spine. How ugly! She was repulsed and mortified. She looked away again.

She would survive. Looking at Dora May made her more determined than ever. She would survive in this land and be a successful businesswoman, and she would not do so in the way Dora May was doing it. She would die first. Watching the woman gave her more determination. The memory of her terror of being helpless and alone on the docks made her even stronger. She could do it and she would. Let everyone think whatever they wanted, laugh as much as they wanted, chide her, ridicule her, dare her. She didn't care. She'd show them all! She had property! She had gold! She had courage and strength. She was Harmony Jones, and she had made it this far. Soon she would be in Cripple Creek, and on her way to her own piece of land.

The trip took two days, and the intervening night was spent at a small stage depot deep in the mountains west of Pike's Peak. Harmony kept to herself, sleeping on a bench in the corner, but not sleeping well. She was too aware of the distant howl of coyotes and the strange, moaning wind. She told herself she must get used to such things, for soon she would be in her own little cabin on her own property—alone amidst the animals and the elements. She would have to get used to these mountains, learn how to survive here. She suddenly wondered if there was even a cabin at her claim. Surely there was, but what if there was not? She certainly didn't know how to build one, and she certainly did not intend to sleep outside.

The coyotes barked and howled again, and in another corner Dora May giggled and whispered with the realtor. What kind of a place had she come to? Perhaps this land was much more lawless, much more wild and dangerous than she had anticipated. Still, she was here, and there was no going back. Harmony buried her fear, her loneliness. Again the awful feeling she'd experienced as a little girl on the docks swept through her, and she wanted to cry. But she dared not. If she cried now, she'd never stop. She'd turn around and run back to St. Louis. She couldn't do that. There was nothing there for her. All she owned, all that could keep her independent and give her security, was here in this place called Colorado.

Morning finally came, and she raised her aching body, sore from lying all night on the hard bench. She boarded the coach, saying nothing to Dora May and the realtor, who both had red eyes and seemed to be suffering from headaches. They slept most of the way the next day, and when the coach rattled into Cripple Creek, only Harmony was awake to watch. The muddy main street was thronged with men, but she couldn't see a woman anywhere. The coach clattered by a sign that said Assayer's Office, and she made a mental note of its location as they headed farther down the street, stopping in front of the stage station.

Harmony put a hand to her chest. She was here. She was really in Cripple Creek! The driver walked around and opened the door, and she ducked her head and stepped out. Several men went thundering by on horseback, mud flying; and she could hear the tinkle of piano music from a nearby saloon.

Chapter Four

Cripple Creek was bigger than Harmony had imagined it would be. Movement and noise abounded, and the muddy main street was lined with saloons, banks, smithies, supply stores, carpenters' shops, real-estate offices, food stores, liveries, everything imaginable. Harmony thought it would be easy for someone to get rich in a place like this just by supplying miners. Already her business mind was whirling. If she could make a success of Brian's claim and get enough money from it, she would not only have a gold mine, she would go into the supply business, something she already knew well. Yes! She was more sure than ever that she was going to make it. Someday Harmony Jones would have all the money she needed to be secure. She turned to the driver, assuming the air of a confident woman.

"Where is the best hotel?" she asked. "One I can stay in and count on not being disturbed?"

The man eyed her closely. "Young lady, you'll have trouble not being disturbed. But you can try the Lone Pine Inn, just up the street a ways."

"Fine. Take my luggage there and I'll pay you as soon as I come back. Would you do that for me? I have to go to the assayer's office right away."

He nodded. "Whatever. Watch your step now."

She turned, lifting her skirts away from the mud and stepping onto a boardwalk. She walked quickly toward the assayer's office, looking at no one but feeling eyes on her. It seemed to take an eternity to reach the door of the assayer's building, but she finally went through it, glad to be out of the street. She approached a well-suited man who sat behind a counter. His eyebrows arched when he saw her, but his eyes shone with pleasure and she knew he was hoping she was a new prostitute come to town.

"Jonathan C. Humes?" she asked.

"That's me," he answered, rising. "What can I do for you, ma'am?"

"I am Harmony Jones. I've come to take over the gold claim awarded me by Brian O'Toole, as stated in your letter to me."

His eyes moved over her, and he laughed lightly. "You serious?"

Her own eyes narrowed. "I am very serious, Mister Humes. Do I need to sign anything?"

The man's smile turned to a scowl. "Yes. I have a claim form for you to sign." He pulled out a form from a file, scanning it briefly. "I had this ready but I didn't think I'd ever use it." He laid it out on the counter for her signature, handing her a pen. "You'd better go tell Wade Tillis you've come to claim O'Toole's property. He's put his own claim on it, pending your not showing up."

"Wade Tillis?" She frowned. She'd heard the name.

"Over at the Mother Lode," the man said slyly, "if a girl like you dares to walk in there."

Harmony's eyes grew colder. She was feeling more determined as each second passed. "You mean Wade Tillis, the man who owns half the town?"

He looked surprised that she would know. "He's the one."

She signed the paper. "Fine. I shall go notify Mr. Tillis that I am here. If he has any men on my property I shall tell him to get them off, and if he has taken any gold from it, he'd better make restitution. I'm not afraid of a gambling man who sits in a saloon all day and sleeps with whores at night." She handed him the claim form. "There. Is there anything else?"

The man looked shocked. "No, ma'am." He knitted his eyebrows in close scrutiny of her. "You sure you know what you're doing, little girl?"

"I know exactly what I am doing." She turned and marched out. She wanted nothing more than to go to her room and soak in a hot tub, and then run right back to St. Louis. But she was here now, and there were things to be done. She walked briskly back up the street, stopping in front of three men languishing on the boardwalk with a bottle of whiskey.

"Excuse me," she said boldly. "Would you please tell me where I can find the Mother Lode saloon?"

One of them grinned. "You gonna' be workin' there, honey?"

"I am not!" she replied sternly, her face hard and cold. "I have business with a Mr. Wade Tillis."

Another rose and came closer. "Yeah? What kind of business might that be, pretty little girl?"

She pulled out her small revolver and pointed it at

87

him. "My business, that's what kind. And I am not what you think, so get away from me or I'll use this."

The man's eyes bulged, and he backed up. "Relax, lady. We won't do you any harm. The Mother Lode is up a ways, just past the stage depot, same side of the street."

She put the gun back into her purse, then turned and headed for the saloon. The three men quickly followed, interested to see what was going to happen, and behind them the assayer also followed, his curiosity compelling him to go and watch a confrontation between little Miss Harmony Jones and the powerful Wade Tillis.

Inside Harmony was screaming with fear, but she would be damned if she was going to show it. She intended to earn respect and cooperation right away. The sooner she did this, the fewer problems she would have later with people who doubted her bravery or determination. And what did she have to lose now? Nothing. She had only herself. No one who cared about her or depended on her. She reached the swinging doors of the Mother Lode, and without hesitation she walked through them, into a room full of smoke and talk and several tables ringed with men playing cards. Peanut shells and cigar and cigarette butts lay strewn on the floor of the otherwise elaborate saloon, which sported an elegant mahogany bar, gaslight chandeliers, and red wallpaper with velvet designs. Someone played a racy song on a piano, but within moments the playing stopped, as did most of the talking, for nearly everyone had turned to look at the beautiful young lady attired in very elegant Eastern clothing, who had just entered. She did not have the look of a prostitute. Even more enticing was the fact that she looked just the opposite—a young innocent, probably still a virgin. Why on earth had she walked into this place?

Harmony's heart pounded furiously, and she felt her cheeks flushing under the stares of what seemed a thousand eyes. She looked around the room, seeing no familiar faces, not even Dora May, who was probably already upstairs in her room with the real-estate man.

"I am looking for Mr. Wade Tillis," she announced.

Nearly all heads turned then, focusing on a tall, dark man who stood at the bar. The man flashed a handsome smile, but something about him, an air of evil perhaps, took away from his handsomeness. He wore an expensive suit with a satin vest from which hung a gold watch chain. His nearly black hair was slicked back, and Harmony guessed him to be roughly in his late thirites. He came closer, his dark eyes running over her and making her feel naked, as Jimmie had sometimes made her feel. Already she did not like this man, which only gave her more gumption. He would not control her any more than Jimmie had. He towered over her then, standing no more than four feet from her so that she had to look up at him, making her seem even smaller and younger.

"I'm Wade Tillis, little girl. What can I do for you?"

"I am here to tell you that I am Harmony Jones, ward of Brian O'Toole and sole inheritor of his gold claim. I have come to legally take what is mine and I will be going there soon to work the claim myself. I am told it's possible you have men up there, taking what belongs to someone else. I want them removed immediately, and if you have stolen any gold from me, it should be returned."

He stared at her quietly for a moment, then began to snicker. Soon he was laughing loudly. The others joined him. The picture of a young slip of a girl standing before them and making demands on Wade Tillis was too amusing to permit them to keep silent, although most of them were already taking the side of the helpless little girl who was so bold and brave. They were laughing at her but also rooting for her. She stared boldly at Tillis, unflinching, not moving back an inch.

Tillis' laughter finally subsided and his smile faded. He stepped closer reaching out and pulling on a blond curl. She jerked her head back and pulled out her little revolver.

"Touch me again and I'll kill you!" she said calmly. The room went silent, and men grinned at each other, rooting even more for the spunky little girl. Harmony knew this was a drastic move, but she was desperate. She must make her stand immediately and firmly. If she showed one ounce of fear, it was all over for her. In the background, standing in a corner where she had not seen him when she'd come in, stood a tall, handsome man wearing a blue scarf at his neck, his blue eyes watching the show with interest. So, that was the girl's name. Harmony Jones. Buck Hanner watched her with intense desire. He liked her spunk, which only enhanced her beauty. And he knew the kind of man Wade Tillis was. Nothing was going to happen to Harmony Jones if he could help it. He put a hand on his gun, quietly moving closer.

Tillis' eyebrows arched in near shock, and he put on a nervous grin. "Well, now, aren't we bold?" He stepped back a little. "I suppose you know I could get

90

that gun out of your hand faster than you could fire it, and that I have a lot of men in this saloon who could come up behind you and carry you off—right back to the stagecoach to send you back where you came from . . . or up to my room."

She cocked the pistol. "Try it. Do you want to risk dying just to see if you can grab me first? They told me this gun might be little, but it makes big holes."

His smile faded again, and she relaxed, suddenly sensing support from several people in the room. It gave her more courage.

"I might remind you, Mr. Tillis, that claim jumping can be a hanging offense. That much I know. There is a code among miners about jumping, and about stealing someone else's gold. So get your men off my property. Send someone up today if you have to. I am told the claim yields roughly five dollars a day in gold. Brian O'Toole died last March fifteenth. It is now June eighteenth. That is three months. Three months times thirty days is ninety days. And ninety times five is four hundred and fifty dollars, Mr. Tillis. Figuring the time it took to get men up there and all, I'll give you the benefit of the doubt and will expect only four hundred dollars. I would prefer cash."

There were several snickers from the crowd, and Tillis flashed them a look of dark anger. He turned his eyes back to Harmony. "What the hell are you talking about!" he hissed.

"I'm saying you owe me four hundred dollars. I have no doubt that you have been sifting gold from my claim over these past three months, since I've had no one there to work it. That is a hanging offense. I think most of the men in this saloon would agree you'd better pay

91

me or be guilty of stealing someone else's diggings."

Buck Hanner grinned. She had him. The crazy little girl had him, and she knew she had a good share of the people there already on her side. She was not only beautiful and brave, but clever and intelligent. She still held the gun on Tillis, whose face was almost black with rage. The man reached into an inner coat pocket, and Buck's hand gripped his gun tighter, but Tillis brought out a wallet. He deliberately let Harmony see that it was stuffed with money. He took out a wad of it and fanned out four hundred-dollar bills.

Harmony snatched the money from him as though she thought his hand might bite her. She backed up then. "Send someone up right away to get your men off my property," she told him again.

Tillis assumed a smile again, pretending not to be too upset, pretending he thought this was all very funny and that he hadn't really lost at all. "Sure, honey," he answered. "I'll send someone up today. Besides, the claim will end up mine. You'll give up soon enough, unless a grizzly gets you first—or the cold or loneliness or some drifter who decides to have you for dessert." His eyes roved her body again. "You could make a lot more money right here in town, if you had any sense." He grinned. "In fact, if you moved in upstairs, you'd be a wealthy woman in no time at all—and you'd have saved yourself all that hard work."

Her eyes hardened, and her cheeks became crimson, but she still held the gun. "I like hard work, Mr. Tillis. I like it just fine. I'd rather work my fingers to the bone twenty-four hours a day than make my money the way you're suggesting. And I'll do it! There is nothing you can do to frighten me or threaten me. That claim is mine, free and clear, and I'll kill any man who steps foot on it without my permission!"

She finally lowered the gun, slipping it and the money into her handbag. Then she quickly turned to leave.

"Miss Jones!" Tillis called out. She stopped but did not turn around. "Good luck, Miss Jones," he said with a sneer. "You're going to need it."

She quickly left, wanting to run as fast as she could, but knowing she didn't dare. She must show no fear. She walked calmly to the stage depot and paid the driver, then went on to her hotel, where her luggage had already been put in a room. She walked up the stairs and through the door, then closed and locked it.

Finally she could give in to her fear. She fell onto the bed. Grabbing a pillow and holding it against her, she curled up into it and wept until she fell asleep from pure exhaustion. She had met and conquered her first challenge, but she knew there were many more to come. It would be hard being strong all alone, but she had no choice.

Late afternoon found Harmony standing at the grave of Brian O'Toole. After a good cry, a nap, and a bath, she had changed into a pale yellow cotton dress and a wide-brimmed hat, then had gone to a bank, where she'd deposited most of her own savings and the four hundred dollars from Wade Tillis; after doing so she'd gone to see the doctor. He had told her of Brian's death and had explained where he was buried. Upon leaving him, she had walked directly north of town, amid stares and whispers. It seemed incredible, but she was certain that news of her arrival and confrontation with Wade Tillis had already spread all over town. Many people gave her friendly smiles, and she smiled back and nodded, certain it was better to win their friendship than to injure their pride by being snobbish. She needed all the backing she could get, although she did not intend to be too friendly with anyone.

As she stood at the grave now, staring at a crude wooden cross, her eyes filled with tears. It didn't seem fair that a man like Brian O'Toole should die in such an unobscure fashion, be buried here with his name already fading on the cross. He had been such a good man. Although she still felt the pain of the day he'd left St. Louis, and the loneliness of his not returning, she couldn't really blame him, for he'd fallen into that great abyss she pictured this land to be . . . and now she was falling into it too. Perhaps one day she would lie in this mass graveyard, among the many who had ended up here due to starvation or freezing to death, too much whiskey, a fight over a claim, a mining accident, or sheer loneliness. In a sense, that was what Brian had died of in the end . . . and Becky. They should have been together. How sad life sometimes was.

She breathed deeply and blew her nose. She would see to it that a proper marker was erected at Brian O'Toole's grave, a nice stone with his name carved into it, something that would last forever. She knelt down, touching the mound.

"Thank you, Brian," she said softly. "I love you. Thank you for taking me in and loving me and giving me a home. And thank you for the claim. I'll work it, Brian O'Toole. I'll work it and I'll do everything I can to get even more gold out of it."

She stood up, wondering why Brian had given her the claim and not Jimmie. Perhaps it was because he knew she was the real worker, that she would do something with it whereas Jimmie would probably have just stayed in St. Louis and sold the claim for far less than it was worth because he'd consider it too much work to come out and pan it himself. If anyone could make it work, Harmony Jones could, and she'd do more than pan for gold. She'd use that gold to get richer by other means. Yes. Brian had probably sensed that, and perhaps he'd felt badly because he'd never legally adopted her or written a will. In any case, he'd assigned his claim to her. That was a tiny bit of a sign that he'd loved her after all. And she still believed that if he hadn't collapsed, Brian O'Toole would have come home, either to stay or to take her back with him. Or maybe, once he'd learned what Jimmie had done to her, he'd have kicked Jimmie out and given everything to Harmony.

There was no use contemplating now what might have been. What mattered was today, this moment. The wind blew the yellow dress wildly about her legs, and she grasped her hat and refixed the hatpins to keep it from blowing off. There was no shade here on this hill, only a few scraggly Yucca bushes and some scrubby sage plants. She wished Brian's grave could be shaded by a nice big tree like the ones back in Missouri—perhaps a nice oak. But in this land there were only pines, and the few cottonwoods that grew along the riverbeds. And here on the hill where the graves were dug, there were none of those.

She looked out at the horizon. In the distance, mountains surrounded her. Cripple Creek was behind

95

her, and before her the creek itself stretched through a broad valley dotted with cabins and mining buildings. In some places great amounts of earth had been dug away, and farther up in the mountains she could make out more buildings and entrances to even more mines. She tried to envision how quiet and untouched the place must have once been, before someone had shouted the magical word "gold." And she wondered how long this would all last—how long Cripple Creek would live.

This was a strange, desolate land, but despite a lack of green and of the big trees she was accustomed to in the East, it was beautiful. There was something in its lonely desolation that made it beautiful. Perhaps she was already growing to like it because it reminded her of her past . . . of little towns loved and then abandoned . . . of wide loneliness. It was a land attacked by miners and settlers, and ravaged. It had no defense . . . was desolate, beautiful, young and taken advantage of. Yet it had a determination and strength. Its mountains defied human progress, creating a constant, natural barrier. She felt as though the rain in this land could be her own tears, the wind her own agony. Had she been destined to come here all along, even when she was only six? Had this land been calling her ever since her parents had abandoned her to come here? She was already feeling attached, feeling a premonition that she was here to stay.

She bent down and laid some wildflowers on the grave, shoving their stems deep into the dirt so that they could not blow away. Yes. She would get a stone put here, right away. She rose then and was turning to go back when her heart jumped and her breath caught in her throat. A man was standing in the distance behind her, watching.

He was tall, wearing high boots that looked worn, and a calico shirt, this time its designs in red. A red bandana was tied at his neck, and the wind blew his thick, sandy hair in every direction. Yet its dishevelment seemed only to make him more handsome.

She had no doubt who it was. Buck Hanner! The man from the train! How did he know she was here? Had he already heard about her confrontation with Wade Tillis? Why had he come here? To spy on her? To attack her? Perhaps he worked for Wade Tillis!

He nodded, stepping closer then, holding his hat in his hands, the gun hanging low on his slim hips, the calico shirt which was gathered at the yoke and shoulders enhancing the powerful muscles that lay beneath it. He flashed his unnerving grin.

"Miss Jones?"

She watched him carefully as he came even closer, feeling no fear, seeing warm friendliness in his amazingly blue eyes. There was so much sureness about him, and an air of gentle strength.

"Yes?" she found herself saying.

"My name is Buck Hanner. You probably remember I was on the same train with you—out of Arriba. I . . . uh . . . I had no idea you were headed for Cripple Creek too. I watched you this morning—at the Mother Lode, facing down Wade Tillis. I want to tell you I greatly admire your courage . . . and I was ready to defend you if necessary."

Her cheeks colored slightly. "You came all the way up here to tell me that?"

He looked around with watchful eyes. "Not exactly.

97

I saw you walking this way. Thought I'd follow, just to keep a watch and make sure some no-good didn't tail you for the wrong reasons. I don't completely trust Wade Tillis." His blue eyes moved over her tenderly, but they did not make her shiver with revulsion as most men's gazes did. "You shouldn't run around alone like this."

She folded her arms, sure she must always be on the defense. "I'll do what I please, Mr. Hanner. I can take care of myself. I think I proved that when I stood up to Mr. Tillis and got the money he owed me."

He grinned softly. "You did. But he couldn't very well harm you right there in front of everyone. I'm not saying he would for sure, but he's a scheming man, Miss Jones, and you embarrassed him in front of half the town today. You'd better be careful."

She looked away, feeling hypnotized by his eyes. "And I am supposed to trust you, just because I saw you on a train, though I have never once spoken to you until this very moment?"

"No. Trust takes time. But a person has to start someplace, and right now you don't have a soul in this town you can trust. You'll have to get supplies, and find a guide to take you to your claim. And someone has to show you what to do when you get there. I'm a trusted man around here. Some of the miners actually give me their gold to bring to town and get assayed or turned in for money. I know the mountains around here, and I know where Brian O'Toole's claim is. Besides I work for the biggest supply house in town. I can get you set up, and I can lead you to your claim."

She finally met his eyes again, having no choice. "How convenient. And why would you be willing to do all this?"

He shrugged. "It's part of my job. I get paid to lead people in and out, show them about panning, take their supply orders, do anything that's required. You're going to need help, and I would like to see you make this thing work."

She turned around. Why did he make her feel suddenly conscious of how she looked and acted? Why did he make her so aware of the strange feelings he stirred in her? She didn't like those feelings. They went against all she had promised herself, and she scowled angrily.

"Why do you bother, Mr. Hanner? I was very rude to you on the train—deliberately. I don't make a habit of smiling and conversing with strange men."

He grinned, wanting to run up and grab and hold her. She was the most beautiful creature he'd ever seen, and his heart went out to her youth and innocence. She needed help so badly but was fighting it. What had happened to make her so determined to survive all on her own? What made such a sweet, beautiful young girl act so cold and unfeeling? And why was she so insistent about going into the mountains all alone to work a claim, to do something she knew nothing about? Why wasn't anyone with her? He wanted to protect her, help her, but she was not an easy person to win over. The worst part of the whole thing was that she reminded him so much of Mary Beth. The thought of the girl he was once supposed to marry stabbed at his heart. Mary Beth . . . cold and dead . . . her love and softness lost forever.

"I understand that, ma'am. And please call me Buck. That's what everybody calls me. All I'm saying is you

99

need help, whether you like to admit it or not. I'm a trusted man around here. Anyone can tell you that."

She sighed deeply and turned again to face him. "Where are you from, Mr. Hanner? I mean . . . Buck."

"All over. Mostly Texas."

She held her chin haughtily. "You're really just a drifter then."

She saw hurt in his eyes and wished she hadn't said it. "I suppose. A lot of things can make a man a drifter, ma'am. And a lot of things can settle him down again. A man has to have a purpose, and right now I don't have any, except to keep working wherever I can find something to do, to see the country and decide where I'd like to light one day."

"No family? No wife?"

The pain in his eyes deepened. "No on both counts. I almost had a wife once, but she's dead now and that's that."

She softened slightly. "I'm sorry. I know what it's like to lose a loved one to death." She thought about her parents. "But there are some losses that are worse than death." She turned back to make sure the flowers on Brian's grave were secure.

"Your guardian? Stepfather?" he asked. "You mentioned in the saloon that you were Brian O'Toole's ward."

She blinked back tears. "He found me . . . on the docks of St. Louis . . . where my parents had abandoned me. I was six years old. He and his new wife took me in, gave me a home. Then he came out here and died, leaving me his claim."

Buck's heart went out to her. How lonely and frightened she must be. But she was determined not to show it.

Harmony turned to face him again. What was it about him that won her trust?

"Do you really think Wade Tillis might try to harm me?"

He frowned. "Hard to say. He's a devious man. If he did intend you harm, he'd not do it himself. He'd send others to do it. But there are strict laws around here about such things, and I doubt he'd try something very soon. Too many people would suspect it was his doing. You have one benefit, Miss Jones, and that is your courage—the way you put Tillis down. A lot of people are rooting for you, even though they might not say so and might seem to be laughing at you. They'd like you to make a go of it; I would too. But I don't think you know what you're in for. You're going to have to trust someone for advice, someone who can get you started right. When I saw you walk into the Mother Lode, I knew then and there fate was telling me to help you. After seeing you on the train, it was too much of a coincidence, don't you think?"

"Not really. We were both headed for Cripple Creek. We were bound to see each other."

He shrugged. "Think what you want. I followed you up here to see that no harm came to you. And you have to admit I could have harmed you myself if that was on my mind."

She put her hands on her hips. "And how do I know you aren't a spy, working for Wade Tillis?"

His eyes turned icy. "Because I hate Wade Tillis' guts, that's why! He's responsible for— It's a long story and I don't care to talk about it. Let's just say that Wade Tillis is the reason I'm a drifter now, and I make

101

a point to drift in his direction, to goad him, to make him nervous. He knows that some day I'll find a way to kill him, or at least ruin him. I like to see him squirm. Now you are one of his enemies, a stumbling block to more riches for him. I intend to help you remain in his way."

She smiled. She was sure he meant every word he'd said. "Now you're being honest. You don't just want to help me because I'm a poor, defenseless girl. It's a way of getting back at Wade Tillis." She nodded. "No one can be trusted more than a man with vengeance on his mind. You just sold me, Buck Hanner. You may help me with my supplies and lead me to my claim. I'll pay you whatever the going rate is for whatever it is you do."

He flashed that handsome grin again, and she felt an odd warmth in her veins. Was this the way Becky had once felt about Brian, when first they'd met? No! She must not allow such feelings! She must be very careful, very wary.

He bowed then. "Glad to be of service, Miss Jones."

"You may call me Harmony."

He nodded. "Harmony. That's a pretty name—different."

Her smile faded. "Well, I suppose I have my parents to thank for that. They were entertainers, from what I can remember. I suppose the name had something to do with their singing together—in harmony—something like that. I couldn't care less. We'd better get back. If you will show me the store where you work, after a good night's sleep I'll come there in the morning and you can start outfitting me for my journey. By the way, I don't know how to ride a horse."

He laughed lightly. "I'll teach you then. You've got to know out here, Harmony Jones."

As they headed down the hill, she was suddenly defensive again.

"You wait behind," she told him. "I'll go on ahead, and I'll see you in the morning—at the store. Don't come to my door as though you're calling on me. Remember this is strictly business."

She walked on ahead.

"Wait!" he called out. "How am I supposed to show you where the store is?"

She sighed and turned. "Just tell me. I don't want to be seen walking back into town with you, as though we'd been out together."

He grinned. "All right. It's on the very end of town, a few buildings south of your hotel. It's called Jack's Place."

She scowled. "And how did you know what hotel I'm at?"

He gave her a wink, sending that unnerving warmth through her veins again. "I found you here, didn't I?"

She felt almost angry at his sureness, at the thought that he'd been watching her, although she sensed he'd done it out of concern and that she didn't have to fear for her person. Was she being too trusting?

"I'll see you in the morning, Buck Hanner," she said curtly, turning and walking briskly back to town while feeling blue eyes on her back.

Chapter Five

Harmony had trouble sleeping, for it seemed to her that the town of Cripple Creek never slept. Street noises, piano playing, and loud spurts of laughter made her jump awake whenever she did manage to drift off, and her nerves were on edge. Would Wade Tillis send someone to sneak into her room during the night to murder her? A hundred thoughts rushed through her mind, about her meeting in the morning with Buck Hanner, the equipment she must purchase, the need to learn to ride a horse.

Most predominant were thoughts of Buck himself. Could she truly trust him, or was she letting his powerful magnetism hypnotize her? She couldn't quite believe that to be true. There was something so sure about him, a quiet honesty, and a hint of loneliness behind his endearing blue eyes. What had he meant by Wade Tillis being a bitter enemy? What could the man have done to him? And what had happened to the girl he'd once intended to marry? How had she died?

There were so many unanswered questions about the

man; yet she had no one else to turn to. He'd been the only one to offer his services. She determined that she must remember he would simply be her guide, a man who was to supply her with whatever she would need and take her to her claim. She was paying him to do so; their arrangement was strictly business. No feelings must be allowed to enter into it. No womanly instincts must distract her from her purpose. There must be no such thing as friendship between them, so she must stop letting his rugged handsomeness keep producing those odd sensations. She'd never felt them before and they frightened her. She must always remember her mission, the promises she had made to herself, her reason for being here in Cripple Creek, and her promise to Brian O'Toole at his grave.

More laughter came up from the streets, and she rose to make sure her door was locked and to assure herself that the pistol still rested on the stand beside her bed. That was her biggest worry this night—her own safety. She went to a window and peeked through lace curtains to the muddy street below. Across the street a man stood looking up toward her window. He could not see her, for her room was not lighted. But she could see him. He wore a tanned buckskin jacket and a wide-brimmed hat. He kept looking from her window to the walk below it, then up and down the street.

Buck Hanner. He was watching out for her, even through the night! But then, perhaps he was only standing there trying to decide just how to sneak up and rape and murder her. No. She could not believe that was the case. The man was determined to guard her, to make sure nothing happened to her. Did he never sleep? She felt warm, protected, much as she'd felt the night Brian O'Toole had taken her hand and led her away from the docks and from the men who had tried to hurt her.

She turned away, going back to her bed and curling into the quilts. Suddenly feeling safe and unafraid, she began to float into much-needed sleep, wondering if it truly was possible for a woman to find pleasure with a man. Surely not. She could find friendship and protection, like what she had had from Brian O'Toole, but the other—the awful things Jimmie had told her—that could never be pleasurable, and no man would ever do those things to her.

Harmony approached the supply store the next morning, surprised to see Buck already there, winding a rope around a flat-bed wagon full of crates. In the cool of morning, he still wore the fringed buckskin jacket. So, she had been right. It was Buck Hanner who had stood across the street the night before. Yet he looked rested, alert. He turned to see her approaching and flashed that disturbing smile, giving her a nod.

"Morning, Miss Jones."

She swallowed. She was so sure of herself until she was near this man. Perhaps she should find someone else to do these things for her, but who would it be? Did she really have any choice now?

"Good morning, Buck," she replied, putting on a cool air.

His eyes roved over her curving figure, which was accented by the wide sash at the waist of her blue dress. A white shawl graced her shoulders.

"Where are your pants?"

She reddened. "My what?"

"You going to ride a horse in that dress?"

She looked down at herself, then up at him. "I have riding clothes—a skirt split and seamed in the center. That is as far as I will go. I'll not wear pants like a man!"

He grinned. "Suit yourself. But you'd better know right now that when you get up to your claim, you'd best forget about dressing fancy. My advice is to buy yourself a couple of pairs of men's pants." His eyes moved over her again, making her redden more. "Better make that boys' pants—small boys."

Why did she feel so beneath him? So stupid? "I'll wear what I please!" she said angrily.

He stepped closer, pushing back his hat. "You're here to take my advice. You'll be sitting on a log or a rock all day, Miss Jones, panning for gold from a cold creek. You'll have a hell of a time keeping skirts out of the water and you'll be wet half the time. If you wear pants, you can tuck them into high boots and not have to worry about it. Skirts will just get in the way, I guarantee. And pants would be a lot more comfortable for riding, but for that I'll allow the riding skirt if you insist. When we're through outfitting you this morning, you can go back and put one on. Then I'll give you some pointers, and pick out a good horse for you."

He turned back and finished tying a knot. When he looked at her again, she was blinking back tears and nervously pulling her shawl tighter. He frowned and stepped closer again. "What's wrong?"

She looked away, her cheeks crimson. "I'll not wear pants!"

She did not see the gentle, understanding look in his blue eyes. He took out some tobacco and began rolling a cigarette. "Are you here to give a fashion show, or to prove to Wade Tillis—and yourself—that you can make a go of it on that claim?"

He licked and sealed the cigarette as she turned her eyes back up to his. "You know why I'm here."

He nodded, lighting the cigarette and taking a light drag. "Then do what I say, and you'll show them all." His eyes dropped to her full bosom, then back to meet her eyes. "Besides, who the hell is going to see you up there?"

She shrugged, breathing deeply to stop the silly tears. "You, for one."

He left the cigarette at the corner of his mouth. "So what? I'm just your guide, and I intend to give you the best advice I can. And seeing a little girl in a lousy pair of boys' pants certainly wouldn't be the most shocking thing I've ever seen. Besides, lots of girls who live and work on ranches wear them. It's no big thing."

He turned and talked to a man who came out of the store to board the wagon. She wanted to ask him if he really thought of her that way—as a little girl. But it would be much too forward.

Moments later he took her by the arm, sending unwanted shivers through her bones as he led her into the store and began taking down various items and explaining them: cooking pans, kerosene, boots, flannel shirts, a heavy, fleece-lined jacket, several pairs of gloves, a shovel and pick and sledge hammer, a coffee pot, three tin "gold pans," which looked more like pie pans to Harmony; glass bottles which he would "explain later;" two knives, one large and one small; canvas bags for packing gear; a rifle and ammunition, another I'll-teach-you item; a tin wash basin; blankets;

109

kerosene lamps; lumber.

"I'll build you a sluice when we get up there. It'll make your job easier," he told her. "I have a suspicion Tillis' men won't leave things undamaged before leaving. If there was a sluice there, it won't be in one piece."

"What's a sluice?"

He sighed and shook his head. "Don't worry about it now. They're also called rockers, or long toms. You'll see."

And they bought food: beans, dried meat, flour, salt, sugar, a little candy—"for when it gets boring and you're feeling sorry for yourself"—and some whiskey.

"Why would I need whiskey?"

He only shrugged. "You never can tell. Whiskey is good for more than getting drunk, ma'am, although that's its most pleasant purpose."

"Well, I don't drink!"

He grinned and kept working. "I'm sure you don't," he muttered. "By the way, Mister O'Toole left a few things at the cabin—some crude furniture, a home-made bed, a table and a couple of chairs, and a big iron stove you can heat and cook with."

She watched him, the powerful shoulders, the tanned face. "Then there is a cabin?"

"Sure there's a cabin."

She frowned. "Did you know him well?"

He stopped and watched her. "No. I only took him supplies now and then."

Her eyes widened with sudden realization. "You! Surely you're the one who took him the message—brought him back to town after he collapsed!"

He sobered. "I am. I got him here as quickly as I could, but it was hopeless." He studied the enticing

110

green eyes. "If it makes you feel any better, he muttered once, 'Harmony. Poor Harmony.' I didn't know then who he meant. He never said anything to me about you, or about any of his personal matters. I just brought him here, and the doctor took care of the rest."

Now she knew she could trust him. Somehow this made all the difference. He had been the last person to see Brian O'Toole alive! Had talked to him! Knew him!

"Why on earth didn't you tell me this before!" she exclaimed.

He shrugged. "I wanted you to trust me on sheer judgment and intuition, not just because I happened to be the one to take a message to your guardian."

She frowned and watched him as he continued to pile up supplies, briefly explaining as he went along, confusing her more with every item.

"How on earth will we get all this up there?" she asked.

"By mule. We'll rent several, or rather you'll rent them from this store. And you can either buy or rent a horse. But I'll have to bring it back down with me. You can't carry enough feed for a whole winter, and there's not enough grass where you're going to sustain a horse. Of course, if you like I can leave a horse up there and come up more often to bring feed for it, but that will cost you more money and probably isn't necessary. Even if you got the idea to leave, you'd never find your way back to Cripple Creek. You'd only get lost and probably die. Your best bet is to stay put. I'll come up now and again to check on you, bring you more food and whatever other supplies you might need. And if you need to come back, you can come back with me."

She felt a gnawing apprehension. "Will I be . . .

totally alone? Won't there be other miners nearby?"

He set down some woolen socks. "Not close enough to call out to. The closest is a three- or four-hour ride away. O'Toole's claim is pretty remote, mainly because most mines in that area are played out. My guess is his isn't worth much either, but we'll see. Now, about those pants." He picked up a pair of heavy woolen pants and held them up, scrutinizing their size, and she blushed. "These look pretty good. Why don't you try them on?"

He held them out to her, and she was angry again, jerking them from his hands. "I'll do no such thing! I'll not wear these until absolutely necessary!" She held them up to her waist and judged the length and size. "They seem to be close enough. Just throw them in with everything else."

He laughed lightly, finishing his cigarette and stepping it out. He added a washtub and scrub board to the pile. "You're going to use up most of that four hundred dollars you conned out of Tillis yesterday," he commented.

"I did not con him out of anything. The money was rightfully mine."

He grinned, taking out a tablet and writing figures on it. "I know that," he replied.

She watched him writing down prices. Apparently he had some education. She hadn't thought drifters had any at all.

"I know all about running supply stores, so you'd better not try to cheat me," she announced.

He looked at her with raised eyebrows. "Oh, heaven forbid I should do that. And how is it you know all about supply stores?" He kept writing.

"I helped run Mister O'Toole's for years. He owned a

big supply store in St. Louis, and a warehouse too. I kept his books for him, and his brother and I ran the store all by ourselves after Mister O'Toole came out here."

Buck frowned and looked at her again. "Why didn't you just stay there? Sounds like a good, solid business to me. It's certainly safer and more secure than coming out to a place like this to pan for gold."

She dropped her eyes. "There was no will. I couldn't prove I had any right to any of it, and Jimmie—Mister O'Toole's brother—he left me no alternative. It was either leave or . . ."

She did not finish but bent down to inspect the fleece-lined jacket. Buck watched her, suspecting what the alternative was: submit or be thrown penniless into the streets. His pity for her was growing, and he didn't like the other feeling that was growing with it. This poor girl who was trying to act so grown-up was afraid on the inside. She had been through hell.

"At least I have the claim," she was saying. "It's all mine. It represents security. I intend to work it and make money off it, and someday I'll open a supply store of my own. I'll be a successful business woman and will depend on no one. I'll never depend on a soul again, not for the rest of my life!"

"Well, Miss Independence, how about paying for all this then? You ready to fork up four hundred and ten dollars?"

She frowned. "I suppose I have to trust that you added everything correctly."

He handed her the pad. "See for yourself, Miss Jones. You say you ran a supply store once. You should know what this stuff costs."

She glanced at the figures quickly, then slapped the pad back into his hand and dug into her handbag, pulling out some bills. "I thought you were going to call me Harmony," she muttered.

"Gladly. I just wasn't sure you'd feel the same today as you did yesterday. And since you get your dander up so easily, I thought I'd be careful."

She handed him the money and smiled a little. "I do seem short, Buck. I'm sorry. It's just that I want this to work. I have to be very careful."

He took the bills, his fingers lightly touching her own when he did so, his blue eyes holding her green ones. "So do I, Harmony. You know, I could possibly get my boss to grubstake you."

"Grubstake?"

"Yeah. Put up the supplies and food in return for a share of your findings."

She thought for a moment, eying all the merchandise. "No. I wouldn't want to do it that way. Whatever I find will be all mine and no one else's."

He shrugged. "Whatever you say. I just hate to take this much money from you."

"I worked hard back in St. Louis, and I made sure I got what was coming to me before I left. I have enough."

He glanced at her as he walked behind the counter, little doubting she'd been very bold in demanding what was rightfully hers back in St. Louis. She had spunk and strength and a willingness to learn. He couldn't help but think what a fine rancher's wife she'd make. He began conversing then with another man who came out from a back room. He introduced the man to Harmony as Jack Leads, the owner of the store.

114

Harmony struck up a conversation with Leads about supply stores while Buck carried her goods into a back room. When he returned, he took her arm and led her outside.

"Go get that riding skirt on, Shortcake, and I'll give you your first lesson."

She looked up at him and blinked. "What about my things?"

"They'll keep. You've got to learn to ride before we can head out. I'll take care of packing everything for you when it's time to leave. But you'll need a couple of days of riding lessons, and after that you might be too sore to go anyplace for a few more days."

"Sore? Why?"

He laughed and gave her a shove. "You'll find out. Now go change. I'll be right here."

She smiled and left, walking toward the hotel. She turned back once to see him kneeling by a hitching post, smoking, watching her. She liked him, more than she cared to admit. It upset her, yet it was good to feel she had at least one friend. And what had he called her? Shortcake? That was a funny name. It made her feel good . . . warm. It had come out of his mouth so naturally, as though that was just what he was supposed to call her. No one had ever given her a nickname, and even though his touch and his eyes gave her those odd feelings, she was not afraid of him. Somehow she knew Buck Hanner would never hurt her or force her or be rude to her. Why, he'd never touch her at all . . . unless she wanted him to.

She scowled then, and marched on to the hotel. How stupid to have such thoughts! She had no time for such things, no desire for them. Besides, he was a drifter. He had probably charmed many a girl with that smile and those eyes and that way of his. She'd better be on guard! She'd not be taken advantage of by any man, especially not a drifter like Buck Hanner! She had higher goals in mind—independence, freedom, riches, success! A man like Buck Hanner didn't fit any of those plans!

Buck had been right. Harmony spent the next few days in embarrassing pain, unable to walk quite properly. She doubted she would ever ease into a saddle with the grace and naturalness that Buck showed. With him a horse seemed just another limb. To Harmony a horse was a giant, awkward, frightening beast, even the gentle mare Buck put her on. The mare seemed to sense her ignorance and fear, and it displayed gentle obedience and utmost patience. Harmony actually grew fond of the dapple gray horse with the white mane, Pepper. Buck was riding a reddish stallion called Indian.

In spite of blisters in unmentionable places and the flush that came to her face at Buck's teasing, Harmony insisted on riding every day, wanting to learn as much as she could as fast as she could, insisting that the soreness would go away more quickly if she rode every day.

Buck set an easy pace. He realized she was hiding a lot of the pain and he admired her courage and determination. Harmony enjoyed the rides, for they took her away from Cripple Creek and the stares and the fear of attack by Wade Tillis' men. That fear lessened every day, for just as Buck had explained,

Tillis didn't dare make a move against her right now. It was against the code. But would he do it once she was alone in the mountains? Surely not there either. People would still know. Besides, it would be easier for Tillis to wait her out, sure she'd never succeed. That only made her more determined. She'd die before she'd go crawling to Wade Tillis to sell her claim.

The surrounding country was beautiful, and Harmony grew to love it more every day. It was so big that she felt a freedom here she'd never experienced in St. Louis. Social codes were not so strict here. People were more relaxed, more uncaring. The country—big, sprawling, free and easy—fit men like Buck Hanner well. Harmony realized that she liked Buck more each day, but she still didn't know much about him. Every time she tried to talk to him about his past, he changed the subject. She knew him well, yet didn't know him at all, and her feelings for him were mixed, confused. She wasn't certain just how a woman was supposed to feel about a man. Could a man and woman be friends without being intimate? Of course! That was the only way it could be anyway. At first, she had not even wanted to be friends, but how could it be any other way when they were forced to spend so much time together?

All her fears of being rudely attacked by him were gone. He'd had plenty of chances. Yet he'd never approached her wrongly, never voiced such desires, never treated her as anything but a young girl he was teaching to ride and was preparing to guide to a mining claim. She supposed that was all she was to a man like Buck Hanner. She now knew that he was twenty-seven, a full ten years older than she was, and he had been on his own since the age of twelve, fending for himself

117

completely. He had not said why, only that he'd been on his own since that age. One thing she did know was that he surely thought of her as only a little girl, and his nickname of Shortcake had stuck, as though she were a little sister of sorts. That was fine with her, she reasoned. It made everything a lot easier, for when they went to the claim, they would be traveling alone, after which she would be left behind to do what must be done and that would be the end of Buck Hanner.

By the seventh day after her arrival at Cripple Creek, Harmony was ready to travel. She found it impossible to sleep that night; her heart and mind were filled with a myriad of emotions and fears. She would be leaving civilization behind, leaving safety for danger, leaving Buck. But it was good that he would leave her once she got to the site. She'd already become too dependent on him despite her vow that that would not happen again. She was looking to him for help as she had once looked to Brian, and that was not good. So, at least that would be settled.

But what about being all alone on a mountainside? What about wild animals? And the rifle? He hadn't taught her how to use it. She must be sure to learn before he left. It was exciting, yet so frightening.

Could she really do this? Could she really survive? Would she die or fail as Wade Tillis had said she would? No. Out of pure spite she would not fail. She would show him! She'd show the whole town! Besides, her whole life she had actually been alone, even though she'd been among people. So what if she was on a mountainside all by herself? What would be so

118

different about that? She had only herself anyway.

She tossed in bed. How would she ever sleep this night? It was then she heard footsteps outside her door, and a scratching sound. Bright moonlight illuminated the doorsill, and her eyes widened as someone pushed a piece of paper with a small object resting on it, under the door. Her heart pounded wildly, and she couldn't even bring herself to reach for her pistol. She lay rigid, staring at the piece of paper, listening to retreating footsteps.

For several minutes she just lay and stared at the paper; finally she found the courage to sit up and light a lamp. She frowned, eying the paper and the object as she stepped closer, then bent to pick them up. The paper bore a note.

"GOOD LUCK, MISS JONES. YOU'LL NEED IT. AND YOU'D BETTER LEARN HOW TO USE ONE OF THESE. LOOK IT OVER WELL. EVERY MINER NEEDS THESE. THIS ONE IS FREE. WHEN YOU GET LONESOME UP THERE, THERE ARE PLENTY OF MEN HERE IN TOWN WHO'LL GLADLY COME AND KEEP YOU COMPANY. MAYBE WE'LL COME EVEN IF YOU AREN'T LONELY."

She shivered at the meaning of the words and blinked back tears. Picking up the object, she walked over to sit on the bed and hold it under a lamp. It was small and tubular shaped, made of copper—and something was stuffed into it. The child in her made her curious, and she took out a hat pin to poke at the contents, but before she could do so there was a knock at the door. Her heart pounded with fear, and she laid the copper tube on her bed and picked up her revolver, pointing it nervously at the door. "Who is it!" she demanded.

"It's me—Buck. You all right?"

She breathed a sigh of relief. "Why do you ask?"

"Somebody was just up here. Now I see your light is on. What happened?"

"It . . . it's nothing. Someone slid a nasty note under the door, and some silly little copper tube. I don't know why, and he didn't scare me."

"Don't lie to me, Harmony Jones. And let me in. I want to see the copper object."

"It's just a little tube, that's all. And I can't let you in. I'm not properly dressed."

"Then put on a goddamned robe! Let me in before I make a scene and everybody in this hotel sees me breaking down the door to get into your room!"

She swallowed. She really was scared. What did it matter if Buck knew it? No one else need know. She carefully laid down the little revolver, glad he'd been watching her room, yet still wondering if his intentions were entirely honorable and she was foolish to continue trusting him. She looked at the copper tube again. What could be so important about a copper tube?

"Harmony Jones, open this door!" he commanded, a little louder.

She quickly got up, pulling on a robe and tying the sash. She felt her cheeks going crimson at the thought of a man she still hardly knew seeing her in her robe, but she didn't want him to make a scene. She unlocked the door and opened it slowly, peeking out at him. The anger and concern in his blue eyes changed momentarily to sudden admiration, and his jaw flexed from restrained desire at the sight of the long, blond hair falling over her shoulders, at the look in her innocent green eyes, and at the knowledge that beneath two thin layers of material lay full, untouched breasts and skin he knew must be soft as satin—a woman's body possessed by an innocent, untouched by man. He suddenly wanted her first man to be himself—her only man, for that matter. But he dared not mention such a thing now, not this soon. She'd throw him out on his ear and hire another guide, and he didn't trust anyone else to take her safely to her claim.

He forced back an urge to grab her and taste those tempting lips, to press her untasted breasts against his chest and feel her lustrous hair twining through his fingers.

"Where's the copper tube?" he asked quietly, coming inside and closing the door.

She glanced at him and then backed away, like a caged animal about to be attacked. She kept her arms folded in front of her and nodded toward the bed. "I laid it over there."

He walked over to the bed, painfully aware of his manly desire. Sometimes he wished he could be less honorable with her. Lord, he had been at times. But something about Harmony Jones kept him in check. She'd been hurt. She was afraid but courageous. Whatever happened to her from now on had to be of her own choosing. She was not a girl to be forced into anything. He picked up the copper tube and sighed.

"Just as I thought." He turned to face her. "It's a

121

blasting cap. They're inserted into dynamite sticks to create the necessary explosion once a spark touches it."

She frowned. "I don't understand."

"Miners throw these around like wastepaper. Many a child has picked one up and played with it, probed around inside it out of curiosity, only to have his or her fingers blown off, sometimes half a hand, depending on how it was held. Someone was hoping the same thing would happen to you, delaying your trip to the claim—or maybe even convincing you to go back to St. Louis."

She blinked in astonishment, then reddened, realizing what a child she really was, for she had started to probe the tube herself out of curiosity. A lump swelled in her throat, and he could see her struggling not to cry. "Why do people . . . have to be so mean?" she said quietly.

"Because bastards like Wade Tillis enjoy such pranks. They enjoy wielding their power, enjoy trying to make people squirm. Don't let him make you squirm, Shortcake. It's just what he wants. You walk out into that street tomorrow smiling and looking entirely confident. I decided a long time ago that he'd never make me squirm, that I'd turn it around. I've been making him nervous for a long time. He's always wondering when I might make a move against him. I'm enjoying doing nothing more than if I went over there and beat the hell out of him, which I'm sure I'll end up doing someday. But it will be at the right place and the right time."

She frowned. "Why? You never said why you hate him."

He sighed deeply, running his eyes over her and making her blush again. "Not tonight, Shortcake. It's hard for me to talk about, and I don't know you well enough to bother you with it. I'm just your guide, remember? You get back to sleep. I'll go get rid of this. And don't worry about anything else happening. I'll be around. Where's the note they gave you?"

"I . . . it's nothing. I don't want you to read it. It's . . . embarrassing."

"Threats against your person?"

She turned away. "I wish you would leave now."

He stepped up behind her, tempted to reach out and touch her hair, but he only watched her a moment. "I'm very tempted right now to walk down to the Mother Lode and call Wade Tillis out!" he growled, his voice husky with anger.

"No!" She whirled about. "What if something happened to you? Who would . . . who would take me to the claim? I don't want anybody else to take me. And I don't want anything to happen—" She reddened deeply then. She had shown too much emotion, acted as though she cared about him. "I mean . . . you're the only person I can trust. If something happened to you I'd have no guide and I'd have to start all over again." She stiffened, deliberately erasing all signs of concern. "I'm paying you well, Buck Hanner, so don't go getting into some ridiculous fight. It was just a scare tactic. Wade Tillis won't really do anything. We both know that. Now please leave my room. Someone might have seen you come in."

He walked toward the door, then stopped and held her eyes a moment longer. "You can give me orders as your guide, Shortcake. But you can't control my personal life. If I think a man has something coming to him, I see that he gets it. I'll let this go, just this one

123

time, for your sake. Since we're leaving in the morning there's no sense taking any last-minute chances. But I'll not stand for you being bothered anymore." He nodded, his eyes roving over her full figure appreciatively. "Good night."

He quickly went through the door, and by the time she got to it, he was gone, the hallway empty. She closed and locked the door, then walked over to her bed. She could sleep now. Buck Hanner would see that no more harm came to her. She touched her hair, wondering how she had looked to him, so plain, her hair unbound, no coloring on her cheeks. She was too innocent to realize she was more tempting to a man the way she looked now than when her hair was drawn up in curls, her face powdered, and she wore her most expensive dress. She curled back into bed and was soon asleep, none of the street noises bothering her now.

Chapter Six

The morning broke, bright with sunshine lighting first the peaks of the mountains to the west, its warmth spreading downward as it peeked over the mountains to the east. Harmony stuck her head out the window of her room to feel the warmth, judging that this first day of her journey would be an almost perfect one, perhaps a little too warm. She ducked back inside, looking again into the mirror. Her hair was wrapped into one thick braid that hung down her back, and her cotton plaid blouse was tucked into a tan riding skirt, her high boots meeting the hem so that none of her leg showed.

She adjusted her belt, not even realizing how enticing she appeared with her full breasts filling out the blouse invitingly. She placed a wide-brimmed felt hat on her head for protection from the sun, then pulled on light leather gloves to keep her hands from getting calloused while handling the reins.

She turned, checking the room and the dresser drawers to be sure she had everything. Then she closed her carpetbag and suitcase. She had already paid the

125

hotel clerk. She had only to leave, but Buck had instructed her not to do so until he arrived to escort her.

She sighed impatiently, tempted just to walk over to the supply store, where the mules should be packed and ready. The event of the night before seemed trivial and silly, now that the bright sunshine lit up the room so cheerfully. This morning she felt no fear. Her heart pounded with excitement for she was actually leaving—riding into the mountains to find her gold claim and make her fortune. She was independent! And in spite of her seventeen years she was as much a woman as any older female. After all, she had been through many hardships—abandonment, poverty, manhandling. She had already learned many lessons that took some people most of their lives to learn. Her experiences had hardened her, prepared her for this very moment. Maybe that was why all these things had happened to her. Maybe way back when she'd been abandoned God had known that someday she would have to work a gold claim all alone in the Rocky Mountains. Perhaps these hardships would make her alert and clever and determined, strong and brave.

Then she heard the familiar footsteps in the hallway. Buck. Maybe she wasn't so brave after all. Maybe Buck helped her feel brave. Again she fought the uncomfortable feelings he aroused in her, fought her growing dependency on Buck Hanner. She must not allow that to happen. He was coming to guide her to her claim, and that was all. He knocked at the door then, and she hurried to fling it open, her eyes dancing, her lips smiling with excitement.

"I thought you'd never get here!" she exclaimed. "I've been ready since dawn!"

Again he wondered how he could hold himself in check once he was alone with Harmony in the mountains. Why did she have to be so beautiful? To wear that blouse? Why did her long, blond hair hang in that thick, beautiful braid nearly to her waist when she turned to get her bags; and how could the hips of such an innocent girl sway so seductively when she walked? In all his experience at guiding miners into the mountains, he'd never run into something like this. He wasn't certain if this trip would be pleasant or painful.

"I did a last-minute check of the gear," he told her. "Here, let me take your bags."

"I can carry them," she insisted.

"At least give me the damned suitcase, Miss Independence."

She grinned and handed it to him, and they went into the hallway and down the steps. When they stepped out onto the narrow boardwalk, the street was bustling with activity: men entering town, men leaving, wagons rattling up and down, horses churning up mud. The smell of horse droppings was extra strong this morning, and Harmony wrinkled her nose. "I think the men who walk the streets picking up horse litter are late this morning."

Buck laughed. "Such things aren't done every day here like they are in your fancy St. Louis, Shortcake," he replied. He breathed deeply through his nose. "Besides, it's a good smell."

"Oh, Buck!"

He laughed again. "I've been around horses all my life—lassoed mustangs, broke them in, cleaned their stalls, rode drag on cattle drives, served as wrangler. I've been breathing in that smell for a long time. A man get's used to it."

She walked rapidly to keep up with his long stride. "What's drag? And what's a wrangler?"

"Drag is when you ride at the back of the herd, keep track of stragglers. You get that job when you're young and inexperienced, and the pay stinks. I made up my mind I'd not do that for long. I worked my way forward to better jobs real fast. A wrangler is the man who takes care of the cavvy, the herd of extra horses they take along on a cattle drive."

"It sounds exciting. You'll have to tell me more."

"Well, God knows we'll have plenty of time to talk once we get out of Cripple Creek. Once you find out how lonely it is up there, you'll probably talk my head off. I'd better tell you now, I like the peace and quiet of the mountains and don't care for nonstop conversation, so save most of it for when we make camp at night. Besides, the more you talk, the thirstier you get, and out here in this dry climate, you get thirsty enough without talking at all."

"Yes, sir."

He led her to a tiny restaurant, where a widowed woman cooked meals for a living and where they had eaten several times before. "Best food this side of Pike's Peak," he had said when he'd first taken her there, and once Harmony had tasted her dinner, she'd agreed. They sat down, setting Harmony's bags beside them, and the widow came over to them, her face bright with smiles.

"So this is your big day!" she said kindly to Harmony. "Oh, you're such a brave girl, Miss Jones."

Harmony blushed a little. "Thank you, ma'am. I'll have the usual breakfast—and lots of the fried potatoes. We have a long ride ahead of us."

"I guess you do! And how about you, Buck? Your usual?"

Buck grinned. "You've got it—and an extra piece of steak. And bring us some coffee, would you, Wanda?"

"Sure thing." The plump, aging woman quickly left, and Harmony noticed several people in the packed little room staring at her, all men. She reddened more, then met Buck's eyes.

"I feel like a side show," she told him quietly.

"You might as well accept it. They've been staring at you all week, and making bets on whether or not you'd go through with this."

Her eyebrows raised in surprise. "Bets?"

"Mm-hmmm. I made one myself."

"You did?" Her green eyes narrowed. "Which way did you bet, Buck Hanner?"

He laughed lightly. "That you'd do it."

She pursed her lips. "It's a good thing."

Wanda brought their coffee and left again, and Buck lit a cigarette. "To tell you the truth, Shortcake, I don't expect to get out of town without some kind of trouble, so be prepared. This is Wade Tillis' last chance to try to change your mind. He won't hurt you, but I've no doubt he's got something in mind."

She sipped her coffee. "What about you? Maybe he'll try to hurt you. You're my guide."

He took a light drag on the cigarette. "It's possible. But he can't go too far without the town coming down on him, even though he is an important man around here. They've all got bets on you, and his interference makes it unfair to those who bet that you'd go. My guess is the most he'll try to do is discourage you at the last minute. If he shows his hand, don't pay any attention to anything he tells you. Got that?"

"Yes. But what about last night? If I had poked at that cap, that would have hurt me."

"Yeah, but he wasn't being observed like he'll be this morning. He could have said some no-good did that."

She swallowed more coffee. "I'm so nervous, Buck. I want it all to work. I want to be able to do this. I want to stay up there all winter and pan for that gold, maybe even dig deeper. Maybe I'll even find the mother lode."

He drank a little coffee himself. "Don't count too much on that, Shortcake. That area doesn't yield much anymore. It was mined out pretty good in the fifties. But you never know. I've seen it happen before, even in the short time I've been at this. Of course I wasn't around in the fifties to see what went on then. But they took a hell of a lot of gold out of that area."

"I don't care. I'm going to make a fortune. I just know it. And neither Wade Tillis nor anyone else is going to cheat me out of what is mine."

He grinned. "That's the spirit. Besides, if you make it, I win two hundred dollars."

She sucked in her breath and her eyes filled with surprise and a hint of disappointment. "Is that the only reason you're taking me?"

He gave her a wink. "Of course it is."

She scowled then. "Buck Hanner!"

He laughed lightly. "You know better than that. I told you I've got it in for Tillis—and I admire your determination. You're just a kid, but I want to help you. And I have the crazy feeling that you're going to do okay, Harmony Jones."

She smiled again. "Thank you."

Their breakfast was brought then, and the next few minutes were spent eating. Harmony wondered why she cared if he might only be taking her to win a bet. It shouldn't really matter, but there were so many things she felt about Buck Hanner that she couldn't quite understand. He was a good friend, yet not in the fatherly way Brian O'Toole had been. Brotherly, perhaps? No. Not that either. She liked him, but she did not desire him the way Dora May Harper desired men. Doing such things still frightened and repulsed her. And yet the thought of Buck Hanner doing those things with some other woman brought an odd burning sensation, almost like jealousy; yet surely it could not be! Why on earth would she be jealous of any woman who might do such hideous things with this man who was simply a casual friend and a guide—a man she had no other interest in? She was sometimes tempted to ask him pointedly if there was a special woman in his life right now, or if he visited the whores often? But a lady could only wonder about such things and never ask.

Breakfast was soon over and Buck insisted on paying for it. After several hugs and much well-wishing from Wanda, who handed them a cloth bag full of fresh biscuits and another full of fresh cinnamon cookies, Harmony was able to leave. They headed north then, toward the supply store, but as they approached it, Buck slowed down and Harmony's heart began to pound with dread and apprehension.

Men lined both sides of the street along the final several yards to the store, and even from a distance, Harmony and Buck could see that Wade Tillis himself languished on the steps, two of his men casually leaning against the support posts of the porch. The store sat on

131

a cross street, at the very end of and facing the main street down which Buck and Harmony now walked.

Harmony swallowed. "Buck?"

He gently grasped her arm. "Take it easy." He guided her off the boardwalk and into the middle of the street, facing Wade Tillis, who stood up from his sitting position on the steps of the store, chewing on a thin cigar. "Keep your chin up, Shortcake," Buck told her quietly. "And keep that determined look in your eyes."

She took a deep breath. "I'd walk right up to that man even if you weren't with me!" she declared.

"That's the stuff. Come on."

The men who had come to watch the confrontation were quiet, watching, listening, curious. Again Harmony felt their eyes on her, some friendly, some belligerent. Buck walked her closer to the store, stopping just a few yards from Tillis and nodding. "Morning, gentlemen."

Tillis chewed the cigar, his eyes roving Harmony, again with the look of a hungry wolf. "Sleep well last night, Miss Jones?"

She looked up at Buck and he gave her a wink. "Go ahead. You can answer."

She turned glaring green eyes back to Tillis. "Very well, thank you."

He grinned. "I heard you had a visitor. Some no-good told me this morning that he slipped a nasty note under your door." He shook his head. "That's a terrible thing to do." His eyes moved from Harmony to Buck and then back to her. "Of course, maybe you weren't alone, and you were too busy to see the note. In that case, the note wouldn't offend you, considering what you were probably up to. Maybe Buck can tell us."

She could not stop her cheeks from coloring deeply then, or the lump from coming to her throat. Extreme anger always made her want to cry. She jerked her arm out of Buck's hand.

"I was alone, Mister Wade Tillis!" she spat back. "And I found the note, which you most likely put there yourself! Perhaps you'd like all these men here to know that the note was a threat to my person. I was threatened with violation! And perhaps they'd like to know that a blasting cap accompanied the note. The person who gave it to me apparently expected me to be young and ignorant enough to toy with it and blow away half my hand! That would have slowed me up a bit, wouldn't it, Mister Tillis! Perhaps long enough for you to take over my claim!"

There was a muttering from the crowd, and Buck grinned as Tillis scowled with anger and humiliation. Harmony didn't know where she'd gotten her courage, for on the inside she was shaking violently. Her anger seemed to give her the necessary fire, and she picked up the suitcase Buck had set down and marched up to Tillis. "I am going inside. Are you going to show me what a big, brave man you are and stop me in front of all these men?"

His dark eyes narrowed. "You need a man to tone you down a notch, Miss Jones," he growled quietly. Then he grinned. "Or hasn't ole Buck been able to do that yet? Maybe he's not man enough for you."

She blinked back tears. "You're despicable, Wade Tillis! And the day any man tries to take me down a notch is the day he dies! Just try me!"

"Harmony!" Buck barked. "Just go on inside."

She shot him a look, her face filled with humiliation

and hurt. Then she marched toward the store.

"Miss Jones!" Tillis called out. "Did ole Buck tell you about all the dangers up there in the mountains? The bears? The wolves? How about the rats that run rampant in the cabin? He tell you about that? You'll find pack rats warming your feet at night, little lady, if you've no man to do it."

She turned and smiled. "I'd rather have pack rats in my bed than the likes of you!" she sneered.

The whole crowd laughed delightedly and shouted to Wade Tillis that he had let a little girl get the better of him again. Harmony marched up the steps past Tillis' two men, and Tillis, fists clenched, turned and started after her.

"Tillis!" Buck called out. "Don't you go another step!"

The man turned slowly, glaring at Buck and pushing his top coat away from his gun. Then he grinned. "You ready to die for your little piece, Hanner? Maybe you've already done to her what you tried to do to Mary Beth."

Buck's blue eyes turned to ice. "Say that name again, or take one step toward Harmony Jones, and you're a dead man, Wade Tillis! You know I don't need much reason to put a bullet between your eyes!"

Harmony stood at the doorway. She set down the carpetbag and suitcase, her heart pounding with fear for Buck. Wade Tillis' two men stepped down off the porch, taking positions on either side of Tillis, all three of them eying Buck.

Tillis grinned. "You intending to take all three of us?" he asked.

"Maybe so. But whether I can or not doesn't matter.

You're sure to go first, no matter what else happens. You'll be dead either way. If you want to die just so your men can shoot me, then go ahead and draw that gun!"

There was a moment of intense quiet, and no one would have known that there were any men around at all, for the only sound was the mountain wind. Wade Tillis swallowed, little beads of sweat on his forehead.

"There will be a better time," he said, lowering his hands and putting his topcoat back over his gun.

One of his men went for his gun, however, and to Harmony's surprise, Buck's gun was out and fired before she even realized what was going on. The man flew backward and sprawled on his back; then Buck waved his gun at Tillis and the second man. The local sheriff came running into the street then.

"What's going on here!" he demanded.

"It was fair, Sheriff!" a man from the crowd shouted. "Cliff pulled a gun on Buck there, and Buck beat him out, fair and square."

Harmony breathed deeply for control, putting a shaking hand to her chest, where her heart pounded furiously. For a brief moment she realized Buck could have been killed, for her! Why had he risked his life if he was simply a guide? Her feelings were even more confused, and she realized she'd have been very sad if Buck Hanner had been killed.

"You tell Tillis to stay away from Harmony Jones and her claim!" Buck was telling the sheriff. "All these men here are witnesses that he threatened her. If anything happens to her while she's alone on her claim, Wade Tillis will be the first man blamed! And we all know what happens to claim jumpers and thieves, men

135

who try to get their hands on someone else's diggings."

Some of the men raised fists and agreed, shouting for Wade Tillis to leave. Tillis glared back at Buck, his dark eyes full of hate. "You win . . . this time," he growled. "But someday it will be my turn. I'll beat you out, Buck Hanner, just like I did with Mary Beth!"

"You as much as killed her!" Buck hissed back at him. "And you watch how you play your hand, Wade Tillis, or you'll be as dead as your friend there!"

"All right, that's enough!" the sheriff spoke up. "Buck, you go on in there and get things ready for your trip. Tillis, you get back to the Mother Lode and stay out of this. Let the girl be on her way. And I'd better not hear that anything has happened to her up there, because Buck is right. You'll be the first man we suspect!"

Tillis smiled. "Why, Sheriff, you know I'm always at the Mother Lode. A lot of people can always vouch for my whereabouts. And I'd never hurt a little kid like that. I was just teasing her—thought I could scare her a little." He looked around, assuming the posture of a good man. "After all, we all know it's foolish for her to try to go up there alone. It's dangerous." He looked back at the sheriff. "I was only looking out for her. Buck here doesn't seem to care. If he did, he'd never take her there. I was just trying to talk some sense into her, that's all. But Buck here got all hopped up, and before I knew it, one of my own men got riled and pulled a gun."

The sheriff sighed. "Sure, Wade. Now get going."

Wade puffed the cigar, eying Buck again. "It's you the men should be angry with," he announced, "taking that poor girl up there to who knows what horrible fate." While he and his other man left, Harmony still stood at the doorway, watching Buck. Was Tillis right? If Buck really cared, maybe he wouldn't be doing this. Maybe he really just wanted to win a bet. He met her eyes then with his kind blue ones, and her emotions were torn by panic at the thought of anything happening to him, admiration for the way he'd stood up for her and had risked his life . . . and a gnawing doubt. Did he really care for her or was this all a game to him. Perhaps he even had some ulterior motive in mind; she would be alone with him in the wild. Sudden, last-minute panic and doubt rushed through her, yet it was subdued as he came closer, reading her green eyes with his hypnotic blue ones, holding her gaze until he was standing very close to her.

"Maybe he's right. Maybe I shouldn't take you up there at all."

"And maybe you're just determined to take me in order to win a bet—and to get me alone," Harmony replied, watching his eyes.

His eyes didn't waver. "Do you really believe that?"

She glanced at the body of the man he'd just shot. Some men were picking it up. Then she looked back at him. "I don't know what to believe. You just killed a man who tried to stop us."

"That had nothing to do with you. Wade wouldn't shoot it out over a half-grown girl and an almost worthless claim. He was just using you as an excuse to get to me. He'd like to see me dead, so he doesn't have to worry about me anymore. But he knew better than to draw on me. He doesn't play that fair, but he needs a better excuse than what happened this morning. He was just testing me—and you. He wants you to fail.

137

You going to let that happen?"

She swallowed. "No. But . . . that man is dead. Doesn't that bother you?"

He frowned. "Some. Bothers any man who's got any decency in him. But he drew on me. I had no choice. He made his move and suffered for it."

She put a hand to her head. "I don't understand you. You mix me up. Why does Wade Tillis want you dead? Why do you hate him?"

"I'll tell you sometime. But not right now, Shortcake." He leaned against the doorjamb. "How about it? You still going?"

She sighed deeply, glancing out at the small crowd that had gathered to see what Harmony Jones would do. She reminded herself why she had come, why she was so determined to make it all work. What difference did men like Wade Tillis or Buck Hanner make? What did they have to do with her promises to herself? She had vowed to claim her piece of land, and she would do so. She had let her feelings interfere lately, obscuring her real purpose for being here. So what if Tillis and Hanner had it in for each other? That had nothing to do with her working her own claim. Buck Hanner simply had to take her there, then leave; and that was that. Half the town had heard Buck and the sheriff warn Tillis to leave her alone, so Tillis didn't dare harm her now. The showdown, and her announcement of what had happened to her the night before, only verified Wade Tillis' underhanded schemes. She had shown him up twice. He'd be wise to leave her alone now.

She met Buck's eyes again. "Yes," she told him. Her green eyes hardened. "And I meant what I said about no man taking me down a notch—and about preferring rats, not just to Wade Tillis but to any man."

That handsome, unnerving smile passed over his lips, almost making her angry. He pushed back his hat a little, and a piece of sandy-colored hair fell over his forehead. "Yes, ma'am," he replied. "But I'm sorry you think I had anything like that in mind, Shortcake. Kind of hurts, after all I've done for you up to now—and after standing up to those men."

She folded her arms. "You said yourself that was something personal. And as far as all you've done for me, you have done for me what you would have done for any person who came along and needed you for a guide."

He held her eyes. "That isn't so, and you know it. I've gone an extra mile for you, Harmony." His smile faded, and she looked down.

"Maybe you have, but I can't help but wonder why."

He sighed deeply. "If you need to wonder, then you don't know people very well, and you sure as hell don't know men. Someday you're going to learn who to trust, learn that there really are some people you can trust. You'll get that chip off your shoulder, Shortcake, and quit believing that all you have is yourself. Nobody just has that. I had somebody once, but I lost her. Yet I know it can't be just Buck Hanner for the rest of my life. Even though at first that's the way I thought, I don't want to live the rest of my life that way, and that person wouldn't want me to go around hating the world and being ornery with everybody I come across just because of what happened. Bad things happen to a lot of folks, Harmony. It's just the way life is. I've got my differences with Wade Tillis, but I don't hate the rest of the world. You've got to learn that too.

Apparently someone hurt you deeply, and you're determined nobody but Harmony Jones will be in your life. But you can't go on that way."

"I'll do what I please!" she snapped as quietly as possible, for others were watching and wondering what they were talking about.

"Yes, you most certainly do that," he answered, sounding angry. He took her arm and whisked her insdie the supply store. "Maybe you should find another guide," he told her. "There are plenty of others around here who know where O'Toole's claim was. I'm sure Wade Tillis' men could show you! You seem to trust me no farther than the next man, so what's the difference?"

He started to leave, and she grabbed his shirt sleeve. "Wait, Buck!"

He looked at her with angry eyes, and her own eyes filled with tears, immediately softening his heart. "I'm sorry! I'm just . . . scared. What happened here—it spoiled everything. It was all going so well!"

"Damn it, Harmony, Tillis is just trying to fill you with doubts. Can't you see that? You're reacting exactly the way he wants you to."

Her breath came in short gasps, and she pressed her lips together to keep from crying. She wiped angrily at unwanted, childish tears. "I trust you, Buck . . . truly I do!" she finally said, her words broken. "Don't go away! I don't want anybody else to take me there, and I want to be friends like before. I just . . . I've never seen a shooting before."

He sighed deeply. "Harmony, I've killed a few renegade Indians. And I killed one other—all in self-defense. I'm not a killer by nature. But I'm not a man to take someone else's bull, either, and if I have to use a gun, then I use it, that's all. This isn't St. Louis, Shortcake. It's Cripple Creek, Colorado, and there's not much in the way of law out here. It's all the sheriff can do to keep up, so a man has to be able to fend for himself. That doesn't make him a cold-blooded killer. I don't exactly forget about killing a man in ten minutes. In my sleep, I'll hear my gun going off and see him falling for quite a few nights, and I could really use this trip and some time alone in the mountains."

She watched his eyes. Yes. It really did bother him. What a confusing man he was—quiet, yet sometimes talkative; easy to know, yet she wondered if she knew the real Buck Hanner at all. There was that mysterious past he wouldn't talk about. He was a gentle man who could turn around and shoot a man down, and she didn't doubt he'd had his share of fist fights . . . and women. But there had been one—someone special called Mary Beth—so special it hurt too much for him to talk about her. She was almost jealous of the girl, even though she was no longer even alive.

"We're wasting time," she told him, forcing a smile for him. "Friends?"

He nodded, saying nothing more. He picked up her carpetbag and suitcase and walked through the store to the back, where Pepper and Indian waited, saddled and ready. Four pack mules stood nearby, loaded with supplies. Buck tied the carpetbag and suitcase onto one of them.

"Mount up," he told her. "You and I are going to ride around to the front so the men can see us leaving. We might as well rub it in a little."

She smiled, excited now, and climbed onto Pepper,

having trouble getting her left foot into the stirrup as she always did because she was so short. But she managed, while Buck eased gracefully onto Indian. He picked up the lead rope for the mules and nodded to her to go out around the side of the store, in the lead. She obeyed, her heart pounding as she came through the alley and made her appearance on the street, followed by Buck Hanner and the mules.

To Harmony's surprise, cheers went up from the crowd. Buck just smiled. He'd expected this. He knew these men, knew they'd be rooting for her. All of them understood the hardships, the dreams, the successes, and failures of those who searched for gold. Now here was a girl not quite a woman, a greenhorn from the East, come here to seek her own dream—alone, no family or friends—and she had even stood up to Wade Tillis, something some men hesitated to do.

Harmony drew her mount to a halt, as three men came forward, holding up a gold pan, this one actually plated with real gold.

"We all pitched in and got ya' somethin' fer good luck, Miss Jones!" one of the men told her. He handed her the pan, and Harmony took it, surprise on her face. Writing was etched into the center of it. "Harmony Jones—Cripple Creek's first female prospector" it read. "That there is real gold plating, Miss Jones," the man told her. "So don't go usin' it on your claim. Jest set it out for somethin' purty to remember us by when yer feelin' lonely."

She smiled and turned to Buck, who winked. "See? Not everybody is an enemy," he told her.

She turned to the man who had handed her the pan. "Thank you so much!" Then she looked out at the small crowd. "Thanks to all of you! I'm going up to my claim and I'm going to work it! I'll see you next spring."

They cheered again, several of them shouting their support of her adventure. Harmony turned to Buck, who was grinning. She didn't know the pride in his heart, the total admiration, and yes, the love that was growing there for her. She wanted nothing to do with such things right now, and he knew it. But he could not help his own feelings, although they frightened him. He had loved once, and had known the pain of losing that love. He was no more ready to love that way again than Harmony Jones was ready to be loved by any man. Yet to be alone with her and not taste those virgin lips, not hold that innocent body and show her that men weren't all bad, that would be a monumental task. He turned his horse and signaled for her to ride beside him.

"As you said, Miss Jones, we're wasting time," he told her.

She grinned excitely, opening a saddlebag and shoving the pan inside. Then she again waved to the other men, shouting a last thank you before they headed out, toward the mountains, toward whatever awaited her, toward the property that belonged to Harmony Jones and the promise of being the independent woman she was determined to be.

Chapter Seven

Harmony experienced a mixture of relief and apprehension as Cripple Creek disappeared behind a ridge and she and Buck Hanner headed into the foothills. Would she ever return? Now she would be alone with this man, in whom she was putting so much trust. Trust. There was that word again, the word that had brought her so much pain. Now she was almost forced to trust this man whom she knew only on the surface, not deep inside. She had no choice but to hope for the best.

"When are you going to show me how to use my Winchester?" she asked.

"In time." He looked ahead, quietly smoking, and she remembered his comment about liking the quiet of the mountains. He probably wanted his peace even more now, after having killed a man that very day. He'd seemed lost in thought when she asked the question, and a little irritated at having to answer.

She decided not to talk unless he spoke first. The horses plodded over gravelly ground, from which sagebrush and yucca sprouted, interspersed with a variety of colorful wildflowers. She wondered how anything could grow in the dry, hard ground. Yet ahead of them, in the higher foothills that approached the mountains, pine trees flourished, some seeming to be rooted in pure rock, some leaning over so that they appeared ready to fall at any moment. Yet they were very old trees and would probably still be there long after her own death.

Harmony rode near the last mule but to the side, not following directly behind because of the dust. When the trail allowed for only one animal, large boulders dotting either side so that were was only one way to go, she moved behind the last mule and coughed from the dust. In no time at all the day grew too warm, but there was nothing she could do about it. Beads of sweat began to form on her forehead and neck, and Pepper shuddered and tossed her head, as though disapproving of the heat. But in front of them Buck Hanner kept going on Indian, seemingly oblivious to the temperature or the time of day. They rode until well past lunchtime. Harmony felt a gnawing hunger but said nothing, not wanting to start complaining on their very first day on the trail. She'd get used to all of this, she was sure. But this was the hottest day she'd experienced since coming to Colorado. It was hard to believe that winter snows might shut her in her cabin for weeks. Right now she didn't even want to think about her heavy, fleece-lined jacket.

For hours there had been only the sounds of hooves against hard earth, an occasional shudder or whinney, the swishing of the horses' tails, the squeak of leather, and here and there the chitter of a prairie dog, which

Harmony thought should be called an "everywhere" dog, because they certainly did not stick to the prairies.

She smiled when she watched the lively little animals, allowing them to take her mind off her physical discomfort and her fear of what lay ahead. She thought of the prairie dogs as friends. For that matter, she decided to think of all the animals as friends while she was alone. That would make it more bearable. She would spend her free time trying to tame some of them—except the horrible rats Wade Tillis had mentioned. She wondered if what he'd said was true. What on earth would she do if they arrived and the cabin was full of rats!

The higher mountains seemed close now, yet they were not. Buck had already told her it would be a good week before they reached their destination. She could see Pike's Peak, but it never seemed to get any closer as they rode on that day.

When Buck finally drew Indian and the mules to a halt, Harmony guessed it was at least three o'clock in the afternoon. She frowned and dismounted slowly, her legs stiff and not wanting to come together. Buck did not seem the least affected by the long ride or the heat. He walked the horses into a little cove, where rocks created shade and the air was somewhat cooler. "We'll eat here and rest a bit," he told her.

"Well, at least I know you really do talk on these trips," she answered, "and you really do stop to rest!"

He turned to watch her come up behind him, walking slowly and rubbing at her thighs. "Sure I talk—eventually," he answered. "Part of the reason I'm keeping my mouth shut is I want you to start getting used to the sounds out here, to know what's a real

147

sound and what's maybe a human signal or something out of the ordinary, like the growl of a grizzly."

"Thank you for eliminating all fear from my soul," she told him, taking a couple of Wanda's biscuits out of the cloth bag she had tied around her saddle horn. "I'll keep my ears open."

"I'm serious, Shortcake. You've got to train your ears in this country."

"Right now I'm still training my legs."

He grinned and opened his canteen, taking a swallow. "You'd better drink a little yourself," he told her, wiping his lips. "I'll pour some in my hat and water the horses. There isn't much in the way of water around here till you get up higher, and you've been perspiring a lot. You'll dehydrate." He gave her a wink. "Drink up. You're small enough as it is. You wouldn't want the mountain winds to blow you away, would you?"

She licked at dry lips. "No. I wanted a drink a long time ago, but I was afraid to ask you. You were so lost in your own thoughts I didn't want to make you angry."

He pushed his hat back and shook his head. "Don't worry about that. If you need something—holler."

She nodded, suddenly reddening. She looked around nervously, and he grinned.

"Got some personal business to tend to?" he asked.

She scowled. "I do."

"Go find a rock. There's nobody to see but the eagles and prairie dogs around here."

She watched him warily. "And you?"

He laughed lightly. "Go take care of it, Shortcake. Then come back here and drink some water and eat a little something. We'll rest in the shade awhile after

148

eating. Now get going, unless you want something more embarrassing to happen because you tried to hold it in."

She reddened more but could not deny the truth to the statement. She took a bite of biscuit, then stuffed them back into the bag and hurried behind a group of large boulders, praying she could trust him not to look. When she returned, he was coming from behind a craggy rock formation.

"Feels a little better, doesn't it?" he said.

She had to grin, and she reddened again. "Don't talk about it," she answered. "I just want to sit down someplace out of the sun and close my eyes."

He motioned toward a lower spot where there was more sand than rock. "It's softer over there. Get a blanket and spread it out. Take your canteen and that bag of biscuits. I could use a few biscuits myself."

She untied a blanket from her gear and unhooked the bag of biscuits, walking to the spot he'd indicated and spreading out the blanket. She set down the biscuits and went back for her canteen. When she returned, he followed her with his own blanket, unfolding it near hers, and they both sat down.

"We'll rest here about a half-hour, then ride till dark," he told her, reaching out and taking a biscuit from her. We can make a fire and eat a real meal once we hole up for night. Can you survive on these things till then?"

"Sure. I'm okay."

He ate three more biscuits, washing them down with water. He leaned against a boulder then, pushing back his hat and looking up into the hills. "You get some shut-eye, Shortcake. I'll keep watch."

She frowned. "Keep watch? For what?"

He glanced at her and grinned. "For a lot of things. I'm just making sure no one followed us, and although it appears desolate and lifeless out here, little girl, there's plenty of life, including rattlesnakes."

Her eyes widened. "Snakes!" She looked around and he laughed.

"Just get some rest, will you? I'll keep an eye out."

"But what about you? Don't you need to rest?"

He rolled a cigarette. "Cowboys learn to rest in the saddle with their eyes open. On a drive a man sometimes has to stay awake a couple of days straight, if the cattle are restless or a storm is brewing, or renegade Indians are stalking you. 'Course there's not much worry about Indians anymore." He licked and sealed the cigarette, his eyes saddening. She watched him light it and take a puff.

"Are there Indians around here?"

He glanced at her with his sad blue eyes and laughed lightly. "Hardly. Colorado chased out the Indians a long time ago. The ones that were here are long gone, on reservations that aren't even in the state. You'll run into no Indians around here, Shortcake, except a few of the civilized ones who try to make a living in a place where they aren't wanted."

She took a drink and then capped her canteen before she lay back, first squishing some sand into a hump under her blanket to make a headrest. "Do you know any Indians personally?"

He smoked quietly. "Not anymore. They're all hidden away on reservations, and most folks, especially those in the government, would prefer to forget they even exist. I had an Indian friend once, down in

150

Texas when I was a kid. We lived near an Apache reservation. His name was Fast Horse. We played together all the time—even cut our palms and held them together to vow to be blood brothers. Then, without any reason, his father got shipped off to a hellhole prison in Florida and Fast Horse got sent to some special school for Indian kids in Pennsylvania. I got one letter from him, telling me how unhappy and humiliated he was because they'd made him cut his hair short and wear hot, scratchy clothes, and he couldn't hunt and ride and talk to the sun anymore. Then I didn't hear from him at all for a long time, so I went to the reservation to ask about him. They told me he'd died in Pennsylvania, of some white man's disease—measles, I think. I don't remember anymore. I only remember that he died in a faraway place that he hated . . . and he was buried there, away from everything he loved."

Buck's voice trailed off, and she wondered if his eyes were red and watery from the heat and dust or from something else. He looked away from her, smoking quietly.

She turned on her side and rested her head in her hand. "I'm sorry, Buck," she said quietly. "I guess I never thought about Indians that much . . . about them being real people I mean. I guess it's just because I never knew any. Back East all people know about them is what they read in dime novels, or rumors they hear. Sometimes there's an article in a newspaper about reservations, about something that happened on one or an argument over whether or not Indians should stay on reservations or be mixed into the white man's world and split up."

151

He sighed deeply. "The government would like to destroy them, but they can't. They want to break up the reservations because they want the land. And they think if they spread the Indians out into white society that will kill the reservations, kill the culture, until one day there won't be such a thing as a full-blood American Indian." He took another drag on his cigarette. "But it won't work. You have to know them to know what I mean, Shortcake. There is a spirit in the Indian that can't be broken, and I'm betting that a hundred years from now there will still be plenty of full bloods and reservations. That land is theirs by treaty, and Indians have to be with Indians. It's the way. They'll never give up their culture, their love of the land, their spiritual beliefs and freedom of soul. And they belong out here, much more than we do. We're the intruders, you know. But then I guess that's just life."

Harmony closed her eyes, thinking about Jimmie wanting to kick her out. "I guess there are always people taking advantage of other people, just because they have more money, more power," she told him. "That's why I'm going to have my own money—my own independence. That's power. Nobody will walk all over me and tell me what to do."

He watched her, wondering if she really knew what she was saying. He had power over her by sheer strength, and it was tempting to use that strength to break her stubborn independence. But a man didn't take a girl like Harmony Jones that way. Someday she would give herself to him without resistance. He was determined to make it happen.

He looked away from her then, finishing his cigarette, thinking about Fast Horse again. It had been

152

so many years, yet he still missed him. Everyone he had ever cared about was gone, and he sensed that it was the same for Harmony. They were a lot alike, although she didn't realize it yet.

Harmony awoke to a hand on her shoulder, gently shaking her. Her first thought was of Jimmie, rudely touching her in the night, and she jumped awake, immediately gasping and moving back like a trapped animal.

"Don't you touch me!" she yelled. She picked up a rock in a shaking hand.

Buck frowned. "Harmony, it's just me—Buck. You fell into a pretty hard sleep. We've got to get going."

She blinked, studying the blue eyes, just beginning to realize where she was.

"Harmony? You awake?" He saw the fear in her eyes. Someone had done something to this girl to make her hate and fear sex and men. That was obvious from the way she had reacted. He could tell she was just now coming back to reality. In her sleep, his touch had reminded her of something else—someone else. "What's wrong, Shortcake? Somebody hurt you once?"

She looked at the rock in her hand, her breathing coming in quick gasps as her startled heart began to slow its rapid beating. "I . . . I'm sorry." She set the rock down. "I thought . . . you were someone else." She quickly got to her feet and picked up her canteen, removing the cap.

"Jimmie?" he asked. "The one who said you had no right to any of Brian O'Toole's property?"

153

She hesitated, then drank some water and recapped the canteen. "I don't care to talk about it. It's no one's business but my own." She slung the canteen over her shoulder and picked up her blanket, marching over to Pepper. He sighed, picking up his own blanket and folding it, then picking up his canteen and loading both onto Indian. He mounted up before he reached down and untied the mules' lead rope from a dying, gnarled pine tree that barely had any branches left on it. He glanced at Harmony noticing she seemed lost in thought as she sat her own horse waiting for his lead.

"Not all men are like that, Shortcake," he felt compelled to tell her.

She met his eyes defiantly. "Meaning you?"

He flashed the handsome grin that made her common sense vanish. "Maybe."

"You keep your mind on the business at hand, Buck Hanner!" she challenged. "I don't care to find out what any man is like! I don't need one, and once I get where I'm going I won't need you either. You promised me—"

"Forget I said it!" he interrupted, his eyes suddenly angry. "Every damned time I try to be nice to you, you turn around and accuse me of having ulterior motives! This won't be the easiest job I've ever had, you know, roaming through the mountains with an ignorant child who hasn't even learned how to shoot a rifle yet! The least you could do is be civil to me and accept it when someone is nice to you without thinking you're being attacked."

He turned his horse and started off with the mules, then glanced back to see her just sitting there, her lips puckered, her face flushed from fighting tears. She looked like a little girl, in spite of her tempting figure.

154

Why did she have to be do damned naïve? This trip could be a lot more pleasurable if she were an easy woman. But there was nothing easy about Harmony Jones; it wasn't even easy to understand her. Again he wondered what had happened to her to make her so afraid of being touched by a man.

He sighed and rubbed at his eyes, knowing that he didn't really want her to be easy. He would have been disappointed, for he liked her . . . too much perhaps. Maybe he even loved her. Who could tell? He couldn't get close enough to her to know the real Harmony Jones. And although this trip would be torture, having to just watch her, it was better than finding out she was wild and easy. Yet he could not help but picture her wild—wild in his arms, in his bed, wild just for Buck Hanner and no one else.

"I'm sorry, Shortcake," he said. "I just wish you'd relax. We'll be traveling for several days, then getting O'Toole's claim back into working order. We can't spend the next two weeks or so together with you blowing up over everything I do and say."

She sniffed. "I know." She rode a little closer. "Don't be mad, Buck. I know there are probably a lot of other things you'd rather be doing. I just—I have bad memories about something that happened. When you touched me to wake me, I thought I was someplace else . . . that you were someone else."

"Well, whether it was Jimmie or some other man, I'd like to get my hands on him. I meant what I said—about all men not being the same. It's true, you know. What about Brian O'Toole? He was good to you, wasn't he?"

She nodded and sniffed again.

"There. You see?"

She wiped at her eyes. "He was like a father to me, and he was married. Besides, I was a little girl when he found me. It wasn't like . . . like . . . you know. It just wasn't the same, that's all."

He pulled his hat down a little. "Well, if you're thinking I've got thoughts about making a woman of you, forget it!" he told her, sounding angry again. "The way you act sometimes, I feel like your father myself, and there are plenty of women in Cripple Creek who can take care of me a lot better than a little girl who knows nothing about men and who has no goal in life beyond getting rich so she can be independent. So put your mind at ease, Shortcake!"

He headed out again, and she watched him for a moment. She did not want him to be interested in her that way, yet when he told her he wasn't and spoke of other women, she felt that painful little ache in her heart again. It confused her.

He did not look back this time, and she rode out after him, following the mules. Nothing more was said for several hours. He didn't even ask if she needed to stop. Toward dusk he halted, telling her to stay on her horse. He pulled his rifle from its boot and took aim. In the distance she saw a rabbit. He fired once but it kept running, and amid a string of curses he quickly cocked the lever of his Winchester and fired again. On the second shot the rabbit flipped over several times, then lay still.

"There's our supper," he announced, dismounting. "Damned fast little buggers. I should have had a shotgun." He ran out to the animal and came back carrying it by its hind legs. She felt relieved when she

156

saw a smile on his face. He was so handsome when he smiled. His blue eyes seemed to match the sky, his sandy hair the earth, his tanned face the rocks. Indeed, his tall, lean body looked as hard as the rocks, and there was an animal-like grace to his walk. Never in her life had she studied a man, compared a man to anything, thought of a man as handsome or otherwise. She had avoided men, never trusted them. For that matter, how could she trust another woman? Hadn't her own mother abandoned her? That left her with nothing and no one, and she was better off that way, better off looking at Buck Hanner in the same way she looked at everyone else.

"You ever clean and skin a rabbit?" he asked her.

"No, sir."

"Well, you'd better learn, Shortcake. You'll be shooting some of your own game once I teach you how to use that rifle. The more fresh game you can kill, the longer your supplies will last. Remember that."

He took a piece of rawhide and tied it around the rabbit's hind feet, then to a strap on his horse. When he mounted up and rode off again, the rabbit dangled from the side of his horse. The sun was nearly gone, and they were in the middle of a broad, green valley, headed into the mountains beyond it, before he finally halted and dismounted again.

"We'll make camp here," he told her.

She looked around but saw no water. "I wish I could take a bath," she commented. "I feel so gritty."

"Most people are that way a good share of the time out here." He untied the rabbit. "You can take a bath tomorrow night if you want. We'll be by a stream then. I know a good place to make camp another day's ride from here."

She suddenly wondered how on earth she would take a bath when there was a man around that she still didn't trust. Worse than that, they were in the middle of a wide, flat valley, with no trees or rocks to shield them, and she had a very pressing personal matter to attend to. She dismounted, watching him begin to unsaddle his horse.

"I'll show you how to clean a rabbit as soon as we lay things out and make a fire," he told her.

She swallowed. "Buck?"

He met her eyes, setting down his saddle. "Yeah?"

"I . . . there's nothing around here . . . to hide behind."

He grinned, his eyes running over her quickly. "Well, Shortcake, I told you not all men are rotten. If ever you're going to trust me, here is a chance for the supreme test." He bowed. "I shall turn around. And then when you're through, you will have to do the same, because then it will be my turn."

Her mouth fell open. "I'd never!" Her eyes narrowed with anger. "How dare you think I would even think of . . . of looking!"

He laughed lightly and turned around. "Hurry it up. I have pressing matters of my own."

She watched him a moment, then backed up and took some paper from her saddlebags. She turned and ran then, as far away as she could, hurriedly taking care of matters and watching him every second. He did keep his back to her, and she began to relax. So far he had kept his word about everything, and she had to admit that when he'd asked her about what had happened to her, what Jimmie had done, his eyes had been filled

158

with only kindness and care. Besides, it was becoming obvious he really did think of her as a child. All well and good.

She ran back to her horse. "I'm back," she said timidly. Then she turned and began unsaddling her own mount, and he walked a distance away. For the first time she wondered what men really looked like. Her encounter with Jimmie had left her thinking they were surely hideous, the things they did to women brutal and ugly. How had Becky gotten used to it? How could she have looked at Brian with such love in her eyes, returned from their honeymoon looking so joyous? And she'd had several miscarriages. There was only one way a woman got pregnant. It gave Harmony a chill to think of it. She would never have a child, that was sure. And maybe children weren't so wonderful after all. Hadn't her own parents hated her so much they'd abandoned her? Hadn't she just been in the way? Harmony Jones wanted no children. She would not bring another life into this cruel world.

"We'll tether the horses," Buck's voice broke into her thoughts. To her relief he didn't even mention what they had just done. She had thought he might tease her. "There's nothing here to tie them to. Take the bridle off Pepper, and I'll drive the stakes into the ground." He removed long stakes from a pack on one of the mules, along with a sledge hammer; then he began pounding them into the ground, allowing each animal room to graze. He tied the front foot of each mule to a stake before he tied Indian and Pepper. The horses tossed their heads and whinnied, as though voicing their gratitude at being unburdened for the night. Buck laughed, petting each of them, talking to them. It was obvious he knew and loved horses, and Harmony was curious about his past.

She thought about Fast Horse. It had hurt him to talk about his Indian friend who had died. Apparently Buck Hanner had suffered some painful losses himself . . . Fast Horse . . . Mary Beth. Maybe he understood her more than she thought. Maybe he had his own hurts and haunts.

"Now for the rabbit," he told her, throwing down the sledge hammer. "Get out a pan and bring it over here."

He walked to where he had laid the rabbit and she hurried over with a pan, kneeling down beside him. She wrinkled her face when he slit open the belly and pulled out the insides. "It's really nothing, Harmony," he declared, suddenly talking to her as if he considered her a responsible woman. Surely he did. Hadn't he said he admired the way she'd stood up to Wade Tillis? But sometimes she did act like a child. She vowed to be more mature from now on, for she wanted him to think of her as an adult. "Clean it right away, and if you can't eat all of it, smoke the meat real good and it will last a long time. Don't be afraid of a little blood and guts. It can't hurt you. Letting it repulse you is foolish. People have to survive." He deftly cut off the head and began skinning the body. "The knife I picked out for you is a good one. It should make this easy for you, even though you're not as strong as I am."

He laid the carcass in the pan then. "Let's get a fire started. It's a good thing I packed a couple of bundles of kindling on the mules. That's why I cut those big pine branches earlier when we were near trees. Sometimes you come to a place where there isn't a damned thing to make a fire with, like this one.

160

Tomorrow we'll have no problem. We'll be up among those pines in the mountains."

He walked to the mules, rinsed his hands with canteen water, then cut one big branch that had been tied to a mule. He dragged it over away from the animals, and retrieving a hatchet, he began to chop it into shorter pieces. "Get out some of the kindling. We'll have that rabbit roasting in no time. It'll make us a damned good supper," he told her.

Harmony quickly obeyed, bringing an armful of small pieces over to the spot. He started to tease her for bringing too much but thought better of it. He didn't want to spark another flare-up and spoil the night. She set the wood down, and he used the hatchet to chop at the ground, pulling away some of the grass to create a bare spot.

"You don't want to make a fire right in the grass or you might burn up the whole valley. And while I'm thinking of it, be damned careful in the pine forests, Harmony, especially later in the year when it's extra dry. Right now the ground is wet and soft, but later, if you build a fire wrong or leave it untended, you'll be roasted girl meat. That's a sorry way to go, and a whole mountain and all the animals on it can be burned up."

He leaned down and carefully lit some stacked kindling. As soon as it flared orange, he added a couple of pine logs. "Not the best wood, but it will do," he told her. "It's a good thing I found a nice dead tree. Green wood doesn't burn. Remember that. Even this stuff is going to make a lot of smoke. If we were in Indian country, we could never make this fire. They'd see us miles away."

He whittled at a couple more pieces of wood, then

161

stuck them into the ground so that Y-shaped ends stood up. He gestured for her to fetch the rabbit, while he whittled a point at the end of a sturdy piece of kindling. Holding the rabbit, he pierced it with the pointed stick and hung the stick so that each end caught in an upright stick. "There." He began to turn the rabbit. "Roast bunny."

He met her eyes and she smiled with delight. "That wasn't so hard," she commented.

"Of course not. I'll let you do all of it next time. You're a smart girl and a survivor, Harmony Jones. You'll do okay."

She studied his blue eyes. "Do you really think so?"

"Sure I do. If I didn't, I never would have agreed to bring you up here. You're young and strong and determined, and you learn easy. That's a good combination. Spread out some blankets and take out the rest of those biscuits. They'll be hard as rock but better than nothing. No sense wasting them. And get out your fleece jacket. It will get damned cold in this valley tonight. It's always cold out here at night. Wear your jacket under your blankets when you sleep."

She nodded.

An hour later found them sitting on either side of the fire, eating roast rabbit. The night was smooth and dark, the sky a mass of stars. Harmony licked her fingers and rubbed at a full stomach; then she lay back, placing her head against her saddle. She looked up at the stars.

"Seems like we're the only two people on earth," she commented.

"That's why I like it out here. A man can really do some thinking on life out here." He tossed a bone aside.

"Even a woman—those who bother to think at all, like you."

She sighed deeply. "Do you think I'm crazy, Buck?"

He laughed lightly. "Sometimes. Mostly I think you're a little mixed up and you've probably had some bad experiences that have made you a determined girl. I admire what you're trying to do, Shortcake, but you are asking for a lot."

A wolf howled in the distance, and she pulled her blankets up closer around her neck. "I know I am. But I don't care. All my life I've never had anyone or anything I could count on, or that was all my own. Even Brian wasn't really mine. He never formally adopted me. But he did leave me the gold claim, and I'm going to make something of it. I'll be rich; then I won't be scared anymore. Nobody will be able to threaten me just because I'm a girl and young and poor."

"Well, Shortcake, sometimes there's more to life than money. Money can make a person hard to live with." He rolled a cigarette and leaned against his own saddle. The fire glowed warm orange in the black night. "I've seen men come out here and get rich, then change so much nobody knows them anymore. Some get rich and lose it all right away, and some—most—never find anything worth coming out here for. I find what some men will do to find gold amazing, what they give up— sometimes their very lives. For most it's just a dream."

She watched the glow of his cigarette as he lit it. "I suppose. Brian left a wife behind—Becky. She'd lost a lot of babies and was depressed. I think they weren't getting along very well when Brian left. Finally she got sick and died. Poor Becky. During the last years she was always so sad. And Brian must have felt terrible, knowing she died alone. That's why he collapsed, I'm sure of it."

"That's what I mean. He left behind security, a wife, a supply store, a brother, and a young ward who depended on him—all for gold. He never found any until he was out here over two years, and even that doesn't amount to much."

"Just the same I'm going to pan it. Five dollars a day sounds like a fortune to me, and I'll get out more than that."

"Maybe. Maybe not."

She studied the various star formations. "You think there's another earth out there someplace, Buck?"

He looked up. "I sure as hell hope not. One mess like this one is enough." He took a drag on his cigarette. "It isn't the earth itself. This land is beautiful. It's the people on it that make it ugly. I think the perfect earth would be one just like this, with all its beauty, and no people except Indians."

"Indians!"

"Yup. They're as much a part of nature and the earth as the animals. Then everything would be in perfect balance. It's the white man that spoils everything."

"Well, you're a white man."

"So? That's still my opinion."

"It's a strange one."

"No stranger than a little girl going into the mountains to pan for gold alone."

She laughed lightly, and his heart skipped a beat. He realized he had seldom heard her laugh. It was beautiful—melodic. What a nice sound! If only he could make her laugh more often! If only he could understand exactly what made her laugh and what made her angry.

"That's a nice sound, Shortcake. A girl your age should laugh more and not be so serious about everything."

She kept watching the stars. "Can't help but be serious when you're in my situation. But you're right. I should laugh more. I've never had much reason. It feels kind of good to laugh."

"It's a release, just like crying."

She nestled down under her blankets. "I've done all the crying I'm going to do. Good night, Buck."

"Sleep tight."

She closed her eyes, deciding she'd just have to trust him. It was too late for worrying about whether she could or not, and she was too tired to worry anyway. She pulled the blankets over her face to keep her nose warm.

Buck smoked quietly, watching her. He thought about getting under the blankets with her. Fact was, they'd both be a lot warmer that way, and he'd be glad to hold her just to keep her warm. But he knew she'd have none of that. He'd scare her clear back to St. Louis if he even suggested it, or maybe get a piece of lead in him from that little pistol she carried. And to think that tomorrow night she even wanted to take a bath! His self-control surprised him, but he knew once this trip was over, he'd best hightail it back to Cripple Creek and pay some prostitute a visit. But it wouldn't be the same, not the same at all. One was lust and the other was love. One satisfied a temporary need, the other satisfied a man to his very soul.

He'd keep his distance—for now. But someday Buck Hanner was going to be Harmony Jones's first man— her only man. He'd make sure of it.

Chapter Eight

Buck brushed down the horses with more vigor than necessary, trying to keep his mind off the fact that Harmony Jones was bathing naked in a stream not far away. He guessed if there were prizes given for self-control, he would most certainly deserve the biggest award. A man couldn't ask for a better opportunity to take advantage of a sweet young virgin, but knowing Harmony, it most certainly would be against her will, and that would take away the beauty of it. He wanted the beauty, wanted her willingness, wanted her first time to be right and good so she'd have no haunting nightmares about it.

Indian snorted and tossed his head, and Buck smiled. "You and me both, boy," he grumbled.

He could hear the roar of the nearby waterfall, which drowned out her splashing, and he envisioned how she must look—silken skin, tiny waist and flat belly; untouched breasts, full and firm; soft, golden hair in secret places. She'd be all pink and white and silken.

He sighed and brushed harder, almost angrily. "If I

had any goddamned sense, I'd never have agreed to this!" he mumbled. He moved to Pepper, brushing her mane. It was then Harmony screamed his name. He dropped the brush, grabbing his rifle and running toward the stream, where she was crouched under the water, only her head visible. For a fleeting moment he realized that if it was daylight, he'd be able to see her through the crystal-clear water, and he quickly cursed his luck.

Harmony was staring at two huge elk standing beside the stream, made visible by the bright moonlight. They were both staring right back at Harmony.

"Make them go away!" she yelled. "They're going to attack me!"

He lowered his rifle and grinned. "You're in their territory, infringing on their water rights," he answered. "And if I let them charge, you'll have to come running out of there, won't you?"

Her eyes widened, and she looked desperately from the animals to Buck. "Make them go away!" she pleaded, starting to panic.

He sighed and shook his head. For some reason, probably because they were in their own territory and haughtily considered any other creature an intruder, the elk seemed unruffled by the presence of humans. Buck splashed into the water, waving his arms and shouting at them, but they just stared back at him, and for a moment he was sure they were going to charge him. He raised the rifle then, firing it three times. He would have preferred to shoot one of them for food, but they had too far to go to carry so much extra weight, and no time to smoke the meat. There would be more elk to shoot.

The rifle fire did the trick. The animals bolted and ran, quickly disappearing into the woods. Buck laughed, then glanced at a staring, shivering Harmony. Their eyes held for a moment, and she saw the challenge in his. "Go back!" she said, actually looking afraid. "Go back like you promised. Don't you come any closer!"

He stared at her another moment, his aching need for her overwhelming. But her totally helpless position tore at his heart. To force her would be like abusing a child. He turned and walked back without saying a word. He kept walking, deeper into the woods, and did not return until Harmony was dressed and had supper cooking over the fire.

"Where have you been?" she asked innocently.

He set aside his rifle, his eyes scanning her lovely form. Her hair was still wet, and hung loose around her shoulders. "You wouldn't understand," he answered quietly. "Let's eat."

As the days passed, Buck Hanner realized he'd gotten himself into a worse mess than he'd expected. Not only would it be difficult to keep from touching Harmony Jones before leaving her, it would be hard to leave her alone out here. He cared about her too much. He'd worry. But he could not come up with a reason for staying that wouldn't make her think he had ulterior motives. Perhaps he could sneak back and just keep an eye on things without her knowing it. This whole venture was turning out to be most difficult for him, and he wished he'd never set eyes on Harmony Jones, never volunteered to guide her, never let himself feel

169

sorry for her. He had not planned to love anyone again after Mary Beth. Love hurt too much. Now he was falling in love again, totally against his will, with a girl ten years his junior, a girl who knew nothing about men and who wanted to know nothing about them. Every muscle in his body ached to hold her, and his heart longed to own her. But he knew the mere mention of his feelings would send her into a tantrum and would make her distrust him. It was an odd situation, because he usually had no trouble attracting a woman. Most of the time they came after him. But he'd never cared about any of them—except Mary Beth. Mary Beth had been much like Harmony, an innocent. But she had loved him. If it weren't for Wade Tillis, she'd probably be alive today and they'd be married and living together on the ranch he'd always dreamed of building. That dream was gone now. He still had money enough to settle down with a woman, but there had been no woman he'd wanted to settle with . . . until now. Someday Harmony Jones would make a man a damned good wife, but she was far from ready for that kind of responsibility. She needed some taming. She needed to learn how to be a woman, how to give a man pleasure and get pleasure in return.

Day in and day out he had to watch her moving, walking, bending, riding, brushing her hair out and then rebraiding it. He responded to her voice; watched her catlike green eyes; studied her full lips. But he was no closer to her than the day they'd left Cripple Creek, nor did he know the real Harmony Jones any better.

"Don't you have any friends back in St. Louis, Harmony?" he asked casually as they rode side by side through a meadow. "Someone who could have come out here and helped you with this?"

"I never had time to make friends. I spent all my spare time after school and weekends helping Brian at the store, and after Brian left and Becky got sick, I spent a lot of time caring for Becky. Besides, it was always hard for me to make friends. I don't trust people."

"That's obvious."

She glanced sidelong at him and smiled a little. "I trust you, though. I was kind of afraid at first, but not anymore. You're pretty nice, Buck Hanner."

He grinned. "Well, I'm making progress."

Her smile faded. "Don't get any ideas. I'm talking about you as a person—a friend. How come every time I say something nice, you get that grin on your face that makes me wonder all over again if I should trust you?"

He shook his head and pushed his hat back. "I guess we're just destined never to be nice to each other, aren't we?" She caught the bitter tone in his voice, and saw a trace of anger in his eyes.

"I think you can like someone and still argue a lot," she answered. "Maybe that's what being good friends is. If you can't say how you really feel, and get mad sometimes, then you can't be really good friends. It's kind of a fake if you're just nice all the time, don't you think?"

"I suppose."

She stared ahead at Pike's Peak, now very close. "Buck?"

"Yeah?"

"Where did you get your name? Your first name is really Raymond, isn't it?"

He nodded. "I've been called Buck since I was about

171

nineteen. Got the name from being able to stay on wild mustangs longer than most men. I was real good at breaking in horses at one time, but I quit doing that after too many broken bones. Wild horses really buck." He shrugged. "Somebody called me Buck once, and the name stuck."

"How long did you work on ranches and herd cattle and all?"

He bent sideways and plucked up a long, golden weed. He stuck the end of it in his mouth and chewed on it thoughtfully. "Most of my life. My folks worked on a ranch down in Texas. My ma cooked for the owner. My pa did general work on the place. Then one night a big barn caught fire, and my folks ran to get the horses out. The barn collapsed on them—killed them both. I was twelve."

He chewed on the weed and stared straight ahead, and she could tell his thoughts were far away.

"I'm sorry. I shouldn't have made you talk about it."

He shrugged. "You didn't know. At any rate, I stayed on there—already knew a lot about ranching and cattle and such. Eventually I drifted away, helped on cattle drives, worked other ranches. The last time I worked on a ranch was up in South Dakota. When I left that place, I'd had my fill of that kind of life and just kind of wandered, worked odd jobs. I ended up in Cripple Creek, learned the mountains, became a guide. It was different, helped me forget."

She frowned. "Forget what?"

He swallowed, staring at the mountains ahead. "Things. South Dakota. Ranching. All of it. I was all ready to settle down once, but that plan got blown to pieces. So I don't plan anymore. I just live day to day."

172

She saw his jaw flex with repressed emotion. She felt sorry for him, then chided herself for having such feelings. But he had suffered losses, just as she had. "Mary Beth?" she asked daringly.

He turned blue eyes to her, eyes that were hard and almost angry. "If and when I talk about Mary Beth, I'll choose to do so," he said coldly.

She looked away. "I was only asking as a friend."

He sighed deeply. "I know that. How about you? You're pumping me, Shortcake. But you never tell me anything about yourself. You get mad when I ask personal questions, so don't ask me about personal things either."

She held her chin haughtily and met his eyes boldly. "Agreed."

Their eyes held a moment; then he rode on ahead of her. Why did he provoke these strange sensations? She had never thought of a man as attractive, seductive. She had never before noticed muscles, eyes, lips, movements, power. She had never been fascinated by the way a man fit a horse or handled a gun, or by his ability to use his fists, which she was certain Buck Hanner could do. It seemed he had been everywhere and had done everything. He feared no man, and knew everything there was to know about survival. She had only the inner determination to survive. But she had to learn the physical aspects of surviving in this land, things Buck knew all about.

What disturbed her most about him, and attracted her, was the realization that he could have violated her at any time. He certainly had the strength, and the opportunities had been numerous. But he had not made such a move, and though he always referred to her as a child, she could not help but see the way he looked at her. His eyes did not see her as a child, but as a woman.

She pursed her lips, wondering just what a woman was supposed to be, beyond being shaped in a certain way. She knew literally nothing about being partner to a man. She'd seen the happy faces of Brian and Becky when first they'd married, though she didn't understand the intimacies of marriage; and she remembered the ugly things Jimmie had told her the night he'd attacked her. The two situations did not match. They didn't go together. How could a woman possibly let a man do such things to her and be happy about it? Surely she would die of shame and horror if a man did that to her, and it would be painful. Maybe that was why Becky and Brian had fallen out of love. Maybe it hurt every time Becky got pregnant, and then when she lost the babies and it was all for nothing, maybe she had started to hate Brian for always hurting her and trying to get her pregnant again.

It was all simply too confusing. She could only vaguely sense that it only seemed right that a woman needed a man for the sheer physical strength he provided, for protection and care—and to have children. But she hated the thought of relying on any man for protection and care. She could provide that for herself. And she wanted no children. Her own parents had obviously hated her, so how could she be sure she'd love a child of her own? She never wanted to hurt another human being the way her parents had hurt her. It was better, much better, never to love anyone. She wanted no one to depend on her and she wanted to depend on no one. Harmony Jones. Just Harmony

Jones. If she kept it that way, life would be simple and concise. Decisions would be easy, because love—emotion—would not be involved. It was all so simple.

She looked ahead at broad shoulders and powerful thighs. She envisioned sky-blue eyes, the sandy curl that sometimes fell across his forehead. Was it so simple for a woman never to have a man? Then she thought of Jimmie again, of his sickening touch on her breast, his revolting breath and ugly words, the horror of his hardness against her stomach. That unknown part of man invaded a woman and brought her pain and humiliation. Yes. A woman certainly could get along just fine without a man!

They were soon climbing, their sure-footed mounts picking their way over large boulders and up a steep, narrow pathway on the side of Pike's Peak. The sheer drop gave Harmony chills. Higher and higher they climbed, through pine and groves of aspen, then pine again, piles of rock everywhere. It was difficult to believe there could be any vegetation amid so much rock, yet there were scrubby bushes, an abundance of wildflowers, and aspens and pines.

Harmony could tell the air was thinner, for her ears popped now and again. Once in a while Buck's horse or the mules would loosen some stones as they marched upward, sending miniature avalanches down the pathway. Pepper always halted automatically, waiting for the rocks to stop sliding, and Buck always looked back to check on Harmony. After a moment Pepper slowly plodded forward.

"Won't their hearts give out?" Harmony shouted to

Buck. "It's so steep."

"They're used to it!" he shouted. "They've all been up this trail before."

"Are we very close?"

"About one more day. You can't go too fast through here."

In shady areas that seldom got any sun, patches of snow lay in lumps. Here and there water trickled over rocks, as the spring runoff continued though it was getting close to the first of July. Harmony was surprised at the chill in the air. She had never realized it would be this cool at a higher elevation. She was sure that down in the valley, and at Cripple Creek, it was a very hot day. She welcomed the coolness. She hated being too hot. It would be nice working in the mountains where everything was so cool and beautiful.

Her surroundings were green and gray, pine and granite. No wonder they called these mountains the Rocky Mountains. They were, and why there were any trees here at all she could not imagine. She breathed deeply of the air, listening to the chirp of birds and the soft moan of a gentle mountain breeze.

They crossed a stream that was packed with giant, round boulders. Water rushed down in a white froth, roaring and splashing over smooth rocks, looking beautiful but dangerous. Buck's horse gingerly picked his way over the rocks, Buck pulling the mules behind. One mule slipped and bayed with great alarm, falling to a sitting position and making the others halt. Buck tugged on the rope, cursing and yelling at all of them. Finally he had to dismount, leaving Indian standing in the foaming water and wading back to the fallen mule. He jerked at the animal's harness, cursing it and kicking its rear until it finally got back on its feet. Then he waded back to Indian, mounted up, and hurriedly led horse and mules to the other side.

He turned then, yelling for Harmony to start across and let Pepper pick her own path. Harmony kicked Pepper into motion, fully trusting the horse to find a sure-footed way over the stream. She did not use the reins at all, but let them dangle while Pepper carefully placed her hooves in the right places, stepping over boulders and smaller rocks until they were on the other side.

Buck looked relieved. "That's our last real obstacle," he told her. "I figured this time of year it might be a problem. Later on, there won't be any water there at all. It's just a snow runoff."

He headed forward, Harmony following as he wound his way along the narrow pathway, over more boulders, through more pine and aspen. Flowers of all sorts—pink, yellow, purple, blue, red, white—bloomed among the rocks, as did green and yellow lichen. There was a damp smell in the cool air.

They rode for two more hours, dipping into tiny valleys, then climbing again. Finally they came upon a rushing stream, and just above it, set against the side of a steep embankment, was a log shack with a stovepipe sticking out through the roof. Buck halted his horse and turned to look back at Harmony.

"This is it!" he yelled.

She stared at the small shack. It stood stark and alone, the back side of it flat against a sheer wall of rock. Her first thought was that she would not have to worry about anyone sneaking in from the back, for there was no back! Wooden steps led from the rough pine door straight down to a rushing stream, with no

177

ground in between. The stream was wide and swollen.

"The water will drop quite a bit over the next month," Buck yelled above the roar. "Then there will be a little bit of space between the steps and the water. For now we'll have to cross the stream and get to the steps from the side.

She looked around. Lonely! So lonely it all seemed! Poor Brian, sitting here day in and day out, dreaming of gold, too ashamed to come home without it, dreaming about Becky and missing her. Had he regretted what he had done? Probably, for he had given up so much to do this. But it was different for her. She had no one—no property and no friends. It didn't matter that she had come to this place and would probably die here.

A few yards farther up the stream stood a crude outhouse, nothing more than a pine enclosure to keep the wind from its occupant. Harmony knew without looking that there would be nothing to sit on. It was simply a place to go without being seen, and without freezing in the winter winds. Her eyes moved back to the shack.

"Won't it blow over in the winter?" she asked.

Buck laughed and urged his horse into the rushing creek. "Well, it hasn't yet." The mules followed, then Harmony. Once across, they both dismounted, tying their horses to a couple of pines, then tying the mules. Buck looked down at Harmony, his heart aching at how small and alone she looked here alongside the mountain.

"You still determined to go through with this?" he asked.

She looked up at him and nodded. Then she looked

178

back at the shack. "Is it true? What Wade Tillis said about rats?"

He frowned. "Probably. They're just mountain pack rats. Keep your food in proper containers and you won't have too much trouble. You can use them for target practice with your pistol. Make a game of it. Put a mark in the wall every time you hit one."

She shivered. "I hate rats."

He grinned. "Believe me, after you're up here alone for a while, you'll be glad they're around. You'll be talking to them."

She scowled at him and headed toward the steps, placing her foot carefully on one as though it might collapse. Then she gingerly mounted them and slowly opened the door.

She gasped. A homemade wooden bed lay overturned, its feather mattress on the floor, holes in it where rats had made a home. The stovepipe had been loosened, and black soot lay on the floor behind the stove. Two chairs and a table had been broken up, and the canned food Buck knew had been left behind was gone.

"Bastards!" he grumbled. "Tillis' men did this!"

Harmony blinked back tears. "Oh, Buck, now I have to clean all this up before I can even move in!" A rat scurried out from inside the mattress and she gasped, stepping back. Buck's gun was out quickly and he fired. The rat flipped and landed against a wall. Harmony covered her face and turned away. "I hate them! I hate them all!" she wailed. She took her hands away then, looking up at Buck in anger. "I'll show them!" she swore to him. "They think I'll come right back to Cripple Creek with you! But I won't!" She marched up to the rat, staring at it, taking deep breaths. Then she bravely bent down, leather gloves still on her hands, and picked up the beast by its ugly tail, walking to the door and tossing it outside. "Our first job is to sit here and kill every rat we see for the next hour or so," she announced.

Buck grinned. "That's the spirit, Shortcake." He walked over to the bed, turning it back onto its legs. He grabbed hold of the mattress and pulled it to the door, then tossed it over the side of the steps to the ground. "We'll punch it around, chase out the rats," he told her. "Then we'll slit it open, sew together some clean blankets, and stuff them with the feathers from this. That way you'll have a clean mattress."

For a fleeting moment he thought about lying on that mattress with her, but matters at hand helped alleviate his hunger for her. Their first few days would have to be spent getting the cabin into shape, and in teaching her to shoot. Then he must teach her to pan for gold, build a sluice, give her survival pointers. He followed her back inside, and she immediately began to put the stovepipe back together. Yes. Harmony Jones had spunk and determination. Maybe she could make this work at that.

For an hour or better, Buck did nothing but sit and wait for an unwanted guest to make an appearance. When it did, he shot it instantly. Harmony retrieved a broom and dustpan from one of the mules, swept up the worst of the soot, and then squished the broom into the sand outside to get the soot off it so she could use it to sweep the rest of the floor. Every time Buck fired a shot, she jumped, for she could not watch him all the time and she never knew when he might fire again. She went to the stream and wet a rag, and going inside, she washed the sooty spot behind the stove. Finally she rubbed it with a dry rag until most of the black soot was gone.

They both stacked the pieces of broken furniture in a corner, to be used as kindling, and then Harmony swept the room.

"This place might be quite cozy at that," she commented. "I brought material along. If I get bored, I'll make curtains for the window." She glanced at the one and only window of the shack. "I brought two braided rugs. We'll make a new mattress, and I have quilts. I'll make a real home here, and it will be all mine. It's so small, it won't take much wood to heat it."

"Well luckily there's some left outside, but I'll chop more for you. I'll be back and forth till the snow sets in, and each time I come I'll stack up more wood. You'll need it this winter. You'll use some at night even now. Just be careful how you use it. You don't want to run out of wood in the middle of winter around here. The snow gets too deep to go find more, and there's no way you'd be able to chop down a tree all by yourself. Besides, green wood doesn't burn worth a damn. You want the good dry stuff. I'll start picking up stray branches and cutting up fallen trees tomorrow. And you have to learn to shoot that rifle. Then we must get a sluice built, and I'll show you how to pan for gold—"

"Oh, Buck, I'll never learn it all!" she lamented.

He winked at her. "Sure you will. Let's unpack the gear. I brought along some rat traps. We'll set them around outside the shack and hopefully keep most of

181

them from ever coming in."

"I hope you're right. I'd hate to wake up to find one crawling over my legs. I think I'd faint."

He laughed lightly. "Not Harmony Jones. She doesn't faint over anything."

"How many did you kill?"

"Hard to say. Thirteen, I think."

She curled her nose. "Oh, Buck, will they go away now?"

"Now that human life is around, they will for the most part. If we set those traps right, you'll be rid of all of them eventually. The newcomers will smell the dead ones and take off. I'll check around the outside for holes and places where they've come in."

They went out together, and as they began unloading the mules, she kept glancing at him, grateful for his presence and know-how. How would she have done this without Buck Hanner? So far she had only succeeded in getting here. Staying was another matter.

Bringing in the food and gear took over two hours. All mining equipment was left outside. Personal belongings, utensils, food, and blankets were brought inside. The mules jumped around and bucked, obviously happy to be free of their load, and Harmony laughed at their antics. Again Buck was struck by the nice sound of her laughter. It triggered in him the awful ache he felt because he had to leave her here alone.

By nightfall cans of food lined the shelves on the wall, and they had set up a crude table made from split logs laid across flour and sugar barrels. Two thick round logs, cut slightly shorter than the height of the barrels and set on end, served as chairs. Harmony's bedroll was laid out over the woven rawhide support of the bed, which served as springs. Buck would sleep on the floor near the stove. She didn't have the heart to make him sleep outside, not after all he had done for her. Yet she felt odd sleeping in the same room with him. It seemed different from sleeping out under the stars. She wondered what people would think if they knew they had both slept inside. Yet who would know, and what difference did it make? If Buck Hanner meant her harm, it wouldn't matter who slept where; he certainly would have done something about it by now.

She built a fire in the stove, while Buck curried down the horses and secured them for the night. Already he had managed to pile some wood outside, and had brought some inside for her. She began to hum. She was home! Home! This was her little house, crude as it was, rats and all. Perhaps she would whitewash it sometime, and she would certainly make curtains. She looked again at the braided rugs on the floor. Already the little shack looked cozy, like a place for humans, not rats. But what a far cry it was from the fancy house Brian had left in St. Louis. How odd that a man would leave such things behind and live this way, just for a dream. If she'd been sure everything back in St. Louis would be hers, she probably wouldn't have left. Her reason for being here was different. It was difficult to understand why men like Brian left homes and families and businesses to come out here to search for gold. Yet she was glad that Brian o'Toole had left her something all her own.

Buck came inside then, taking off his hat and hanging it on a hook on the wall.

"Tomorrow I want to figure out what part of this place is really mine," she told him. "Maybe after a while

I can dig deeper, or into the side somehow, and find a whole vein of gold."

"Now you sound like all those other dreamers who come out here."

"Well, you never know." She set a pan on the stove and put some grease in it, watching it melt. "I'll cook that squirrel you shot," she told him.

"Sounds good." He stretched. It had been a very long, tiring day. He walked over and sat down on the bed, bracing his back against the wall. He watched her, envisioning what a fine wife she would make. She was strong and sturdy, yet beautiful. She was willing to learn, unafraid. She could cook. She was smart. The only thing she lacked was an understanding of men and a womanly attitude toward them.

"You ever cook squirrel before?" he asked.

"No. But it can't be much different from chicken or anything else. I'll roll it in a little flour first."

The room was quiet for a few minutes; then it was filled with the crackle of frying meat as she laid the pieces of squirrel in the hot grease. It was a big squirrel, filling most of the pan, plenty for two people. When she wiped her hands and turned around, she caught his blue eyes watching her. She reddened slightly and tore her eyes from his, looking around the cabin.

"I think I'm going to like it here, Buck," she told him. "It's beautiful . . . peaceful. I have a lot of things to think about. It will be nice being all alone, without worrying about a supply store, or poor Becky, or men like Wade Tillis"—she turned back to the pan—"or Jimmie," she finished.

He watched her turn the meat. "What happened with Jimmie?" he asked again carefully.

She did not reply right away. She poked at the meat, then took a deep breath and shrugged. "He attacked me one night, while I was sleeping," she told him. "He tried to . . . do things. And he told me . . . about men and all . . . said he wanted to marry me. But the way he told me . . . the horrible way he touched me." She shuddered. "It was ugly. I got away from him and got hold of a poker stick."

She turned, her eyes afire with anger and humiliation. "I'd have killed him with it if he'd tried to touch me again! He knew it! He backed off, and he never bothered me again!"

His eyes were full of sympathy. She had half expected him to laugh, but he only frowned. "I'm sorry you had to be told such things that way. Don't get mad, Harmony, at what I'm about to say. I only have your interest in mind, because I care about you. I'm not after anything. I just want you to know it's true what I said—that it isn't that way. Jimmie gave it to you all wrong."

Her cheeks colored and she turned back around. "It doesn't matter. It isn't anything I care to find out about either way. Do you like salt?"

"What?"

"Salt—on your meat."

He sighed. "A little." He sat up straighter and rolled a cigarette. "Is that when he told you to give him what he wanted or get out?"

"Not exactly. Becky was still alive—and Brian. I told him I'd tell Brian and he'd come home. Then Becky died, and Brian died. That was when he knew he had a hold on me, because everything was his and I had nothing and no one." She set down the fork and turned to face him. "You aren't being fair, Buck. I've talked

185

too much. I didn't want to tell you that. So now it's your turn. What is between you and Wade Tillis? And who was Mary Beth?"

His blue eyes looked up at her as he finished lighting his cigarette. They were cold again. "Not tonight, Shortcake. I said I'd pick the time." He got up from the bed. "I'm going out to check on the horses."

She scowled, putting her hands on her hips. "Do you always run away from your feelings, Buck Hanner, and from your past?"

His eyes ran over her tempting form. "No more than you do," he answered. He turned and left, and she watched him go. She wished she could tell him more—about how afraid she really was sometimes inside, how mixed up her feelings for him were, how lonely she was. But to do that would be to admit she needed him, maybe even cared about him. Lately it seemed she kept straying from her vow. She chided herself, recalling her purpose and reminding herself that it was dangerous to trust anyone too much.

She turned the squirrel meat again, while outside Buck Hanner chopped wood with only the moonlight to guide him. He needed to do it, needed to vent his anger and frustration. He pretended the wood was Jimmie, although sometimes it was Wade Tillis. He could smell the squirrel cooking, and he repeated his vow that someday Harmony Jones would belong to him.

Chapter Nine

"Put on those boys' pants you bought," Buck ordered, rising from his log chair. "We're going to do a little panning this morning, Shortcake."

Her eyes widened, and she gulped down a swallow of coffee. "Now?"

"Why not? That's why you're here, isn't it? Might as well get started learning."

She set down the tin cup. "Yes, but— Well, I thought you were going to teach me how to shoot my rifle."

"We'll get around to that." He frowned. "I thought you'd be excited."

She stood up. "Oh, I am! I'm just kind of nervous." She smiled, rubbing her hands together. "I'm really going to pan for gold?"

He chuckled and shook his head. "You really are. Now get into those pants. I'll be outside." He turned to leave.

"Buck?"

He glanced back at her anxious face. "What?"

"Do I have to put on the pants?"

He sighed. "We've been through this once, Harmony. Now put them on. I'll get things ready outside. This afternoon you can practice shooting your rifle while I build a sluice. Tillis' men destroyed the one Brian built. Now quit wasting time. I have to get back to Cripple Creek before winter sets in!"

"But it's only the first of July!"

He put his hat on. "Well then maybe you get my meaning."

He walked out and she stared after him a moment before hurriedly removing her riding skirt. She picked up the pants, heavy, dark cotton ones, making a face at the sight of them. Deliberately she pulled them on, buttoning them and realizing she'd better get out a belt, for they were too big in the waist. There wasn't one part of them that fit her right. They were baggy, and too long. She tightened the belt, then rolled up the legs and pulled on her boots.

She took a deep breath then. If he was going to see her in pants; it must simply be done. She marched to the door, feeling awkward and ridiculous. She felt her cheeks go crimson when she opened the door and stepped onto the wooden steps. Buck looked up from the edge of the creek where he stood, able to tell more now about the shape of her hips and legs even though the pants were too big. He suddenly ached to run his hands over the gentle curve of those hips, to touch places made more inviting by the pants. But he covered his desires with a smile, then a chuckle.

"You look absolutely ridiculous," he told her. "Believe me, Shortcake, if you think wearing those baggy things is being too forward, think twice. You'd be more inviting in a gunny sack. Come on. Let's

188

get started."

She slowly approached, her lips in a pout. "I look that terrible?"

He wanted to tell her she was beautiful. But he didn't dare. "That terrible," he answered. "But practical. You'll see soon enough why you need those pants." He looked closer into her green eyes. "Don't tell me you care how you look to me," he teased. "It's not supposed to matter, remember?"

She reddened even more, and the now-familiar anger began to rise in her green eyes. "Buck Hanner, you know I don't care how you think I look—not the way you mean!" She stuck up her chin. "I just like to wear nice clothes and look like a lady, that's all. No lady dresses like this."

He grinned. "That could be answered in a lot of ways. I think I'll leave it alone. Just remember there's not anyone here to see you except me, and I don't care. Nor do the horses or the mules. Now get over here and sit down on this board. Put your feet up on the rocks."

He led her to a place where he had laid a flat board over the stream. In order to sit down on the board one had to straddle the stream. She placed her feet on the rocks as he directed, and the pose was almost more than he could ignore. Never had he seen a prettier, more innocent, more tempting girl in such an inviting position, made more so by the pants rather than a skirt. He cleared his throat, averting his eyes as he took a gold pan and dug deep into the loose sand and gravel of the creek bed, scooping up a panful of dirt.

"Believe it or not, there is probably gold right here in this dirt," he told her. He began swirling it, tipping the pan and spilling out a great deal of water, mud and small rocks.

"What are you doing?" she asked. "If there's gold in there, you're losing it."

He shook his head. "Gold is very heavy, Shortcake. It settles to the bottom. All you do is keep swirling, gently spilling out all the dirt and rocks that come to the top. You keep doing that until you get down to what is called drag. Some men call it dregs. Whichever, it's a heavy, black-looking sand, and if you look real hard, you'll see some very obvious gold specks, and if you're real lucky, some tiny nuggets. You'll see a few red stones, also. Those are garnets. They're worth keeping, although they'll not bring you anything near what the gold will bring you."

He kept swirling, spilling out, gently dipping the pan just enough to get a little more water into it, then swirling what was left, spilling out, and dipping for more water. For almost ten minutes he continued the procedure, until a small amount of black residue was left.

"There, see?" he told her, holding it up close to her. She looked hard, her face very close to his own, and he allowed himself the pleasure of looking more closely at her soft, peachlike cheek. He could smell her, a clean, soapy smell. He wanted to nuzzle her hair, kiss her soft cheek. She was so lost in looking at the drag that she didn't even realize he was looking at her.

"I see some!" she said excitedly.

He tore his eyes from her face to look at the pan. "Yup. Touch the specks with your finger, Shortcake. Just let one stick to your finger, then touch it to the water in the jars beside you there. It's heavy. It will float right to the bottom of the jar. That's how you capture it."

Her face was bright with delight and excitement. She touched a flake, then put it in the jar of water, watching it float to the bottom. "It really does go down!" she exclaimed.

He washed the drag a little more, and she picked out more flecks of gold, and a few garnets.

"There's even a little silver there," he told her. "Pick that out, too. See it?" He pointed some out, putting it on the end of his own finger. She didn't notice the strong hands, the powerful forearms that worked the pan, the handsome face that was watching her. She saw only the pan—the gold.

"Let me try it!" she said excitedly.

He grinned and handed her the pan. She dipped it, scooping soil from the bottom of the stream, and she began to swirl it, letting just a little run off before refilling the pan with water.

"You can get rid of more than that first round," he told her. "And don't put too much water back in. You need just enough to work it, make it swirl lightly. Dump out more dirt next time."

"I feel like I'm throwing away gold when I do that."

"You won't be. Remember, it goes to the bottom. You won't lose any."

She smiled. "This is fun!" She swirled more, dumped, dipped, swirled. She did it clumsily, but he let that go. He'd learned to be diplomatic with Harmony Jones. He liked being on speaking terms. He'd let her find her own way a little, then gently point out what she was still doing wrong.

"Oh, Buck, I'll be rich!" she told him, picking out a few gold flecks after several more minutes of swirling the drag. "If I sit here every day and do this for six months or so, I'll have a ton of gold!"

He chuckled. "Not exactly. But you'll do well enough. Just be careful to pick out the right stuff. There's a lot of gangue in the drag."

"Gangue?"

"Worthless minerals. All you're interested in is the gold and silver. The garnets are okay, but nothing to worry about."

She dipped the pan again. "This is easy," she bragged.

"Do it for a few hours and you'll change your mind. You'll be mighty sore the first few days." He began to roll a cigarette, then sat down on the ground next to her, watching her swirl the mud and rock. "Gently," he spoke up, "and get rid of all that junk on top." He lit the cigarette. "Later on, after you've panned this way for a few weeks, you'll want to dig down into the ground at different spots along the creek. Use the shoveled dirt to wash out in a pan. Chances are good you'll find a lot more. And maybe—just maybe—you'll discover a bonanza."

"What's that?"

He took a drag on the cigarette. "A very rich vein of gold—or silver," he answered. "There could be one around here, but like I told you, don't be too sure of it. You'll work a lot faster once I build that sluice for you. I'm glad I brought a little lumber."

"What will a sluice do? How does it work?" Harmony asked.

"It will speed you up. It's kind of a rocker. You shovel the dirt into it, and we position it along the creek so that the water runs right through it all the time, keeping the dirt washed. You rock the dirt back and forth and it gets constantly washed away until all that's left is the drag with the real stuff in it, just like in your pan, only on a bigger scale. You can use shovels full instead of little pans full."

"Oh! Then build one right away!" she said excitedly, picking out more gold from her pan.

His eyebrows arched. "I intend to, but not until I smoke this cigarette."

She laughed lightly. "You know what I mean."

He leaned over and studied the drag in her pan. "You've got quite a bit in that one. Lots of color. Keep up the good work."

"I could do this forever!" she commented, shifting slightly on the board.

Again he noticed her hips, the roundness of her bottom against the hard board, the way the pants fell around her thighs, outlining slender legs he knew must be silken. The way she sat, her knees bent, dipping the pan between her legs, her face alight with enthusiasm, he wondered if he'd ever seen such beauty, or ever wanted so badly something that he could not have. Yes, he had. Once before. Mary Beth. But she had wanted him back, and if it hadn't been for Wade Tillis, he'd have had her for his own. Harmony, on the contrary, wanted nothing to do with men, not in that respect.

"You'll talk differently after doing it for a couple of days. Your back and arms will regret that statement, Shortcake."

He got up and walked to the stack of lumber he had brought, retrieving a hammer and nails. For the next few hours he pounded while she swirled dirt and water. Once or twice she glanced at him, noticing his sureness and strength, grateful for his constant help and patient instruction. Buck Hanner was a pretty good man, if there was such a thing as a good man. Of course there was. Brian had been a good man. But Buck was different. Buck made her look at him the way women looked at men who were desirable. That made her angry, not at Buck but at herself. She kept forcing back her feelings, the little urges she didn't understand. They frightened her. Panning for gold helped tremendously. This was exciting! Real gold! All her own! She really did own this claim; and this really was her gold.

She settled in and panned right through lunch, forcing herself not to look at Buck Hanner as anything but a friend. The work helped. Soon he would be gone, and that would be even better. She'd be fine then. She'd forget him and that would be that.

Harmony stared at the blurry cards. "I don't care if the ace is worth more than the king, or the other way around," she complained. "I'm too tired."

"I'm just trying to teach you a few games you can play alone, Shortcake," Buck answered. "Believe me, you'll need to know them, because you will get so lonely you'll be talking to the rocks. Did you bring some books like I told you to do?"

"Yes. Can I go to sleep now?"

He took the cards from her hand. "If you had stopped panning when I told you to, you'd not be so tired now. Tomorrow you'll practice with the rifle and not do any panning. Give your back a rest. After that I'll be about done with the sluice. I'll teach you how to use that, then we'll see if you can shoot yourself some

194

game. Then it will be about time for me to get going. Luckily Brian left quite a bit of wood. I'll chop some more over the next couple of days, and more when I return in a couple of months."

"A couple of months?" She met his eyes. She had grown used to his friendship, his companionship—perhaps too used to it. "I'll kind of miss you, Buck."

He smiled almost sadly. "I'll kind of miss you too, Shortcake. Go on to sleep now."

Somehow she walked to the bed and Buck tucked a blanket around her and she wasn't afraid. The next thing she knew it was morning. Buck Hanner was making the breakfast. Two huge kettles of water were heating on the stove, and a washtub sat in the middle of the floor partially filled with water.

"Good morning," he said when he caught her staring at him. "You can eat whenever you want, after which you can take a bath. I heated some water for you. I figured you'd like a bath again—a real one. I'm going out to finish the sluice. When you're ready, come on out and I'll give you some pointers with that rifle."

She sat up, rubbing her eyes. "I have to pan for more gold. I should do it every day."

"Yes, you should. But you did two days' worth of work yesterday, so take today off. Do as I say. I give the orders until I'm gone, at least when it comes to how you should operate up here. I'm supposed to be teaching you, right?"

"I'm supposed to be the boss. You're just a guide."

"And I'm guiding you in how to pan for gold and how to survive. So do what I tell you." He winked at her and then left.

Harmony nibbled at some bacon and drank some

coffee. Then she undressed and poured the hot water into the tub, easing herself into it. He was right. Her back and neck and shoulders ached. The warm water felt good. Maybe she would take a day off from panning at that. Besides, he was nearly through with the sluice. She could use that tomorrow and catch up.

She sponged herself off, looking at her body and wondering what a man like Buck Hanner would think of it. Would he think she was pretty? Womanly? She scowled. Yes. She would miss him, but it was a good thing he would be going soon.

She finished bathing and dressed, and soon the mountainside echoed with her own rifle shots. She struggled to ignore the pleasant warmth that moved through her when Buck had put his strong arms around her to show her how to hold the gun. Everything about him was strong and sure. That was not good. It made her forget how strong and sure she had to be. She must not let someone else be strong for her. That was dangerous.

She practiced most of the day with the rifle, while Buck finished the sluice and chopped wood. The day grew warm, and he removed his shirt. She glanced sidelong at him occasionally as she reloaded her gun, catching the ripple of muscles as he chopped, the glisten of sweat on his tan skin. She still didn't know what a man really looked like, not completely. Seeing Buck Hanner's bare chest gave her mixed feelings. She was fascinated and frightened. She didn't like the thought of a man's hard muscles and bare skin against her body, yet there was a distinct animal quality about Buck Hanner that evoked desires she did not understand. There was a power about him. She felt that he knew exactly what to do with a woman, just as he knew exactly what to do about everything else. And that was all the more reason to stay clear of him. Nothing and no one must control her, nor should anything or anyone interfere with her plans to become economically independent.

The day passed quickly, and finally it became too dark to do any more shooting. Her neck and shoulders still ached, and now her arms as well, from holding the rifle. But her aim had vastly improved by the end of the day. She got up from where she sat and walked over to set up some woodchips for targets.

"I'll practice more tomorrow," she called out to Buck, who set aside his axe. "It's getting too dark."

"Agreed," he answered. "Time for more cards, then bed."

Their eyes held a moment before she marched past him into the cabin. She sat down at the homemade table while Buck washed at the stream. He came inside then, still shirtless. She glanced at his broad, powerful shoulders, then quickly looked away.

"I don't feel like cards," she told him. "I'm too tired."

"All right. Just go to sleep then. Tomorrow I'll teach you how to use the sluice, and maybe we'll do a little hunting. In a couple more days I'll have to get going, Shortcake. Be thinking about anything you might want me to bring next time I come."

She nodded, suddenly wanting to cry. She didn't want him to go. She was terrified of his leaving. It was like her parents abandoning her, like Brian leaving. They, too, had said they would come back. Now Buck Hanner was saying it. But would he? Probably not. No one else ever had. Buck would go, and she'd be alone . . . forever. She'd never even be able to find her way back, and she wouldn't even have a horse to ride. She had to trust him to come back, or she would probably die on this mountain. *Trust,* how she hated the word! *Leaving,* she hated that word too! She swallowed back tears and went to her bed, lying down and curling up on the mattress they had fashioned out of clean blankets and feathers from the old mattress. She pulled a blanket over her shoulders.

"What's wrong, Shortcake?" he asked. "You having second thoughts about staying up here alone?"

She sighed deeply. "No," she finally answered.

"It's only natural if you do," he told her. He ran a hand through his thick, sandy hair. "Do you want me to stay longer, or do you want to go back with me? Nobody would blame you for either, Harmony."

"I'm not going back," she said in a tired voice. "I'm not giving up. And there's no sense you staying any longer than necessary. I have to be alone sometime, so what's the difference?"

He leaned forward, resting his elbows on his knees. "I don't want to leave you here. I suppose you know that."

She met his eyes. "Why? I'm just another customer. You've left plenty of other miners up here."

"You damned well know what I mean, Harmony Jones. They aren't seventeen-year-old girls who know nothing about survival in the mountains."

"You've taught me what I need to know. And some seventeen-year-olds are as mature as full-grown women. Anyway I'm too stubborn and unfriendly for any human or animal to get the better of me."

He grinned a little. "You're probably right there. But

I still don't like it. Leaving you here will be the hardest thing I've ever done."

She was tempted to tell him that letting him leave would be the hardest thing she had ever done, but she thought better of it. She didn't want to give him ideas. There was already too much hope in his eyes when he looked at her, too much admiration, too much desire. If she had been more mature she'd have realized that all of that added up to love, but love was something she'd had little of and did not fully understand, for love also meant trust, and she had learned to never trust.

"Well, I'm just another miner like the others," she told him. "So rest your conscience, Buck Hanner. Leaving me here is what I want and that's that."

"You sure about that?"

"Just as sure as I am that I want to go to sleep now."

He sighed and stood up. "All right. I'll see you in the morning, Shortcake." He walked over and patted her head. "Sleep tight."

She watched him walk out, then turned over and wept. Why, she wasn't even sure. Perhaps it was fear. Perhaps it was loneliness. Perhaps it was even . . . love.

The next two days were filled with panning, shooting, chopping wood, skinning and cleaning small animals, and long talks about the perils of living in the mountains, about safety precautions. Harmony learned to work the sluice. It was exciting to see how much more earth she could filter with the sluice than with a pan. Neither of them spoke about Buck's leaving. Neither of them wanted to think about it, each secretly wishing they did not have to part, neither fully convinced it was right to stay or to go.

Another day was spent just riding, exploring the side of the mountain on which Harmony Jones would spend many long months alone.

"Watch out for places like that, especially in the spring." He pointed out a rocky ledge. "At that time of year a good rain can bring down a lot of soil and rocks. Everything is already softened up from the melt. Fact is, this is a dangerous spot right now." He rode farther into some pines. "Trees will protect you some if you do get caught in a rock slide. Try to get into a stand of trees. Brian did right building that shack where he did. There's a shelf above it and the ground goes back a way before going up again. That ledge will protect you if anything does come sliding down." He looked back at her. "And don't be afraid of the thunderstorms. Up here they can sound pretty scary. You're right in the clouds sometimes and the storm is beside you rather than above you. But it's still just thunder and lightning and rain. Stay inside till it's over, then be sure to check right away for signs of fire. If you see any signs of it, watch the wind, Shortcake. Don't run into the wind, because the fire will be coming right on it. Run with the wind—and I mean run. If there's no escape, get into some water, if you can find any, or lie flat in a creek."

He halted Indian and lit a cigarette. "Now, about bears," he added. "You've got to keep your head if you see one. Do you know the difference between a regular black bear and a grizzly?"

She patted Pepper's neck. "I think so. Grizzlies have big humps on their backs. But if one was chasing me, I wouldn't care if it was grizzly, brown or black. I'd be scared to death!"

He grinned. "Well, never stray far from that shack without a rifle. If a bear chases you uphill, you'd better stand and shoot, and hope that if you miss, just the shot will scare it away. If it's chasing you downhill, chances are you can outrun it. Most bears are very clumsy running down steep embankments. Remember that. You can almost always lose one that way, and if you're headed downhill, you're better off running than standing and shooting, because the bear will reach you too fast. A black bear will give up quicker than a grizzly. Grizzlies are more persistent. Keep fresh meat inside the shack, not outside where it can attract other animals. And if you ever see bear cubs, stay away from them, no matter how cute they look. I know how women are about soft, cuddly little things, but if you touch a bear cub, its mother will have you for supper. Remember that."

"I'll remember."

"You'll probably end up making pets out of some of the small animals. There's no harm in leaving food for the squirrels and such. You'll welcome their presence after you've been alone long enough."

Their eyes held and she felt a rush of warmth. She looked away, turning her horse in another direction. Never had her emotions run so high or been so confused. It seemed a million thoughts and feelings were rushing through her, for although she did not want Buck Hanner to leave, she was excited about being alone here on a mountain, learning to fend for herself, facing a challenge few girls her age would even consider. She was anxious to prove to all of them at Cripple Creek that she could do this. But more important, she suddenly wanted to prove it to Buck.

Deep inside she knew he would admire her more for trying this venture and for succeeding at it. If she went back now, Buck Hanner would be disappointed in her and she would be disappointed in herself. She could not live now without knowing whether she could survive, and perhaps find a mother lode and become independently wealthy.

"Maybe I'll even have a rat for a pet," she joked.

"Maybe," he answered with a light laugh. "You remember how to set those traps?"

"Of course. I can shoot a Winchester and actually hit something. I can pan for gold and I can work a sluice. I can clean animals for eating and I can chop wood. I know enough to stay away from rocky hills and to remain inside when it storms, to watch for fires and run downwind of one, keeping to water. I know I should kill all the small game I can for food to preserve my canned supplies, and I know I should not leave raw meat outside, especially at night. I have plenty of bandages and whiskey and medicine, even some laudanum, in case I should be in a lot of pain. I know I must always stay calm and think rationally, that I should never leave the shack without my rifle. And I even know how to play poker against myself, and how to play solitaire and other card games."

She turned around and looked at him. "Maybe when I go back to Cripple Creek, I'll sit in on some card games. Maybe I'll even gamble against Wade Tillis and win some money from him. That would be fun."

Buck laughed. "I'd like to see that. But I wouldn't like to see someone as nice as you sitting in a saloon gambling with men."

"Well, I'm doing everything else like a man."

202

He studied the round hips beneath the pants, as she sat straddled her saddle. The movement of Pepper made her hips sway sideways. "Maybe you live like a man, but you will never resemble a man in any other way," he teased.

She looked back, reddening slightly, not sure if she should smile or be angry. "I think that is supposed to be a compliment. If it is, I'll accept it. But you'd better be careful how you talk, Buck Hanner."

He didn't doubt that if he told her his true feelings and desires, she'd turn around and use her Winchester on him.

"I'm the most careful man ever born," he answered.

She looked ahead again. "Is that all you ever did before this, Buck, work on ranches and herd cattle?"

"All I ever knew. Then when the railroads came in, there were fewer jobs for trail men. And I was a little tired of it anyway. I'd been working up in South Dakota. I even considered settling down. But a few things happened that changed all that, so I started wandering, ended up at Cripple Creek doing this."

"You said once you made a point of following Wade Tillis around. He must have had something to do with you not settling in South Dakota. I know from the way you talked that day you stood up against him that he had something to do with Mary Beth. Were you going to settle down with her?"

When there was no reply she halted Pepper and turned the animal to face him. He was just staring at her, quietly smoking.

"You don't play fair, Shortcake," he told her. "I asked you not to bring up that subject."

"But you know almost everything about me. You

203

made me tell you about Jimmie."

"That's different."

"Why? Aren't we good friends now?"

He threw his cigarette stub down, dismounting to smash it with his foot, then remounting. "All right. Wade Tillis owned the ranch I worked on in South Dakota. Mary Beth was his niece. Now, are you satisfied?"

"That's it? What happened to make you hate him?"

He pushed back his hat and sighed. "For one thing, Wade inherited the ranch from his brother. His brother was a good man, worked hard all his life. Wade was always no good. He used people, took anything he could get the easy way. He came to the ranch acting high and mighty. His sister-in-law was already dead, so he became Mary Beth's guardian. He was suddenly a rich landowner, and everyone else was beneath him, including all the ranch hands, like myself. By the time he came to take over the ranch, I was already in love with Mary Beth Tillis, and she loved me. I'd saved like crazy, had enough money set aside to start a place of my own. We were going to get married. Then along came Wade Tillis. When he found out about our plans, he quickly put me in charge of a cattle drive, never revealing what he really had in mind."

Buck dismounted again, walked to a rock shelf, and looked out over the valley below. "As soon as I was gone he carted Mary Beth to the nearest train station and put her on a train East, sent her to a finishing school. I wasn't there, but I know she didn't want to go. It must have been torture for her to be sent away like that, without being able to explain or say good-bye. When I got back she was gone, and for a long time I

204

couldn't even find out what school she was attending. Tillis told me I wasn't good enough for her. The only reason I put up with his insults and stayed on was because I knew Mary Beth would come back sooner or later. Why Tillis didn't fire me, I'll never know, except that I think he enjoyed seeing the pain in my eyes, enjoyed lording it over me."

He began to roll another cigarette, and Harmony dismounted, walking up to stand beside him. "Gosh, I'm sorry, Buck. I guess maybe I shouldn't have asked."

He looked down at her, the pain still there. Then he shrugged and lit the cigarette. "I managed to correspond with her finally, through a maid who sympathized with us. Then word came that . . . that Mary Beth had come down with some kind of fever." He swallowed, smoking quietly for a moment, looking out over the valley. "Then we got the news that she had died." He swallowed again, cleared his throat. "It was just like Fast Horse—someone I cared about being sent away, to die alone and never come back. I never saw Mary Beth again, never got to . . . hold her . . . talk to her . . . make her my wife. From that moment on I never hated anyone the way I hated Wade Tillis! And he knew it! He made damned sure he stayed out of my way—had me fired. I wanted revenge, but I knew there would be a better time and place to seek it. It's pretty hard to get revenge against a man with power and money. And Mary Beth was gone, so nothing mattered anymore. I drifted off. I heard that Tillis had found gold on his property, mined it, and then sold the mine and the ranch for a tremendous amount of money. Other strikes followed and he bought more land, set up supply stores, owned a good share of the towns he occupied—and charged exorbitant prices for his goods. That's how he got so rich. He's a good businessman, but he never did a hard day's work in his life. If he hadn't inherited that first ranch, he never would have made it and probably wouldn't be worth anything today." He took a drag on the cigarette. "At any rate, I kept track of him, stalked him, began following him. Wherever he went, I showed up, making him nervous, reminding him of what he did to poor Mary Beth. I know it bothers him some, and I'm glad. I want him to squirm, to worry. I enjoy that. And someday the time will be right—just right. I'll know when that day comes, and when it does, I'll have my revenge!"

The words were spoken bitterly, almost in a hiss. His jaws flexed with repressed anger, and his eyes were watery. She felt out of place, unable to console him, guilty over bringing back memories he would rather forget.

"I'm sorry, Buck. I didn't know it was anything that bad." She toyed with the reins of her horse. "Sometimes I feel like that about my parents. I was only six when they abandoned me. Sometimes I wish I could do something to hurt them. I wish I could find them just so I could tell them I hate them, but they probably wouldn't even care. It's a terrible feeling to know somebody you love is just . . . gone . . . and that they'll never come back."

He looked down at her, throwing down the cigarette and stamping it out. He suddenly grasped her arms. "That's why I don't want to leave you here, Harmony," he told her, his grip tight and desperate, his blue eyes suddenly pleading. "I'm afraid if I go away, I'll come back to find you gone. I don't want you to be gone! I want you for my own, Harmony Jones. I haven't cared this much about a woman since Mary Beth."

His grip frightened her, and suddenly his face came closer. His lips covered her own, searching, pressing, his strong arms pulling her close, pressing her against his hard-muscled chest. He crushed her to him, searching her mouth hungrily, pressing that strange hardness against her belly—it had frightened her so when Jimmie O'Toole had done the same thing—telling her what he would do to her. She suddenly realized that if Buck Hanner thought for one moment that she wanted him, he'd do awful things to her too.

Her heart raced with panic. Not this way! Not this soon! Not at all! She began pushing at him, but his grip was powerful. More and more it reminded her of the night Jimmie had held her wrists, pressing himself against her, kissing her against her will. She had wanted Buck Hanner to kiss her. She knew secretly that she had. Yet now it frightened her.

She twisted her face away. "Stop it!" she gasped. "What are you doing!"

"Damn you, Harmony Jones, I love you!" he said in a husky voice. "Do you know the hell it's been being up here alone with you and never being able to hold you, touch you? Don't you have even the smallest idea—"

"You let go of me!" she screamed. "Let go! Let go!"

She kicked his leg hard and his grip lightened enough for her to wrench herself loose. She pushed at Pepper, urging the horse a few feet away from him, and yanking her rifle from its boot, she turned it on him.

"Did you think you could get me by making me feel sorry for you first?" she raged. "You go on back to

207

Cripple Creek, Buck Hanner! You've already over-stayed your welcome. Now I know why you took so long in showing me everything!"

He stood there, staring at her, looking like a lost little boy. He cursed himself inwardly. What had made him do that? It was not at all the way he'd intended to approach her. He was going to be so careful, so gentle, so tender. He was going to very calmly tell her he loved her and wanted to make her his wife—to take care of her, love her, protect her.

"I'm sorry, Shortcake!" he said, total devastation in his voice. "I . . . I don't know what came over me. It was just . . . talking about Mary Beth—"

"You just thought you'd give it one hell of a try before you left!" she yelled, tears coming to her eyes. "I knew all men were the same—just like Jimmie, pushing and grabbing and hurting! You can leave now, Buck Hanner! I don't need you anymore!"

Their eyes held. He knew damned well she'd never shoot him . . . or would she? Sometimes she acted like a crazy child, at others she was a rational woman.

"I mean it, Harmony," he spoke up. "I'm sorry. I never meant—" He turned and mounted up. "I do love you, Harmony. You think about that. You think about it real good while I'm gone. I'll ride back now, get my things and get the mules together. You'd better bring Pepper. I'll be taking her too. There's still some daylight. I'll leave today."

He kicked Indian's sides, charging past her at a gallop. She turned to watch him go, then put the rifle back with shaking hands. She was not shaking from fear, she realized, but from an awakened desire she'd never known she possessed. She touched her fingers to her lips, still able to taste the kiss, the sweetness of it, the power of it, the message in it. Buck Hanner was all man and could undoubtedly answer her questions about whether or not it was pleasurable to be with a man, but every time she considered finding out, she remembered Jimmie—the ugliness of his touch and the horror of his words. No. Let Buck Hanner be angry and leave. It was best.

She turned and mounted up, sure she could still smell the scent of him even though he was gone—the smell of man, fresh air, leather. She shivered with a feeling she could not even understand, feeling suddenly weak and out of control. Why did the little inner voice tell her it might be exciting to give Buck Hanner his pleasure? Why did she have this terrible curiosity about him, about being with him? Yes, the timing was right. It was good that he leave, right now. It was best.

When she got back to the cabin, he was nearly packed, tightening straps angrily, cursing when something went wrong. He said nothing to her. She realized he had said he loved her. Loved her . . . How could that be? Nobody loved Harmony Jones. Everyone left her. Surely he'd only told her that to have his way with her.

Her lips puckered. "Go ahead and leave!" she pouted.

"What the hell do you think I'm doing!" he grumbled.

"Good! I have to be on my own sometime. And you obviously have been here too long, Mr. Buck Hanner! You've shown me you're just like all the rest! Don't talk to me about love! Love hurts! People love you and then they leave you! I want nothing to do with love, and I don't care to have a man tell me he loves me just so he can do bad things to me!"

He jerked at a strap, then looked up at her. "Well this man doesn't tell any woman he loves her unless he means it!" he barked. "And I never would have done 'bad things' to you against your will, even though I stole a kiss, for which I apologized! If you were more woman than child you'd understand they aren't bad things at all! They're good things, Harmony Jones; someday you'll understand that!" He mounted up, whirling his horse. "And I'm the one who'll make you understand it!" He picked up the lead rope to the mules. "Now get down off that horse and get your gear off so I can leave!"

She blinked back tears, suddenly wanting to beg him to stay. But that would mean losing the present battle, and she did not like losing. She dismounted, taking off her bedroll and her rifle and canteen.

"I'll leave the saddle on," she announced. "It's rented anyway, and I won't need it."

"Fine!" He rode his horse closer and yanked the reins from her hand. "I'll be back in a couple of months."

"I'll be here!" she replied. "I'll be rich by then, and I'll be thinking the same way I'm thinking right now!"

Their eyes held, and he suddenly dismounted. When she backed up a little, he came closer to her anyway. "I love you, Harmony," he said quietly. He bent closer, and she let him kiss her again, she didn't know why. It was a quick, gentle kiss, soft, sweet, delicious. Then he simply turned and mounted again. "I'm betting you won't feel the same at all when I come back," he added.

He turned his horse, taking up the rope attached to the mules and to Pepper's reins. "You be careful now!" he called out. "Remember everything I told you—

everything! I'll be back, Harmony Jones! You think I won't be, but I will. You'll find out you can trust me after all. And by then you'll know you love me just as much as I love you."

She watched him ride away, screaming inside for him to come back but making no move and saying nothing. Soon he disappeared amid a thick stand of pines, and the last mule followed.

Tears ran down her cheeks then. "Good-bye, Buck," she said quietly.

Chapter Ten

When Buck got up from the bed, he stared down at the young prostitute with whom he'd spent the night. It had been a long time since he'd been with a woman, and he was hoping this one would make him forget about Harmony Jones. But if anything, she made him want Harmony more. Surely bedding a woman would be more fulfilling if she were someone like Harmony. He didn't feel satisfied, not satisfied at all. Actually he felt more frustrated.

He let the girl sleep while he pulled on his underwear and pants. Then he poured water into a washbowl and washed and shaved before he pulled on a clean shirt. The girl slept through it all, and when Buck finished dressing, he laid a two-dollar bill on the pillow beside the girl, wondering why such a young, pretty thing did what she did. Perhaps she had no choice. It might be a matter of survival. For Harmony, survival was working her gold claim. Who could tell which way she would have turned if she hadn't inherited it? He grinned then. No. Harmony Jones would never turn to this! She was too smart, for one thing. She'd find a way into some kind of business. Selling her body was the last thing she would do. It would be hard enough for any man to get her to give that body freely and willingly. Harmony Jones would die before she sold it.

He shook his head and donned his hat, picking up his gun belt and strapping it on. Then he quietly left the room, to walk downstairs and outside into the bright sunlight. He had work to do for Jack Leads as soon as breakfast was over. And soon he had more trips to take, but none that would bring him close to Harmony's claim. He would just have to pray for her health and safety, and hope for the best until he could get back to her.

Thinking of her, worrying over her, was torture. He loved and respected her enough to let her do what she thought she must, realizing she had a need to prove something to herself and others—a need to feel free and independent. But his manly instincts nipped at him constantly. He should be with her, providing for her, protecting her, helping her work the claim. Yet, if he went back there and offered his help, she'd accuse him of trying to get a piece of the claim—and a piece of her. The claim he didn't care about, but she'd be right about herself. He didn't want just a piece of her; he wanted all of her, from the top of her pretty blond head to the tips of her tiny toes—and everything in between. He wanted it all for himself, not just as a matter of conquest. He wanted her because he loved her and wanted her with him forever. He never dreamed he would love another girl, not after losing Mary Beth. But now there was Harmony. Harmony Jones. A delightful name. A delightful girl. The next two months or so without her were going to be painful and lonely. He missed her companionship, even missed her quick temper.

He walked into Wanda's restaurant, and several people looked up at him. Some began to whisper. He knew what they were thinking, knew they were curious. They were wondering if anything had happened when he and Harmony Jones were alone up there on the mountain. He sat down, and Wanda brought him coffee.

"Morning, cowboy," she said.

"Morning, Wanda. Bring me the usual."

"Anything for Buck Hanner. When did you get back?"

"Last night."

She set the pot on the table and looked at him with concern. "That little gal okay?"

Buck shrugged. "She was when I left her. I think she'll be just fine. She learns quick. When I left she could pan, work a sluice, shoot a rifle, clean and skin small animals." He gave her a smile. "She'll be all right. Fact is, I wouldn't want to be the man who might decide to go there and give her a hard time." He said it loud enough for others to get the message. "Harmony Jones is an independent girl, and she'll use that rifle right quick if necessary."

Wanda laughed. "She is an independent one." She gave him a wink. "And my guess is you wouldn't mind her being a little more dependent—on you, maybe?"

Buck laughed lightly and rolled a cigarette. "I wouldn't mind at all. But right now I'm just her guide, Wanda. Nothing more."

"Well, good luck to you," she offered, turning to

215

pour coffee for someone else.

"Just a guide, huh?" A man to Buck's left sneered. "I'll bet."

Buck lowered his cigarette, laying it in an ashtray and turning to face one of Wade Tillis' men, a big, burly brick of a man who usually followed Tillis around like a bodyguard. Tillis himself was nowhere in sight, however. Two other men sat at the table with the big man, who was called Buffalo. The three of them eyed Buck, grins on their faces.

"When are you going to collect on that bet?" Buffalo asked him loudly. "You took the little filly up there and left her. I guess that means you win two hundred dollars. There's a lot of others who bet on her. They're all over at the Mother Lode, waiting for you to make the official announcement."

Buck leaned back, eying all three of them steadily. "I'll not go over there and make an announcement. I'm sorry it all turned into such a circus. The girl doesn't deserve that. You can go tell your friends she's there and she's fine and she's making a go of it. Forget my own bet. Just return the money I put down. I don't want any profit."

Buffalo laughed. "Maybe you already made your profit, while you were up there alone with the little filly."

The words were barely finished before Buck was out of his chair and landing into the man, half dragging and half throwing the much heftier Buffalo out the door, knocking over two tables in the process. A couple of women screamed, and Wanda came running in time to see Buck Hanner forcing his huge opponent through the door.

216

The two men struggled on the boardwalk, then fell together into the street, and in an instant it seemed half the men in town were ringed around Buck and Buffalo, who rolled in the mud for a moment, then got to their feet. They circled then, fists clenched, eyes smoldering.

Buck charged into Buffalo then, ramming a shoulder into the man's gut and shoving him backward, while Buffalo pounded at Buck's kidneys. Suddenly Buck rose, slamming the back of his head into Buffalo's chin. The bigger man reeled backward, and Buck straightened, grabbing Buffalo's shirt and hanging on while he landed blows on the man's face several times. Finally he let Buffalo slump to the ground and stood over him, panting.

Men cheered. Many of them were surprised at the way he had handled the much bigger Buffalo. Buck was a big man, a good fighter, and hard muscled, but compared to Buffalo, even Buck Hanner looked small. Nonetheless, Buffalo lay prostrate in the mud, blood running profusely from his nose. Buck turned. His blue eyes, icy with anger, ran over the onlookers.

"Some of you made bets on Harmony Jones!" he roared. "Well, she's up there, working her claim! So those of you who bet on her can collect!" He stopped to get his breath. "But I'll tell all of you right now! Anybody who gets the idea of going up there and bothering that girl, or bringing her harm, he'll answer to me!" he roared. "And I won't just stop with a bloody nose! The next man who accuses Harmony Jones of being anything but a respectable little girl will be dead! That's all she is—a little girl, with more guts than most of you will ever have!"

He bent down and picked up his fallen hat; then he

pushed his way through the crowd back to the restaurant, stalking inside and up to Wanda. "I'm sorry about this. I'll pay the damages," he told her.

"There's no real damage, other than a little spilled food, Buck," she answered, frowning with concern. "You go clean up and come back here, and breakfast will be on the house. You deserve it. That man shouldn't have insulted that little girl."

As Buck ran a hand through his tousled hair, he felt pain in the knuckles of his right hand. He looked at them. They were already swollen.

"I think I'd better see a doctor too. Hitting Buffalo is like hitting a cement block."

Wanda clucked, touching the hand lightly. "Oh, dear. I hope it isn't broken, Buck."

"I don't care if it is. It would be worth it. Listen, I'm going to clean up and see the doc. Then I'll be back. I really am sorry about the mess. I couldn't help myself."

"No problem. I don't blame you at all." She studied the handsome blue eyes, longing for her own youth. "You love her, don't you?" she asked quietly.

She was sure his eyes actually teared. He nodded. "I do," he answered. He turned and left, and she looked after him, shaking her head.

"I hope it all works out for you, Buck Hanner," she said softly.

As Harmony worked the sluice, she hummed. She liked this life—liked the privacy, the independence, the freedom. Here there was no one to answer to. Here she was just Harmony Jones, her own woman. She had been here two months now, and had stored up a lot of

218

gold nuggets already. The weather had been good, the clear, bright days broken only occasionally by five- or ten-minute thunder showers. The nights were quiet, and she was usually so tired from working all day that she slept soundly.

Everything would be perfect, if not for the fact that she missed Buck Hanner terribly. She hated to admit it, hated to acknowledge that his kiss had left a lingering sweetness on her lips, a lingering longing in her soul, a lingering warmth that was very pleasant in her.

She still had no idea why she had let him kiss her again, after being so angry about the first kiss. Perhaps it was because the first kiss had stirred in her a furious curiosity that overwhelmed her anger. Buck . . . She wished she could figure him out, wished she didn't feel sorry for what had happened to him and Mary Beth, wished he weren't so handsome and sure—wished she'd never met him at all. Yes. That would have been best, never to have met him at all. It infuriated her that he made her think of things she had never before considered, made her more aware of her own body. She wondered how it would feel to have a man like Buck touch her breasts, press her naked body against his own.

Never had she entertained such thoughts. They had always revolted her. For the first time she considered some of the things Jimmie had told her in a new light. Perhaps it wasn't the things a man did to a woman, but the man himself that made the difference. To think of Jimmie touching her made her nauseous. To think of Buck touching her set her on fire. Yet a stubborn voice inside her told her she should never—ever—submit to any man. That would be letting him get the better of her. She wanted no master. She was in charge of her own life. Besides, she still had that gnawing doubt, that continued inability to trust. Maybe Buck Hanner wanted more than Harmony Jones. Maybe he was just playing games with her, proving he could break her down. Maybe he wanted part of her claim—or all of it. Maybe his hatred of Wade Tillis was just staged. He might be working for the man, be some kind of spy who was waiting for her to fail so he could inform Tillis and Tillis could move in.

Yet when she closed her eyes and pictured his face, she saw him talking about Fast Horse and Mary Beth, saw the love his face revealed. She knew he must be telling the truth. And, after all, true hatred had blazed in his eyes when he'd spoken of Wade Tillis. His story seemed very believable, and he had killed one of Tillis' men before they'd left, unless that gunfight was staged.

No. She envisioned the sky-blue eyes; the handsome, tanned face; the quick, brilliant smile. He had done so much for her, been so patient with her; and above all, he'd been so respectful of her. He could have had her anytime, by sheer strength. Yet he had never used that strength against her, except that last day when he'd kissed her so savagely. Even then she'd known he wouldn't have done more if she hadn't wanted him to.

She sighed deeply and picked out some gold particles from the drag. In her usual routine, she spent the evenings picking out the gangue from the gold, so that she had one sack with only gold in it, and another with pieces of garnet and some silver. Now she was getting tired, and decided to call it quits for the night.

In the evening shadows she caught a movement, and she reached for her rifle, but Amber appeared then, the coyote with whom she had made friends.

"Hi!" she said quietly. "You hungry?"

The animal watched her timidly, carefully stepping a little closer, then standing rigidly.

"Don't go away," she told him. She picked up her rifle again and walked slowly to the shack, climbing the steps and going inside, where three freshly killed rabbits lay. She cut one in half and carried one part of the carcass outside. Going down the steps she waved it teasingly, while Amber just stared apprehensively.

"I know I shouldn't do this. I need my food, you know," she told the animal, watching its yellow eyes look longingly at the fresh meat. "But you're such a pretty fellow, and I like talking to you. Someday you're going to come up and eat right out of my hand, Amber. Why not try it now?"

The coyote did not budge, and after a few minutes she sighed and threw the meat toward him. It landed just inches away, and in a flash it was in his jaws and he was off, disappearing into the woods.

"You could at least stay and talk awhile!" she called out to him. "You aren't a very grateful coyote!"

She smiled and sat there with her chin in her hand. She was proud of herself—shooting rabbits, making friends with a coyote, working a sluice. She was surviving very nicely, sitting here on her very own property on her very own mountain. At least it seemed like her mountain. After all, she was the only human inhabitant. In addition to the coyote, a squirrel came around so often that it was now by the cabin most of the time. She didn't have the heart to shoot it. There was other game, and she needed the friendship of the animals. Besides, she could also fish. At the mouth of the creek that ran past her cabin, about a half-mile away, her own small creek fed into a larger stream, which in turn ran down the mountain and joined the South Platte River, far to the west. At the junction of the two creeks, trout were so abundant she could catch them by hand and have fish whenever she wanted it.

She was proud of the fact that she had discovered that abundant source of fish on her own. But when she went fishing she kept her eyes open and her rifle nearby, for she remembered Buck's warning that bears love fish and can often be found where they swim close to the surface in clear water. So far, however, there had been no sign of any bears, either at the fish pond, or near the shack.

She turned toward the rumbling sound behind her, noticing heavy black clouds moving her way. It seemed to rain at least once a day in these mountains, quick, sudden storms that hit fiercely, then were gone. She felt a slight chill in the air, and her heart filled with a mixture of fear and awe, for the rumbling sound that came with the clouds echoed fiercely through the mountains, seeming to shake the very earth. She never failed to be amazed at how swiftly these storms could sneak up on her. Moments ago she had seen no clouds, yet now thunder boomed, as though a great monster had rushed in to pounce on her.

She ran to the sluice, picking up her jars of minerals, and hurried with them to the shack, where she set them on the homemade table. The entire cabin shook as thunder clapped again, and she jumped. Storms didn't usually frighten her, but this one seemed to envelop the shack in its powerful embrace. The thunder made her feel alone, reminding her that she was just one small person against a vast mountain and mighty Mother Nature. At such moments she was aware that choosing to live alone meant she had no one to turn to, and she missed Buck Hanner.

If Buck were here, she knew she wouldn't be afraid. He'd be laughing right now at the storm, joking about it, teasing her. She got out her cards. Perhaps if she played solitaire, the storm wouldn't bother her as much. When she began to lay the cards on the floor, a rat ran from under the stove, crossed the room, and scuttered out the door. She reminded herself to check the traps again, but she wasn't upset. Buck had been right. Even the rats seemed like friends now. They didn't really bother anything. All they wanted was a crumb or two that she might drop. As long as she kept all food up high, there was no problem. Still, they were the only animals she didn't welcome. She would keep the traps set.

The storm raged and whipped around the cabin, rain coming down in torrents. But as usual it lasted only minutes. Suddenly everything was calm again, and the sky brightened with the sun. Wondering why she had been afraid, Harmony opened the door and stepped out to smell the clean, damp air. When the pine forest was wet, it was pungent with sweet smells. She went back inside to get a bucket. With the water stirred by the rain and the stream slightly swollen from it, perhaps there would be more fish than usual at the mouth of the creek. She was hungry for trout, and she didn't feel like doing anymore panning that day. After all, the place was hers. She could work it as much or as little as she chose. At the moment she preferred to go catch fish.

She walked down the steps, for once forgetting her rifle. It was the first time she had done anything so foolish. She marched down the mountainside with the bucket, calling for Amber. But the coyote made no appearance.

"He'll be back," she muttered to herself. "And he'll eat out of my hand."

The sun grew hot on her shoulders. It was strange how fast the weather could change in these mountains. She wondered how it would be in the winter. Surely it was going to be even more lonely, for she wouldn't be able to take these walks and go catch fish. She mused on what she could do in the winter to keep herself entertained. Perhaps she would build snowmen all around the shack, or make snowballs and throw them at Amber. Would the stream freeze? How would she pan for gold if it did? But no. Buck had said it could be very cold in the winter, but the days were warm enough to thaw the stream and most days brought sun, even in winter.

She was over halfway to the mouth of the creek when she realized she'd forgotten her rifle. She stopped and considered going back. But it was a long climb, and it surely wouldn't take her long to get the fish. She'd been this way so many times, and had never had trouble. One trip without the rifle would not be the end of the world.

She began to hum. Yes, she was happy. What she would do about her feelings for Buck she wasn't sure. She liked him more than she cared to admit. She couldn't exactly say that she loved him, even though he'd told her he loved her. She wondered if he'd really meant that. Why should he love her? She was hardly more than a girl, and she'd been mean to him most of the time. She'd given him absolutely no reason whatsoever to love her. Were his words just a ruse to make her submit?

She tightened her lips. She'd never submit! She'd never fall for Buck Hanner's clever words and handsome smile . . . or his tender kiss. Yet the thought of his touch made her shudder with an odd, heated excitement. She would have to be very careful when he returned, for she must have feelings for no one, allow no one into her life. Besides, whether she liked the man or not, what all men did was the same. It would be humiliating and painful beyond description. No man would do that to her except by force or trickery, and she'd make sure Buck Hanner used neither one on her.

She looked up and smiled at the birds that sang and flitted from tree to tree, made happy by the new-fallen rain. Then she studied the surrounding area and glanced back toward the cabin. She saw no sign of fire from the recent lightning. She was glad of that. She did not want to have to leave this mountain and her claim. She liked it there, even though it was lonely.

She turned and half skipped the rest of the way to the mouth of the creek. The swollen waters rushed over smooth, round boulders in a loud torrent, roaring so loudly she could hear nothing else, not the birds or the wind or the animals that might be nearby. She didn't check the area, for she was enthralled by the churning white water. It was all so beautiful. She laughed out loud and jumped onto a large boulder, clinging to the bucket. All around her trout jumped and splashed, so many the water seemed black with them, more than she had ever seen there. She decided to fill the bucket to the

225

brim if she could. After all, she could always smoke what she couldn't eat. Then she'd have fish for several days—even weeks. She'd never dreamed she could be so practical, so self-sufficient.

She jumped into the icy cold water, not caring that it soaked her high, leather boots. She could tell it was cold, even through the boots, but it was exhilarating. She set the bucket on a wide, flat rock, then began dipping into the cold water with her hands, sometimes catching a slippery meal, sometimes missing a fish.

She fished for forty-five minutes, laughing and screaming at the way some of the fish wriggled in her hands. She'd quickly toss each one into the bucket, paying no attention to her surroundings, behaving like the child she truly was but had never been allowed to be. All around her the water pounded and rushed. Once she dived for a fish and fell into the water face first. She laughed and shivered, telling herself she'd better get back to the cabin and change before she took cold. The worst thing she could think of was being sick up here alone, maybe dying of pneumonia with no one to know until Buck came for her.

The thought suddenly sobered her, and she caught three more fish, throwing them into the bucket and deciding to head back. She straightened. When she picked up the bucket, she was surprised at how heavy it was. Good! She must have at least twenty trout. She could almost taste them without even cooking them. She moved toward the bank, then stopped, feeling an eerie presence, a sixth sense telling her she was not alone.

She turned to scan the other side of the larger creek. A grizzly sat there on its haunches, lazily chomping on

226

a big fish, the remains of its snack hanging limp and torn in its great paw. For a moment Harmony simply froze. How long had the animal been there? Had it noticed her? Surely it had. She had been screaming and laughing and splashing in the stream for close to an hour.

The rifle! She had no rifle! And she'd have to run uphill to get to the cabin. Should she just slowly walk away? Or should she run? Should she stand still? Perhaps if she didn't move at all, the bear would simply waddle off, leaving her alone. She stood transfixed, holding the bucket so tightly the knuckles on the hand that gripped it were white. The grizzly finished swallowing the rest of the fish; then it looked at her. It stared directly at her for what seemed hours to Harmony, and finally it began to sniff, wiggling its nose and making snorting sounds. It splashed at the water, then slowly rose to its hind feet. Standing, it looked a hundred feet tall to Harmony.

She didn't wait to see what it was going to do. She turned and started running, so much fear in her heart it pounded wildly, actually hurting her chest. For some strange reason she clung to the heavy bucket. In her panic she didn't even think to set it down. She was reacting in the strange way of panicked people. They became irrational, and brought more trouble on themselves.

She ran! Fast! Faster! Was the bear behind her? Should she have stayed put? But how could she, when it had reared up on its hind legs and sniffed her? She scrambled up the path, slipping several times, skinning her hands. Each time she fell, a fish or two slipped out of the bucket. Still she clung to it, not even realizing she was doing so, not stopping to think that she was leaving a tempting trail for the grizzly. If she had thought of that, she'd have left the bucket and all of the fish. The grizzly would most likely have stopped and sat down to enjoy a hardy meal, letting the foolish girl run on.

But her flight only intrigued and infuriated the grizzly. He followed the small creature who was carrying his meal away. He lumbered after her, his excitement building as the human creature ran on ahead of him, spilling fish out here and there. It was like a game. Now he wanted to catch her. Occasionally he stopped to pick up a fish and savor it, quickly swallowing the delightful morsel. Then he'd run on again, to see if she would drop more, intent on catching the little creature that was fleeing him. Perhaps that creature would make a tasty meal. Perhaps it would taste better than the fish. Perhaps this creature was an enemy. Hadn't she been at his creek, catching his fish? Wasn't she running away now with those fish, trying to keep them for herself? Of course! He must catch the human creature and give her a swat—teach her a lesson! Perhaps he should even sink his teeth into her throat and kill her, as he would kill any enemy!

Harmony ran faster, tears of fear filling her eyes. She prayed silently and desperately that she would make it to the cabin. But what if she did? Was it strong enough to protect her from the fierce power of a grizzly if the bear wanted to come in after her?

She had been so foolish. Why had she played like a child, paying no attention to her surroundings? Why had she forgotten her rifle? She had done all the things Buck had warned her not to do.

Her breath came in quick, frightened gasps, and

tears blurred her vision. The half-mile to the cabin seemed more like ten miles now! She was drenched in perspiration and as the hot sun shone down on her, her wet clothes seemed to steam. She screamed for Buck, knowing he wasn't there, yet unable to stop herself. If only Buck were around! He'd come! He'd shoot the grizzly and she'd be all right!

Run! Run! Her legs felt like lead. She could hear rhythmic snorting behind her now—the bear was grunting with every heavy breath—and she could hear crashing sounds. Yes, he was running! He was chasing her!

"Oh, God!" she whimpered. She could see the cabin ahead. If she could just get to it . . . It was late afternoon. If she could get to the cabin the bear would hang around awhile, then give up and leave when darkness came. She'd be all right if she could just get to the cabin! She ran hard, stumbled, got up and ran again, still clinging to the bucket. At last the cabin was only a few yards away. She headed for it, running across an open space, splashing through the creek that ran in front of it, almost feeling the bear's breath on her neck, smelling his awful stench.

She pounded up the steps, dropping the bucket inside the cabin and quickly slamming the door and lowering the crossbar that latched it. A split second later something landed against the door and she screamed and jumped back. The grizzly let out a fierce roar.

Harmony looked around the room. If she could shoot him, perhaps right through the door . . . The rifle! Where was the rifle! More tears came to her eyes, as she realized she'd left the rifle leaning against the railing outside. There was no way to get to it, for the bear was on the steps. She would have to wait for the right moment. The huge beast roared again and scratched viciously at the door. She screamed and covered her ears, cowering back against the farthest wall, glad the back of the cabin was flush against rock and that there was only one window. The window!

She ran to it, looking out. She could see nothing, for it was on the side of the cabin. The bear was still at the front door, clawing madly, growling, angry. She did not even stop to think he might be after the fish. She searched the room for something to put over the window. It was high from the outside, but perhaps it was not high enough to keep a tall grizzly from looking inside, perhaps reaching inside. To her the grizzly seemed a monster now, huge and snarling, capable of ripping the cabin to shreds, then doing the same with her. Why didn't he just go? She hadn't done him any harm. Why was he so persistent?

She could find nothing that would serve to cover the window and protect her. Just nailing a rug or a blanket over it would do no good. But maybe that would keep him from seeing inside. She screamed again as he clawed once more at the door, pushing, growling, adamant. Then she grabbed a hammer from the corner of the room and tore a blanket from her bed. Hurriedly she nailed the blanket across the top of the window, finally moving back into a corner, the hammer, her only weapon, in hand. As she did so, she remembered the big knife Buck had bought for her. It lay on the table. She ran to it, grabbed it, and moved back to the corner again . . . to wait. Either the bear would leave, or it would get through the door and come for her.

For what seemed hours she sat in sheer terror, unable to get to her gun, afraid to move. The bear would not give up. It snorted and wheezed and growled, constantly clawing and scratching at the place where the human creature had disappeared with the delicious fish. He wanted both. Harmony whimpered, her eyes wide, her heart pounding wildly. She thought that she would go crazy. Never had she felt this alone, this abandoned! This was much worse than the docks of St. Louis! There was absolutely no one to help her, and the grizzly seemed stubbornly determined to get inside and claw her to death.

Finally everything was quiet. The cabin was dark then. For hours the bear had kept up his furious rage, long past sundown. She blinked, listened, trying to control her own breathing, feeling a little demented. Had the grizzly gone? She watched the door for a long time, then slowly started to rise. As she did so, there was a crashing sound, and a huge paw was thrust through the window, ripping down the blanket and reaching out at nothingness, trying to grab on to something.

Harmony screamed, over and over, covering her ears, "No! No! Go away!" But the bear would not give up. It kept roaring and clawing, grasping the window sill and bringing up its hind legs, trying to climb inside, but it was too big to get in. For what seemed hours the grizzly hung there, one paw inside, its hideous face sticking through. Growling furiously, its long sharp teeth bared in anger, it was determined to get into the cabin, to get the good-smelling fish . . . and the enemy creature who had stolen them away.

Chapter Eleven

A soft wind moaned through the pines as Buck approached the cabin. He expected to see Harmony already busy with the sluice, but as his eyes scanned the area from a distance, he could not see her anywhere about the place. Had she decided to take a walk or go hunting this early in the morning?

"Harmony!" he called out.

There was no reply, and experience told him before he got any closer that something was wrong. There was an eerie silence in the air, and he drew his horse and pack mules to a halt when he saw her rifle lying outside on the ground, as though dropped or knocked over.

A tight feeling came to his chest. He'd never forgive himself if something had happened to her, and if some man had harmed her, he'd die!

"Harmony!" he called out again. Then he dismounted, tying Indian and the mules, and removing his rifle from its boot. His eyes scanned the area as he jumped across the creek that was now much narrower. It was nearly the end of August, and some creeks were

233

completely dried up.

As he approached the steps to the cabin, a sickening dread overcame him. The door was covered with claw marks. He looked around again. There was no doubt in his mind that the marks had been made by a grizzly. A few fish skeletons lay about.

He charged up the steps and pushed against the door, but it was bolted shut. "What the hell!" he muttered. "Harmony!" he yelled. There was no reply. He pushed against the door again, but it would not give, so he ran down the steps and around to the side window. It was too high for him to see inside, but he noticed that it was broken and there were claw marks in the logs around it. "My God!" he groaned. Had the grizzly gotten inside? Surely the window wasn't big enough. But a determined grizzly could do just about anything.

A lump came to his throat. Was she lying dead inside, mauled to death? What a terrible way for his Shortcake to die! He looked around for something to stand on, then grabbed a barrel, rolling it over under the window. He told himself to be careful—the bear could be inside—as he stood the barrel on end and climbed onto it, his nose curling at the smell of bear that still lingered on the logs of the cabin. He grasped the window sill and looked inside.

"Harmony!"

She sat shivering in a corner, her wet clothes and boots still on, her hands still clinging to the hammer and knife. She stared at him, and he could see by her eyes that she didn't realize it was he. How many hours had she sat staring at this window, watching a furious grizzly trying to get inside to claw her to death? He could imagine her terror.

He set his rifle inside, then pulled himself up and scrambled through the window. "Harmony," he said softly. "It's all right, Shortcake. It's me—Buck."

Her breathing quickened as he came closer, and she raised the hammer, drawing back. He made a quick dive, grabbing the hand that held the hammer and wresting it from her, grasping the other wrist tightly at the same time and squeezing until she dropped the knife. When she began to scream and claw at him, he quickly pinned both arms behind her, holding her wrists with one hand and drawing her tightly against him with the other.

"Harmony, it's just me—Buck. The bear is gone, Shortcake. He's gone. He won't hurt you now." He stood, pulling her up with him but keeping a grip on her wrists until she was on her feet and he could grasp her arms firmly. Then he gave her a shake. "Come on, Shortcake. Don't do this. Where's my brave girl?" He shook her again. "Harmony, it's okay."

She blinked, looked around the room with a desperate stare. "The bear! The bear!" she yelled.

"He's gone," Buck repeated. "I just got here, Shortcake, with new supplies. And I'm damned glad I arrived when I did. It's okay, Harmony. The bear is gone. And I'm here."

She looked up at him then, meeting his blue eyes. She felt as though she were coming out of a trance. Buck! It was Buck! She broke into sobs of relief and loneliness, throwing her arms around his neck and clinging to him like a little girl. He gladly embraced her,

235

relishing the feel of her body against his, grateful for the opportunity to hold this woman-child he so cherished.

"Don't let him come back!" she wailed.

"I won't let him hurt you, Shortcake. I'll stay till I find out what he's up to. He'll probably come back, and I'll be ready for him. I won't leave till he's taken care of, one way or another."

"Buck, he's so big! So awful! If you go after him, he'll sneak up on you and kill you!"

"Don't you worry about that."

"Oh, Buck, I did everything wrong! I went to catch fish without my rifle, and I didn't pay any attention—"

"Hush," he told her, petting her hair. "Tell me about it later. Your clothes are wet and you're shaking. You'll be sick if you don't get into something dry and get some rest. You must have been up all night."

"I thought he'd never go away!"

She clung to him as he picked her up and set her on the bed. "You get this stuff off, and I want no arguments. Forget your damned modesty. You're shaking, and you feel hot. If you don't get pneumonia from this, you'll be lucky."

He pulled off her boots and threw them aside, then peeled off her long stockings, forcing himself not to look at her slender legs despite the desire he felt. Her health was all that mattered right now. He reached up and took a flannel gown from a hook beside the bed; then he helped her to stand. "Come on. Out of this stuff right now and into bed. I'll clean up around here and make you something to eat. Then you sleep, as long as you need to."

He unbuttoned her shirt.

236

She felt dizzy and confused. She wanted to stop him, but she was too weak and too glad that he had come. "Don't look at me," she heard herself saying.

"Jesus, Harmony, do you think I'd take advantage of you after I thought I'd find you mauled by a bear? What the hell do you take me for?"

It was strange. He'd been gone two months, yet they could pick up their friendship in a matter of seconds, as though he hadn't even left. And even though her clothing was coming off, she wasn't afraid. He slipped the warm, dry flannel gown over her head. It felt wonderful to be out of the wet clothes. The next thing she knew, he was pushing her into the feather mattress and covering her with quilts, saying something about heating some soup for her. She felt safe now, protected. Buck would take care of everything. And he'd kill the bear so it would never come after her again.

She snuggled down into the quilts. She could hear movement, but didn't know what Buck was doing. She drifted into an exhausted sleep, and Buck stood and watched her for a while. He'd seen—only briefly, and unintentionally—enough to know she was everything he'd pictured and more. He almost felt guilty, as though she were just a little girl and he had no right to look at her with anything but a fatherly attitude. But he couldn't be fatherly, and he wondered if he could go back this time without claiming Harmony Jones for himself, or if he could go back at all.

Now he had the bear to think about, and cleaning up; and most of all, he had to think about her health. She definitely had a fever. First things first. He'd keep her warm and rested, and pray she didn't get too sick from this. He was not going to lose Harmony Jones—not to a bear or to sickness or to her damned independence. He'd not love and lose again as he had with Mary Beth.

He stepped closer, gazing down at her. How he'd missed her! Had she missed him? Surely she had. He bent down and lightly kissed a soft, babyish cheek. "I love you, Harmony," he whispered. But she did not hear.

For the next several days Harmony lay abed, feverish, her throat aching, a cough racking her lungs. During the worst of her sickness she was not aware of Buck's presence, did not see the concern and fear in his eyes, wasn't embarrassed because he sometimes unbuttoned her gown and bathed her with a cool cloth, trying to keep the fever down.

Sometimes she would dream about the bear coming back, and she would wake up screaming. Then someone would hold her. Was it Brian? Was he saving her from the men on the pier? When she smelled the familiar scent of him, she knew it was Buck. She wasn't in St. Louis. She was in a little cabin in the mountains, and Buck Hanner was holding her.

He fed her, he carried her to the outhouse, he bathed her, and sometimes he talked to her, telling her funny stories from his own past in order to make her forget about her sickness. Sometimes he rubbed a strong-smelling liniment on her chest and throat, his hands gentle, never rude, never touching places he should not touch.

Ten days passed before she began to feel normal. The fever had left her, as the dizziness had and her head was now clearing. She had a lingering cough, but she knew she was getting better. She awoke from what had seemed an odd dream. Had there actually been a bear? Had Buck really come? She sat up, her mind clearer than it had been since the grizzly had terrified her. She looked around the cabin. It was clean and tidy, and something that smelled very good was on the stove. Steam rose from the pot.

She put a hand to her head, wondering what she must look like, beginning to remember all of it—the bear, Buck's arrival. She moved her hand to her flannel gown. He'd undressed her! He'd bathed her and nursed her, fed her, put liniment on her. Put liniment on her! Had he looked at her, touched her while she was so sick she didn't know what he was doing?

He came in then, glancing at her with his blue eyes, sandy hair dangling over his forehead, his smile bright and warm. No. She had not been that far gone. She'd know it if he'd been rude to her, taken advantage of her. It was an odd feeling, to look at a man who had actually seen her, touched her, doctored her, yet to think of him only as a friend. That was still all she really wanted him to be, wasn't it? But the look in his own eyes revealed much more than friendship. Had he really whispered once or twice that he loved her, or was that just a dream?

"Well, Shortcake, you look brighter this morning. You feeling better?"

"I feel much better. I feel almost normal."

He set down some wood. "Good. But that doesn't mean you can jump right up. You stay in that bed two or three more days, no matter how good you feel. I want no relapses. You scared the hell out of me. I thought I was going to lose you for a while."

239

He walked over and stirred the soup. She watched him, lean and hard, a man most women would probably consider perfectly formed. "Would you really have cared, Buck? If I died, I mean."

He turned to her, a frown on his face. "Of course I'd have cared. I love you."

She reddened, pulling the quilts up closer around her neck. "Don't say that. You're just saying it to— I mean, don't say it, unless you mean you love me like a friend . . . or a daughter . . . a sister, maybe. I guess I love you too . . . in a way. Having you around is like . . . like having a big brother."

He snickered. "A big brother!" He shook his head and stirred the soup again. "I'm not sure whether I should be grateful for that comment or insulted by it. As he turned to her, he put his hands on his hips, his broad shoulders and masculine stance evoking feelings in her that she did not like. "Well, I don't love you like a daughter or a sister or even a friend, although we most certainly are friends. I love you, Harmony Jones, like a woman I want to have for myself, like a man loves a wife. Now maybe you don't like the sound of that, but that's the way it is and I'll be damned if I'm going to hide it anymore. But I'll not push you. Whatever happens between us is up to you, Shortcake. In the meantime we will go on as we always have. I've brought you your supplies, and as soon as you're well and capable of taking care of yourself again, I'll be heading back. I'll return midwinter, if I can get up here."

She sighed, lying back on the pillow. "I'm sorry you feel that way, Buck, because I don't love you that way. But I hope you'll believe me when I tell you how grateful I am that you came, and that I truly appreciate your taking care of me the way you did. It feels funny, having a man who's half a stranger taking care of me. But I don't know what I'd have done without you, so I guess I can't argue about that. I might have died if you hadn't come. I realize that." She turned on her side to look at him. "But that doesn't give you any more rights with me than you had before. You're still just my guide—and a friend."

He smiled and shook his head, stirring the soup. He wondered if she had any idea of what it meant to truly love a man—to truly love anyone. She'd been without love so long, she didn't even understand it. He wanted to hit her for hurting him with her words, yet he realized she didn't even know what they were doing to him. She had no understanding of passion, no awareness of the deep love he held for her, the reverence. She didn't comprehend his need to provide for her and protect her. Yet he must not crawl to her. He must simply and boldly state his feelings, leaving the rest up to her. If he pushed her, it would only take him that much longer to break her down, for she'd throw up those barriers again and shut him out completely. He'd wait. The time would come when she'd want him, when she'd get frustrated over the fact that he made no moves toward her. Yes, he would wait.

Three days later Harmony was panning again, but she had strict orders not to work more than three or four hours. Buck began a search for the grizzly, for he suspected it was still in the area and would probably come back. He wouldn't feel right going back until he'd taken care of that bear. He didn't want a repeat of

241

Harmony's last experience with the animal. Her condition when he'd found her, and her ensuing sickness, had been harder on him than Harmony realized. If only she knew how much he loved her. If only she knew he'd prayed for her, even wept once when he was sure she wouldn't make it. But it would do no good to tell her those things. She'd probably think he was making them up. In spite of all he'd told her about himself so she would learn that they were very much alike, he hadn't gotten through to her. She was still stubborn and independent, still determined to work her claim and be her own woman, still convinced she wanted no man sexually, wanted nothing to do with marriage or anything that involved trust and dependency. The only way he could bear being around her and not having her was to go off on these hunts, to pass the time keeping as busy as possible.

For the fifth day in a row he sat quietly at the mouth of the creek, where Harmony told him she'd first seen the bear. The waters were heavy with trout. The grizzly would come back, he was certain of that. He kept his rifle loaded and cocked, waiting. Later that morning, his perseverance and patience finally paid off. His daydreams of Harmony were interrupted by a loud splashing that came to his ears above the roar of the foaming waters. He heard a grunting sound.

Immediately all his instincts were alert. For a moment he crouched behind the huge boulder on which he'd been sitting, out of sight of the rushing waters. Then he crept around the rock to see a huge grizzly slapping at the water, catching fish in its great paws and chomping on them eagerly. Buck shivered at the size of the bear. No wonder her night of terror had nearly made Harmony lose her mind. How the cabin door had held back such a monster he could not imagine. Perhaps the animal hadn't realized that if he pushed against it he could have bashed it open. Thank God all he'd done was claw at it. And thank God he'd been too big to get through the window. If he had gotten to Harmony . . .

Buck crouched on one knee and raised the rifle. This monster would not go down with one bullet, that was certain. He'd have to hit it two or three times before it would give up, and he'd better make the shots count, get them in the right places. Nothing on earth was more vicious than a wounded grizzly, and this one was vicious enough as it was. He took quiet aim, his heart pounding, beads of sweat on his forehead. Then he squeezed the trigger. The gun went off and the bear roared and fell backward. Buck had aimed for the head, but he couldn't be certain he'd hit what he'd aimed for. Nonetheless, he'd hit the huge creature.

He cocked the rifle and aimed again, as the bear rolled onto its four paws, roaring and groaning. He fired, this time hitting it in the side of the head. Again the bear howled and fell. It lay panting and clawing at the ground. Buck walked toward it. If he could get two or three more shots into the head while it was temporarily stunned, he'd have it.

At the cabin Harmony jumped at the sounds of rifle fire. "Buck!" she whispered. Despite the distance, she could hear the bear's horrible roar. There was no mistaking the sound. It seemed to echo over the mountainside. Her night of terror returned. She could see the huge claws, the white fangs; hear the horrible growling, smell the putrid stench. "Buck!" she whim-

243

pered. She could not believe anyone or anything could kill such a monster. Was it attacking Buck right now, mauling him, murdering him, chewing him up like a huge fish? Would it come for her?

There had been two shots. Now three more were fired, and her heart pounded. Was it chasing him? Perhaps he had missed and only angered the bear. She could hear more growling and roaring. Another shot. Her breathing quickened, and she ran for the steps, picking up her own rifle. She climbed up the stairs, intending to go inside the cabin for protection. Buck had nailed split logs over the window opening, so there was no longer a window for the bear to get through. But now, when the door was closed, the cabin was almost completely dark. A lamp had to be lit during the day, or the door had to be left open for light. Still, she would rather have it that way. She felt safer.

She considered going to Buck. He might need her. Perhaps he was bleeding to death. She waited for what seemed an eternity. The growling had stopped. Was it because the bear was busily eating Buck Hanner?

Then he appeared, walking up the path, carrying his rifle. He looked up at her, a grin on his face. "How about some bear meat tonight?" he called out. "It's pretty good. 'Course he's an old, tough one, so I can't guarantee the flavor."

"Buck!" She set her rifle aside and ran to him, hugging him tightly, surprising him by her obvious concern. He eagerly embraced her, wondering if he could hope that perhaps she was beginning to love him the way a woman should love a man.

"Well! Remind me to go shoot a grizzly every day if I get this for it."

"Oh, Buck, don't joke!" she wailed. "I was afraid for you! I was going to come down and see if you needed help! I thought the bear had attacked you and was eating you!"

He laughed lightly, patting her shoulder. "Bears often kill people in anger or what they think is self-defense, Shortcake. But they don't eat them! They'd rather have fish or berries." He gave her a squeeze. "Your worries about that ornery bastard are over. I'm going to gut him and bring back some of the meat. Tonight we'll celebrate. We'll roast some bear meat and we'll have the ultimate celebration of the conquerers—we'll eat the enemy!" He laughed, and with his arm around her, he walked toward the cabin. "Maybe we'll even break out a little whiskey. If you're going to work like a man and live like a man and be independent like one, you've got to learn to drink like a man, Harmony Jones. Tonight you will share some whiskey with me."

She frowned, feeling suspicious again. She stopped walking. "You know I don't like whiskey," she declared.

He pushed back his hat. "Listen, Harmony Jones. Do you know what it took for me to stalk and shoot that damned thing? It isn't exactly something I'd like to do every day. I've been through hell for you since I got back up here, and most likely I've saved your life. Can't you even share one drink with this good friend who nursed you, taught you everything you know, and killed a grizzly for you? What do I have to do to get one ounce of fun and laughter and relaxed friendship out of you?"

She studied his unnerving blue eyes. "All right. I guess I owe you a celebration. You deserve it. But don't expect me to drink as much as you probably can."

He gave her a wink. "Just one," he replied, going inside to find a bigger knife than the one he carried on his belt.

Harmony shrugged and went back to the sluice, a little apprehensive, for she knew what whiskey sometimes did to men. She remembered smelling it on Jimmie's breath the night he'd attacked her. But that was Jimmie, not Buck Hanner. Buck would not hurt her.

Never in her whole life had Harmony Jones felt so gloriously happy. The first drink of whiskey had gone down hard, but moments later she'd felt a marvelous warmth, and everything Buck had said seemed funny. She felt delightfully free and relaxed, and she was sure she could do anything. She had survived up here for over two months. She would survive the winter. She took another drink, for she loved the way it made her feel. She had had no idea it could do this to a person, remove the fear and gloom that shadowed her life.

She stuffed herself with bear meat, then drank more, laughing meanwhile at Buck's stories. She was oblivious to the fact that he, too, was feeling his whiskey, that he was looking at her with a painful longing, listening to her laughter, wanting her as he'd never wanted her before. Her hair was unbraided, and hung loose and flowing over her shoulders. She had put on a dress, announcing that if they were going to "wine and dine" she should dress for it.

Harmony paid no attention to the fact that he moved closer, and when he told more stories his arm was around her shoulders. They sat outside, roasting the bear meat over an open fire. It was a pretty night, quiet and silky, with a million stars overhead. For two hours they had sat, drinking and eating until Harmony felt giddy and dizzy. Her head often lolled against Buck's shoulder, and he wrestled with his conscience. He'd never gotten her drunk. Perhaps he should have tried this a long time ago. In his own condition, his protective instincts were not operative. The whiskey only heightened his desire for her, removing all thought of what was right and wrong, awakening only his burning need to have her.

"Oh, Buck, I'm so glad that bear didn't get you," she was saying. "I was so afraid for you."

She looked up at him. How handsome he was in the moonlight! In the next moment his lips were covering hers, and for some strange reason she did not want to stop him this time. The kiss tasted good. She was happy . . . and she was curious. All the womanly things he had awakened in her were brought to the surface by the whiskey. She was on the brink of changing from a girl to a woman. Her feelings were awakened, and her eager young soul yearned to discover man. Hadn't Buck promised it could be good? Surely it wasn't always the way it had been with that terrible Jimmie! She felt silly and daring. Was it the whiskey? She couldn't think straight. She returned his kiss with newly awakened passion, wanting suddenly to see if she could be a woman, feeling almost challenged to prove she was not a little girl.

Yet down inside her a voice tried to warn her that this was wrong. Her deep-seated fears reasoned that this man was only taking advantage of her, that he would desert her like everyone else she had ever cared about. He was breaking her down!

"No," she mumbled the word between passionate kisses. She meant it, yet she could not seem to make herself push him away. She wanted to fight him, but his tongue moved in the most enticing way between her lips. What was this he was doing? Why did it make her feel so weak? She tried to pull away, but his mouth would not leave hers, and a gentle hand moved from her waist to one of her breasts, gently squeezing and massaging it. Fire swept through her blood. That wasn't the way Jimmie had touched her. It didn't repulse her at all. It only made her breathing quicken, her heart pound furiously! What had he done to her? What was this magic? Was it his touch, or just the whiskey—or both?

"Buck, please don't," she whispered, as his lips moved to her throat. Yet the words sounded pitifully weak.

"Why not?" he answered, his voice husky with desire. "I love you, Harmony. I've never loved anybody so much in my life. And I want you. God, I want you, Harmony!"

"No. Don't say that."

But he was already picking her up and carrying her toward the cabin. She rested her head on his shoulder, her arms about his neck. Somewhere deep in the recesses of her mind she knew what he intended to do, yet the womanly curiosity he had aroused would not permit her to fight him.

They were inside the cabin then, and he was kicking the door shut. She felt herself being laid on the bed. Her head swam. She wished she could think straight. He lit the lantern, keeping the flame low. Then he came and stood near her, unbuttoning his shirt. Why did she watch? Why did she want to see him? Why was she doing any of this?

"I want you, Harmony, and I'm going to have you," he told her, removing his shirt. "There will be no more arguing about it. You need a man, and I'm it. I'm the only man who's ever going to touch you."

He threw down the shirt and loosened his gun belt, then his belt. He removed both, then his boots. He unbuttoned his pants and pulled them off, then he removed his long johns. She felt giddy and afraid and curious, passionate yet childish and confused. He stood in front of her for a moment, and she drank in the glorious man who was Buck Hanner. She had thought a man would look ugly. But he looked beautiful, like a finely bred stallion.

He sat down on the bed beside her, then leaned over her. "Now you've seen man, and soon you'll experience man," he told her. His lips came down over her mouth again, and an almost painful desire swept through her. She heard someone whimpering. Was it her own voice? Was it she who was returning his kiss with such hunger and such a sudden rush of curious passion?

Gentle! So gentle he was! She knew her clothing was coming off, yet it seemed that it was happening by magic. Buck! This was Buck, her friend, her guide, her protector. He was so sweet and kind, always so patient. And he had said he loved her, hadn't he? How long did she think she could go on without once being a woman? And was there a nicer man to show her than Buck? He wouldn't hurt her, not Buck. Gentle hands massaged her virgin breasts, and she could not help crying out

249

when his tongue toyed with nipples that had never before greeted man. Then his fingers moved over her bare hips, caressing her slender thighs, moving between them. Why couldn't she stop him? Why didn't she want to stop him?

He tasted her sweet, full breasts, groaning with hunger, while his fingers worked their way into the silken, moist softness that lay in that secret place never before touched by a man. She cried out his name, fanning the fire of his passion. Harmony! This was Harmony, not some two-bit whore! This was Harmony Jones, the beautiful little girl that he loved beyond all reasoning. How long he had dreamed of having her. Was this really happening, or was he still dreaming? If this was a dream, he never wanted to wake up.

His breathing was quick, his body heated, his nerve endings were on fire. He moved his lips down over her flat belly, lightly kissing the golden hairs that surrounded the most womanly part of her. When he explored it with his fingers, she cried out and arched upward, and he knew she was responding passionately for the first time—and she was ready for him.

He moved on top of her, smothering her with kisses, kissing her mouth, her eyes, her cheeks, her throat, her shoulders, her breasts, and then returning to her mouth; priming her, building her desire so his first thrust would not be too painful. He was glad she was full of whiskey. It wouldn't hurt as much that way. He did not want to hurt this small woman he loved so, yet he must. She even wanted him to do it.

He smoothed the hair back from her face. "Harmony, my Harmony. I love you so much," he whispered.

"Buck, I don't know what's happening. I . . . it feels so good."

"Of course it feels good. You're just enjoying a man, that's all—the man you love, whether you know it yet or not." He moved on top of her, pushing her legs apart with his own knees.

"Don't hurt me!" she whimpered, fear now showing in her eyes.

"Hey, Shortcake, this is Buck, remember? Have I ever hurt you?"

Their eyes held. "I shouldn't be . . . doing this. I don't know what happened."

He held her with his hypnotic eyes—beautiful eyes, too beautiful to belong to a man. "Do you want me to stop?"

As he pressed his hardness against her belly, she swallowed, torn between fear and terrible desire. "No," she whispered.

His mouth met hers again, tenderly, so tenderly. Then he moved slightly, and pain suddenly shot through her loins. She cried out and dug her fingers into the hard muscle of his arms. There was no stopping it now.

"Hang on, baby," he whispered. He moaned with the want of her, the glory of taking her—finally. He thrust deep, even though he hadn't meant to. Now there were tears in her eyes, yet she didn't seem afraid. Determined was more like it. She wanted this. She finally wanted it, and she was determined to do it right, just as she had been about everything else.

He reached under her hips and pushed her up to him, moving gently in her to ease her pain. In moments it was over, but Buck's ecstasy was not. He moved off her, his body sweating, his breathing hard, his heart gloriously satisfied. He ran a big hand over her belly.

"Did it hurt bad, Shortcake?" he asked, kissing her neck.

"Not so bad. I . . . I don't know. I can't tell. I feel so . . . dizzy . . . so strange."

"It's just the whiskey. It's better this way—less pain. I just hope I didn't do any damage."

She met his eyes, reaching up and touching his handsome, tanned face. "I want to do it again," she told him, her blood still hot with whiskey and newly awakened desire. "Can we do it again?"

He grinned. "Again and again. All night long. I'll never be able to get enough of you." His lips covered hers then, and passion swept through her.

"Oh, Buck, I think I love you," she whispered.

"And I love you—every inch of you," he answered, his lips moving to her breasts again. "By morning I'll have seen every inch of you, tasted every part of you. You'll belong to Buck Hanner body and soul."

Buck awoke to cold water on his face. He jerked away, sat up slightly, and shook his head, which screamed with a hangover. Then he opened his eyes to see Harmony sitting nearby on a log, her rifle pointed right at him, her cheeks stained with tears.

"What the hell?" he muttered.

"You get out of here, Buck Hanner!" she ordered, her voice shaking. "I hate you! I'll hate you the rest of my life for what you did!"

He sat up straighter. "What I did? What the hell are you talking about?"

Her lips quivered and more tears spilled down her cheeks. "You know what I'm talking about! You took advantage of me! You got me drunk on purpose, then raped me!"

His eyes narrowed with anger and disappointment. "Raped you!" He threw back the covers, not caring that he was naked. "I made love to you, Harmony Jones, because I'm in love with you! And you wanted it! Don't deny it! So what if I used a little whiskey to make you see the light!"

She sucked in her breath, backing away. "See the light! You . . . you bastard! Get your clothes on and get out of here! You don't love me! You just wanted to get me into bed! That's all you've ever wanted! How much did you bet this time, Buck Hanner! How much will you win when you go back to town and announce that you conquered Harmony Jones?"

He frowned, telling himself to calm down, to move carefully. He pulled on his long johns, then sat down on the edge of the bed. "Do you really believe that? Do you think I'd make bets on a thing like that, or that I planned to make love to you when I got up here?"

"Yes!" she retorted. She rubbed at her belly and he watched her with concern.

"I hurt you."

"Yes, you hurt me!" she whimpered, her face red with anger and embarrassment. "I hope you're satisfied."

He sighed and rubbed his eyes. "Harmony, it always hurts at first, but then the hurt goes away." He met her eyes. "It goes away, Harmony, and after that it's all pleasure. Don't do this, honey. I love you."

"I don't want your love! I just want you to go away! I

know all about love! You love people, and then they leave you! I loved my parents, and they left me on the docks. Two men came, drunk like you were last night! They were going to do to me what you did to me, when I was only six! That's all men think about! That's all they care about! If not for Brian . . ." She sucked in a sob. "And then Jimmie . . . he got drunk and tried it too. The only thing different this time is I was drunk along with you! Why did you do that? Why did you make me drink that whiskey? I didn't want that to happen! I want you to go now! I'll not love any man or be dependent on one. Do you hear? I came up here to pan for gold and to get rich. I'll never, never trust or love anybody again, least of all a drifter like you who tricks a girl into his bed—a girl who's never drunk whiskey before, never been with a man before!"

He just watched her. She was so mixed up. He hated her damned parents, hated Jimmie, hated the men on the docks who had scared her to death so early in life, hated Brian O'Toole for leaving her.

He stood up and began to dress. "I'm sorry you feel that way, Harmony, but put down the damned rifle. I'd never deliberately hurt you and you know it. Even in my drunken state last night, I'd have stopped if you'd asked me to. But you didn't. And I'll tell you one thing: whiskey makes most people tell the truth and follow their desires. You wanted me, and I think you still do. You told me last night you loved me."

"Well, I didn't mean it!" she retorted angrily. "And I'll never forgive you for making me drink, for getting me all mixed up like that. You did it on purpose, Buck Hanner! You know you did!"

He finished dressing, saying nothing. When he put

on his hat, he turned to look at her. Then he walked straight up to her, yanking the rifle from her hands and throwing it on the bed. He knelt in front of her.

"I'm damned sorry, Harmony. Does it hurt bad?"

She reddened deeply. "Just go away."

"I don't think you really want me to go. But I'll go, because that's the only way you're going to realize you need me . . . and love me. And I love you, no matter what you say or do. Last night was the most beautiful experience I've ever shared with a girl. It didn't happen just because of a challenge. It happened because I love you, Harmony Jones, and someday it will happen again, many times over, because someday you're going to be my wife, when you think you're woman enough for it."

He rose and walked to the door. He could only convince her that she loved and needed him by leaving her. It was the last thing he wanted to do now, but to stay would make her angrier. He wanted to hit her, yell at her, say things that would just make her hate him more; but he loved her too much to do any of these things. He hadn't really intended for it to happen last night, but he was glad it had. She'd sure as hell have something to think about now, and he'd finally made sure he was Harmony Jones's first man. It felt strange to bed a woman and still be challenged to win her over. If it weren't so painful it would be almost humorous. Harmony Jones was truly the most stubborn person he'd ever met. He turned to her. She still sat pouting.

"A hot bath helps," he told her. "After I leave, heat some water and soak yourself." He waited for her to look at him, but she didn't. So he sighed and shook his head. "I'm sorry I hurt you, Shortcake. But I'm not sorry for making love to you in the first place. I love and respect you more now than I ever did, and there's one thing you can't change. I've laid my claim on you. You're Buck Hanner's woman now, not just little Harmony Jones. And you wanted me. I don't give a damn how much you deny it this morning. You wanted me and you love me. You'll realize that once I'm gone."

He walked out and closed the door.

The cabin was dark, and tears welled in her eyes. She wanted to call him back, wanted to run to him, wanted him to hold her. What stopped her? Was she that afraid of trusting someone? Of course she loved him. But her mouth would not open, and her legs would not move. Moments later she heard the sound of hooves striking the hard earth. He was leaving, taking the pack mules.

"Buck!" she whimpered. "Don't leave me."

Chapter Twelve

Harmony wondered whether she would ever stop crying. Every day was the same. Rise, try to eat, work the sluice, fill the jars, feed Amber sometimes. The coyote seemed to be her only friend. While she went about her chores, tears came sporadically, in sudden, unexpected bursts. She wanted desperately to hate Buck Hanner, for loving him went against everything she had promised herself when she'd come out here. Yet he'd been right about whiskey making people admit the truth. It had been so easy to do then. Why was it so difficult when she was sober to say what she really felt? Was that due to fear?

The tears came again. Of course it was fear—fear of being deserted. What if she admitted she loved him? What if she dared to trust him, gave her heart and soul to Buck Hanner, and then he left her? There was no forever in Harmony Jones's life. Forever might be for some, but it was not for many. The mountains were forever, day led to night forever. But people were not forever, and she knew that if she opened herself to Buck

Hanner, if she admitted her true feelings, she would have to admit she was desperately in love with him, more in love than she'd dreamed she could be. Her desire for him was wild and passionate, despite her vow never to entertain such feelings for a man.

Day in and day out she worked, and she argued with herself. She loved him, but she shouldn't. She trusted him, but she shouldn't. She wanted him, but she shouldn't. And through it all she saw his handsome, tanned, rugged face; his bright smile; his sky-blue eyes; his thick, sandy hair; and his broad, muscular shoulders. She could feel his strong arms around her, protecting her, keeping her safe from all harm. She could taste his sweet kisses; she shuddered with rapture at the memory of his velvet touch in secret places. Only Buck Hanner had seen and touched those places. That knowledge gave her a warm feeling that made her cheeks redden. She knew deep in her soul that what he had done meant she belonged to him, and she liked the idea of belonging to him. Yet that thought brought back her old fears.

On and on her thoughts whirled, in a vicious circle. Buck Hanner had awakened cravings in her that must now be satisfied. One night had not been enough. Her curiosity had been temporarily satisfied, but doing so had awakened her passion. That was what must be satisfied.

Yes, she must admit she had enjoyed his touch, his tender kisses. She hadn't even minded the pain all that much. It was gone now, and that softened the memory of its severity. Could he be right when he said it hurts less each time? Surely it was true. Doing some things for the first time did cause pain, but after you got used to doing them, the pain usually went away. And there had been such a pitiful sorrow in his eyes when he'd realized he'd hurt her. He really seemed to be sorry. Maybe he did love her. He seemed so sincere. But why did he love her? No one had before. And why had he resorted to getting her drunk to make it easier to bed her? That was a dirty trick. If he loved her he wouldn't have tricked her that way.

Still, maybe he hadn't intended any of it to happen. He'd sworn he hadn't planned it, and in her state, she had made herself flagrantly available to him. If he really did love and desire her, how could she have expected him to turn away from her vulnerability and curiosity? But, she reasoned, because he had taken advantage of that very vulnerability and innocent curiosity, he could not love her.

For a month her thoughts whirled, day in and day out; yet each day she missed him more, became more afraid he wouldn't come back. Maybe he would send someone else with supplies. But she didn't want anyone else. She wanted Buck Hanner. Her attempts to convince herself that he was not worth having, that he was a drifter, that he had tricked her, that he could not be trusted, that he wanted some of her gold—all were to no avail. For she always came back to the same unwanted conclusion. She loved Buck Hanner, every beautiful inch of him, and every gentle, kind, generous part of him. He was a wonderful man, a good man, who had suffered many hurts and losses himself. He understood a shattered heart. He, too, was lonely, and she knew by his eyes that he meant it when he said he loved her.

On top of all of that, he had made her a woman, his

woman, and despite the pain that experience had been more gratifying than she had thought possible. The pain that lingered had frightened her, as did the realization of what she had done, and the knowledge that he had gotten her drunk. Because he had, she had thrown him out, had shouted hurtful words at him, words she now regretted. But he was not here for her to tell him so. She longed to feel his arms around her, to cry against his chest and to admit that she loved him. She was tired of fighting everything and everyone, of trying to be strong all by herself. Maybe it really was possible to love and trust. Maybe she really could belong to someone. Maybe she didn't have to be afraid all the time, worried all the time.

But then there was the gold claim to think about. She would not give it up. It was hers, Buck Hanner or no Buck Hanner. That was one thing that must not change. If he wanted her, he would have to let her keep working her claim. But maybe that was all he was after in the first place, a piece of her claim, a share of her gold. That was her biggest worry. Would he be as interested in her if she didn't have this claim? All men lusted after gold. All men would do anything to get it.

Reason told her that Buck Hanner was not like all men. He was one of the few who was different. He was his own man, strong and sure. He'd been in these mountains for a long time, yet he'd never bothered to prospect. He seemed to have no interest in doing so. He was simple, hard-working, very sure of himself—not one to wander the mountains searching for gold and leaving behind loved ones as Brian had. Somehow she sensed Buck would never do that. Every argument she gave herself was answered by the memory of the man

260

himself, his gentleness, his sincerity, and the eyes—so true, so full of love. Yes, Buck would want her, gold claim or not. It wasn't the gold, not with Buck, surely not with Buck.

All that was soft and womanly about her had been aroused, stealing away her determination to be independent. She had been awakened by a man. She had learned that being with a man was very pleasing, that being a woman in the truest sense was extremely satisfying, and that wanting and needing a man was very sweet and very natural.

But her reasoning, her admission of love, her resignation to her womanly feelings were to no avail, for Buck Hanner was gone. Once she had admitted her own feelings and had decided to believe that he loved her, she felt terrible about the way she had treated him. There was no mistaking the love and hurt in his eyes the morning she'd sent him packing. He'd been hurt many times, and now he'd been hurt again. She felt cruel, and she wondered if he thought of her that way. She couldn't blame him if he did. Her tears of shame and doubt began turning to tears of love and remorse. What if he didn't come back? What if she never saw Buck Hanner again! Maybe he would reach Cripple Creek and just keep riding, deciding that if she hated him so, he might as well forget her. After all, he had been a drifter for a long time, a lonely man, and he was a very proud man. She had injured his pride badly. She wondered if her own hurts and fears had turned her into a mean person. She felt like one, and she began to pray that Buck Hanner would come back. But there was no way of knowing whether he would, for winter was approaching, and soon he wouldn't be able to get into the mountains at all. The weather was nice enough now, but what would it be like in two months, when he would normally return?

September and October passed in autumn splendor, the aspen turning to brilliant gold, other foliage changing colors, the air crisp and clear. The nights became much colder, and she began using more wood. She worried about having enough. Buck had cut more for her, but she had sent him hopping so soon that he'd hadn't had time to build up much of a store of it. She dressed warmly at night and used the wood conservatively.

She allowed herself no spare time—no time to think and dream. That hurt too much, for all her lazy thoughts were of Buck Hanner and of the night he had done beautiful things to her, awakening her to splendor and ecstasy. She must not think about that, for Buck Hanner might never come back. She used all her spare time to hunt, smoking and storing up more meat; to fish; to cut more wood herself; to read; often just to pour out all the gold she had discovered and just look at it. At least if Buck Hanner did not return, she had this. Yet it was cold and hard to the touch. It could not love her back. It could not hold her or protect her, talk to her, laugh with her, kiss her, invade her. It could make her rich, but suddenly the thought of being rich and alone did not sit well with her young heart. Something more precious than gold had been presented to her—love—and she had thrown it away.

She vowed that if Buck Hanner ever returned, she would never hurt him again, never send him away. She wanted to be his woman. She wanted to be loved and held. It was a nice feeling, a little frightening to be so

262

trusting, but nice.

By the end of November it had snowed often. Sometimes several feet had fallen overnight, but it melted away within hours because of the dry air. Then it got colder, and snow began to accumulate. She trudged through it, dug through it, did everything necessary to keep panning. She wondered who would help her if Buck had ridden off somewhere. She began trying to harden her heart a little against the possibility that he would never come back, that some stranger would come riding to her cabin to tell her he was her new guide and supplier. How could she trust anyone new? Such a man might be sent by Wade Tillis.

She realized more and more that there were many reasons to hope Buck Hanner returned with the supplies. There was no way she could possibly trust anyone else. Buck Hanner had made her more dependent on him than she realized, whether she loved him or not.

Yet what did any of it matter? If he didn't come back, she didn't care what happened to her. Nothing would matter anymore without Buck. And he'd been gone longer than the first time. Maybe something terrible had happened to him. Or maybe the worst had really happened—he had left her, left Cripple Creek forever, because she had hurt him so deeply. Hadn't she told him she hated him?

Again tears came too often. How could a person love and hate someone at the same time? But that was the way it was with her and Buck. She had hated him, but now she knew she loved him. He had loved her, but now maybe he hated her for being so mean to him. Why didn't he come? Why was he taking so long this time?

263

Her loneliness knew no bounds.

Buck struggled with a long train of mules. In winter he took along more provisions than usual. The miners in the hills always needed more in winter. It felt good to be back out here alone, where he could really think. Jack Leads had sent him to Santa Fe with a huge order of supplies for an Apache Indian reservation. The trip had taken longer than he'd thought it would, for he'd been instructed to wait there for a load of supplies from Mexico, as well as trade goods from the Indian reservation.

He'd been glad to be kept busy, so he wouldn't go up the mountain to Harmony. She needed to be without him, the longer the better. It was hard staying away, hard not going to her and begging her to love him, but he didn't want her that way. It had to be her decision, her need, her desire. She had to know, inside herself, that she loved and wanted him. She had to admit to it and take him again without the help of whiskey.

But to be away from her was the worst torture he'd ever experienced. Every inch of him ached for her. Every manly instinct told him he should be with her, holding her, protecting her, making sure nothing happened to her. But it was too painful to be around her and have her look at him with such hurt and hate. He couldn't have picked a worse way to take her for the first time—getting her drunk first. It had only made her distrust him more. She was sure he'd tricked her. If only she hadn't been so vulnerable, so sweet that night, so curious and easy . . . if only he'd had more willpower . . . But his own consumption of whiskey had broken down any resistance he had left. He'd loved and wanted her for too long, and now every part of him screamed for Harmony Jones.

The memory of her sweet lips, her luscious body, her softness, roundness, the virgin nipples, the aching glory of invading her for the first time, all of these kept torturing him, invading his thoughts, his dreams, disturbing his sleep. He tried the whores, but that did no good. How could any woman satisfy him after he'd been with Harmony? No one was prettier or softer. No one was able to carry him to the heights of ecstasy he'd found the night he'd made love to the woman-child he thought he might never touch that way.

Why had she come into his life? He had been stupid to volunteer to guide her. He should have known the moment he saw her in Cripple Creek, when she again aroused his desire as she had on the train, that he was headed for trouble. He'd vowed never to love again the way he'd loved Mary Beth, yet he wondered if perhaps he loved Harmony even more. Yes, he did. For he'd bedded Harmony, claimed her. He'd never had the chance to do that with Mary Beth. And his manly instincts told him that Harmony Jones belonged to him now, no matter what happened after this. She could never deny that, never deny that Buck Hanner had invaded her, made a woman of her. And he'd been direct and sincere when he'd told her he loved her.

Why did she have to be so confused and stubborn? She carried that barrier of fear like a shield. She was so afraid to love and trust. If only she could bring herself to do those two things, she'd be perfect. But he could see that Harmony Jones would always be haunted by the day her parents abandoned her on the docks of St.

Louis. That terrible experience would always undermine her ability to trust. And then there was that bastard Jimmie. He'd scared her to death, made her think all men wanted only one thing from a woman. The memory of his attack made her think Buck had deliberately tricked her.

But he hadn't. He would never trick her. He loved her, and he'd go back and make her understand that. Maybe it was good that he'd been gone so long. It was early December, over three months since he'd left her. Still, he wondered if she was all right. He was almost crazy with curiosity, yet his hurt and pride told him to stay away as long as possible. She must miss him, long for him. She must have plenty of time to calm down, to think, to realize she really did love Buck Hanner. He could only hope that when he did get back to her she would have decided she loved and wanted him, for he doubted he could leave a third time or face her denial again.

He could not move from camp to camp as quickly now. The weather did not allow it. Sometimes he was held up for days by a blizzard. Then it would get so warm he'd ride through the drifts with only his shirt on, actually sweating from the warm sun, yet trudging through deep, dangerous snows. Everything took longer, for the mountains were full of danger at this time of year. Every step Indian took had to be carefully gauged, for snow often covered crevices and boulders that could send horse and rider tumbling to their deaths. There was also the danger of avalanches. He only hoped Harmony had sense enough not to stray too far from the cabin in this weather. At least during these months there was little to fear from bears. They were hibernating. But other animals would be tempted to come close to the cabin in search of food, if the snow got too deep to find it elsewhere. He was glad there were no horses at the cabin, for they would attract wolves. And although she'd made a near pet out of a coyote, she'd have to be careful of that too. Amber might bring several friends at this time of year, all of them hoping for a handout, and she could not afford to hand out too much.

Harmony. Always his thoughts returned to Harmony. How could they not? What would he do if he returned to find her dead? And how would he handle himself if she still hated him? He hadn't meant to hurt her, either physically or emotionally. Yet he'd done both and he hated himself for it. She was so precious, so delicate. He had not intended things to happen the way they did. He was going to win her over, then ask her to marry him, then make her his woman. It had happened all backward. His urgent need of her, his intense love for her, had made him move too quickly, but he loved her just the same. Marriage didn't matter; the lack of it didn't take away any of his respect for her. He already felt that she was his wife, and if she loved and wanted him when he returned, he'd marry her just as soon as they got back down the mountain. He had always intended to marry her, anyway. Perhaps the horse had come before the cart, but who knew, and what did it really matter when two people really loved and needed each other? In his own heart he had already married her, already devoted himself to her. He loved her as much as any man loved a wife. Actually making her his wife was a simple legal matter. The important thing was that she belonged to Buck Hanner, body and soul, and hopefully her heart also belonged to him. That was the only part he doubted. In the meantime, no one need know what happened. Out in this wild land a lot of things happened backward. People married for the craziest reasons, or they didn't marry at all. This wasn't St. Louis. This was Colorado, much of it still wild and untamed although it was now a state. Breaking social codes was a common occurence. But his intentions were good and he'd do right by her, for he loved her dearly. That was all that mattered.

He headed Indian and the mules into the camp of Hank Fisher, a prospector who'd used dynamite the past summer to blast into the side of the mountain where his claim lay. Fisher was searching for a mother lode, but so far he'd done nothing more than bore a cave big enough to work with a pick. Although he spent as much time there as in his little cabin, he'd still not found the vein, but he would not give up. Fisher had been here for longer than Buck had been delivering supplies. Buck could not imagine how the man stood the loneliness. He couldn't understand what kept these men going, where they got their constant hope, or why making a strike was so important to them.

"Hank!" he called out. "It's Buck Hanner!"

For several minutes there was only the sound of the winter wind, which was cold again today. Buck wore a heavy jacket, yet just the day before he'd worn only a shirt. Fisher finally appeared at the entrance of the mine, waving to Buck. The man had aged since Buck had known him, but he ran toward Buck now, apparently happy as hell to see another human being.

"What do you know, Hanner? Did you bring me some old newspapers?"

"Sure did. I wouldn't forget that, Hank."

When Fisher laughed, he looked far older than his forty years and a distant longing appeared in his eyes. Buck had seen it before. Men came out here and changed, searching forever, never going back home, some going a little crazy. Hank sometimes had that crazy look in his eyes.

"Come on in, Buck! I've got the cabin warm! Come and set a spell. I've got somethin' to tell you."

"You got a list of needs?" Buck asked. "I really can't stay long, Hank. I get slowed down this time of year."

"I know. I know." The man led him inside and brought out a bottle of whiskey. "Now this is what I need most," he said with a chuckle. He poured two drinks and sat down. "I'm close, Buck. I can feel it. I'm close to the mother lode, and soon I'll be comin' down off this mountain a rich man."

Buck nodded, sipping some whiskey. "I hope you're right this time, Hank." How many times had he heard that statement, not just from Hank, but from others? And how badly did Harmony want the same riches? Perhaps she would stubbornly refuse to come with him, would insist on staying and working her claim. Perhaps she would turn into an old-looking woman before her time, be always searching for something that was not there, become a crazy woman. She seemed to have gold fever almost as bad as most of the men who came up here, but her reasons made more sense than those of most of the men.

"I know I'm right." Fisher took a long drink of whiskey, then set his glass down and wiped at his lips. "Tobacco. Tobacco and whiskey, and some canned beans and jerky. You got them things?"

269

"Always do."

"I could use a new axe too." The man sniffed and poured himself some more whiskey. "I got to tell you to be careful Buck. Some men was here, ornery lookin' sons of bitches. I think they had in mind to do me in and jump my claim, figured this time of year nobody would come around for a long time and they'd make up some kind of story about what happened to me. But I was onto them quick, and I holed up in here with my rifle. I told them to move on or I'd open their innards to the winter winds."

Buck frowned. Harmony's camp was only a three-day ride from Hank's claim. He'd been saving her for last on this trip so he could stay longer. "How many?" he asked, "Which way did they head?"

Hank rubbed his whiskered chin. "That's why I thought I'd warn you. They headed around the west ridge, far as I could tell. You done told me about that nice little gal around that way you had a hankerin' for. I've been hopin' that turned out okay for you, Buck; wasn't even sure she was still over there. It was too far for me to try to get to her at this time of year, without a horse or anything. There was four of 'em. Bad-lookin' sort, you know? You'd best go check on that girl next, if she's still there."

Buck quickly swallowed his whiskey. "I'll get your supplies right away," he told the man. "I'd stay, Hank, but Harmony is still up there." His heart raced with fear for her. "You think they're just riding the hills looking for easy jumps?"

Hank nodded. "That's what I think. And there wouldn't be nothin' easier than takin' somethin' from a little girl, let alone what they'd do with her, bein' all

270

alone up here and all. They didn't look like the considerate sort."

Buck moved fast then, hurrying out to get the supplies and leaving them on the ground. Hank followed him out.

"I'm sorry, Hank, but I can't stay and visit this time."

"I understand, Buck. You want me to go along?"

"No. I can handle it. But I can move faster without the mules. I'm leaving them here. Can you watch over them for a few days? I know there isn't much around here for them to eat—I usually keep them moving, so there's always something—but they'll probably do okay for a week or so. I've got to get to Harmony as fast as I can! I'll come back in a few days for the mules. She'll need the supplies." He mounted up. "If she's still alive," he added quietly.

"Sure, Buck, I'll take care of them."

"How long ago were they here?"

Hank scratched his head. "About two days ago, I guess. I'm glad you came through when you did."

"Well, I know exactly where I'm going, and they'll be riding slower just hunting around. If I'm lucky I'll get to Harmony before they do. I don't intend to stop to rest or make camp."

Hank nodded. "Good luck, Buck. I'll be waitin' for you to come back."

Buck nodded and rode off, praying nothing would happen to Harmony. If the claim jumpers harmed her, there would be hell to pay!

Chapter Thirteen

Harmony sifted through a pan of drag, so lost in her work she was oblivious to the new but very quiet sounds around her. These last few weeks had been especially hard, for some days the snow had been so deep she was unable to go beyond the creek right outside her door. Even Amber hadn't shown up for a long time, and she wondered if he was still alive. Worse than that, did anyone care whether she was alive? She had always thought she knew what loneliness was, but this was unlike anything she had ever experienced. The only thing that kept her going was working long hours, in spite of the cold. The snow would come in huge amounts, then disappear in two or three days, but a lot of it was beginning to stay on the ground, making everything seem even lonelier, for it muffled sound. There were no birds about, and seemingly there was no movement anywhere.

She had heard stories of prospectors going crazy, and she was beginning to understand how it could happen. She had looked forward to being alone, but human nature demanded some companionship, someone to talk to. Now all she had were a few rats, and even they did not make daily appearances. It would all be so much more bearable if she could get Buck Hanner out of her mind, and out of her blood. But the memory of him would not leave her, especially the memory of his lips on her own, of his gentle hands claiming her body. Even the memory of the pain he had left behind seemed beautiful now. She had given herself to a man, then turned him away. What if that man never came back?

She blinked back tears and kept working. It did no good to dwell on what had happened. Buck was gone and that was that. He'd been gone three months, and it would be better for her if he didn't show up again. Yet a searing pain in her chest told her she didn't want to go on living if he didn't. The thought of seeing him brought a rush of warmth and anticipation. What would she say? What would he say? She would surely die of embarrassment, realizing he'd seen her, touched her, been intimate with her. Would he be embarrassed too? After all, she'd seen and touched him. But then, a man like Buck wouldn't be embarrassed. She felt a terrible rush of jealousy at the thought of other women in his life. Had he turned to the whores of Cripple Creek for what she had refused to give him after their one night of lovemaking?

Buck. Her every thought was of him. Every part of her tingled for him. But she had driven him away, and she must now work this claim and make her little fortune. She most certainly had no one, and wanted no one except Buck Hanner.

A soft wind moaned through the pines, and the snow shrouded the sounds of quietly approaching horses. All she heard was the rushing of the creek, and the wind, until suddenly a rope came over her head and around her arms. She gasped, then screamed as the rope tightened hard and she was yanked away from the sluice, falling to the ground with the force of the tug.

Her mind raced as she rolled in the snow, then struggled to get up, her arms pinned to her sides, laughter echoing in the background. What was happening!

"Got lots of gold there, do ya, little girl?" It was a man's voice.

She coughed and got to her feet, shaking snow from her long hair, which hung loose this day. She blinked and raised her eyes, looking at the three men who stared back at her, all with several days' growth of whiskers. Two of them looked to be about thirty; one seemed younger. The younger one was slender and filthy, and some of his teeth were missing. The other two were not ugly, nor were they handsome. They were a little cleaner looking than the younger one, but all three wore soiled buckskin jackets.

They leered at her, their expressions ugly, and her heart pounded with fear and dread. Buck! If only he were here now! Had he betrayed her? Had he sent them?

"Well, now ain't she about the best-lookin' thing in these parts?" The voice came from behind her.

She turned to look at the man who held the rope that had trapped her. He was huge, wide and very fat. His teeth were yellowed, and he wore a buckskin jacket and a coon hat.

"She's a young one," one of the others put in. "Maybe even untouched."

The fat one grinned. "Yeah." He leaned toward her. "Where's your pa, blondie?"

She blinked, the horror she'd experienced on the docks flashing through her mind, then Jimmie's ugly treatment. She was wiser now. These men had one thing in mind, and it wouldn't be like being with Buck Hanner, that was sure. The thought of them touching her brought a sick feeling to her stomach, and horror to her heart.

"I . . . he . . . he'll be back soon!" she stammered, taking deep breaths and telling herself to be bold and sure. Perhaps they'd leave without bothering her.

"No, he won't," the young one spoke up, eying her up and down. "We heard tell there was a young girl up here, workin' her claim . . . alone. Might you be the one, missy?"

She eyed her rifle, but it was too far away and her arms were pinned. "No. I . . . I'm not—"

Before she finished the fat one jerked her closer to his horse and yanked off her hat. He grunted out a laugh, then fingered her golden hair.

"Boys, we found more than gold nuggets here. We found a golden girl!"

They all laughed as the fat man dismounted. He walked around in front of her, towering over her. Her heart screamed for Buck, for help. But there was no one to help her, and now the other three were dismounting.

"Let's take her inside, Frank," one of the others said to the fat one.

Frank loosened the rope, then backhanded her hard and shoved her to the ground. "We will," he answered, plunking his incredible weight on top of her thighs so that she could not budge or kick. "But let's get a look at

276

the goods right here and now."

Sheer terror enveloped her as he began to unbutton her coat, and she scratched out at him, only to have someone else grasp her wrists. The fat one threw open her coat, then ripped open her shirt. She wore no undergarment, finding little necessity for one up here all alone in the mountains. Why be uncomfortable when there was no one around to see or care?

Now someone touched her breasts in that ugly way again. She heard screams, horrible, gut-wrenching pleas. Was it her voice? The only reply was laughter. Someone was dragging her then, and she felt the weight lift from her thighs. Her head still spun from the hard blow to the side of her head, and every part of her screamed for death rather than what they had in mind for her. But she was aware of their laughter, ugly words, and talk of doing her in later and taking her gold. She began fighting then. She'd not let this happen! Not Harmony Jones! She screamed and kicked. No one would take her by force, and no one would take her gold! It was her gold! Hers!

But one of them struck her hard. There were too many . . . they were too strong! She felt herself being shoved up the steps toward the cabin door. Then came the gunshot.

In the crisp winter air it rang out extra loud, and they all jumped, even Harmony.

"Jesus Christ!" someone yelled. "Clyde's been hit!"

Someone tumbled past her, down the steps. Then came another gunshot, and the fat one clumped down beside her on the steps, groaning and cursing.

"Run, Harmony!" she heard someone yell. Buck? Was that Buck's voice? Everything was confused,

277

unclear, as though she were dreaming all of it. But somehow her legs moved and she obeyed the command. "Away from the cabin!" came the voice. "Don't let them get you inside!"

"Circle around, Hugh, and get that bastard!" she heard someone say.

"Buck!" she squeaked, deliberately rolling off the side of the steps and scrambling under them. She threw snow onto her face and shook her head, trying to clear her thoughts. If Buck was out there she had to help him. Quickly she buttoned her shirt and the jacket, while all around there were gunshots. Buck! They were firing back at him!

Through the openings between the steps she could see the huge body of the one called Frank. He wasn't moving. She crawled around to the side, and saw another man lying at the bottom of the steps, blood staining the snow around his head.

She scanned the surrounding woods, but could see nothing. "Buck!" she screamed. "Buck, is it you?"

"Stay under the steps!" The reply came from behind a huge pine trunk. Buck! Yes, it was his voice! He'd come!

Suddenly he darted from behind the tree, running to another. She saw the flash of the sun against his gun barrel, then heard a shot. The man at the corner of the cabin cried out and fell forward, but just then another shot was fired, and Buck's whole body was thrust forward, his rifle flying from his hands.

"Buck!" she screamed. "Oh, God!"

He lay flat on his stomach, arms outstretched. Harmony ran from under the steps toward the sluice to get her own rifle, and as she did so Buck suddenly

278

lurched forward, grabbing his gun and managing to cock it. He quickly rolled onto his back, and when Harmony turned to aim at the last man, who was heading toward Buck, ready to finish him off, Buck's own gun fired at the last minute, and the man flew backward, his face exploding in blood.

Buck laid his head back then, groaning and rolling to his side, and Harmony ran to him. As she knelt beside him she saw that the back of his buckskin jacket was already covered with blood.

"Buck! You're shot!"

"Watch them!" he groaned. "They might . . . still be alive." He moaned, then struggled to his knees as she looked around desperately, seeing no movement.

"I . . . I think they're all dead, Buck. This one is, and the one by the steps is! The others haven't moved! Oh, God, Buck, you're shot! What should I do!"

"Help me . . . inside," he muttered, his voice already weak.

She grabbed his arm and gave him support as he got to his feet, throwing back his head and grimacing. "I've got . . . to get inside . . . and you've got to get it out of me!" he muttered.

Her eyes filled with tears, and her heart with panic. "Me? Buck, I don't know anything about taking out bullets!"

His breath came in desperate pants, and he looked down at her, putting a hand to her hair. "You . . . want me to die?"

Their eyes held, and she carefully hugged him around the middle. "Oh, Buck, I love you! I do! I don't want you to die! You came back! You came back!"

He held her with the arm that hurt less. His whole

279

body seemed to be exploding with pain, from just the one bullet which had entered under his right shoulder blade. He guessed no vital organs had been hit, or he'd never have been able to get to his feet, but a bullet was a bullet. It had to come out—fast.

"Time for talk . . . later, Shortcake," he said in a near whisper. "But that's all I need to hear . . . to hang on. Now help me inside . . . and fill me up with whiskey . . . and get this damned bullet out of me, or there will be five men to bury instead of four."

She felt his weight pressing on her as he weakened and seemed ready to pass out.

"Oh, Buck—"

"Pick up our rifles," he told her. "Let me . . . lean on you . . . till we get inside. Get me some whiskey . . . and then come back out here and pick up every weapon you can find . . . while I drink up. After that . . . stoke up your fire, and lay your best knife in it . . . understand? You've got . . . to do everything . . . fast as you can."

She wiped at her tears and nodded her head, quickly bending to pick up their two rifles. He put an arm around her shoulders.

"Did they hurt you bad, Shortcake?" he asked, as she helped him toward the steps.

"No. Not bad. They didn't have a chance."

"I saw that big one . . . hit you."

"I'm okay. Really, Buck. You're the one to worry about."

"He . . . mauled you."

"I'm all right, Buck. Please don't talk so much."

They reached the steps; the fat man still lay on them.

"I wish . . . I could have had time . . . to make him

280

suffer," Buck hissed.

Harmony shuddered. "I'll . . . get him down some-how later," she declared. "Please get inside, Buck."

He groaned as he slowly mounted the steps, and Harmony struggled to hang on to him as they made their way around the fat man. "Later," Buck muttered. "Just . . . drag them to one side for now . . . if you can even do that. It will be . . . hard, Shortcake. You're so . . . small. Don't try . . . to bury them. I'll do it . . . later, when I'm better. It's cold . . . will be for a long time. They'll keep."

She felt a chill at the thought of four dead men lying around the cabin, but she could never dig a hole big enough to bury them all. She had no choice but to do what he said, and she was glad it was winter.

"Buck, please stop talking." She got him inside, and he stumbled to the bed, flopping face-down on it. He groaned again, as he wriggled to get his legs onto the bed. Then he turned onto his side at her prompting, so that she could unbutton his coat and flannel shirt and the top half of his long johns. She managed to get the sleeves off one arm, then rolled him onto his other side to get the other sleeves off, throwing aside the coat and shirt and peeling the underwear down to his waist.

"Hurry, Shortcake," he muttered. "Hurts bad."

"Buck, I can't cut into you! I'll kill you! I don't know what to do!"

"Just . . . heat the knife . . . like I said . . . and dig till you find the bullet and get the damned thing out of there. Then just . . . throw whiskey in there and wrap it tight. That's all you can . . . do, honey. I'm strong. I'll . . . heal . . . after a time."

She fought new tears as she scrambled to find her

knife, then laid it into the hot coals inside her stove. She grabbed a bottle of whiskey and took it to him.

"My horse . . . Indian . . . down the creek a ways," he mumbled. "Left him . . . behind . . . no noise. Get Indian."

"I will! I'll get him soon as I'm through with you!" she replied.

"Get the bodies . . . together. I'll drink . . . some whiskey." His back was covered with the blood that oozed from a small hole beneath his right shoulder blade. She wondered if she would vomit.

"Buck, I can't!"

"Got to." He rolled to one side again and took the whiskey from her, trying to smile for her. "You've learned to do . . . everything else. Might as well learn to take out a bullet." His face was covered with perspiration as he pulled the cork from the bottle with his teeth and took a long, long swallow. She watched him, staring apprehensively. She had hated him for drinking that night he'd taken advantage of her, and for making her drink. Now the whiskey would be a godsend. His blue eyes moved over her, from head to toe, then back to her face, on which a bluish-red welt was appearing. "I should be . . . helping you, Short-cake . . . not the other way . . . around." He took another long swallow.

"I'm okay, really, Buck."

He gripped the bottle tightly as hot pain ripped through him. "Go see . . . about the bodies," he told her. "And get Indian . . . quick. I left the mules . . . at another man's cabin. He told me men were headed this way. I had to . . . hurry. Mules would've slowed me down." He took another long swallow, then fell face

282

forward, his arm hanging down over the side of the bed but still clinging to the whiskey. "Hurry, Shortcake!" he groaned.

Her breathing was quick and labored. How could she do what he was asking? She fought panicky tears and ran out the door, grabbing the fat man and yanking as hard as she could, grateful now for the snow, for once he'd tumbled down the steps, the snow made it easier to move him. But she still had to use all her strength to get him to the corner of the cabin where the body of another man lay. It filled her with horror to think she'd have dead men lying so close to her door, but there was no way she could tug the fat man any farther. She went back for the first man who'd been shot. He still lay at the base of the steps. She pulled and tugged at him also, until she had him near the first two. The fourth man, who lay farther in the woods where Buck had shot him, she would just leave him alone. At least he was farther from the house.

She ran down the hill then, following the creek until she found Indian. She untied the stallion and rode him back to the cabin, tying him on the opposite side of the shack from the bodies so he could not see them and get skittish.

"I'll tend to you later, Indian," she said quickly. "I just hope your owner lives to ride you again!"

She removed Buck's canteen and bedroll and ran back inside, closing and bolting the door. Buck lay quiet, not moving. She wondered if he was dead. "Buck?" She moved closer. The bottle lay on the floor, its contents spilled around it. "Buck?" she cried.

"Leather," he groaned. "Get me . . . something leather . . . to bite on." His voice was barely audible.

She was relieved that he spoke at all, but the thought of cutting into him and bringing him more pain tore at her heart. She looked around the room, then remembered an old bridle that had hung on the wall when she'd first taken over the cabin. She had stuck it under a cupboard. She hurried to the cupboard and took it out; then she took her butcher knife and hacked off a piece of the thick leather. She dunked the leather in the washbowl, wiped it with a piece of cloth, and hurried back to Buck. She bent over him, for his eyes were closed and he didn't even seem aware of her presence.

"Here, Buck. Put this in your mouth."

"Tell me . . . again first . . ." he mumbled. "Tell me you . . . love me."

Her eyes teared. "I do! I . . . I didn't know it till you left, Buck. And I don't know what I'll do if you die on me! Please don't die, Buck!"

He grinned a little. "After . . . hearing that? I've got . . . some lost time to make up for . . . with my Shortcake." He grimaced then. "Use . . . lots of whiskey on it . . . and don't pay attention . . . to me if I . . . yell. Just dig . . . and douse it with whiskey. Give me that rawhide . . . to chew on, Shortcake . . . and get busy."

"Buck, you should swallow some laudanum."

"No . . . might put me out. I should stay awake . . . help you know what to do. Give me some laudanum . . . when you're done. Come on. Let's . . . get this over with."

She swallowed and touched the leather to his lips. When he opened his mouth, she shoved it inside so that he could bit on it. She went to the stove then, taking a towel and grasping the handle of the knife, which was very hot. She dipped the handle into the washbowl to cool it, being careful not to get the blade into the water.

She laid the knife on the edge of the table, leaving the blade over the edge and untouched, while she hurriedly moved one of the log chairs to the edge of the bed. Then she poured some heated water from the stove into a pan and set it on the log. Putting some whiskey into another pan, she put that nearby before taking some bandages from a saddlebag that hung on the wall. These she set on the bed near Buck, putting a towel under his right shoulder. Her heart pounded with dread when he moaned from the slight movement.

She did everything as quickly as possible. Her mind racing, she struggled to keep back tears that would blur her vision. There would be time later for crying. Buck needed her. He'd risked his life for her, and now she had to try to save that life. What else could she do? If she didn't try, he'd probably die anyway. She forced herself to concentrate. The whiskey. She grabbed the second bottle from the table and poured some of it over the wound. Buck jumped and moaned, and her breathing quickened. What would he do when she cut into him?

"Dear God, help me!" she whimpered. She dipped a clean cloth into the hot water, wringing it out and gently washing away as much blood as possible from the wound so she could see it better. The bleeding had slowed, and she was thankful for that. She dropped the cloth back into the water, which quickly turned red. Then she dipped her fingers into the pan of whiskey before picking up the knife from the table. Nothing had touched the blade. She knew that whatever she did must be done with clean hands and a clean knife. Infection was the biggest danger, if she got the bullet out without killing him.

She gently felt around the hole, but could feel no foreign object. She would have to cut into the wound, make it wider, then feel inside with her fingers. She could think of no other way.

"Buck, I'm ready," she told him.

His right hand grasped the support board of the bed tightly, and his left hand grasped the quilt. She closed her eyes and said a short prayer. She must be quick, for the pain would be terrible. She dare not hesitate or be afraid to cut deeply. If she didn't go down far enough, she'd have to cut him again, and she didn't want to do that. She thought about the force she'd had to use cleaning rabbits and squirrels. Surely a man's muscle would take the same force, if not more.

She struggled against the terrible urge to scream and cry and run away. She couldn't do that. She couldn't desert him. She placed the point of the knife at the center of the wound, then cut in and down, deeply, quickly, before she could vomit and run away from it all. Buck grunted, then moaned pitifully, biting hard on the leather, his fist completely white where he grabbed the board. Sweat immediately poured from his face, and he shook.

"Oh, dear God!" Harmony whimpered. "God! God help me!" She threw the knife into the pan of whiskey, quickly dipping her hand in it again before gritting her teeth and exploring the enlarged wound with her fingers while Buck groaned. She felt a strange object nearly two inches down, and she grabbed it. It came out easily.

"Buck! I got it! I got it!" She dropped it into the whiskey pan and rinsed her fingers once more. Then she took the bottle of whiskey and poured some over the wound, relieved that as far as she could tell, she'd cut into only muscle and had not interfered with any vital organs. She doused the wound with whiskey once more before setting the bottle aside, after which she rinsed the cloth in hot water, folded it and layed it over the wound to soften some of the dried blood around it. She'd wash it good, then bandage it.

"Buck, it's out! It's out! I did it!" She leaned down, noting that his eyes were closed and his mouth was slightly open, the leather strap hanging loosely from it. She gently removed the strap. "Buck?" There was no reply, and her heart pounded. Had she killed him? She bent close, her cheek against his mouth and nose. She could feel a shallow breathing. Apparently he had passed out. She wasn't sure whether he'd lost consciousness before or after the bullet had come out.

Quickly she washed the wound. It would be harder to bandage it while he was unconscious—he couldn't sit up for her—but she picked up the bandages and struggled to roll him onto his left side. Then she placed her knee against his chest so he would not slip down again. She placed the bandage across his left shoulder, bringing it around and under his right arm and then crosswise up and over the wound under the right shoulder blade, winding it around the top of his left shoulder again, having to lift his drooping head slightly each time. She wrapped and wrapped, lifting his head each time, struggling to keep him from rolling onto his back or his stomach until the bandage was heavily wrapped around him. Finally she split the end, put one edge under the bandage, brought it up, and tied it tightly to the other split end. As she gently let him roll back onto his stomach, she realized he was still wearing his boots and gun.

"Oh, dear!" she lamented. He needed to rest, and

such impediments wouldn't help. She gently worked off each boot, then reached under him to unbuckle the gun belt. Having carefully removed that, it occurred to her then he'd rest even better if he wore only his long johns. Even though he was unconscious, she reddened as she reached under him again, unbuckling the belt securing his trousers, and unbuttoning them.

Memories of their time together rushed through her mind. She had known this man, and the woman in her knew she must know him again, if and when Buck Hanner ever got well. She wasn't afraid anymore. There were men like Jimmie and those who had attacked her, and there were men like Buck Hanner. She carefully pulled off his trousers, then brought some extra quilts and gently laid them over him. It was very cold outside, and she worried about what a chill might do to him so she stoked up the fire in the stove, adding plenty of wood. That done she pulled off her own boots and eased herself under the quilts. Snuggling up beside him and putting her arm around his waist, she kissed his left shoulder.

"You'll be all right, Buck," she said softly. "It's all over now. I won't hurt you anymore, and I'll stay right here beside you and keep you warm till you wake up."

She kissed his shoulder again, pondering its firm muscle, very aware of the masculinity of Buck Hanner. Yes, she loved him. And she wouldn't let him die. She lay as close to him as she could, closing her eyes and praying again. Then the tears came. She struggled not to cry too hard, for each sob racked her body, making the bed shake.

"Don't you die on me, Buck!" she whimpered. "Don't you dare die on me!"

288

Chapter Fourteen

For the rest of the day and throughout the night Harmony lay beside Buck, keeping him warm, praying, crying, waiting for a sign of recovery. It wasn't until the wee hours of the morning that he stirred, groaning as he did so. She rose a bit.

"Buck?"

He moaned her name in reply.

"Buck, I'm right here. I've been right here beside you all the time. You awake, Buck?"

He managed to raise himself just enough to turn his head to face her, but winced and broke into another sweat as he did so. "You . . . get it out?"

She smiled and lay back down, her face close to his. She kissed his cheek.

"I did, Buck! I got it out! I think you passed out before it even happened."

He studied her green eyes, her beautiful face. "I wish to hell I felt better right now. You're a hell of a pretty sight to wake up to . . . and me all . . . full of pain and not even able . . . to move."

She smoothed back his thick, sandy hair. "That's all right. You'll get better."

He managed a faint grin. "And then?"

Their eyes held. "I love you, Buck. I just want you to live." Her eyes teared. "I was so scared you'd die on me."

"After hearing . . . what I think I heard, and now hearing it again? You sure, Shortcake?"

She sniffed. "I missed you so much," she whimpered. "I'm almost glad you got hurt, because now you have to stay a long time."

His grin widened. "I didn't need a bullet in me . . . to make me stay." He closed his eyes. "I've never . . . had anything hurt like that before."

"I'm sorry, Buck. I did the best I could. I hope I didn't do any damage."

"Don't worry . . . about that. If there's any damage . . . it's from the bullet . . . not you. You did what you could, Shortcake. I . . . probably owe you my life."

"But I owe you mine, so we're even."

His eyes opened again, but they looked more cloudy, and his voice was drifting. "They . . . hurt you. I can't stand . . . the thought of . . . anyone abusing you. I'm glad . . . they're all dead."

She kissed his hair. "You want anything, Buck?"

"Thirsty. Damned . . . thirsty."

She carefully moved out from under the quilts, tucking them around his neck and then checking the bandages. There was a bloodstain on them, but an old one. The bleeding had stopped, to her great relief.

She got a tin cup and dipped it into a bucket of drinking water she'd brought in from the creek and had already boiled. She returned to the bed, bending over and gently lifting his head slightly.

"Here, Buck. Try to drink some of this. I'll probably spill some."

His face was hot, and that worried her. When she held the cup to his lips, he managed to gulp down some of the water in spite of his awkward position. She set the cup aside and bent over him again, gently smoothing back his hair. His eyes were closed again and he didn't speak.

"Hang on, Buck," she whispered near his ear. "Hang on for me."

By noon of the following day, Buck was able to help Harmony bring him to the head of the bed, and turn him so he could lie back against a pile of pillows and quilts, in a half-sitting position, to eat and drink. Whatever embarrassment her modesty caused, she ignored, for Buck Hanner was a sick man and during those first few days he could not think about getting out of bed. She kept towels on him at first, until he was awake enough to relieve himself by using a pan. There was no longer any mystery about him for Harmony Jones, only womanly concern and, in her new maturity, a realization that some things had to be ignored when other things were more important, like the life of the man she loved. Perhaps it was best this way. Seeing him again and touching him without making love gave her a chance to understand and not be afraid of the mystery of man.

By the fourth day Buck was much more alert. He was able now to begin moving his right arm, whereas before pain had prohibited such movement. His biggest fear had been that he would lose the use of his arm, at least the ability to raise it, for that necessitated using his back muscles. However, he'd found that he could raise the arm slightly, and he was determined to raise it a little farther each day, in spite of Harmony's admonishments.

"You're trying too soon," she scolded. "Let it heal, Buck. You aren't out of the woods yet."

"I'll be all right, Shortcake. And I'll be damned if I'll be a cripple. I need this arm, for shooting—and punching."

"Well you don't need to do either one right now, so rest it."

They heard a long "Hellooo!" from outside then, and Buck frowned. Harmony picked up her rifle and went to the door. She opened it a crack.

"Be careful," Buck warned her.

"It's a bearded man, walking with some pack mules," she told him. She squinted. "Buck, some of the gear has Jack's Place stamped on it. They're your mules."

Buck grinned. "Must be Hank Fisher. He's okay. Call out to him."

She opened the door a little wider, cocking her rifle. "You Hank Fisher?" she yelled.

"That I am!" he called back. "Lookin' for Buck Hanner. I got worried. He left his mules with me to come up here."

The man stopped to stare at the dead body near the edge of the trees. He frowned then, and looked back toward the doorway, noticing more bodies near the cabin.

"What happened?" he yelled.

She stepped out a ways. "They attacked me. I'm

292

Harmony Jones, Mister Fisher. Buck shot them, but he got hurt. He's inside."

"Bad?"

"Yes. Pretty bad. But he'll make it. You're welcome to come inside. I have coffee and fresh bread."

"Sounds good!" The man came closer then. As he tied the lead mule to the railing, he eyed Harmony. No wonder Buck Hanner was determined to save her. She was the prettiest thing Hank Fisher had seen in all his born days, and just looking at her, he realized he'd been away from town too long. When he came up the steps and nodded to her, Harmony lowered her rifle, then extended her hand.

"Buck says you're okay, so I'm trusting he's right."

He gave her a wink. "Little girl, I ain't about to cross Buck Hanner over a woman. Them's fightin' words, and lookin' at these here dead bodies tells me who'd win, wounded or not." When he laughed and shook her hand, Harmony smiled. Then she ushered him inside.

"Hank!" Buck had a grin on his face. "You crazy old prospector. Thanks for coming to check on me."

Hank shook his hand. "Well, I figured if somethin' had happened to you, that meant maybe somethin' bad had happened to the little girl too, and maybe she needed help to get back to town or somethin'." He eyed the bandages. "How bad is it?"

Harmony poured some coffee for all of them, and she cut Hank a slice of bread. "Bad enough. I probably wouldn't have made it if Harmony there hadn't had the guts to cut into me and dig the bullet out. One of those bastards out there back-shot me. I'm damned lucky it was a good piece away from the spine, or I wouldn't be sitting here."

Hank shook his head, taking the bread and coffee from Harmony. He ran his eyes over her appreciatively as he thanked her. "You must be some gal, Miss Jones. Looks like you took good care of ole Buck here."

Harmony sat down. "I don't know if I could do it again. I was in a panic, Mr. Fisher. I didn't have much choice. I didn't even know what I was doing. I just dug for the bullet and got it out somehow, then prayed I hadn't killed him."

"Well, you did a right good job, it appears." He bit into the bread while Buck carefully set his coffee on the bed and began to roll himself a cigarette, using the tobacco and papers Harmony kept beside him.

"She's good at everything," Buck told the man, grinning a little. Harmony blushed deeply, knowing what he meant. Her instincts and desires were beginning to make themselves painfully evident as Buck got better. "She can shoot, clean animals, pan for gold, cook, and take out bullets."

"Sounds like everything a man could want in a woman," Hank joked. He stuffed the rest of the bread into his mouth. "You're right about the cookin'. Best bread I ever ate."

"Listen, Hank, I'm glad you came." Buck lit his cigarette and left it in the corner of his mouth as he talked. "What are the chances of you taking those mules into town for me? I'll be held up here awhile. You could explain what happened to Jack Leads. He'd pay you for your trouble, and they've got to go back."

Hank rubbed his chin. "Well, I reckon I could do that." He glanced at Harmony again, then back at Buck. "Yeah, I could. It's been too long since I hit town anyway and seen civilization. I could use a trip like

294

that, and I reckon I could make the trip and get back in time to keep my claim in order."

Buck took a drag on the cigarette and then took it from his mouth. "I'm also hoping you'll consider helping Harmony bury those men out there. She can't do it by herself, and it's not much fun for her to look at dead bodies every time she goes out the door. I'd like to get rid of them. You could take any identification you can find off them and explain the situation to the sheriff in Cripple Creek. Take their horses too, but leave one here. When I finally come down, Harmony might come with me and she'll need a mount."

Hank nodded. "Sure, Buck. You've been a good friend. And no decent man would refuse to help a pretty little gal like Harmony here—I mean Miss Jones."

"No, call me Harmony," she answered.

Hank grinned. "Well, you call me Hank."

Buck watched her. She was different—kinder, friendlier, less defensive. She was finally turning into a woman instead of a stubborn little kid. He had broken the barrier when he'd invaded her that one wonderful night, and having to help him the last few days had helped even more. She was finally beginning to trust him—and she loved him! She loved him! He was determined to get well as quickly as possible, for he intended to refresh his memory of the one passionate night he'd spent with her. And this time he'd be stone sober, so he could remember every moment, every word, every kiss, every lovely inch of her.

Hank rose. "I'd say the sooner we get the buryin' over with, the better," he was saying. "I'll go get a shovel and we'll get started."

295

Harmony rose as he headed for the door. "Thank you, Hank. I'll be right out to help."

After Hank nodded and went out, Harmony turned to look at Buck, feeling a rush of warmth and passion at the look in his provocative blue eyes. She knew instinctively what he'd been thinking. Buck Hanner was getting better, and this was the first time since he'd been wounded that he'd looked at her with desire.

"Come over here, Harmony Jones," he gently commanded her.

She reddened, but she went over and sat on the edge of the bed. He reached out with his left arm, his good arm, wrapping a big hand behind her neck and pulling her toward him. Her long, blond hair fell over his bare chest as she came closer, showing no resistance. She parted her lips, wanting the kiss as much as he did, and she was sure flames were shooting through her veins instead of blood when his mouth met hers hungrily. His tongue, lightly teasing, reminded her of the things he could do to send her into a world of ecstasy.

She returned the kiss, terribly curious and deeply in love, great joy and relief flooding her at the realization that she was a woman, that she loved a man and could trust him, that he loved her back! Yes, Buck Hanner loved her! Finally someone who would not leave her loved her. Finally she had learned about man, had learned it really was possible to enjoy being with a man. A spark of fear nudged her at the thought of the pain she would probably feel when he made love to her again; but he'd promised it wouldn't hurt as much next time, and she believed him. She believed everything Buck Hanner told her, for he'd been true to everything he'd promised so far—and he'd risked his life for her.

When his lips left her mouth, she cradled his head against her breast and through her clothing he kissed at the fullness there.

"Oh, Buck, I'm so happy," she whispered.

He breathed deeply of her sweet scent, moving his hand around from her back and gently cupping one breast in it as his lips moved to her throat. "You're so different, Harmony, so sweet and giving." He kissed her throat. "I loved you before, but I love you even more now." His hand moved to her neck again. "When I saw those men . . . abusing you . . ." His voice drifted off and his lips met hers again, in groaning hunger. She whimpered, returning the kiss almost savagely. Then she gently pulled away, her face crimson, her body warm.

"We shouldn't be doing this. You aren't well enough, Buck."

He grinned and put a big hand to her soft cheek. "I will be soon, but I agree. I don't want to risk doing damage and having to wait even longer to make love to you. I'll hold out a couple of more days. But I don't think I can go much longer than that."

She smiled and took his hand, closing her eyes and kissing his palm. "I'm so glad you're here, Buck. I was afraid you were mad and wouldn't come back."

He squeezed her hand. "I knew you were just scared and confused. I stayed away to give you time to think, and I prayed every day that when I did come back you'd know you love me. I sensed that the whiskey made you tell the truth that night, Harmony. I wouldn't have done what I did if I'd thought you didn't love me. I didn't do that just to take advantage of you and then leave you. I did it because I love you, and I felt that if I laid my claim on you and broke down that last barrier, you'd realize you love and need me." He let go of her hand and gently pressed his own against her belly. "I worried about you, about hurting you like I did. I take it no real damage was done."

She shrugged. "I guess not." Her face was still red, and she averted his eyes. "I was okay after a while."

He sighed and took a drag from the cigarette he held in his other hand. "I told you it would get better, and that's true, Harmony. You believe that, don't you? You aren't afraid?"

She shook her head. "I'm not afraid. Not if it's you."

He grinned, putting his hand to her cheek again and forcing her to look at him. "Hey." He pulled her close again and kissed her lightly. "It will be all right. I'll make it all right, okay? Trust me?"

She studied the intense blue eyes. "I . . ." It was so hard for her to say. "I trust you, Buck."

He kissed her again. "Go on and help Hank. In a few days I'll be better, and we'll pick up where we left off. Then we'll go back to town and get married."

She frowned and straightened. Marriage. That did scare her a little. That meant giving up independence.

"What . . . what about my claim?"

He shrugged. "We'll work it together, if you want. Or better yet, we'll sell it. What the hell? You don't need this, Harmony. I have plenty of money. We'll settle down in the valley, have a ranch, kids."

Her stomach tightened. Again she remembered the docks, parents who hated and abandoned her. She wasn't ready for children. She wasn't even sure she wanted to give up her claim. She'd had it such a short time. It was hers. It was all she'd ever had that was just hers.

Buck saw confusion come into her eyes; he felt her apprehension. Harmony Jones was still wrestling with something, something his love had not yet conquered.

"Harmony, you do whatever you want with this claim. I'm not marrying you for this claim. I don't know what's going through that pretty head of yours, but don't let it keep you from loving me."

"I . . . I just don't think . . . I don't know about marriage, Buck," she said quietly, staring at the floor. "Kids and all. And this . . . this claim . . . it's all mine . . . all I've ever had that's mine."

He frowned. "I'm yours too, Harmony. And everything I have is yours."

She shook her head. "That's not the same. You don't understand. Marriage and kids . . . my parents . . . they didn't want me, and—"

"Harmony!" he spoke up more sternly, grasping her hand tightly. "Settle down and listen to me."

She blinked back tears of confusion. How she loved him! Yes, she wanted to marry him, and yet . . .

"Harmony, we'll take a step at a time, all right? I don't want to lose you before we even get started. I've apparently said something that upset you, and we've got a lot of talking to do. You have some pretty deep wounds inside that pretty soul of yours, some bad memories under that blond hair. I don't give a damn if you keep this claim or sell it. I don't even give a damn if you don't marry me right away. Just relax and trust me, Harmony, do you hear? Trust me and let me love you . . . let me make love to you . . . be a man to you and show you how to be a woman. I'll make no other demands on you, Harmony. I'll even stay up here with you and dig out some ground for you if you want. We might even blow a hole in the rock behind this cabin. It belongs to you. Maybe we'll hit a mother lode. Who knows? Apparently that's more important to you than anything right now, so we'll go from there. Just don't turn away from me, Harmony. Don't stop loving me."

She met his eyes again, tears on her cheeks. "I get so mixed up sometimes, Buck," she said softly. "I love you. I do! But marriage . . . children . . . that scares me right now!"

He petted her hair. "Then don't worry about it. Just don't worry about it. We've got plenty of time. I'll stay up here with you for the rest of the winter. To hell with what anybody thinks. We'll talk . . . do some exploring around the property"—he ran a thumb over her lips— "and we'll make love whenever we want."

She sniffed. "You'll think I'm bad!"

He grinned. "No. I'd never, ever, think that of Harmony Jones. But come spring I'm going back to Cripple Creek, and by then it will be time for a decision, Harmony. We can't hole up here forever. Come spring I'll want you to marry me. That gives you some time to think about it . . . to learn to trust me. Come spring we'll make some decisions—about this place and about marriage. Agreed?"

She nodded and stood up. "I'd better go help Hank." She rose and walked to the door, then looked back at him. "I do love you, Buck. I never loved anybody the way I love you. I just want to know this place is all mine . . . just a little while longer."

She saw the manly pride and determination in his eyes. Buck Hanner would not be toyed with. "If that's what you want. But I won't let this place take you from

300

me. I can see by those green eyes that you still think independence and wealth are your only security, Harmony. It isn't so. I'm your security. Buck Hanner will be your security, your protection, your happiness. That's so and you know it. Don't forget that. Don't let your priorities get mixed up. Don't let bad memories keep you from understanding what real happiness is. I came back. I'll always come back. Buck Hanner will be a part of your life forever, and don't think you can ever turn away from that, for any reason."

Her eyes teared again. "Don't be angry, Buck. I just . . . this is the first time I've let myself trust somebody. Don't be lying. Please don't be lying!"

He smiled softly, his blue eyes full of love. "Buck Hanner never lies," he assured her.

Oh, God, how she wanted to believe that! How she needed to believe it. This was such a new feeling, love and trust. It was all she could handle for now. They'd take a day at a time, just like he'd said. She turned and went out to help Hank bury the bodies—bury the men Buck Hanner had killed to save her. Yes, she could believe him. She could trust him! And she did love him!

Hank buried the bodies and left the same day, wanting to get to town and back as quickly as possible. He took along a supply of Harmony's fresh-baked bread. That same evening Buck came down with a fever, and it was soon evident that his wound was infected, much to Harmony's distress. The area around the wound reddened and swelled, and his fever worsened to the point of near delirium. She had no choice but to cut open the wound again, but this time she made just a surface cut to drain the infection, so the muscle that was healing deeper down was not interfered with.

But the ordeal brought renewed pain to Buck, followed by four more days of weakness and healing. In a sense Harmony was glad, for that prolonged the time they had before he sought what he would want once he felt better. She wanted him, but the reality of their coming together made her apprehensive. It had seemed something they would talk about, not really do, until their burning kiss the day Hank was there. Yet the thought of Buck Hanner looking at her with desire again, touching her that way, invading her, brought a flushed nervousness to her skin. Did he compare her to other women? Would he like her as much when he was sober? Would it hurt as badly as the first time? She wanted him, yet she did not want him. It seemed that since Buck Hanner had come into her life, she was constantly confused.

She loved him, but why couldn't that be simple? Why did it have to mean trust and marriage and children, allowing him to take liberties with her body and she wanting his? Why was love so frightening and complicated? She had been so certain of how she would conduct her life when first she'd come out here. She'd had no doubts whatsoever. Then she'd seen Buck Hanner on that train, and for the first time the look of a man had aroused feelings better left buried.

Meanwhile Buck's conditioin slowly improved, and on the tenth day after he'd taken the bullet, Harmony came in from panning to find him standing beside the stove, wearing only his long johns and pouring himself a cup of coffee. She looked surprised when he turned to

302

meet her eyes. Then she closed the door and stomped off snow.

"You're up! Are you sure you should be?" she asked.

"It's about time, don't you think?" His eyes roved over her as though she wore nothing.

She swallowed. "I suppose." She smiled then. "I'm glad."

Buck frowned teasingly. "I'm not so sure you are."

She removed her coat hesitantly. "I just . . . it was nice feeling needed."

He set the cup down on the table and walked over to her, grasping her arms, his bare chest and shoulders close, so close. "You're still needed, Harmony Jones. You'll always be needed."

She raised her eyes to his, and he could feel her tremble. He sighed and shook his head. "What did you think? That as soon as I was on my feet I'd throw you on the bed and expect to have my way with you?"

"I . . . wasn't sure."

His lips met hers gently, then moved to her forehead. "Relax, Shortcake. You've got to learn to let things happen, like they're supposed to. And right now I'm so dizzy that if I wasn't hanging on to you I'd be on the floor."

"Oh!" She put an arm around his waist and helped him back to the bed. "I told you it was too soon," she chided.

"A little bit each day. Give me one more week and I'll be good as new. I guess my original plan for you went a bit astray, doctor."

She smiled. "That's all right. I can wait."

"Thanks."

"Oh, Buck, you know what I mean. I just get all

303

shaky and unsure again."

He sat down on the bed. When he tried to pull her down to kiss him, she pulled away.

"You rest like you're supposed to do, Buck Hanner. I'm going back out to work."

He frowned. "You work harder than a man. You rich enough yet?"

"No. I'll never be rich enough."

She went out the door and he stared after her, wondering if Harmony Jones would ever know what she really wanted. How many ways did a man have to prove his love and loyalty?

For the next four days Harmony made herself scarce, only coming in long enough to feed him and to prepare a bath for him, then leaving before he took it so she would not be in the same room while he undressed. He knew she was running again, fighting her feelings, being defensive. She'd come inside after dark, then sit and count her gold until he was asleep, and she made a bed for herself on the floor.

The fifth night after he'd gotten on his feet again, Buck could see that if he didn't do something, she'd revert to the old Harmony, allowing her fears to overtake her wants. He waited, pretending to be asleep as she counted her gold again. When she rose to turn out the lamp, he called her name as she leaned over it. She met his eyes, looking surprised.

"I thought you were asleep," she told him.

"I know what you thought. Leave the lamp lit, Harmony." It was a gentle command again. She could feel his masculine magnetism, knew by instinct he was much stronger—nearly healed—knew what he wanted. She stood rigid, in love but afraid. "Take off your clothes. I want to look at you."

She swallowed, shaking. "I . . . can't."

He reached out to her then, and her eyes teared. She made her legs take her around the table, and she grasped his hand. "Help me, Buck," she whispered. "I'm so scared."

"You love me?"

She nodded. He pulled her closer then, wrapping an arm around her waist and pulling her onto the bed. His broad, strong shoulders hovered over her then, and he gently kissed her forehead, her eyes, her cheeks, her throat, her lips. The kiss on her lips lingered until he could tell her curiosity and love were again overcoming her fears. Then she began to return the kiss, suddenly eager with passion, the child in her making her move almost too quickly. He kissed her harder to calm her down, pinning her beneath him, his renewed strength reminding her of the man Buck Hanner was. If a woman wanted to pick the best—the most strong, brave, and handsome—man in the world, she guessed that would be Buck Hanner. And here he was, in her arms, wanting her, loving her—hers for the taking. She wondered if she would ever truly be woman enough for him? She'd learned much since she'd met him, but lingering fears kept her from fully blossoming.

He began unbuttoning her shirt. "Wait," she told him. "I'll do it." Their eyes held. "Don't hurt me, Buck. I . . . I don't mean just physically. I mean . . . don't leave me. Don't stop loving me."

He smiled softly. "Never. Never, never, never."

She kissed his cheek. "I do love you." She sat up then and unbuttoned her shirt, braver now, excited, wanting to please him. Her cheeks turned scarlet when she exposed her firm, lovely breasts, and his eyes glazed as he watched. When she lay back and unbuttoned the boys' pants she had begun to prefer to dresses, he sat up and took hold of them, gently pulling them down over her slender thighs, hot fire in the tips of his fingers as they touched her skin. Her underwear came off with the trousers, and he threw both to the floor. Then he just sat, looking at her. Finally, he ran a big hand along her leg, up the side of her hip and over her belly. When he lightly brushed the secret place only Buck Hanner had ever seen or touched, she drew up her knees.

"You're like an angel, Harmony," he told her, his voice husky with desire. His hand moved to her breasts, gently massaging them until the nipples became full as her passion grew. He bent lower then, to taste them, and her breath came in little gasps.

She wondered why she had put this off, why she had been afraid. This was Buck, her protector, her friend— her lover. There was not one promise he had not kept. She reached around and tangled slender fingers in his thick hair, whispering his name as she felt his warm breath against her breasts. His lips moved to her throat, while the hand that was so calloused and strong caressed her secret places with surprising gentleness. His lips met hers at the moment his fingers invaded the nest of love that was silken with moist passion, and she could not help whimpering with aroused passion as fire built and then raged deep in her abdomen until moments later an explosion of feeling ripped through her. She cried out his name, ecstatic now. Yes! It was more wonderful than she had remembered. Buck had made it wonderful. Buck! Beautiful, wonderful Buck.

He'd come back! He'd saved her, had almost died

306

doing it! Buck! He moved on top of her now. Why, oh why had she avoided this? Her legs parted willingly as his lips moved to her throat again, that most manly part of him probing, pushing.

"Hang on, Shortcake," he groaned. At almost the same instant he was invading her, thrusting deep, reclaiming that which he had already claimed. She cried out then, from the pain; but it was not as bad as before, just as he'd promised. Everything was just as he'd promised. Yes, she could trust him!

"Buck! Buck!" she whimpered, arching up to him. In all his years he'd never experienced such sweet glory with a woman. It was better this time, for she was sober and willing, and he could tell she was enjoying it. She loved him. He could tell by her voice, her eyes, by the wanton rhythm of her body.

He moved with her, and she with him, each alive with savage desire. Alive and in love! Before long his vital fluid poured into her and he groaned, slumping down onto her in sweet release, exhausted.

For several minutes they lay there, neither speaking. Then he raised up on his left elbow, favoring his right side which was still sore. "Don't you move," he said in a near whisper. "Stay right where you are, Shortcake. I don't want to break the spell. You're staying right here all night. I'll never get my fill of you."

With her fingers she traced his finely chiseled lips and straight, handsome nose. "Am I the best . . . of all the girls you've been with?"

He laughed lightly and kissed her nose. "You're the best, the very best. I'll never want another woman the rest of my life."

"Promise?"

"Promise."

She smiled. Buck Hanner had never broken a promise yet, and suddenly thinking of him with any other woman brought rage to her soul.

"I love you," she whispered. "I want to do it again."

He sighed as though she were asking him to do a chore. "I suppose, if you insist."

She giggled. "I insist."

He kissed her tenderly. "You're a demanding woman, Harmony Jones."

"Am I? Am I really a woman?"

He grinned and bent to kiss her throat. "Oh, yes, my love. You are indeed a woman."

She closed her eyes, tingling at the touch of his lips. What a beautiful man he was! Surely nothing could go wrong now. Nothing could take Buck Hanner from her, and he loved her, so he'd not desert her. Not Buck.

"Oh, I love you, Buck!" she whispered. "I love you so!"

Chapter Fifteen

Harmony had no idea one person could experience such happiness. For two weeks they worked by day and made love by night. The snow had melted enough to allow the horses to nibble wet grass, but Buck was worried about the animals. He'd asked Hank to leave Indian and one of the other horses, thinking that he'd soon be going into Cripple Creek to marry Harmony. But his wound and her fears had prevented that. He knew that the horses must be taken into the valley where there was more to eat.

But like Harmony, he hoped the animals could find enough grass for a while, for he didn't want to leave this place where they had found so much happiness and love. This was their little world, and doubts or not, Harmony Jones had admitted that she loved him, and he had had her in his arms every night. That was enough for now. If she wanted to keep working the claim awhile longer, he'd work it with her.

When he began digging near the high rock behind the cabin, he found a few large stones that were rich with specks of gold which could be pried from them with a knife. Harmony began spending the days separating the gold from the rocks while Buck shoveled deeper and farther. He intended to set off some dynamite at the base of the rocky hill behind the house and then start tunneling inward. If Harmony Jones was determined to see what was here, he'd help her. The sooner they found out the better, for he wanted to prove or disprove the claim, then get her to town to marry her. This would be a bonanza or a washout. He almost hoped for the latter. He wanted her to forget about the gold and the claim, to marry him and settle down. But her tenseness every time he suggested she do that told him to be careful.

Still, he could see the love and trust growing in her eyes every day, and it felt good to allow himself to love and trust in return. He never thought he could love anyone this much, not after Mary Beth. But Harmony Jones was everything a man could want—young and beautiful, intelligent, hard-working, level-headed— and in bed he'd never known such ecstasy. Her innocent eagerness and curiosity excited him. She was clay in his hands, to be molded as he wanted. He enjoyed teaching her things, and he experienced great pleasure each time he broke through that little wall of resistance she still put up whenever they started to make love. He liked to release all the passion and sweetness that was stored up inside this young woman who was so full of hurt and bad memories. He was determined that his love for her would eventually overwhelm her fear and hesitation, for she often woke up shaking and crying, saying nothing, only clinging to him. There was nothing he could do at those times but hold her tightly and reassure her of his love.

A fierce storm hit on the first of February, just before Buck was about to do some experimenting with the dynamite. The cabin was literally buried in snow, and Buck had no choice but to untie the two horses and whack them, hoping they would have sense enough to head downward until they reached the valley where they could find food. Harmony stood beside him at the top of the cabin steps, which they had had to dig out, and they watched the two animals struggle through the deep snow, their hunger forcing them to head for warmer places. In the valley the snow would disappear quickly—it usually did in this part of Colorado—but at the elevation of Harmony's cabin, it would be around for a while.

"Do you think they'll make it, Buck?"

He watched Indian with concern. "I hope so. I don't like to see horses suffer. I should have taken them down a long time ago, I guess." He put an arm around her shoulders. "But for some reason I just couldn't seem to get away." He looked down at her, and she blushed. He loved to see her blush, in spite of all their intimate moments. "Looks like we're really stuck here for a while now, Shortcake."

"Do you mind?" she asked seriously.

He grinned. "What do you think?" He bent down and kissed her lightly. "Fact is, I can think of a damned good way to keep warm and pass the time as long as the snow is too deep for anything else."

She smiled and pulled him back inside. "Do you think you'll find Indian again?" she asked, as he closed and bolted the door.

"I'll sure as hell try. I wouldn't be surprised if Indian

found me instead. I think we'll get together. He's a damned good horse. I hated turning him loose like that, but I'd rather lose him than have him die of hunger. I couldn't live with that."

He removed his jacket and walked over to stoke up the fire in the stove that served for both heating and cooking. A pot of stew, flavored with squirrel meat, was simmering. Harmony stirred it while Buck put more wood in the stove. After he'd closed and latched the iron door, he just watched her for a moment. Yes, she was a perfect mate. He began to untie the rawhide strip at the end of her braid, laying it aside and unwinding her thick, golden hair.

"Buck Hanner, I just fixed that braid!"

"I know. But I like it loose, and you can't go out and work today anyway."

She smiled and sighed. Why did a simple thing like his loosening her hair stir her? He was so manly, yet sweet and gentle though rock-hard strong and sure. It made her heart flutter to think she could actually please such a man, one who had had lots of women and who seemed to have been everywhere and done everything.

"Buck?"

"What?" He ran his fingers through her hair to smooth it out.

"Come spring, we'll . . . we'll sell the claim, for whatever we think it's worth by then. We could use the money toward a real nice ranch and get set up. That would make it nice for you."

His heart swelled with love. "You saying you're ready to get married come spring?"

She sighed. "Fact is, if it wasn't for this storm and not being able to get to the valley, I'd marry you right now. I don't know what I was so afraid of."

Reaching from behind her, he grasped her wrist so she stopped stirring, and he turned her, studying her green eyes. "You serious?"

She smiled softly. "I'm serious." She rested her head against his chest. "I wish I could explain how I felt when I was little, Buck, when my folks left me in St. Louis. I've never forgotten how it felt and I never want to be that afraid or that alone again. That's why it's been so hard for me to put all my love and faith into one person. Can you understand that?"

He kissed her hair. "I've always understood that. Why do you think I've been so patient with you?"

"And the other . . . kids, I mean. You'll have to help me there. I'm so afraid of children, Buck. What if I hate my own, the way my parents hated me?"

He held her close, rubbing her back. "You won't hate your own children, Harmony. People don't usually do what their parents did. They were very selfish. You aren't a selfish person, and there is usually nothing stronger than a mother's love. I guarantee if and when we have children, you'll be amazed at how much you love them. You'll love them even more than you love me."

She looked up at him. "I could never love anyone more than I love you."

He picked her up in his arms. "You'll love our children more, and I won't mind. You're a sweet, wonderful girl, Harmony, full of love but just afraid to share it. Now you're doing that, and when you have a baby, love will come flowing out of you like water from a overfilled barrel."

He laid her on the bed and unbuttoned her shirt.

"Buck, it's morning."

"So? Is there a rule about the time of day people are supposed to enjoy each other?"

She smiled. "I guess not."

"Well, with those winds howling out there, can you think of anything else to do? I'm a little tired of cards."

He opened her shirt and bent down to kiss her breasts.

"Buck Hanner, I shouldn't be doing these things."

"Why not?" He pulled her to a sitting position and slipped the shirt from her shoulders and arms. "You're going to be my wife, aren't you? As far as I'm concerned, you already are. I made you my wife that first time I took you. I don't need a preacher to tell me you belong to me."

He kissed her then, a sweet, wonderful kiss that made her lose all ability to reason or object. She was putty in Buck Hanner's arms; she knew it and she didn't care. It was wonderful to love and be loved, wonderful to make a real decision about her life. There was no more wondering and worrying now. She would sell the claim in the spring and marry Buck; then they would ride off to find their own dream. It was much nicer to dream together than it was to dream alone.

She never tired of just lying there while he worked his magic with her. Within moments he lay beside her, her clothes off now, his own body naked and urgent, hard muscle pressing against her, commanding, demanding. the man in him ordering her to be the woman she was, yet doing so very gently. The things she allowed him to do amazed her—things she'd once thought ugly and repulsive had become beautiful and desirable. With Buck everything was different, wonderful, glorious.

His lips were warm and sweet, not just against her mouth, but in other places, intimate places that belonged only to this man. It was wonderful to truly enjoy being a woman and to give this man his pleasure, and to take her own pleasure in return. Yes, this was what it was all about. This was why people fell in love and married. This was true joy and ecstasy. This was what was intended for a man and a woman in love—to be one, to give and take and give again.

They moved slowly, glorying in one another, no one to hear their passionate whispers and groans or the rhythmic movement of the homemade bed. There was only Buck—Buck and Harmony and the little cabin on the mountain. The lamp dimmed as the oil ran low, and the stew simmered, waiting to be eaten . . . later.

For two weeks the winter winds blew, and for two weeks Buck Hanner and Harmony Jones made love, talked, made love, played games, made love, ate, made love, counted gold, made love. They became intimate not just in body, but in spirit, understanding one another, learning to be the best of friends as well as lovers. Harmony felt so alive, so free—free of fear and sorrow, free of loneliness. She had Buck Hanner, and sometimes she wished they could stay together on the mountain forever, alone. If it were not for their desire to be legally married and their need for supplies, she would never leave this place. Often at night he caught her crying. Then she would cling to him, vowing she would never forget this place, this mountain, the things she had learned here.

Finally one night the wind stopped howling, and it

was deathly still. Harmony could hear dripping, and she knew the warmth of the cabin was melting snow from the roof.

"Buck?" she said softly.

He stirred, nearly asleep. Then he stretched and pulled her closer, enjoying the feel of skin against skin, for they slept naked together. "What?" he asked sleepily.

"Will you still love me when we go back?"

He kissed her hair. "Why shouldn't I?"

She sighed. "I don't know. I just . . . maybe it will be different. Up here it's just you and me—no problems, no one to bother us. In town, you'll see other girls, and—"

He laughed lightly. "Harmony, don't be silly. We know each other inside and out. Do you think my love is that shallow?"

She kissed his chest. "No. It's just scary. I've been up here so long, away from people and all. It will seem strange to be around them again."

"Well, we have to get back to real life eventually. You just remember that you and I are the same, no matter where we go or what we do. We're still Buck and Harmony, and nothing can change our love for each other. You remember that, Shortcake. Nothing can make me stop loving you. Nothing."

She rested her head in his shoulder. "Do you think people will talk about us, about our being up here alone this long? Will they think I'm bad?"

She felt him tense. "The first man who suggests such a thing will feel my fist in his face," he grumbled. "You're the woman I love and intend to marry. You've not done one bad thing, Harmony, and don't ever think you have. All you've done is love me. You've been sweet and wonderful and good, and any man who tries to say otherwise will wish he hadn't!"

She smiled, feeling protected and safe. It was a nice feeling, the only way a woman could feel in Buck Hanner's arms.

"I'll be eighteen next week, Buck. I guess I'm a full-fledged woman now."

He squeezed her close and nestled into the quilts. "You're a full-fledged woman, all right. You've grown a lot since you first came here, Harmony. I'm proud of you. And I did my share of waiting for you to grow, I'll say that. I wanted you right off, you know. Fact is, the first time I saw you on that train, when I didn't even know who you were, I wanted you. You were the prettiest little thing I ever saw, and something deep inside told me I'd see you again."

"I felt the same way, but it scared me. When I came out here I was determined to be an independent woman, wealthy and secure, on my own. Then you had to come along." She pushed at him teasingly. "Now my whole world revolves around you. You messed up my thinking, Buck Hanner."

He laughed lightly and rested a hand against her breast. "And I've enjoyed doing it," he answered, running his hand down over her belly.

They both lay there quietly for several minutes. "I still hate the thought of going back, Buck. I'll never forget this place, the months I spent here, the beauty, the quiet. It was fun being alone, for a while, except that awful day the grizzly came after me, and then the day those men came. It seems every time I needed help, you were there, like God led you to me or something."

317

"God did lead me to you. We're supposed to be together."

"I just hope it can be the same when we go back. I'll hate leaving here. This is our place, Buck. It's special. If we sell it, men will come up here and tear it up, blow out the side of the mountain."

"Hush, Harmony. So what if they do? This place will always be here—in our hearts and memories. That's all that matters. Nothing can change these last few months. Nobody can take away our memories, or our love. Whenever we want to be here, all we have to do is close our eyes and remember. Now go to sleep."

She closed her eyes. Yes, as long as she could lie in his arms, life would always be like this, wherever they might go, whatever they might do.

The weather cleared, and enough snow melted for Buck to dynamite away portions of the cliff beside and behind the cabin. He was careful to set the explosives in such a way that the cabin would not be buried under rock slides. The first few blasts brought an avalanche of snow down from above, however, and they spent the next few days digging their way to the place where the hole had been blown.

Several times Buck repeated the process, dynamiting inward to create a tunnel in which they could work out of the wind and cold. They used a few timbers left behind by Tillis' men to shore up the small cave they had created, and since the snow and cold were still too intense to permit them to journey down the mountain, they continued working. They decided to dig out as much gold as possible, and to get a good idea of the value of the claim before returning to Cripple Creek.

"Might as well get everything we can out of this," Buck told her. "The more we make, the more land we can buy—and cattle and horses."

She agreed, fully trusting him, glad to share her wealth with him, for this was the man she loved, the man who would soon be her husband. It was exciting to know she'd soon be Mrs. Buck Hanner. She liked the sound of it. It now seemed right to be a wife and mother instead of a business woman. She needed Buck, and he needed her. They should be together, should unite and create children. She felt that was God's way.

Days turned into weeks, and the snow melted more quickly. The nights were still cold, but by the end of March the days were much warmer. Harmony was certain they'd passed the supreme test of knowing whether they could be happy together, for if they were going to get on each other's nerves, they would know that by now.

That hadn't happened. There had been only a few friendly arguments, always ending in sweet kisses and teasing. She wondered if any two people could be better suited for one another, and she had to laugh when she remembered the times she had argued with Buck Hanner, had been stubborn and resistant, distrustful and defensive. She was different now. That Harmony was gone.

Then came the day Buck yelled to her from inside the cave. She was beside the stream, picking gold out of rocks. She dropped her knife and ran to him. He was furiously hacking away with a pick at a sparkling vein in the rocks.

"My God, Harmony, look at this!" Chunks of

sparkling rock fell to the floor of the cave, and she picked them up.

"Pyrite?" she asked carefully.

"No! It's too soft, Harmony. I think it's the real thing!"

Her heart pounded. "Buck, are you sure?"

"Take a look! You can make a nail print in the stuff!"

She pressed it with her thumb nail, then sat down, staring at it. "Buck, I think you're right."

"If I am, there's enough here to buy up half the state of Colorado!" he muttered. "I'll be a bigger rancher than Wade Tillis ever thought of being!"

She watched him, the old distrust nipping at her. Was that all he was really after, enough money to outdo Wade Tillis? Was he using her? No. Not Buck. Not Buck.

"Baby, we'll be the biggest ranchers this side of the Mississippi!" he told her, still hacking away. "I'll shove a load of this stuff into some saddlebags and find a way to get it down the mountain and have it assayed."

Her heart tightened. "Just you? I thought we were both going back."

"We both will go back, once I get this assayed and file the proper papers for you. This is it, Harmony, the mother lode. If I go back alone, no one will suspect anything, don't you see? I'm just coming back to report back to Leads. If you go down, everyone will be watching you." More chunks fell on the floor. "The minute you go into that assayer's office, they'll suspect, and Wade Tillis will buy up everything that surrounds your claim in ten seconds flat! This way it will be our secret. Nobody need know what we've discovered here. We'll secretly buy up more claims, then hire someone with the right equipment to come up here and mine it right. Eventually we'll sell out to a bigger mining company and take our money and settle on the finest ranch in Colorado!"

For several more minutes he hacked away, while Harmony just watched him. Why did distrust consume her so easily? This was Buck. He kept saying "we" and "our," and he still spoke of settling on a ranch. But he was so excited. Was it because he'd hoped all along this would happen, that her claim would pay off and he'd get rich because of it? Perhaps he was just using her after all. He might have asked her to marry him because he knew she'd refuse, but asking would give him more time on the mountain with her. And he had mentioned Wade Tillis. He might have helped her in order to outdo Wade Tillis, not because he really cared about her.

Again her old fear of being unloved crept over her. Would Buck Hanner change if he got his hands on her claim? Maybe she shouldn't marry him after all. Maybe—

"Hey," he said, interrupting her thoughts and setting aside the pick. He knelt down beside her. "What's wrong?"

She shrugged, her eyes tearing. "I don't know." She met his eyes. "You . . . you wouldn't just . . . use me, would you, Buck?"

He frowned. "What the hell does a man have to do to make you trust him, Harmony? I believe I almost died a couple of months ago to save you from a fate worse than death." His blue eyes were angry.

"But a man will do a lot of things if he thinks he might get rich," she answered, a tear spilling down

321

her cheek.

He stood up and kicked at a piece of ore. "I don't believe you, Harmony! I thought I had you figured out, but I guess I didn't!" He stormed out of the cave, and she ran after him, following him up the steps.

"Where are you going!" she yelled.

"Back to Cripple Creek!" he barked. "You can have your damned gold—and your independence!" he roared. "I don't want any of it! Finish digging it yourself! I'll walk back right now and freeze to death if I have to. But I'm going!"

Her heart filled with remorse. "No!" she screamed. Quickly she went up the remaining steps and into the cabin, where he was throwing his things into saddlebags. "Buck, I'm sorry! Don't go!" she begged. "Not this way! I trust you! Really I do! Please don't go!"

He cast her an angry look, his blue eyes icy. "I can't live my life always being doubted, Harmony. I love you, but damn it, I have my pride! How can you think your gold is the only reason I've stayed up here! I thought we had that all straightened out! I don't need your damned gold! I have plenty of money. I just thought the gold would make it that much easier for us, that's all, but I'll do fine without it!"

When he reached for his gun belt, she ran over and grabbed his arm. "Buck, wait!" She was crying now. "Please, please don't go! I really am sorry! If you go you won't come back! I'll die if you don't come back! I can't live without you!"

He studied her eyes. Why did he love her so much? Why did he understand her fear and feel sorry for her? Suddenly she was a little girl again, and the thought of leaving her tore at his heart. He sighed, grasping her arms.

"Harmony, you've got to trust me to take some of the gold down and get it assayed. I'll be back. You've got to believe that I'm doing it for us, not for me, for us! Why should we pass up the chance to have a good life? I can make it good for us without the gold, but the gold will make everything much easier, don't you see? I can build you a fine house, and our children can have the best. But it's your gold, not mine, so it's your decision."

"Do whatever you want! I don't care, Buck! You've always been right, and you've never broken a promise. Just promise me that when you go down with the gold you'll come back!"

His jaw flexed with anger. "I don't need to promise that, Harmony. You should know by now that I'll come back. You should know how much I love you."

"Don't be angry! Please don't be angry! I get scared when you're upset with me—scared that you'll leave and never come back. I . . . I don't want to have to wait for you . . . like on the docks!"

A spasm shook her body, and she sobbed. He closed his eyes and sighed, pulling her close. "It won't be anything like that, Shortcake," he told her, squeezing her tight.

She cried harder, relieved. When he called her Shortcake, she knew he wasn't angry anymore. She wept against his chest, and for several minutes he just held her, his strong arms reassuring her until she finally quieted. Finally he held her a bit away from him.

"Harmony, look at me," he told her quietly.

She raised her eyes to meet his, but his face was a blurred by her tears.

"I'm saying it one more time. I love you. I don't need

323

your gold, so it's up to you, what we do with that. But I love you, and I want you to be my wife, to bear my children. Do you believe that?"

She sniffed and nodded, and he bent to kiss her lightly.

"I love you," he repeated. He kissed her again. "I love you. How many times and ways do I have to say it?"

"I believe you," she said pleadingly.

"Then you must also trust me, Harmony. Now if you want this stuff assayed, it's much better that I go back alone, understand? It won't take me long. I'll file the proper papers and then come back for you. It will look very natural if I go into town. I'm in and out of these mountains all the time; sometimes I take gold down for other miners. No one will think much about it. I'll get things all set, then come back for you. When I do, we'll go down to Cripple Creek and get married, and we'll live there until all this is straightened out and we sell the mine. Then we'll take your money and mine and we'll go search for the prettiest piece of land in Colorado. How does that sound—thousands of acres, all ours. You said you wanted to own property and all. Now you'll own more than you ever dreamed of. After all, it won't be just mine if you're my wife, right?"

She nodded, watching his eyes—so true and devoted. "Oh, Buck, I'm so sorry! I love you so much. I didn't mean to be so stupid."

He kissed her forehead. "I know that. Now let's get busy. You get some sacks for the ore. I'll take a good sample down with me so we know that much is safe. Then I'll be back. I might even bring some other men with me, men to mine this thing while we go down and get married. That way the claim won't be unprotected.

Then we'll just take it from there, Harmony. We mine it awhile or sell it, whichever you want. I'll file all claims in your name and won't have anything to do with the gold. It's your decision."

She wiped her eyes. "I . . . I'd like to do it the way you suggested. If you go back first, no one will suspect. You go, and I'll wait for you." She hugged him tightly. "But don't take too long, Buck! I'll miss you so!"

"I'll go as fast as I can. But remember I'll be on foot going down, so allow me extra time. And while I'm gone, you be damned careful, understand? Forget about fishing and all that. Stay close to the cabin. Spring is a dangerous time of year up here."

She pulled away. "Oh, Buck, I don't want it to end! I don't want to leave here!"

He kept one arm around her waist, while he gently smoothed back her hair with his other hand. "I won't be leaving immediately, but we have to face reality sometime, Shortcake. We have to get back to the real world, to life. And we have to start living a normal life. We can't stay here forever. You know that."

She closed her eyes. "I know. But it's been so wonderful here, alone together."

He kissed her tenderly, then held her close. "Yes, it has. But we have each other, Harmony. Wherever we go, we'll take our love and the peace of this place with us, in our hearts." He patted her bottom. "Come on, now. Let's get to work. Get the bags."

She nodded and he left her, hurrying back outside. As Harmony watched him go, she realized how empty and horrible life would be without him. It would not be easy to let him leave. It would test her ability to conquer her fear of abandonment. If he came back this time, she'd never distrust him again, never be afraid again.

For several more days they dug, picking out the best pieces of ore and filling several sacks. To their surprise and delight, Indian reappeared, and the reunion of man and horse was touching. Harmony was delighted for she knew Buck had been worried about his horse. And she was very relieved. Now he'd have an easier trip down. He could take more gold with him, and he'd get to Cripple Creek and back much faster. Still, her heart was heavy with apprehension. After having him with her for so long, she hated the thought of being without him. Her loneliness would be magnified now, but she could be here awhile longer, while it was still peaceful and just her own, before men came in to blow away the mountain.

She was tense the night before he was to leave, unable to eat, unable to think of anything but Buck Hanner going away. He sat down on the bed and removed his boots and shirt.

"Hey," he called to her. He'd been watching her as she sat at the table, just staring at the floor. "Come over here, Shortcake."

She walked over to him, her head hanging, and he pulled her onto his lap. "You okay?"

She shrugged. "I guess so." She placed her arms around his neck. "Oh, Buck, I'll miss you so!"

He patted her back. "You've been up here a long time—too long. I'll be glad when I get back to take you down from here. But while I'm gone, I'll miss the hell out of you. You can bet I'll be back damned fast,

Harmony Jones. I don't relish spending the nights away from you." He kissed her cheek. "You trust me to come back, don't you? No more doubts?"

She met his eyes, so blue and loyal. "Yes." Their eyes held, and in the next moment his mouth met hers and he was laying her back on the bed.

"This is one night we won't sleep much," he told her, nuzzling her neck. "If we're going to be apart, let's make it a night to remember."

"Oh, Buck, it's been so beautiful here," she whispered. "Make love to me. Don't stop making love to me!"

She didn't need to ask. He moved over her, savoring every part of her, his lips lingering, teasing, carrying her to the heights of ecstasy and passion, his lovemaking made more sweet by the knowledge that he was going away. Harmony felt she had to show him her love, to make him remember, make him come back out of sheer need of her; while Buck seemed to be equally determined to be sure she·did not forget him. She sensed his fierce possessiveness as he moved over her, felt a hot branding as he surged inside of her, as though to say "This woman is mine and everyone had better know it!" She thought she'd already been to the heights and depths of lovemaking, but this was the most passionate night she had spent with him and by the wee hours of the morning her body was spent and exhausted. Yet it was a sweet exhaustion, a glorious weariness.

They both slept soundly then, oversleeping, in fact, so that Buck had to rush around when they did wake up, for the sun was higher than he'd expected. He planned on covering a good many miles that first day.

Harmony felt panicky. It was all happening too fast now. He was going! How she hated moments like this! They frightened her! He dressed and ate quickly, packed, saddled Indian, and was ready to go. She could do nothing but watch. Finally he swept her into his arms.

"Stay close to the cabin, understand?"

"Yes."

"And keep the rifle with you at all times."

"I will."

"No walks. No fishing. Don't even dig or pan while I'm gone. Someone might catch you off guard, like those men did. I've got enough of a sample to get a good assay so there's no sense in digging right now."

"I'll just keep to the cabin."

"Good. Don't take any chances. I'll worry about you enough as it is. But I want to protect what's yours, Harmony, and the best way to do that is to go back alone. I'm seen around all the time, taking other men's samples in and all."

"But they know you've been with me."

"Yes, they do. But I saw plenty of others before I got up here, and I won't go directly to the assayer's office. It would arouse too much suspicion. As for my being up here this long, let them think what they want. To hell with them. I love you, Harmony Jones, and you're going to be my wife. While I'm gone, think about what you want to do with the mine. When I get back, you'll be registered as the owner of the bonanza and some of the land around it. What you do after that is up to you. Just promise me you'll marry me, no matter what."

"You know I will, Buck. I love you."

He kissed her, over and over, both of them declaring

328

their love. Then he could put off leaving no longer. Gently, he set her from him and mounted Indian, reaching down to tousle her hair.

"Good-bye, Shortcake," he told her, flashing his handsome grin.

"Good-bye, Buck. Be careful!"

"You do the same. Don't worry about me. I plan to make good time, Harmony, so don't be surprised if I'm back in eight days or so."

"The sooner the better."

He backed Indian, and she thought her heart might explode when he turned the horse and rode off, turning back once to look at her.

"I love you!" he called out.

"I love you!" she called back.

He rode on then, soon disappearing into the thick pines.

"Good-bye, Buck," she whispered. "Please come back! Please, oh please, come back!" Memories of her parents waving good-bye flashed into her mind, followed by the memory of saying good-bye to Brian. None of them had come back. Now she was saying good-bye to the most important person in her life, the person she had dared to trust with her love and devotion—and a good share of her findings.

She shook with fear of being deserted again, yet never had trusting someone been more important to her than now. She sat down on the cabin steps, while the wind moaned through the pines, a tiny girl on the side of a big mountain, her fear and loneliness knowing no bounds. She had wanted so much never to depend on anyone, but she knew that if Buck Hanner did not return she would not want to live. She would never love again, never smile again.

She looked up at an eagle flying overhead, envying the huge bird its freedom from human feelings. Then she touched her belly. She didn't know much about having babies, but she did know when a girl went six or eight weeks without flowing, it could mean she was pregnant; and she had not had her time for at least that long. Perhaps that had something to do with being so young and a virgin and then making love so often and with such intensity. But common sense told her otherwise. Common sense told her she might be carrying Buck Hanner's child. She hadn't told him. For some reason she'd been afraid he'd be angry about it. There were so many things about men that she still didn't understand. Perhaps Buck didn't want a child right away. He had so many other plans. She'd been afraid if she told him before he left, he might be angry and wouldn't come back. Somehow she knew deep inside he'd never be angry about such a thing, yet her old fears prevented her from taking that chance. She'd tell him later, after he came back for her, after they were married. It would be different then. Buck wouldn't care. There was plenty of time. She couldn't be more than two months pregnant, and he'd be back in less than two weeks. There was no sense in burdening him with the news now. The most important thing was that he came back.

The wind howled again, sounding almost like groaning voices, matching the loneliness and fear in her heart. She closed her eyes and her body moved spasmodically as she sobbed.

"Oh, God, take care of him and bring him back!" she prayed, her words carried off by the groaning wind.

Chapter Sixteen

Eight days turned into ten. More snow melted, and it was April. Harmony told herself not to panic. Perhaps some small thing had gone wrong. Three weeks had gone by, and she was getting low on supplies. He would come. He'd had some kind of snag, but he would come—soon.

When a month had gone by, her feelings drifted from terror to hurt to depression. No! Buck would not do this! Something had happened to him. Yes, that was it. He might have been hurt. Buck! Poor Buck! What in God's name had gone wrong? Only something terrible would keep him from coming to her or sending a messenger. Maybe he was dead! No! How would she live without Buck Hanner? And what about the baby?

She rested a hand on her stomach. She had no doubt now that she was pregnant, probably at least three months along, maybe more. Pregnant by Buck Hanner. Pregnant from those wonderful moments she'd lain naked beneath him, his woman, enjoying her man, giving and taking. Buck! Sweet, beautiful Buck.

Surely he was dead. How would she live if that were so? What could have happened? An avalanche? A rock slide? Bandits wanting his gold? A hungry grizzly just coming out of hibernation, fierce and ornery? In this wild, savage land he could have been killed in a hundred ways.

The ache in her soul was fierce, but she clung to the belief that he was dead or horribly wounded. Awful as that thought was, it was better than the fear that Buck Hanner had lied to her all along, that Buck Hanner had taken her gold and left, never having intended to marry her in the first place. Still, sometimes she wondered if he was using the gold to start the ranch he'd dreamed about.

Surely such a thing could not be true! Not after all they'd been through together—all their talks, their sweet friendship, his love and protection. He'd risked his life for her, hadn't he? But then a man would do a lot of things if he thought there was gold to be had. She could not forget the day he'd struck the vein, his excitement, his almost evil laugh at the thought of being richer than Wade Tillis. Surely though, if it was the gold, he'd stay with her and marry her, for then it would all be his, not just the nuggets he'd left with. But then, Buck was a drifter, perhaps he didn't like the thought of being tied to one woman. Perhaps he had lied to her about Mary Beth. Perhaps there was another side to the story. But his eyes! Those blue eyes were so true and sincere when he spoke of her, and when he whispered words of love to Harmony.

She had never been in such a fix. What was she to do? She couldn't stay here forever. She was pregnant. How would she hide it once she got back to civilization?

What would she tell people? She didn't even know how she could get back there. She couldn't walk all the way, not in her condition. Yet if she didn't do something, she'd die of hunger. There were only a few cans of beans left, and a little flour.

Terror gripped her. Again she felt abandoned. Was this her eternal fate, to be forever left behind, unloved, unwanted? Whether Buck was dead or had deserted her, no man would want her now. She was a spoiled woman. She was carrying Buck Hanner's bastard child. And what of the child? She didn't even want it! A child! What on earth would she do with a child?

She felt as though she were going crazy. She knew she had to think, but she couldn't. Nothing made sense without Buck. He'd become her whole world. She had severely broken her own rule of never depending on anyone but herself. She had dared to love and trust, and this was the result. The quiet loneliness of the mountain began to eat at her, and horrible visions of Buck riding away, laughing, floated through her mind. They alternated with visions of a grave with a marker that bore his name. What had taken him from her? If only she had gone with him that day! She no longer cared about the gold or the mother lode. Buck was gone, though he'd promised to come back. He'd never before broken a promise to her, only this time. Why?

She began moving about as though in a daze. She must keep busy—dig out more gold and then walk down the mountain in the hope of finding Cripple Creek. She had only enough food left for a few days and a little for the trip. She was even low on ammunition. She decided to save what remained for her journey, in case a grizzly attacked her, and to shoot fresh game to eat.

Yet why did she want to eat, to live? There was nothing to live for without Buck. The baby? She didn't want the baby, not now. She might have wanted it if Buck had returned, for he'd have been happy to know she was giving him a child. Or would he? Maybe he didn't want the responsibility. Maybe he'd only wanted the gold after all. If only she knew what had happened, she'd know whether to love or hate the baby. If Buck had been killed, she wanted the child, it would be a part of Buck Hanner; a little piece of Buck would go on living. But if Buck had deserted her, she couldn't possibly love the child.

She began to work frantically, feeling like a crazy woman. "Fill the bags! Take as much as you can carry or drag!" she told herself. "You can build some kind of travois to drag along instead of carrying everything on your back." She worked hard—too hard. She didn't want to sleep, couldn't sleep. She didn't like the things that floated through her mind when she tried to rest. Buck! Buck! God, how she had loved him, trusted him, and she needed him so. If only he would appear over the ridge. If only she could hear him call out to her. But day after day it was the same. No Buck. Only silence. She began to hate this place, to hate the ugly little cabin, to hate everything and everyone. The bitterness that was growing in her soul far surpassed what she had felt because of what her parents or Brian or Jimmie had done. This was worse than any other hurt she'd felt.

But the day came, despite her youth, when overwork and the lack of food and rest took their toll. The pain gripped her just as she was undressing for bed, determined that this night she would get some rest, for she intended to leave in the morning. Her body buckled and she cried out, gripping her abdomen and barely managing to limp over to the bed.

What was happening! She crawled onto the bed and eased the quilts over her body, shivering as pain slashed through her again. As she lay moaning, clad only in underwear and her shirt, she felt a wetness between her legs and pulled the covers back. Looking down, she saw blood staining her legs and her underclothing.

The baby! Something was wrong. She was losing it! "No!" she screamed aloud. Terrified, she wondered if she would die. She did not know how to stop the bleeding.

"Buck!" she screamed, long and loud. "My God, where are you? Where are you?"

Then she fell into bitter weeping, interspersed with groans provoked by terrible pain. For most of the night she writhed in pain and terror and aloneness. By morning it was done. The life Buck Hanner had spilled into her had spilled back out of her, lifeless. Yet its very tiny shape could not be mistaken. Remembering Becky's miscarriages, Harmony massaged her stomach, not sure why, only knowing that it was supposed to be done. More strange nothings came out of her.

She was in a trance now, feeling only hate for the world and everything in it, including herself. This was her fault. She hadn't wanted the baby, so God had taken it from her. This was her punishment, and she deserved it. Why she was doomed to a life of loneliness, she didn't know, but apparently that was the case. She wrapped herself in towels, noting that her body was thinner now, too thin. She was weak, so weak! She managed to get off the bed, and taking another towel, she carefully wrapped it around the lifeless object that had come out of her. That done she sobbed pitifully. It wasn't fair that her own hatred and bitterness had been directed at this little thing that would have been her baby. And she knew in that moment that Buck Hanner had been right about one thing: if she had a baby, she'd love it beyond measure. She would not forget her guilt over causing this child's life to end before it could even begin. Now that it was too late, she realized that she had wanted it, more than anything she'd ever wanted. But she could not have it.

How long she cried, she wasn't certain. She wondered if she would ever stop, for she was weeping for more than the lost baby. She wept for her own desolation, and for Buck, her mind reeling with a mixture of love and hate. If he'd simply left her, then what she had just gone through was all his fault. Was this why Becky had begun to lose her love for Brian? How many times could a woman go through this pain for nothing without resenting the man who put the life in her belly in the first place? Still, if Buck were dead, she'd have wanted that child.

She carefully laid the wrapped object on the table, so weak she could barely stand up. It must be buried. But how was she to do it? She looked back at the bloody bed. She didn't even have the strength to clean it up. She simply removed the blanket that had been under her; it took all her strength just to do that. Then she put down one of the top quilts. She would lie on that, although it would mean one less quilt to cover herself with, and she was cold—so cold. She glanced at the door. She had not latched it the night before. She had intended to, until the pain hit her. Now she didn't have the strength to walk over and bolt it. What did it matter anyway? She almost hoped a man or a wild animal would come inside and kill her. Death would be better than what she was going through. She crawled under the quilts and soon fell into an exhausted sleep.

Harmony awoke to a hand on her shoulder. She was groggy and weak. Perhaps everything that had happened had been a horrible nightmare. "Buck?" she groaned.

"No, honey. It's me—Hank Fisher."

She turned and slowly opened her eyes. Hank's chest pounded with fear. She looked terrible! She was so thin and pale, and there were such dark circles under her eyes!

"You sick, Harmony?"

She blinked, reality beginning to sink in. "Buck!" she whimpered, her eyes welling with tears. "Where's Buck?"

Hank frowned. How could he tell her what he thought? He'd found it hard to believe himself. He'd figured he'd known Buck Hanner well, had thought him a dependable man. That day Hank had visited Harmony Jones's place and had seen Buck and Harmony together, they had seemed to be so in love. Buck had even been wounded when he'd risked his life to save her.

"He . . . he ain't here, little girl," Hank replied. "I got to worryin' about you two, wonderin' about ya. When I went down to town them months back, I brung a mule back with me on account of I decided I'd mine a little more through the rest of the winter, then head back to

337

Cripple Creek and sell my claim for what I could get. I've been away from civilization much too long. When I went on down to Cripple Creek I heard Buck had been there and gone, but not you. The whole town's been wonderin' about ya, so I come up here to see what was what. I . . . uh . . . I thought I might find Buck here," he lied.

His words were partially lost to her, for her mind was unclear. "Buck"—she groaned—"The . . . baby. I . . . lost it. Our baby."

Hank frowned. He knew nothing about women having babies, nothing about miscarriages. She looked terrible. Was she bleeding to death or something?

He touched her warm forehead. "What's that? You lose a baby, honey?"

"Last . . . night," she whispered. "I've got to bury . . . my baby . . . table."

Hank looked at the table, where a towel lay. He rose and carefully opened it, grimacing at the little bloody mess that lay within. "My God!" he whispered. Then he looked over at Harmony. The girl was obviously very sick. He quickly got some water. She had lost a lot of blood, and she would need water. Gently, he raised her head and helped her drink.

He wondered why Buck had left her here alone. The whole town was whispering about why, after seeing an assayer, Buck Hanner had ridden out of Cripple Creek and never returned, about why he hadn't stopped to give Jack Leads an explanation of his departure. And the whole town was wondering about Harmony Jones. She'd been on the mountain ten months. If Buck had gone back up to her, he'd told no one. Now Hank could see that Buck wasn't here. Apparently he hadn't come here when he'd left Cripple Creek, for the cabin was nearly empty of food.

To Hank's relief, Harmony drifted off again. He hadn't the slightest idea what to do for her so he decided to wait until she was conscious and could tell him. In the meantime he'd get some food together for her and make a pot of soup. But first he would bury the baby. He picked up the little package with a heavy heart. Surely Buck hadn't deliberately deserted her. Not Buck Hanner. But what else was one to think? There was no other answer, yet it made no sense. No sense at all.

He shook his head, and picking up the partially formed infant, he walked out of the cabin. Now he knew why the door hadn't been bolted. She must have been too weak to do it. "Poor child!" he muttered. He'd watch over her, for Buck. He couldn't believe Buck wouldn't be back.

Harmony sat up in bed sipping the hot soup gratefully. But there was no softness in her green eyes. They looked lifeless and bitter. It was over now. Done. She would revert to her old independent self.

"There is really no other explanation," she told Hank coldly. "Buck Hanner isn't coming back. I would like to believe that he's dead"—she met Hank's sorrowful eyes—"but there's been no report of his body being found, has there?"

The man sighed and shook his head. "This is a big country, Harmony. A man can die and not be found for days—weeks."

"Buck was good with a gun, good with everything.

That leaves only one conclusion. He took my gold and left."

Hank scratched his head. "I can't believe that, honey. I just can't."

"I can," she said matter-of-factly. "People have been walking away from me all my life. My parents abandoned me when I was six years old, Hank—left me on the docks of St. Louis. If a kind man hadn't come along when he did, I'd have been hauled off by a couple of thugs and sold into some kind of slavery, but my parents didn't care." She sipped more soup. "Don't worry about it, Hank. I'm used to it."

He watched her finish the soup. He didn't believe her. She was building a wall around herself, hiding her feelings. She was turning from a sweet child into a cold woman. There was even a cruel streak about her now, a hardness despite her smallness and her youth.

"I'll be well enough to travel in a few days, Hank," she was telling him. "I'd like you to take me to Cripple Creek, where I'll find help in getting good men up here to mine my claim. I've hit a mother lode."

"I . . . uh . . . I seen that. I was scratchin' around out there. You hit it big, Miss Harmony, right big. You'll be a rich lady."

"Of course I will," she answered. "That's what I had in mind when I came out here, to be rich and independent. Buck turned my mind for a while, but he's done me a favor. He's really taught me not to trust anyone but myself. I take it you didn't stuff any of my gold into your pockets?"

She saw the hurt in his eyes and hated herself for making such a remark. She didn't know why she was behaving this way, but she couldn't seem to stop

340

herself. If felt good to hurt someone else. It actually felt good. It relieved some of her own hurt, hurt that she refused to fully recognize. She had forced herself not to think of Buck Hanner with anything but hatred, but that hatred was being directed at the wrong people. It was Buck she wanted to hurt most of all, but he wasn't here. Hank was.

"I'm sorry, Hank," she declared, leaning back. "I didn't mean that. You've been good to me, nursed me. You could have taken advantage of me, but you didn't. I guess I'd have to say you are one person I trust, but not completely. I'll never trust anyone completely again."

He came over and took the bowl from her. "It's all right, Miss Harmony. You've been through a lot. But I wish you wouldn't draw your conclusions yet. I just can't believe Buck would up and leave you like that. I've known him a long time. He's a good man, dependable—"

"He's a drifter," she cut in. "A drifter with a dream. I gave him just enough gold to realize that dream without having any responsibility attached, and I gave him something more precious than my gold. I'll never get that back. He stole my pride, Hank—my pride, and my faith, and whatever love I had inside of me. There is nothing left for me now but my gold, and I like to keep busy. So I will decide how to spend my money— get into some kind of business, perhaps. I'll go to Cripple Creek, maybe give Wade Tillis a run for his money. That would be fun."

Hank sighed. "If that's what you want," he answered.

"That's exactly what I want. I helped run a very large

341

supply store back in St. Louis. I know all about business, Hank. It's time I applied my knowledge. And do me a favor."

He looked at her with sad eyes.

"Don't mention Buck Hanner again," she told him firmly. "He's gone, and that's that. I'm trying very hard to forget him, so the less you talk about him the better."

He frowned. "You're the one who brung up his name," he reminded her.

Her eyes flashed angrily. "You just remember what I said!" she spat out. Then she turned over, pulling the quilts up around her neck.

Harmony Jones was not even halfway through town before most people were in the street, staring at her and shouting questions. "How'd you do, little girl? Where's Buck Hanner?" There was a little laughter, but she kept her eyes straight ahead. She sat astride Hank's mule, while he led it. It had been a long, hard journey back, and she just wanted to go to the assayer's office, then get a room and sleep. "Glad you're back!" someone shouted. "We've been rootin' for you!" "Hey! It's Harmony Jones!" someone else yelled. "Harmony Jones is back!"

Just before they reached the assayer's office, Wade Tillis stepped out in front of them. He was taller and more handsome than Harmony had remembered, but he still had that scheming look about him. He nodded to her, removing his hat. She remembered what Buck had told her about him. Had that, too, been a lie? Perhaps there was more to the story. This was the man Buck Hanner hated with a passion. Harmony smiled at him. If Buck Hanner hated this man, then she would like him, just for spite.

"Hello, Mr. Tillis," she said pleasantly.

He studied her beautiful but too-thin form. "You don't look well," he told her. "Is there anything I can do?"

Her eyebrows arched, as half the town stood around and watched them talk. "I was . . . sick. I'm better now," she answered. "And after I see the assayer, there is something you can do for me. I need men . . . lots of them . . . men who know how to dig tunnels and mine a rich vein."

His eyes lit up. "I suspected as much. Buck Hanner put your name on a lot of land around your mine before he left town with some heavy-looking bags."

She flinched at the pain that swept through her heart. The mere sound of Buck's name tortured her, and she hated her weakness. Her eyes glared coldly. "Well, at least he had the courtesy to do that much. I would like to talk to you about Buck Hanner, Mr. Tillis, but I need to rest after I see the assayer. Would you consider dinner tonight, at the hotel? We can talk then."

The man grinned broadly. "I would be honored," he replied. "And . . . uh . . . congratulations, Miss Jones. You did what most of us thought impossible. You not only struck it rich, you survived. We all admire you."

She smiled sarcastically. "Yes, Mr. Tillis. That is one thing I have learned about myself. I am a survivor."

He winked. "And a shrewd businesswoman, I'll bet. I can help you there."

"We'll see," she answered. "Seven o'clock, tonight." She looked at Hank, who appeared distressed by the

343

conversation. "Let's go, Hank."

Fisher sighed and walked on toward the assayer's office, while Wade Tillis watched. Already he was hungry for Harmony Jones's gold and brains and body. Now that Buck was out of the way . . .

He grinned. Only Wade Tillis knew that Buck Hanner would never again grace Harmony Jones's doorway. He chuckled. Harmony Jones was now free for the taking, but she was smart. He'd have to be careful with that one.

Harmony wore a plain skirt and a white, high-necked blouse that had puffed sleeves. She nodded to Wade Tillis as he entered the restaurant, whereupon he removed his hat and then walked briskly to her table.

"What would you like to drink, Mr. Tillis?" she asked curtly. "I'm buying tonight."

He looked surprised. "You? That isn't very ladylike."

"I couldn't care less what is ladylike. Not anymore. Besides, this is a business meeting, Mr. Tillis."

"Won't you call me Wade?" he said smoothly.

When a woman came to take his order, he asked for white wine. Harmony sipped a little from her own glass, for one brief moment remembering the first night Buck Hanner had made love to her, both of them drunk from celebrating the killing of the grizzly. Hadn't Buck saved her from that too? She shook away the thought.

"All right," she answered. "And you may call me Harmony. But that is as far as your privilege goes."

He shrugged. "I had no intention of pursuing it any farther."

344

She blushed a little, realizing she had been too forward. "I am willing to pay you, Wade, to arrange to have my claim mined properly. I obviously can't do it by myself. I've hit a rich vein, and the claim is good. We'll need the proper papers signed, and you'd better realize I know a good deal from a bad one. Don't try to cheat me or I'll have you hung. You'll be managing the mine. I'm told you do a lot of that around here, and you do it well."

He nodded. "Thank you. You're absolutely right. Who told you about my business dealings? Buck Hanner?"

Her eyes flashed and she felt her cheeks flush. "Perhaps you can tell me what happened between you and Buck," she replied.

He grinned, leaning back and taking a sip of the wine the waitress had brought him. "What did he tell you?"

"Never mind what he told me. I want to hear your side."

Wade's smile faded. "I did what was best for my niece. How was I to know she'd get sick and die? The point is, Buck Hanner is a no-good. He was a drifter, never stayed in one place more than a year, had a woman in every town he hit. I had him checked out. There was only one thing Buck Hanner really wanted, and that was a big ranch of his own. He would have used my niece to get it. He only wanted her money." His eyes narrowed. "And if you think real hard, you'll see that was all he wanted from you. I'm sorry."

Her heart throbbed with pain at the memory of the assayer's words. "Yes, Miss Jones, Buck Hanner was here. He had the gold assayed, and I must say it was worth a fortune. I offered to take it and hold it, to give

345

him money for it, but he refused. He said he had someplace to go with it, and he set me to getting you access to more land around your claim. Then he left."

"Did he say where he was going?" she asked.

"No, ma'am. Only that he needed the gold for something else. Plenty of others saw him leave town, but he didn't tell anyone where he was going. He said you'd be down soon to finish up these claims. We thought maybe he'd gone back up the mountain to you."

She had trouble hiding her bitter disappointment. "He didn't come back up the mountain," she answered quietly. Then she looked directly at Wade Tillis. "If all he wanted was my money, Mr. Tillis—I mean . . . Wade—then why did he leave right away? If he had stayed and married me, he could have had all of it."

Wade laughed. "He didn't need all of it. He'd earned some himself, cheated others to get more, then he cheated you. To stay would have meant taking on the responsibility of a wife, maybe children. Buck Hanner doesn't want those things."

The pain came again, a terrible, stabbing pain that almost took her breath away. Would she ever forget the sight of the tiny life she had expelled?

"Buck had enough gold to get him off to a good start," Wade was saying. "That's all he wanted. He certainly isn't the kind of man to settle down with one woman, not Buck Hanner. I'm afraid you let his looks and his gentle way fool you, Harmony."

She stared at her wine, wanting to cry. "Is it that obvious?"

"That you thought you loved him? Of course it is," he replied quietly. He realized he had only to be kind to her, to befriend her, and he might be able to move in on a fortune. This girl had been badly hurt. He'd done the right thing, getting Buck Hanner out of the way. "Everybody in town knew what was probably going on up there. Not that they blamed you. Buck is quite the ladies' man when he wants to be. Don't worry about it. No one thinks any the less of you, believe me. We're all glad to see you buck up and come back to town determined to make a go of it in spite of Hanner. To hell with him. You're here, and you have a gold mine. And yes, I will help you mine it, on whatever terms you state."

She studied his dark eyes. It was all happening so easily, perhaps too easily. He was so ready to help her now, yet when she'd left Cripple Creek Wade Tillis had been her enemy. Perhaps he'd only been trying to help her after all. Maybe he'd been angry because it was Buck Hanner who had taken her up the mountain. Perhaps he knew Buck would hurt her.

"All right," she replied.

He reached over and lightly patted her hand. "Don't you fret one more minute about Buck Hanner," he urged. "I know it hurts. But the hurt will go away. Besides, you're a damned smart girl. You have more to do than settle down on some ranch with a no-good like Hanner, wasting away in some forgotten place with ten kids toddling after you. You're too beautiful and too talented. Now that you have a real gold mine, a whole new world is opening for you."

She smiled. "Yes, I know. I intend to get into some kind of business," she answered. "You had better be careful, or I might end up owning more of this town than you do."

347

He smiled, but there was a coldness in his eyes. "Well, well. And here I am trying to help you. Maybe I shouldn't be so obliging."

She picked up her menu. "Maybe you shouldn't," she answered. "You're lucky Buck Hanner hated you, because the way I feel about him right now, I'm actually beginning to like you."

Wade Tillis laughed again as he picked up his menu, but he was contemplating her shrewd business mind. She was a determined woman now, one to watch out for. But there was one way to insure he'd not have to worry about her taking over the town. If he married her . . .

"I think I'll have the T-bone," he told her. "Some fresh meat just came in yesterday, so maybe this time it won't be tough."

She kept her eyes lowered, struggling momentarily against tears. Buck! He kept looming in her heart and mind. She must forget him! She swallowed and breathed deeply for control.

"Fine. I'll have the same," she answered. She raised her wineglass and held it out. "Here's to a profitable business relationship," she told him.

Tillis raised his own glass, drinking in her beauty appreciatively. He touched her glass with his. "I'll drink to that," he answered. Their eyes held for a moment before they sipped their wine.

Chapter Seventeen

Harmony stood on the porch of the small home she'd rented. It was August, 1897, and a heavy hailstorm was in progress. She didn't care that lightning was flashing around her, nor did the rain and hail bother her for the porch roof was over her head. And she hardly heard the furious thunder that rumbled and echoed through the mountains.

Nothing really mattered. She even contemplated running out into the storm to risk being hit by lightning. The hail came down in ever-bigger balls, pounding against the roof. She heard something break. Was it a window? It didn't matter. It seemed as though the fury and thunder of the storm only matched the fury and thunder in her soul.

She stared at Pike's Peak, far in the distance, sometimes shrouded by heavy black clouds that were moving very fast. She remembered when she'd first come to this place, over a year ago, young and ignorant and determined. It had seemed so frightening to go to the mountain and stay there alone. But she'd had Buck

Hanner with her, to guide her, teach her, protect her. She clearly envisioned his face now: his sky-blue eyes, sandy hair, high cheekbones and tanned skin; his straight, handsome nose and wide, provocative grin. Why couldn't she stop thinking about his powerful shoulders and hard-muscled arms, his strong, firm thighs and hips. She recalled the scent of him, the feel of his arms around her, the glory of being one with him.

Over and over she told herself that he had loved her, that he would not have abandoned her. But he was gone and she had heard nothing from him. He had left Cripple Creek with her gold, and without so much as a glance backward. Despite all the men she had hired to search for Buck Hanner, there had been no word of him, nor had anyone found him dead. He must have gone far away, perhaps to Montana or back to the Dakotas, or maybe down to Texas, where he was originally from. By now he probably had a fine ranch going, thanks to the extra money her gold had brought him. When she had even checked with the local bank, she had been told Buck Hanner had withdrawn all his savings. So, she could only conclude that he had left her to go his own way. He had used her heart and body, had conquered her, and was probably laughing about it right now, while he held some other woman in his arms. She had been a fool.

The storm raged on, and she continued to stare out at it. Someplace up there men were digging out her mine, bringing down a fortune in gold every week. She was rich, richer than she'd ever dreamed she could be, and the town of Cripple Creek had grown considerably. Its population was now approaching twenty-five thousand. And out of all these people, she and Wade

350

Tillis were the richest. But somehow her riches meant very little. Being wealthy didn't feel as good as she'd thought it would, yet at the same time she could not get enough money. Somehow she continued to believe that the only relief for her loneliness lay in obtaining even more wealth. She'd show them all! She'd show her parents, Jimmie O'Toole, even Wade Tillis! And if Buck Hanner ever returned he'd regret not staying around to marry her! He could have been the richest man in Colorado!

Again sweet memories came to her as the top of the Peak was brilliantly lit by the sun which peeked out from behind a cloud. Their special place was up there— the little cabin! She had known so much happiness there, had become a woman there, at the hands of Buck Hanner. It could have been so wonderful, so beautiful. If only she could go back to the way it was, to that sweet, wild winter on the mountain. She wouldn't even care if the grizzly came back.

Her eyes teared when she suddenly remembered Amber. Did he still come around looking for food? Had one of the miners shot him? Poor Amber! She wanted to see him again. She remembered wishing he were not so wild so she could have hugged him and cried into his thick fur. Everything was gone. Even Amber. And she doubted that the cabin was still there. Her mining crew had probably torn it down to get to more of the mountain. The thought of it lying in a heap tore at her heart, and her body jerked convulsively. It seemed everything was destroyed, including her own heart and soul. She was just a shell, with a business mind that kept the money flowing. She was apparently unlovable. Why, she would never know. But there was something about her that drove people away.

Now she didn't even want friends. What good were they? People could not be trusted. She made no effort to befriend any of the women in town, having no use for the prostitutes and feeling awkward around the wives, who talked of things that did not interest her. Her only interest now was money and obtaining more of it. She already owned a supply store, having bought out Jack Leads, which pleased her greatly. Let Buck Hanner come back. She'd be his boss! She had enlarged the store and had then purchased yet another one located in Colorado Springs, hiring others to manage both stores. Yet she had rented a modest home, for she didn't spend enough time there to worry about anything fancy. On the hill above her sat a much more elegant home, belonging to Wade Tillis. She contemplated building one to out-do his, but hadn't had the time to fuss with that. She did, however, keep an eye on her supply store in Cripple Creek, as well as the real estate office she now owned, and she often visited the bank and the assayer's office, and her attorney to see that things were in order. Now she was contemplating opening her own bank.

Ironically, it seemed that her only friend was Wade Tillis. Because of their original business deal and his subsequent help in other dealings, they had developed a friendly working relationship. She realized that because of her association with him, others had withdrawn from her, surprised that she had turned to the most notorious man in town for help. But she didn't care. What she did was her business. Let them talk. Let them shun her. Some local businessmen were cordial to her because they were friends of Tillis. But whether

352

anyone was cordial or not mattered little to her. Wade Tillis had been Buck Hanner's enemy—all the more reason for her to be Wade Tillis' friend. And Wade was good to her, patiently teaching her many new things about handling her new wealth and about business. She'd hated him when she'd first come to Cripple Creek, but after all, he was a good businessman, and his original desire for her claim was understandable. Why shouldn't he try to discourage her? Her determination to keep the claim and her bravery in standing up to him had won his admiration and respect. He didn't treat her like a stupid little girl now. He treated her as an equal. She suddenly smiled at the realization that Wade Tillis probably considered her a threat to his own wealth.

That was good! That was power! It was something she'd always wanted. It was her only defense now. No one could hurt her as long as she had wealth and the power it brought. She was totally independent and in control. At eighteen she guessed she must be the youngest independently wealthy woman in the country. How many other eighteen-year-old girls were rich due to their own determination and hard work? She hadn't inherited it, she'd worked for it. And no one would ever take it from her. Money didn't desert a person. Money didn't abandon you. Money could be a friend, the kind of friend on which someone could depend.

She stared at the mountain as the storm began to taper off. The trouble with money was that it was cold. It couldn't hold her in its arms. It couldn't love. It couldn't make her feel like a woman. Never again would she know the kind of happiness she had known

353

on the mountain. How wonderful it had been to feel loved and to love in return. How sweet it had been to think she could trust in someone. She had given herself to Buck Hanner with such sweet abandon.

She looked away, turning to go inside. And what had that brought her? Nothing but pain and humiliation. A tiny life lay buried up there, a life she had expelled that lonely night. It had been planted in her womb by Buck Hanner and forced from it by her own hatred and desolation. The depression that had followed the miscarriage had never truly left her. She had built her own little world of wealth, put on her own armor against the hurt of remembering, but deep inside her the depression and pain remained, screaming to get out. But she would not let them surface. She was too proud and stubborn. She would not let Buck Hanner hurt her that way. If she gave in to the hurt, he would have won the final victory. She was through with crying. She had cried her last when she'd wept over her lost baby.

Buck Hanner tugged at the leg irons that held him, knowing his efforts were futile yet too stubborn and angry to give up. The last several weeks had left him emaciated. Despite having only bread and water to eat, he clung to life, refusing to give in, as he knew Wade Tillis wanted him to do.

How could he have been so foolish as to ride alone toward Colorado Springs, carrying Harmony's gold? He should have realized that the assayer would tell Tillis what was going on. Instead he'd left a note with the assayer, telling him to get word to Harmony that he'd be back just as soon as he'd found the best men in Colorado Springs to handle her mine. He hadn't trusted Wade Tillis to run her claim.

Now he realized Harmony had never received his message. That was the worst part of all of this. Here he was on a stinking fishing boat on its way to China, where he would probably be sold off like a slave to some sea captain who needed deck hands on his merchant ship. Rich traders often owned ships manned by slave laborers. That way they made even more of a profit on their trade goods. He had guessed that China was where he was headed after he'd listened to the talk of other shanghaied men on the boat. In the meantime, poor Harmony had been left alone on the mountain. He knew what she would think when he never returned, and when she later learned he'd left Cripple Creek with her gold.

The thought of her being alone and thinking he had deserted her brought him more pain than anything his captors could inflict upon him. Harmony! Sweet, trusting Harmony! If only he could find a way to get to her, to explain. If only he could hold her once more, tell her he loved her and would never deliberately leave her. What Wade Tillis had in mind was obvious. The man had probably already set her against him. He'd probably told her what an undependable drifter Buck Hanner was, and had made her believe Buck had deserted her.

Buck did not doubt who was behind all of this. He'd gotten only a glimpse of the men who had waylaid him, for they had sneaked into his room in Colorado Springs, and had quickly put a strong-smelling rag over his mouth. Blackness had overcome Buck, but not before he'd seen one of their faces. It was Buffalo's. He did not doubt they were Tillis' men, all well paid to keep silent about what they had done, just as the assayer had been paid for giving out information on the gold Buck had brought to Cripple Creek.

When Buck came to, he'd been chained in a boxcar, amidst hay and cattle, animal droppings all around him. For days he was left there in the smelly darkness, his ankles firmly cuffed, having to relieve himself nearby and share the stinking train car with his own feces and those of the cattle. Soon more men were brought inside, always after dark, all of them unconscious at first. They were chained and gagged. The gags came off only at night, while men stood guard as the prisoners ate. One prisoner dared to call out for help, and immediately his throat was slit.

"We'll lay him under the wheels when the train leaves," one guard muttered. "Nobody will know once he's in pieces."

Buck knew then that he would bide his time before attempting to escape. He'd figured a better time would come, but it had not. He wasn't even sure where he was then, at some stop on the Kansas Pacific, no doubt. The train had soon left, rumbling on for days while the smelly car got worse and Buck Hanner got weaker from lack of food and water.

Finally, one night they were moved to a smelly fishing vessel, shoved into the dark hold of the boat, and crammed together. One man tried to resist, and he was severely beaten. Days later they were moved again, to the hold of an even bigger ship, where Buck was now, his stomach lurching as the ship pitched and rolled on great waves. The ocean, no doubt. He'd heard men talking about China. Buck had been around enough to know what that meant. If he lived and managed to get back to Harmony and Colorado, doing so could take months, even years. By then it would be too late to undo the damage that had been done. But few men survived the ordeal he would suffer. Most were deliberately killed once their wasted bodies no longer served their captain well. He received a taste of what was to come when a man came below to begin "training them into submission" to make them "good servants and good shipmen." Using Buck as his "example," the man laid Buck's back open with several cruel lashes, yet Buck refused to cry out, even when they dumped salt water over the cuts.

The only thing that kept him going was his love for Harmony. He thought of those beautiful months on the side of the mountain, when he'd held her sweet body in his arms and been one with her, teaching her all the glories of man and woman, listening to her whispered words of love, gazing into her provocative green eyes and wrapping his fingers in her golden hair. Harmony! What would become of her? How terribly hurt she would be when he didn't return! Abandonment had been her biggest fear, and it had taken him so long to win her love and trust.

Wade Tillis was probably moving in on her now. The thought that the man would probably talk Harmony into marrying him ate at Buck like an acid, making him furious. He couldn't stand to think of Wade Tillis bedding his Harmony.

God, how he missed her, needed her, loved her! It was agonizing to picture her waiting alone on the mountain. If only he could hold her, comfort her . . .

357

But he could only try to live through whatever lay ahead. They had been at sea for weeks, perhaps months. He had lost all track of time, sometimes he was not even sure whether it was day or night. Soon he would be in China. What would happen then, he could only guess. He wondered how he would even have the strength to get to his feet. Perhaps he was already useless, and he would be shot.

No. He would not give up. He would refuse to die, no matter what they did to him. And he would somehow, someday, make an escape. If he thought about nothing but Harmony, he could do it.

Harmony opened the door and stepped aside for Wade Tillis to enter. He was more handsome than usual on this night. He wore a dark, expensive suit, and his thick, dark hair was freshly cut. The forty-two-year-old man's looks belied his age. He bowed low to Harmony, now nineteen. She had been back in Cripple Creek for a year, and she'd blossomed into a shrewd woman, cunning in business dealings and so cold and sure that she seemed much older than she really was. Wade was beginning to wonder if the girl ever smiled, for he couldn't recall having seen her smile in many months.

"I'll get my shawl," she told him. "Where are we going?"

He watched the gentle sway of her hips as she walked away from him. He had wanted her since the first day she'd walked into the Mother Lode and demanded what was rightfully hers. Perhaps Buck Hanner had broken her in first, but if she had had a taste of man, perhaps she needed her taste buds reawakened.

"Well, our burgeoning city has a new playhouse, which is opening tonight. Of course you're aware of that, since you own half of it."

She turned about, her eyes cold. "I'm aware of it. But you might tell me, Wade, why you're asking me to more than business meetings lately. I don't mind. I do get a little bored in the evenings, but I've never totally trusted your motives for anything."

He laughed lightly. "I don't blame you. Not many people trust a wealthy man. And since you and I are just alike, you have all the more reason not to trust me."

"I'm waiting for an answer."

He took a hand from behind his back and held out a fistful of wildflowers. "For you."

Her eyebrows arched, and a tiny wave of other times and places rippled through her at the gentle look in his eyes. She'd have taken that look for love had it not been bestowed by Wade Tillis. She reached out and took the flowers, watching him suspiciously.

"I have a proposition for you," he told her.

She turned and placed the flowers in a vase. "I'm listening."

He straightened his shoulders. "You're the richest woman in Cripple Creek," he told her. "and I am the richest man."

She folded her arms and stared at him. "So?"

"So if we pooled our wealth, we'd both be even richer, and neither of us would mind that."

She frowned. "Pooled our wealth?"

He stepped closer, looking down at her as he gently touched her cheek with the back of his hand, bringing back more memories. "A woman needs a man, Harmony. And I'm at an age where I like the idea of having one woman—a wife. Why don't we get married and stop this little tug of war between us?"

She reddened slightly and stepped back. "I have no desire to marry you or any man."

"Come now, Harmony. You're lonely as hell, and so am I. We couldn't be a better match, you and me. Surely you don't intend to spend the rest of your life without . . . well, without being a woman again, in the best sense."

She snickered. "The best sense?"

He stepped closer again, this time daring to envelop her in his arms. "You know what I mean. Surely you don't really want to live out your life alone. Surely you aren't going to let Buck Hanner do that to you. If you do, he's won his game, don't you see?"

She sighed and shook her head, looking up into his dark eyes. "And I suppose you're going to lie and say you love me?"

He grinned. "You'd know it was a lie, just as it would be a lie for you to say you loved me. But we get on well, we're good friends, and we'd both be much richer." He rubbed at her neck. "And I wouldn't be cruel to you, Harmony. I may be a lot of things, but I'm not a man who abuses women. You'd play the role of Mrs. Wade Tillis well. And who knows? Maybe we'd learn to love each other. In the meantime, we'd be the wealthiest people in these parts. We could travel. Wouldn't you like that? Maybe see Europe? I'll take you there if you like. I'll do whatever you want. I'd only ask . . ." He swallowed, his eyes glazing with desire. "I want you, Harmony Jones. I admire you. If that's love, then I do love you. Every woman needs a husband, and I'd not be demanding or cruel."

She closed her eyes and rested her head against his chest. He was, after all, a man, and he had been good to her, in spite of his murky reputation. He had not cheated her in any way, and he had become her only friend. The nights had become so unbearably lonely that she wasn't sure how much longer she could keep going. And what better way was there to forget Buck Hanner than to be in some other man's arms? What better revenge than to have those arms belong to Wade Tillis? Wade was right about one thing. Buck had awakened the woman in her, and at nineteen years old, she wasn't certain herself that she could truly go all her life without taking a man again. Buck had made her aware of her womanly needs and of her desire to share her life with someone. She would not let what Buck Hanner had done ruin the rest of her life.

"I'll think about it," she said quietly.

He drew her closer with one arm while he lifted her chin. She kept her eyes closed, knowing what he would do, afraid of it yet wanting it. His lips met hers gently, hungrily, but she felt no passion, not the kind Buck Hanner had stirred in her soul. Still . . .

"Think hard," he told her. "The waiting will be very difficult for me."

She met his eyes again. "I could never put all my faith and trust in you," she told him coolly. "I learned long ago not to do that with anyone. It would have to be a kind of business arrangement. Certain assets would remain mine alone, but I will share some profits with you because you would be my husband. I would be a wife to you in the best sense, but basically out of duty. I admit I would enjoy companionship and wealth, but there will be no lies between us, Wade Tillis. It would be a marriage of convenience, and for profit."

He stepped back, looking her over. "Agreed. But I will make one part of your 'wifely duties' something more than just a chore for you, Harmony. Someday you will truly want me."

She wrapped her shawl around her shoulders. "I'll never truly want a man again. We will simply relieve our sexual needs. As long as you are kind to me, I can put up with that much. Just don't expect me in your bed every night."

He smiled a crooked smile. "I never considered such a thing. Are you saying yes then?"

She finally smiled back. "No. Not yet. I said I'd think about it. I'm only spelling out the terms. I'll give you an answer in two weeks."

He put on his hat. "Fine," he replied as he followed her to the door, wondering what had happened to Miss Harmony Jones to turn a warm, sweet woman-child into something akin to a bitch. Surely it was more than Buck Hanner's supposed desertion. She'd never told him anything about her early life, but being married to her would be interesting indeed, a fascinating challenge and one promising tremendous profits.

Europe was beautiful and interesting, and it kept Harmony's mind off memories better forgotten. She had a new husband now. She was traveling the world, meeting prominent people and seeing famous places. For weeks they traveled by ship from port to port, she playing the role of the beautiful new wife. But she was seldom a wife in the sexual sense. She had allowed

Wade Tillis his husbandly rights on very few occasions since their wedding night, a night that had brought her little pleasure. She had planned on allowing herself to enjoy it, but in the darkness and in a man's arms, she kept picturing herself with Buck. If Buck were making love to her she could enjoy it; she could bring passion to the act.

With Wade, she felt nothing, except a brief moment of carnal release. She wondered if this was how it felt to be a prostitute. She thought it was not for she believed that prostitutes generally enjoyed sex. Harmony did not, unless she was with Buck Hanner. But Tillis had kept his promise to her. He was not demanding or cruel. That kept their marriage civil, and they did enjoy one another's company.

They traveled half the world, it seemed, while back in Cripple Creek Harmony's mine continued to pour out gold and the couple's businesses continued to flourish. But nowhere did Harmony find the peace and pleasure she'd known in the little cabin on the mountain. Her mental picture of that place, and of Buck Hanner, recurred with disturbing frequency. She had not been back there since she'd come down, for she knew if she returned she would probably lose her mind. If she didn't see it again, she would be all right. Eventually the picture would fade, and perhaps some day she could even be a real wife to Wade Tillis.

Until then, their relationship would be all business, with a moment of carnal pleasure here and there. When they returned to Cripple Creek, a huge party was thrown for them at the Mother Lode, and Harmony didn't even care when Dora May Harper hung all over Wade, telling him how much she missed his visits. The laughter and well-wishing all seemed far away to

Harmony, who smiled but felt no true happiness. She did not doubt that Wade Tillis would do whatever she wanted, that he would be a friend and hold her when she needed holding. But she simply did not love him. What she derived from the marriage was a traveling companion—with Wade she could see half the world as a proper lady—and increased wealth.

But the few times he'd made love to her had left her empty and longing for the one man who had been able to truly awaken her passion, the only man she had ever wanted in return. Always she had turned over and wept silently for another, for the mountain, for those golden moments, for her baby, for Buck. It had been over two years since he'd left her on the mountain and he had not been heard from. More and more she realized that he really had abandoned her. All this time she had fought acknowledging that, but her hope of ever seeing him again had now dwindled to nothing. It was best that she had married Wade. She needed and wanted a companion, and her reputation was enhanced by having a proper husband. Single wealthy women seemed to be branded by society, but once she'd married Wade, despite his reputation, others were kinder to her. Women began inviting her to teas and luncheons; men seemed to look at her with more respect.

All but Hank Fisher. Hank had stayed in town while making a small profit off his claim, which Harmony eventually bought up. He ran a livery, and was present the day of the party at the Mother Lode. Harmony smiled and opened gifts and thanked people, but all the while she felt Hank's sad eyes on her. Hank had been the only person to continue to trust Buck Hanner. He was certain Buck wouldn't run out on Harmony, whereas Harmony's own great love for Buck Hanner had not been enough to overcome the damage done to her when she'd been abandoned as a child by her parents. All the fear and horror of that early time had surfaced when Buck had not returned, and in her mind, his continued absence had only proved her suspicions to be right. But Hank Fisher was not convinced. He'd warned her before she'd married Wade Tillis that Buck Hanner would come back, but she had only laughed at him and told him to leave her alone, which he had promptly done; for Harmony Jones Tillis was a changed woman—calculating, bitter, hard. Now she was the wife of Wade Tillis, and that could only destroy her more.

The limited sexual life of Mr. and Mrs. Wade Tillis did not last long. How could that aspect of their marriage endure when she had no such attraction for the man she had wed. Not long after their return to Cripple Creek Wade Tillis showed his more evil side, coming home drunk from the Mother Lode and crawling into Harmony's bed. They kept separate bedrooms, which the servants thought nothing about, for many wealthy couples did so. But the separate bedrooms of Mr. and Mrs. Wade Tillis served another purpose than sleeping in luxurious privacy. When Harmony awoke to Wade's urgent kisses and fondlings, she was angry. She'd already been asleep, and she could smell the liquor on his breath.

She fought him, telling him to get out. But Wade Tillis didn't feel like being obliging that night. He was full of whiskey, and he was tired of making love to a woman who lay beneath him like a dead fish. He wanted her to respond passionately, and he intended to make her. His hands clawed at her, ripping away her nightgown, while his lips searched her body hungrily.

She scratched and kicked, but he hit her hard, startling her, making her dizzy.

"You're my wife!" he growled. "I don't always have to ask your damned permission to take my pleasure with you!"

"We made a pact!" she declared, despite her stunned condition.

"To hell with that!" he hissed. "I want you. I love you."

"You don't love me!" she whispered angrily, afraid of waking the servants. "You love my money! I'd like you better if you were honest about it! When you say you love me, it makes me want to laugh!"

He pinned her against the bed, keeping his huge frame on top of her. "All right, Mrs. Tillis. I love your money. But I've not been a bad husband. Admit it!"

She started crying. "Please, Wade, don't do this. At least we must remain friends!"

He sighed deeply, then ran a hand over her bare breasts to her throat, squeezing it until she thought he might choke her to death. "You and your damned Buck! That's it, isn't it! In all this time you've never forgotten that worthless drifter! What was so great about Buck Hanner, my love! Was he bigger than your husband?" He sneered.

Her eyes widened with rage at the ludicrous remark. Then he got up from the bed and began to dress. "Sleep with your goddamned memories from now on!" he told her. "I'll not crawl for you! I'll take my pleasures over at the Mother Lode. You can have your privacy! I want you, but not badly enough to beg!"

"Go ahead!" she spat at him. "Go to Dora May! She'll let you grovel over her like an animal!"

"At least she knows how to make a man feel like a man!" he grumbled. He tucked in his shirt and stared down at her. "I wonder if you'll ever be a real woman, Harmony." His tone was contemptuous. "I suppose big Buck Hanner made you one, but he's gone now and life goes on!"

"Stop it! You talk about what Buck and I had as if it were something ugly! It was beautiful! We were in love!"

"You were in love!" he shouted. "He used you, you stupid bitch! I've married you! I've given you respectability. Well, we'll keep the outward appearances of a proper man and wife, but I'll not disturb your sleep anymore. If you want a sleeping companion, go draw out a bundle of money and sleep with that! That's what you married me for!"

She glared at him. "And that's what you married me for!"

He grinned. "Exactly! Pardon my moment of drunken desire. I almost forgot myself. But remember that Buck Hanner was a no-good, and I've done right by you. Remember who's been the better man, whether it was for love or for money! Your Buck Hanner is never coming back, and someday it will be Wade Tillis you pant for!"

"Never!" she screamed.

"You stupid little bitch!" He put on his coat and turned to the door, then glanced back at her. "Right now I ought to tell you—" He caught himself. How tempting it was at this moment to laugh at her and tell her the real truth, that it was Wade Tillis, her own husband, who had seen to it that Buck Hanner would never share her bed again, never have access to her wealth. He'd made a fine profit from selling Buck to the

367

slave dealers, and he'd ensured Buck's death at the same time. But the ultimate glory had been in marrying Harmony Jones and taking what Buck Hanner had claimed for himself. He'd had his satisfaction. He didn't need her that way anymore.

"Tell me what?" she asked suspiciously.

He just grinned. "Forget it. Go to sleep with your pillow and pretend it's good ole Buck!" He walked out, slamming the door behind him.

Harmony collapsed into tears, disobeying her vow to never cry again. Finally exhausted, she curled up, hugging her pillow and calling Buck's name softly. She hated him for what he'd done, yet she still loved him, wherever he was! How could a woman love and hate with equal passion? And what had happened to the sweet little girl she'd once been before her parents had abandoned her? That little girl had vanished a long time ago. The sweet shyness, the gentle desire to give and please had been reawakened once, on the side of a mountain in a little shack in the middle of winter—by a man. Buck. Sweet, beautiful Buck. But he had betrayed her in the worst way, just as everyone else she'd loved had. Why? If only he would come back, hold her again, give her some kind of explanation. But she had stopped actively hoping for that, and she knew she'd never believe him now. Besides, she was married to Wade Tillis. She would never again know love and happiness in a man's arms. Buck had done this to her. Buck and Jimmie and Brian and her parents. They all had contributed to her bitter unhappiness. She had nothing left now but her wealth, and she fell asleep thinking about other ways to make more money.

Chapter Eighteen

Jimmie O'Toole looked up from his desk when he felt a presence. His eyes widened at the sight of the beautiful woman who stood before him, wearing a gored skirt and bolero jacket, in the latest fashion. The entire outfit seemed like a sea of green silk, the short jacket fitted at her slim waist, the puffed sleeves making her waist appear even thinner. He hesitated for just a moment, studying the beautiful green eyes and the upswept blond hair graced with a round straw hat. She held a parasol that matched the rest of her clothing.

"Harmony?" he asked, almost hesitantly.

She looked him over slowly, as though studying an ugly bug that she was about to squash.

"Hello, Jimmie."

He rose, frowning, his curiosity piqued. "Hello." His eyes roved over her as he stepped back slightly. "Well, you look like a pampered woman. Your little claim must have done right by you."

She smiled, the kind of evil, glittering smile Wade Tillis would bestow on someone he was about to cheat or destroy. "It did quite well, thank you. A million, so far. But it's dwindling now. All mines play out eventually." She turned and began walking down one of the aisles of the supply store. Jimmie followed eagerly, his heart swelling with jealousy, but his mind hopeful that she'd come to bail him out of his own bankrupt situation. Perhaps she'd give him a good deal of money. After all, his brother had raised her and taken care of her all those years.

"At any rate," she was saying, "my husband and I have invested wisely, so when the mine goes, it will be no problem. We own a great deal of Cripple Creek, and have made other . . ."—she looked around the store—"investments."

She turned to face him haughtily. "And how are you doing, Jimmie?"

He just stared at her, wary of the feeling of hatred and revenge her eyes revealed.

He swallowed. "Uh . . . fine . . . just fine."

She laughed lightly. "No you're not. You never could tell the truth, Jimmie O'Toole. And I knew you'd never last three years with this place once I left. That's how long it's been, hasn't it? Let's see . . . I left in the spring of '96 and now it's the spring of '99. Yes, three years."

"What the hell are you after?" he suddenly growled from where he stood behind her.

She turned and frowned, pursing her lips. "Why Jimmie! Is that any way to talk to your long-lost . . . h'm . . . what was I to you, anyway? A niece, perhaps?"

He breathed deeply for control, realizing if he lost his temper he'd never get a thing out of her.

"I always thought of you as a friend," he lied. "Brian

370

took care of you, was good to you. He gave you a home, food and clothing. And you and I worked this store together."

She smiled softly. "We did, didn't we?" She turned and began walking again, stopping here and there to inspect the merchandise. Her behavior made him uneasy, as though she were some kind of buyer, and jealousy raged even higher in his soul at the realization of how rich she had become off his brother's claim. "Aren't you going to ask about my husband?" she was asking.

He followed behind. "All right. I'm asking."

"His name is Wade Tillis. He was the richest man in Cripple Creek, and I was the richest woman. So, it was a logical union."

He let out a quick snicker. "You married each other for your money?"

She turned, wanting to hurt him as much as possible, remembering the night of horror he'd inflicted on her. "Of course," she replied softly. "But there were other reasons, the usual reasons a man and woman get married. I must say it's been quite enjoyable. Wade is forty-three, old enough to know how to handle a woman . . . properly." She faced him. "How about you, Jimmie? You married yet?"

He glared at her. "No."

She looked him over scathingly. "I'm not surprised. You probably still don't know what to do with a decent girl. You've spent too many years with the whores, my darling."

He glared at her, his fists clenching. "Why don't you just tell me the real reason you're here?" he asked. "I don't suppose you're going to do the right thing by me and lend me a little of that million you've made?"

A customer entered, and she stepped closer to him, talking softly. "Do right by you?" Her green eyes turned to slits of hatred, and she spoke in a near whisper so the customer would not hear. "If I did right by you, I'd kill you!" she hissed. Instantly her face changed to a pleasant smile again, and her eyes had evil laughter in them. "You better go wait on your customer, Jimmie dear."

He just stared at her a moment, then left. She roamed the store while he waited on two more men, her ears picking up his words when he told one of them he'd have to refuse him credit.

"I need the money, Bill," she heard him saying. Harmony smiled. Yes, indeed. She'd had her revenge on Buck Hanner by marrying his hated enemy and becoming the richest woman in Colorado. Now she would get her revenge on Jimmie. Slowly but surely she would hurt every person who had ever hurt her. If only she could find her parents, she'd find a way to hurt them too. But at least in her own mind she felt revenged for their abandonment by surviving and becoming a wealthy and powerful woman. If only they could see her now!

She walked out then. Wondering what she was up to, Jimmie wanted to stop her, but he had more customers. The rest of the day his mind dwelt on Harmony. Why had she come, and why had she left again so abruptly? For the rest of the day he worried. His night was sleepless. Where had she gone? Why hadn't she returned?

The next day at the store seemed endless. Every time the door opened he hoped it would be Harmony so they could finish talking. He wanted to tell her he needed money, to apologize for how he'd hurt her years before. Maybe that would work—an apology. Customers came and went, but she did not appear. He didn't even have an address for her, other than Cripple Creek. He wondered where she was staying. If he knew, he'd go and see her. Deep inside he wanted to do more than see her. He wanted to give her what he'd never been able to give her, a sound thrashing, after which he would rip off her clothes and show her he knew exactly how to handle a woman. So, she was married, was she? She'd taken a man, had she? Maybe she'd be easier now, maybe curious. Sometimes the married ones—

The door opened. It was late and he was already closing the store. "You'll have to come back tomorrow," he called out.

There was no reply so he walked around the end of an aisle and looked toward the front door. Harmony stood there with two men, one of them a law officer.

"Hello, Jimmie," Harmony spoke quietly, a sly grin on her face.

His heart pounded and he slowly approached them, sweat breaking out on his brow. She was wearing a deep blue velvet suit, one that enhanced her beautiful shape. He remembered the sweet, innocent look he'd often seen in her eyes years ago. There was no trace of that look in them now.

"What's going on?" he asked cautiously.

"This is my store now, Jimmie. I'm here to warn you not to come back in the morning."

He frowned. "Your store!" His breathing quickened. "I don't recall selling it, or signing anything!"

"Oh, I've brought papers. And you had no choice in

selling it. I happen to know you were going bankrupt. I had it all checked out before I even came to St. Louis. The bank owns everything—not you. So I paid them off. Now, if you'll just sign the papers I brought, I'll give you five hundred dollars to tide you over until you find some other source of income."

He stepped closer, his fists clenched, but the two men accompanying her stepped forward threateningly.

"Five hundred dollars?" he hissed.

"Yes. I think that's being quite generous, considering I don't have to pay you a thing—and considering what you did to me a few years ago. I believe there was a time when you gave me no ultimatum, Jimmie dear. Now I'm doing the same with you." She held out the papers, her eyes suddenly icy. "Take it or leave it!" she said coolly. "Five hundred is better than nothing, isn't it?"

He stared at her for several seconds, then grasped the papers. He looked at the men accompanying her. "There must be some kind of law that gives me a couple of weeks to get things together, to try to get a loan."

The man smiled. "Sorry."

Jimmie stared at him, suddenly getting the whole picture. Harmony had paid them off! That was it! She'd paid them to help her kick him out of his own store! He turned his eyes to the other man, who smiled.

"I'm Jonathan Brodie, a partner in your own attorney's law firm," he informed Jimmie. "There's no use going to your lawyer, Mister O'Toole. He has already agreed to all of this. I would suggest you go along with Mrs. Tillis. Do you understand?"

There was a warning look in his eyes that Jimmie understood only too well. So, Harmony had thought of everything. She'd paid off all of the right people. He looked at her.

"You hate me this much?"

Her eyes glittered. "Obviously I hate you enough to ruin you, and perhaps to go even farther," she said threateningly. He swallowed. Realizing she just might do that, he broke out in a sweat as he walked to the counter and began signing the papers, not even really seeing what he was signing. He felt like crying, but he would save that for later. He looked at Harmony with bloodshot eyes and handed the papers back.

"I . . . I don't suppose it would help to tell you . . . I'm sorry?"

She folded the papers. "Not in the least." She shoved the papers into a folder. "Oh, be sure to gather your things at the house, Jimmie. It's mine now, and I've rented it to someone else, including the furnishings. So be sure to take only your personal belongings."

His eyes widened. "What! But I . . . I don't have anyplace to live! I don't have a job!"

"That is your problem, Jimmie dear. I've given you five hundred dollars to tide you over." She looked at the attorney. "Mister Brodie, we almost forgot. Give him the money."

Brodie dug into his pocket and handed five bills to Jimmie, who took them with a shaking hand.

"There now," Harmony told him. "We're all settled. Good luck, Jimmie dear. I hope you find something. Just don't apply here, though. You never did know how to handle this store and I don't care to employ you, not under these circumstances. You understand, of course."

Their eyes held in mutual hatred. "Of course," he replied curtly.

"Fine. Now if you will hand me the keys to the store, we'll all leave . . . you first."

In a near daze, he went behind the counter to get the keys. Then he handed them to her and walked out without another word.

She frowned and shook her head. "Poor Jimmie," she chuckled. Then she looked up at the two men. "Shall we go, gentlemen?"

Harmony casually walked along the busy St. Louis street. It felt nice to be back in a civilized city. She and Wade had done what they could to bring some culture to Cripple Creek, but there was something about Western towns that kept them from seeming truly refined and graceful, even Denver. The cities in the West grew too quickly to establish cultural backgrounds. They were all still babies, and they usually died before reaching maturity. She could see that beginning to happen to Cripple Creek, and she and Wade had already begun investing in businesses in Denver, a more stable city.

She thought about Wade. He hadn't really been unkind to her, except the one night when he'd had too much whiskey. She knew he didn't love her, that he'd simply wanted to enjoy her in bed a few times and to reap the benefits of her money. Their marriage was a fake, yet it had benefited both of them. It did give her respectability and companionship. After his abusive behavior there had been a few days of angry looks; then they had come to civil terms again; and although he spent most of his time at the Mother Lode, and many of his nights in the upper rooms of that notorious saloon, they remained good friends. He had not touched her since the night she'd told him to leave. She felt a little guilty about that. She was, after all, his wife; and at the moment she was feeling exhilarated over the way she'd handled Jimmie O'Toole. Perhaps when she returned to Cripple Creek she would be more obliging to her husband. Wade Tillis was the only man in her life now, and she was, after all, only twenty. Perhaps she could learn to enjoy his touch. At any rate, she felt like celebrating, and she wanted to thank Wade for letting her come here. They would both have a good laugh over how she had handled things; she knew Wade would toast her victory, again stressing their similarity.

A little voice deep inside tried to tell her she was nothing like Wade Tillis, that her hardness was all just show, her way of covering up the bitter hurts deep in the recesses of her mind and heart. But that little voice was muffled by her determination to get revenge, and her belief that security lay only in money and power. She had that now. No one could hurt Harmony Jones again. She had been a sweet and giving and trusting woman only once; she had experienced real love only once. It had brought her the worst heartache and depression she'd ever known, and there was no man she hated more than Buck Hanner.

She walked into a store that sold both men's and women's hats and began to try a few on. It was then she saw him, reflected in the mirror, his back to her. Broad shoulders, cotton plaid shirt, and thick, sandy hair. From the back he looked so much like . . .

She turned, setting down the hat she held. The man was paying a clerk as Harmony rose, her heart pounding. She hated him, didn't she? If she did, why

377

was this terrible, heated flutter making her feel faint? Why did she suddenly envision falling into his arms? Why did the old Harmony who had loved Buck Hanner surface so quickly and easily? Everything about the back of this man reminded her of Buck Hanner, and fire ripped through her veins.

He turned around then, frowning a little at the lovely young woman who stared at him as though he were a ghost. "Ma'am? Anything I can do for you?" he asked.

It was not Buck. She felt like crying. What had made her think she would casually run into her old lover in the streets of St. Louis? Surely he was out on the plains of the Dakotas, or maybe in Texas, running his fine ranch. Her cheeks reddened.

"I . . . no. I'm sorry," she stammered. "I thought . . . you were someone else."

The man smiled, a pleasant smile but not nearly as handsome as Buck Hanner's. His teeth were not as white and even, his eyes were not the beautiful sky blue that Buck's were. He nodded to her and walked out the door, and Harmony grasped the counter for support. She stood there a moment, regaining her composure, before she managed to move her legs to walk out the door.

The day was spoiled now. She'd been cruelly reminded of Buck Hanner, sharply made aware of the fact that she was not over him at all. Perhaps she never would be. She blindly called a carriage and half stumbled into it, directing the driver to take her to her hotel. Minutes later she descended from the equipage, and made her way to her room. In its privacy, she collapsed onto the bed and wept.

Buck! Why? Why had he left? Again the tiny voice

378

warned her he never would have done so deliberately. But everyone she loved and depended on had left her. That was what was so pleasant about Wade Tillis. She didn't love or trust him, so it didn't matter if he left. But Buck! She'd been so sure she was over him, that if she ever saw him again she could look him straight in the eyes and flaunt her new marriage and her wealth. She realized she must train herself, keep her senses and realize she might someday see Buck Hanner again, and if she did she must be ready for it. She must hurt him in any way she could, and never show her own hurt.

Still, this encounter with someone who merely resembled Buck had undone her. She was angry with herself for reacting as she had, for thinking she could still love Buck Hanner even a bit. How could she be such an ignorant fool?

She turned on her back and stared at the ceiling, tears running down the sides of her cheeks. She would be nice to Wade when she got back. Maybe that would help. She got revenge on Buck Hanner by taking Wade Tillis back to her bed and learning to enjoy being intimate with him. There was nothing wrong with that. After all, they were legally married. Why did she feel like a bad woman when she was in bed with her own husband? She had not felt that way when Buck Hanner had bedded her, and she and Buck had never even married. Yet he had told her they were married, in mind and heart. Maybe that was it. She had never "divorced" Buck Hanner. He still owned her, even though he'd never married her and had run out on her. He was the only man who had awakened her true passions and desires. Apparently there were two kinds of marriages: the legal ones, without love; and the ones with love but no legal papers.

How long she lay there, she wasn't certain, but finally she sat up and walked over to the dresser, sitting down and staring into the mirror. So, in her mind and heart she was still married to Buck Hanner. That was the problem. She would simply have to forget him, erase him from her mind and heart, learn to face facts. She took out a handkerchief and wiped at her eyes and nose, angry that she had let herself cry over a man who had been so cruel to her. At least Wade had not done that. She would go home to Wade, and she would be a wife to him. She would let him erase Buck Hanner from her soul.

She became aware of fire bells then, which she had been hearing for more than an hour. She walked to the window of her room. Several blocks away black smoke curled. She frowned. It was in the area of her supply store. But she was too tired to bother to go and check on it. When there was a fire, it was best to stay away. She walked back to the bed and sat down, wondering what Jimmie had done with himself since she'd kicked him out of the store the night before. She smiled at the memory of the look on his face—so shocked and devastated. That was good. She liked that. She began removing her shoes. She liked the power she had now. If she could just find a way to use it against Buck Hanner someday, she'd be happier. Perhaps she should hire men to search for him. Perhaps she could find Buck's ranch and figure out a way to ruin him.

She had just taken off her shoes when a knock sounded. She lifted her dress and walked on bare feet to the door, hesitating before opening it. "Who is it?"

"Police, ma'am."

She unlatched the door and opened it a crack. "Yes?"

"We came to tell you, ma'am, that a store you just purchased is on fire. One of the employees who came running out gave us your name, said you'd just hired him and several other people and that you'd be here a few days yet."

She opened the door wider. "Is it bad?"

The two policemen removed their hats. "I'm afraid so, ma'am," the spokesman replied. "It's going right to the ground. The firemen are working hard to save the buildings beside it. And . . . uh . . . we think it might have been set deliberately."

She frowned and motioned for them to come inside. "Deliberately?"

"Yes, ma'am. Some man came there all drunk, according to the employee. He was bragging about how he'd once owned the store and still did as far as he was concerned. The young man stormed toward the back of the store, and the next thing he knew, there was a fire. The firemen dragged a body out later. It was burned pretty badly, but the man had probably died from inhaling to much smoke. The employee told us it looked like the man who'd come storming into the store earlier. He thinks that man set the fire on purpose, then got caught in his own flames. We took identification from him. His name was Jimmie O'Toole. You know him?"

Her eyes remained cold. At last—the ultimate revenge! "I knew him once. I came here a few days ago to buy the store. He was quite upset, but I can't help that."

The policemen waited for some sign of remorse about what had happened to O'Toole, some voiced pity. But Harmony did not refer to O'Toole.

"Well," she declared, holding her chin high, "I'll just have to have the store rebuilt, won't I?"

Buck threw water across the deck of the merchant ship and began to mop, watching his guard out of the corner of his eyes. This was the first time in months he'd been allowed on deck and freed of iron cuffs, the first time since he'd tried to escape when they'd docked in San Francisco. He didn't want to be punished as he'd been then. Such pain and torture was not something easily forgotten. His back and legs would forever bear the scars of the brutal lashing he'd suffered, and how he'd lived through the ensuing infections and filth and near starvation he didn't know, except for his dreams of the mountain . . . and Harmony.

Every bone and muscle in his body raged with a need to get away, to get to Harmony and explain, whatever her circumstances were now. Even if he could not have her back, he had to tell her what had happened so she wouldn't think he'd abandoned her as others had done. His determination to prove himself, and his love for her, kept him going when other men would have succumbed.

For over two years he had lived in this hell, watching others around him die terrible deaths. He'd endured whippings and humiliation, filth and backbreaking work, wormy bread and brackish water. His strength came from his enduring determination not to die, but to live and to escape, face Tillis again and watch the man pale with fear before he killed him with his bare hands. That he would surely do.

He was thin now, and not very strong. It would take weeks of eating good food and of resting before he could begin to resemble the old Buck Hanner. He had lost a lot of other things that had been a part of the old Buck Hanner too: his casual attitude toward life, his gentle side, his easygoing nature. There had been only ugliness in his life for too long, too much brutality, too much pain. The only beauty left was a memory—of a mountain, and of a beautiful girl with blond hair.

Somehow he had to touch land again, to live like a normal human being. He had to find his precious Harmony. Land! People! The mountains! How sick he was of ships' holds and the stench of mold and the sea. He was not made for such a life, nor was he made to be another man's servant, treated like a pig, beaten for every wrong move. Seldom was there a chance for escape, for most of the time he was at sea, but here, on deck, docked in San Francisco, he had his first chance in months. San Francisco! America! He was home, and he was determined that this time he would not leave this land, even if he had to remain here as a corpse.

He looked at his guard again. A huge man with bulging muscles, he was well fed and in much better physical shape than Buck. But Buck Hanner's driving desire for freedom would give him strength. He slowly worked the mop, grateful that the docks were bustling with activity. The movement often took the guard's eyes from him. He looked down the dock and saw several gaudy women approaching. He grinned. If ever there was a good diversion, it was women, especially after a man had been at sea for months. He would have taken pleasure in watching them himself if he hadn't had more urgent matters to deal with. He waited until the women came closer, cautiously watching his guard as the man's eyes strayed to them. Obviously they were whores looking for customers, hungry men from the sea who would pay a fortune for their first night with a woman in months. The women wore bright dresses, cut low to reveal an abundance of cleavage, and the guard watched them like a hungry wolf, ogling them as they went by.

Never had opportunity been riper. Why it seemed so easy, Buck wasn't sure. Perhaps God was helping him, although he'd stopped praying a long time ago. He would have to move fast, very fast. He swung the mop hard, its metal clamp landing on the guard's temple and sending the man reeling. Instantly Buck jumped over the side, and just as quickly several more guards ran to the rail and began firing into the water.

Buck desperately swam deeper under water, aware that bullets were skimming the water all around him. He hadn't had a chance to take a good deep breath, nor was he strong enough to swim very far. He headed in the direction of the docks, keeping under water as long as possible and finally coming up for air beneath the wet, wooden docks.

He could hear running and shouting overhead. Some of the guards had disembarked and were running up and down the dock, waiting for him to emerge. He soundlessly sidestroked to a concrete wall, then hung on to a slippery post jutting out from it. Gasping for air, he slipped very quietly along the wall, keeping far back under the docks. Whenever the footsteps were right overhead, he dived, continuing to feel his way along the concrete wall, his heart beating with excitement. He was escaping this time. Home! He was home, in America! If he could just get through this, he would go back to Colorado, to the mountains, to Harmony!

When he came up for air again, he spotted part of an old boat, half its small hull still intact, which had drifted up under the dock. He headed for it, turning it over his head, creating a pocket of air but hiding himself. He stayed beneath the remains of the hull for what seemed like hours, until it was finally dark. Then he worked his way farther down the docks. He felt like a shriveled prune, and he was shivering from the cold of the water and chilly night. He had on nothing but his trousers now for he had slipped off his boots shortly after he'd hit the water. He kept moving until he knew he was well away from the hated ship, at least a half mile, he thought.

Darkness brought safety. Taking courage from the dim light and the fewer people on the docks, Buck moved cautiously toward the edge of the pier. Grasping at the overhead boards, he slowly moved out, hanging on to the ends of the boards and raising his head. He almost laughed aloud, for no one was in sight. He knew his own ship was due to make for the sea by early morning. They'd not spend a lot of time searching for one man. They'd gotten their money's worth and then some out of Buck Hanner anyway.

But he couldn't be too careful. He worked his way even farther down, then hoisted himself up and hastily crawled into an alley. He was chilled, quivering. He wondered if he would die of pneumonia after all he'd gone through to be free again. He moved quietly through the alley and into a back street. He heard voices and music in the distance, but he had no money and was wearing only his trousers. He could think of only one kind of person that just might help him. He hurried down the street toward the booming piano music and the mixture of men's and women's voices shouting and laughing.

Buck awoke to soft sheets, thinking at first he must be dreaming. He rolled onto his back and stretched, rubbing his eyes and opening them to view gaudy wallpaper, pink with red roses. He curled his nose and blinked, then allowed his tired eyes to meet the brilliant wallpaper again. Finally he glanced around the room, which held only the bed and a dresser, and a few flashy dresses that hung on hooks on the walls.

He ran a hand through his hair, sitting up slightly and trying to remember where he might be. This was certainly not the hold of a ship. Even the scent of cheap perfume in the air smelled wonderful. He moved his aching legs back and forth against the wonderfully soft sheets, then realized he was naked. He looked down at himself in surprise, seeing also that he was very clean. Someone had bathed him. He felt his face, and it was shaved smooth, without even a cut.

He settled back and smiled. Whatever this was, it was certainly not a prison. Tears came to his eyes at the realization that he must be free. It was glorious to awaken to a clean body and clean sheets and a real room on land! This room did not sway and lean. It did not stink. A breeze came through the open window then, carrying with it the scent of the sea and creating momentary panic in him. He was starting to rise, to go to the window and make sure he was on land, when the door opened and a young girl with raven black hair entered. She was wearing a silk robe that was obviously her only covering. The points of her large breasts were clearly visible beneath the cloth as she came closer.

"Hello," she said with a soft smile.

He nodded, and she sat down on the edge of the bed. "How do you feel?"

"I . . . I'm not sure yet," he replied, looking her over. She wasn't really very pretty, yet after his long imprisonment he supposed she was the most beautiful thing he'd seen in a long time. She had an Oriental look about her, but she wasn't a full-blood. "Where am I?"

Her smile widened and she put a hand to his face. "You're at Madam Lucy's saloon and boardinghouse," she replied. "Don't you remember coming here?"

He blinked. "I remember . . . a door . . . a woman opening it and smiling and telling me I was the sorriest-looking thing she'd seen in a long time. I remember following someone . . . up some stairs . . . some remark about how maybe I'd not be a bad trick . . . if I was clean."

The girl laughed. "That was Madam Lucy." She ran a hand over his chest. "We all took turns bathing you," she added seductively. "From what we saw, there's quite a man dwelling in that too-thin frame. We all decided to fatten you up and see what we'd end up with. That was two days ago."

He grinned, looking around the room. "Is this real?"

His eyes moved back to her as she opened the robe, letting it fall to her waist and revealing a huge bosom. "It's real," she answered, leaning toward him and kissing his chest. He grasped her arms.

"Wait. Look at me."

She frowned and met his eyes. "Is this some kind of trick?" he asked. "I may be a wanted man."

She giggled. "You're wanted, all right. We drew straws. I won."

He sighed. "You don't understand. I have to be careful. Am I still in San Francisco?"

She leaned over him again, resting her weight on an elbow. "Of course. We knew you might be in some kind of trouble. Who could miss the scars on your back and legs. We bathed you, remember?" She took his hand. "Look, mister, we aren't stupid. We've worked these docks for a long time. We know a shanghaied sailor when we see one. It isn't our business how you got away. We're glad you did, that's all. We've helped men in trouble before. Madam Lucy doesn't mind. All we ask is that you stay around a little while, work off whatever you feel you owe us"—she smiled then, kissing his chest again—"and . . . service those of us who find you irresistible."

She kissed him lightly, but he only frowned. "Look, I'm pretty weak. I don't feel so good. I think I need to eat something."

She sighed and sat up. Looking disappointed, she retied her robe. He grasped her arm as she rose.

"What's your name?"

"Tillie."

"Mine's Buck."

She nodded. "All right, Buck. I'll get you some food."

He continued to hold her arm. "I'm sorry, Tillie, but you don't know what I've been through. And it's been . . . it's been about two years since I was . . . with a woman. Do you understand? I need some time. And I need to get my strength back."

She sat back down, putting a hand to his hair. "I understand. Don't worry about it. Just promise you'll stay a little while after you're stronger, and promise you'll pick me when you're ready for a woman."

He grinned, and even the loss of weight could not hide his handsomeness. "I promise. But I can only stay long enough to work off my debt, and maybe earn a little extra to get me to Colorado."

"Colorado?" She studied him closely. "A woman, I suppose."

His eyes teared with a mixture of great relief and joy. He'd done it! He was free, and in time he'd be strong enough to head for the Rockies—and Harmony! "Yes," he answered in a near whisper. He swallowed in an attempt to regain control of his emotions, and even the whore Tillie was touched. She leaned over and kissed him again.

"Well then, we'll help you get strong enough to go to her. In the meantime, you can get practice on how to handle a woman again, with me. I'm sure it will all come back to you with no trouble."

She expected him to laugh, but he suddenly pulled her close, clinging to her. "Stay a while," he whispered. "Just stay a while and hold me."

She wrapped her arms around him and kissed his hair. "Sure, honey. Everything will be all right. You'll see."

Chapter Nineteen

Harmony stayed in St. Louis long enough to organize the rebuilding of the supply store and to hire the best men she could find to manage the enterprise once it opened. She did not attend Jimmie O'Toole's funeral, and since he had no family left, only a few of his acquaintances attended. Harmony was not concerned. She merely reflected that there was no problem with the distribution of his property, for he had none left to distribute. Everything now belonged to Harmony Jones Tillis. She surmised that Wade Tillis would get a good laugh out of how it had all worked out. Unlike Buck, Tillis had shown no particular concern or sympathy when she'd explained what Jimmie had done to her. He'd only laughed, and told her if it would humor her to go to St. Louis to see if she could buy out Jimmie O'Toole, she was free to go. To her delight, she'd discovered Jimmie was already losing the business. The rest had been easy.

Now she would go back to Cripple Creek, and as she had promised herself, she would be a better wife to

Wade. She truly did feel like celebrating. She boarded the Kansas Pacific in elegant attire, riding in a private compartment. It was late July, 1899, and the compartment was warm, but comfortable. The train lurched forward and was off; Harmony was headed back to Cripple Creek.

She glanced out the window, thinking how different things were now. On her first trip to Colorado, she had been so young and stupid, so innocent and determined. She'd had no money, but she had made up her mind that her claim would make her rich. It had all worked out just as she'd planned, and she was even married to the very man who had tried to stop her, the man she had boldly faced down on her arrival at Cripple Creek. Things couldn't have turned out better for the naïve woman-child who'd had nothing to go on but courage. Only one thing had gone wrong . . . Buck Hanner.

She watched the scenery fly past. Buck Hanner . . . where was he now? Was he happy? And why did she care whether he was or not? He certainly didn't care about how she was, or he never would have deserted her. Yet there were times when she remembered vividly the feel of his arms around her, the sweetness of his kiss, her happiness at hearing his whispered words of love. It had all been so beautiful. Why had he crushed her so cruelly? That had happened over two years ago, and she was just beginning to get over him.

Yes, she was getting over him. Of that she was certain. She actually was looking forward to going home to Wade. She was different now, much different from the Harmony Jones who'd first come west. She was older, wiser, more hardened, hardened the way a businesswoman had to be hardened. Living on the mountain had hardened her physically, and Buck Hanner's desertion had hardened her emotionally. Perhaps she should thank Buck for throwing reality into her face. Because of Buck Hanner no one could ever hurt her again, because she would never allow that to happen . . . and because she would never love again. Love was dangerous to those who wanted only wealth and power. Wade understood that. Harmony was now beginning to understand it herself. Love only complicated matters. It made people stray from their true goals, stray from what was really important.

She smiled at the thought of Jimmie O'Toole, remembering the look on his face when she'd pulled the store out from under him, thinking it ironic that he'd been caught in the fire he'd set to get revenge. Jimmie O'Toole had lived to regret trying to rape Harmony Jones. Now she would like Buck Hanner to know she'd married Wade Tillis, and if she ever learned where he was, she'd find a way to destroy him. That left her parents. She'd probably never locate them, never be able to tell them what she thought of them for abandoning her on the docks, but to her dying day she'd remember that feeling, that night. It haunted her. Sometimes she still woke up screaming.

She settled back in her seat, which folded out into a bed for sleeping. This train was faster than the first one she'd taken, making fewer stops and rumbling on right through the night. By the third day of her journey she'd be in Colorado; then she'd take the Denver & Rio Grande to Colorado Springs, and again travel by stage to Cripple Creek. It would be the same old journey, but not the same old Harmony.

On the third day, as the train clattered through the

393

Colorado plains, more tender thoughts of Buck Hanner disturbed Harmony. Occasionally she spotted one or two men riding on the golden, rolling hills, herding a few cattle ahead of them. Buck had once been such a man, a cowboy. At first glance it seemed every man she spotted on a horse was Buck Hanner. She recalled his easy manner in the saddle—he might have been born on a horse—and she thought about Indian and Pepper. She missed them. Pepper had been sold when she'd purchased Jack Leads's supply store, because Harmony could not bear to look at the animal. The little mare had made her think of Buck. Indian had not been seen again, nor had his owner, Buck Hanner. The disappearance of the horse had coincided with that of the man, and to Harmony that was a good reason to believe Buck had run off. If he'd been attacked, Indian would probably have shown up sooner or later. But then, he might have been stolen.

She scowled, feeling like kicking herself. It was ridiculous to be looking for an excuse for Buck Hanner. He was gone, yet her mind had strayed to thoughts of him. Her heart had fluttered at the mere sight of cowboys in the hills. What was wrong with her? One moment she was strong and sure, the next weakened by memories. It was a constant merry-go-round. If only Buck Hanner's memory were not so powerful . . . if only he'd been uglier, perhaps cruel to her . . . If the memory of being with him was not so beautiful, it would not stir passions long buried. She had been foolish to allow herself to fall in love with him.

Life was so full of irony. She'd been determined never to love or trust, yet she'd quickly fallen for sky-blue eyes and a tanned, handsome face, the security of powerful arms and the sweet words that had made her trust him so explicitly. Then he had turned on her. Her greatest fear had been realized. She had had a cruel lesson in not trusting. It was probably as much her fault as Buck's. She'd been weak. She had allowed the softer side of her to show. The love that Harmony had been unable to show for her parents as a little girl had come out through loving a man, and it had been spurned as her love for her parents had been.

She disembarked in Denver, and pampered herself by staying at the finest hotel and eating a sinfully expensive meal. She knew Wade wouldn't care. He'd want her to live high. The next morning she boarded the Denver & Rio Grande and was off again, the train's whistle and the clattering wheels echoing back from the nearby mountains. She gazed at peak after snowy peak, remembering another time, another mountain. It was quiet up there, and one could pretend there was no world down below, no people, no civilization, no pain and sorrow, no heartache, no tears. A mountain stood fast despite adversity, oblivious to human emotion. She wished she could be like that.

Perhaps she should go back into the mountains, where she could think quietly. But then she would remember . . . another time, another Harmony, and a man. It was a different Harmony who had lived in the mountains. Sometimes it seemed that time had never really happened. Perhaps if Buck hadn't been her first man . . . if she hadn't given herself to him in such trust . . .

She gritted her teeth. She was doing it again. This had to stop. The memory of Buck Hanner, of the grave up there in the mountains—the tiny grave that held all that remained of the love affair between Buck Hanner and Harmony Jones—she must erase them from her mind. She'd never spoken to anyone about that affair, except Wade, and she'd seldom mentioned it to him. Yet she knew others talked about it. She was aware of their whispers, of their remarks: "It's too bad" or "How sad." Once she had even heard a man singing of her love on a corner. He'd strummed a guitar, and the words of his song told about "the lady on the mountain," with the "golden hair" and the "cowboy who'd loved her and had gone who knows where." "Oh, where is the cowboy, who left his true love?" the song had asked. Harmony had not lingered to listen, but deep inside she had felt the ballad was incomplete. It would never be complete until she discovered what had happened to Buck Hanner, and gotten her revenge for his cruel trick that destroyed her trust, her most precious possession, and for stealing her virginity . . . and her gold.

For four days after his awakening at Madam Lucy's, Buck lay abed, sleeping away the time between the huge meals that were brought to him on trays. He had not eaten such wonderful food in two years, and he ate everything in sight. He was determined to get his strength back as quickly as possible.

In the quiet moments when he was awake and alone, he would sometimes just stare at the gaudy flowered wallpaper in the room, appreciating its colors in spite of its ugliness. At least this place and its women represented softness and caring and gentleness, things he had not known for a long time, and the women here had been good to him. Somehow he'd find a way to pay them back, but first he had to get his strength back so he could go to Colorado and find Harmony—and kill Wade Tillis. He did not doubt that he must do it, no matter what the consequences. But the tired face and the thin arms he saw in the full-length mirror beside the bed told him he must be patient. He looked like a skeleton, and now that he'd had a chance to rest, he wondered how he had survived the rigors of the ship, how he had escaped. Even now, when he tried to stand he felt so weak and dizzy he crawled right back into bed.

He sighed and closed his eyes. Harmony. She had kept him going—kept him alive. Sweet, beautiful Harmony Jones. Now that he was safe and knew he could return to her, his survival instinct had surrendered to extreme exhaustion and malnourishment. He could afford to relax now, to give in to his body's need to rest and rebuild itself. He no longer had to force himself to get up and work for fear of a brutal whipping. He didn't have to force down slop instead of food, because it might keep him alive. Now he could go back to Colorado in time, so he allowed himself to think about Harmony and the winter he'd spent with her. On the ship, he hadn't let his thoughts dwell on that time, for it hurt too much to remember it. Now he was free to dream, and to remember. He could allow himself to visualize Harmony's emerald green eyes, her thick blond hair, and her soft curves. He could remember the feel of her full, young breasts, the sweet taste of them, the softness of her lips, the glory of surging inside her. On a ship full of men with no hope of escape or even survival, a man learned to turn his mind from such things, or he might go mad. After two years of such a life, he wondered if he could be a man again. He had wanted to try with Tillie, but it had been so long that he'd felt maybe he couldn't do it right anymore. She'd been very understanding though, assuring him that he was just too weak and exhausted. He could only hope she was right.

After twelve days at the saloon it was obvious that Buck was regaining strength at a rapid pace. He dressed and walked around, helping in the kitchen and eating everything he could lay his hands on. Madam Lucy, a pleasant older woman with graying red hair and a painted face, told him he was costing her a fortune in food, but she said it was worth the cost just to look at him and to help give him baths those first few days. When the other women laughed at her comments, Buck would smile sheepishly, but he was beginning to feel long-buried urges slowly surfacing.

Sixteen days after his arrival, Buck was lifting boxes of supplies, partly to pay back Madam Lucy by working and partly to help strengthen his muscles. He ran errands, helped move furniture, carried wood, and spent most of his nights watching over the saloon, checking the gambling tables and helping to keep things in order. In public he used the name John Hanover, for he was afraid some customer might know the name of the man who'd escaped from the Chinese freighter. After what he had been through, it was difficult to trust anyone. He was suspicious of every man who came through the door. He practiced drawing his gun over and over, practiced shooting it behind the saloon during the day, determined that no one would waylay him and force him back onto a ship. But after three weeks at Madam Lucy's, his fears began to fade, and his savings for the trip back to Colorado had grown. Madam Lucy paid him ridiculously high wages. He knew she was just being kind. He'd mentioned that he needed train fare to get back to Colorado Springs, where he could work at a couple of odd jobs to earn enough money to buy a horse and ride to Cripple Creek. What happened after that depended on whether or not he could find Harmony, and on what had happened to her. Then, of course, there was the matter of Wade Tillis. If he managed to keep from being hanged for taking his revenge, and if he could find Harmony and get back to living again, he'd find a way to pay back Madam Lucy for the extra wages he knew she was paying him.

But now he would not argue against it. He had an all-consuming desire to get to Colorado—the sooner, the better. Physically he was probably not ready to go, for he'd not regained his normal strength or his normal weight, but now that he was free and getting well, he must soon deal with his desire to get to the Rockies and to find Harmony, even if he wasn't quite ready. He had only waited this long because he'd wanted enough strength and health to assure that nothing would go wrong, and he'd wanted to be in good enough shape to face down Wade Tillis.

After twenty-five days he felt like a new man, except for one thing. Although he was surrounded by prostitutes who teased him and flirted with him, he had not overcome his fear of being with a woman again. Did two years of abstention affect a man in such a way that he could never perform again? He did not want to go back to Harmony as half a man. If she was still free and still loved him, he wanted to be a man for her in every way.

He had begun to sleep on a cot behind the kitchen, so that Tillie could use her old room to entertain customers. Tillie had been kind to him. She had nursed him those first few days, and she'd held him when he'd needed comforting. He felt indebted to her; he liked her. And he'd often seen desire for him in her eyes. Several times she had undressed and offered herself to him; it had bothered him that he could not perform unless a woman teased and persuaded him. When the time came, he wanted to be in control, to choose the time and not need any prompting. He was becoming more and more worried. He felt that something was wrong with him, as a result of the brutal beatings he'd suffered. He was ready in every other way to go back to Colorado, but he would not go until this final healing occurred.

On a warm night in late September, he sat wide awake, on the edge of his cot, smoking, thinking. In the wee hours of the morning the "boardinghouse" had finally quieted, and it was a good time to think. Some customers were spending the night with their chosen partners, but the saloon was closed and the kitchen was quiet. Buck took a drag on his cigarette, then watched it glow in the dark. He heard a noise in the kitchen then, and peeked through the door to see Tillie looking through the cupboards. He said nothing at first, only watched her. Her long, dark hair was disheveled, and her thin silk robe was tied loosely so that her breasts were partially exposed. She took out a pie then and cut a piece, putting it on a plate and turning to sit down at the table.

Buck opened his door farther. "You having trouble sleeping too?"

She glanced up at him, her eyes running over his broad chest and flat belly, then dropping to that part of his body that was making him so concerned.

"I got hungry," she answered. "I had a busy night."

He left the cigarette in the corner of his mouth as he emerged from his room to sit at the table with her. "Want me to heat some coffee?" he asked.

She shrugged. "I don't think so. I'll just drink some water."

"I'll get it." He got a glass from the cupboard, filled it, and set it in front of her. Suddenly, he felt jealous, not because he cared for her, but because she'd had customers that night and he wondered if he could out perform any of them. If he could please this woman who'd known all kinds of men, he could please anyone, and somehow, sitting at the table in the wee hours of the morning, worn out from her "busy night," she looked vulnerable. She was not the aggressor now. In fact, she'd probably had her fill of men for the night. She might not be in the mood for anymore sex. He was curious as to whether he could cajole her into one more round.

He sat down across from her again. "I can't sleep lately myself," he told her. "I've got to go to Colorado soon. I'm a lot stronger now. Do you think Madam Lucy will mind?"

Tillie smiled, then swallowed some pie. "I doubt it. She knows that's what you've had in mind all along."

"I owe her a lot. I'll repay her. I'll repay all of you somehow."

401

Tillie's smile broadened and she shook her head. "It's not necessary." She sighed then, sobering. "We've taken in others like yourself. Lucy always feels sorry for them. We all do. Someday there will be laws about such things. Of course, when there are, there will probably be laws against women like us, which will make things a little difficult."

"I don't think men will be in any big hurry to outlaw prostitution, especially out west where women are hard to find."

She laughed lightly then, finishing her pie. "You're probably right there." She drank some water, then rose. "Well, you try to sleep, Buck. I'm going back to bed. I've had it."

He stood up as she headed for the door. "Tillie," he said softly.

She stopped and turned. He almost looked like a little boy pleading for something.

"Come to bed with me," he told her. It was a gentle command. Her heart raced, for she'd wanted nothing more than to be bedded by Buck Hanner before he went away. But she instantly reminded herself that his situation was a delicate one. She had not come after him, had not exposed herself or thrown herself at him. Did he need to feel he had talked her into it? If so, she was willing to cooperate. She knew men well, and had suddenly realized what this one needed.

"I'm pretty worn out," she answered.

He walked up to her then, pulling the robe off her shoulders. "Then I'll do all the work. You don't have to do anything." He gently grasped her shoulders, and she could feel his hands trembling. "Please, Tillie." He bent down and kissed her eyes. "I've got to know." He pulled her close, pressing her bare breasts against his chest. "Something is different. I want you this time. Maybe that's all I needed, just to want you and not force it. Seeing you sitting in here alone after being with men who just used your body all night and didn't care about the woman inside of it, I wanted you."

She felt a hardness against her groin and a rush of desire swept through her, true desire, not just a mechanical reaction. She looked up at him. "Buck?"

He met her lips, gently at first, then savagely, all the pent-up needs suddenly flooding his bones, his blood, his nerve endings. Harmony! If only this could be Harmony! . . . But he could pretend, couldn't he? After all, perhaps someday soon he could be making love to her. He must be ready. Of course he couldn't know what he might find when he went back to Cripple Creek. Perhaps Harmony could no longer be his. But he had to get these things out of his system before seeing her again. Perhaps he couldn't have her back right away. How could he control his furious desire for her unless he vented his lust, even his rage, on someone else first?

His mouth left her lips to move down over her neck in heated passion, and he lifted her in his arms and kissed her breasts as he carried her to his cot. When he laid her down, he moved over her, tasting the large nipples of her breasts with urgent hunger.

"Buck!" She ran her hands through his thick hair. "Be careful. You're hurting me."

He left her breast, moving over her throat again to her lips. "I'm sorry," he whispered. "It's all happening so fast. I don't know why—"

"Who cares why? I've never had a man want me just

403

for me before. It's wonderful to be wanted—needed—in a real way." She leaned up and kissed his breasts, then reached down to gently caress the part of him that told her he would be a man again. "It's been a long time, Buck. Don't hurt me."

He straddled her, opening her robe the rest of the way. "I'd never hurt you." Why did those words sound familiar? Harmony! She'd said that to him the first time, and he'd answered the same way. Harmony! God how he needed and wanted her! He eagerly kissed the soft hair between Tillie's slender white legs, and soon he was giving her more pleasure than she had experienced in a long time, despite her profession. This was different. This was Buck, a friend, a nice man she knew well—and he needed her. No man had truly needed her in a long time. She opened herself to him, glorying in the expertise she suspected he had all along. She envied the nameless woman who waited for him in Colorado, as she panted his name over and over, grasping at his hair, on fire for him as he moved back up her body then surged inside her, plunging deep, shuddering and groaning at the wonderful release. It seemed only seconds before he exploded inside her, so fiercely that she could feel his life flowing into her in urgent pulses.

They lay there quietly then, both of them perspiring and out of breath. "Goddamn, I'm sorry," he groaned. "It was too quick, too goddamned quick."

"It's all right, honey," she soothed. "The point is, it happened. That's all that matters. We'll just lie here awhile, just be together, and I'll bet before the sun rises we'll set a record, you handsome stud."

He half rose so he could see her in the pale light that

shone through his slightly open door from the lamp in the kitchen. "Was it good, Tillie?"

She smiled. "Are you kidding? My God, Buck, how did something like you go without for two years? Welcome back to the world of the living."

His eyes teared and he kissed her lightly. "Don't take any other customers the next few days, will you? I want to be with you all night every night. Besides, I made you a promise that when I was ready, you'd be the one."

She ran a finger over his handsome lips. "And I'm glad as hell you promised. I'll take no other men as long as you're still here, Buck Hanner." She grinned. "What a fitting name. Buck. You're a big buck, all right."

He buried his face in her dark hair. Yes, he was about ready now. He'd spend some time with Tillie; then he'd be healed in every way, ready to go back to Cripple Creek . . . and Harmony.

Harmony Jones Tillis was a different woman when she reached Cripple Creek, much to Wade's delight. She was more receptive, seemingly happier. Wade Tillis felt he had achieved the ultimate success, for not only had he molded Harmony Jones into a scheming power monger, he had apparently won her heart. Suddenly she was inviting him back to her bed. That was just fine with him, for Harmony Jones Tillis was a beautiful creature indeed, made more beautiful by her cold heart. And getting along with her, convincing her they were made for each other, would help him slowly but surely siphon off her fortune. Quietly, paper by paper, he would make sure her name was removed from the ownership documents for their many investments. One day, Harmony Jones Tillis would have to stay with Wade Tillis whether she loved him or not. She would have to submit to him in every way, if she wanted to keep enjoying the fruits of their fortune. If she chose to leave him, fine. But he was protected from any loss, and from having to turn over anything to the haughty little girl he'd talked into marrying him.

He would probably let her keep the store in St. Louis. He cared little for it. That was just one of her flings at revenge; marrying him had been another one. He hated Buck Hanner all the more because his was a rebound marriage. Still, he had won in the long run, for he'd legally bedded Buck Hanner's woman; and he was secretly stealing her blind so that one day it would not be her decision as to whether or not he came to her bed, it would be his. But for now, she was willing. Why spoil a good thing? He was happy enough, and so, apparently, was Harmony. She made a fine wife for such a prominent man. He'd keep her as long as they got along so well—and as long as she didn't look at younger men.

He often wondered when and where Buck Hanner had met his death, and how. Under the lash, he hoped. That would serve Hanner right, for harassing him, tailing him, threatening him. And for what? Over his stupid little niece, who had been foolish enough to fall for a ranch hand. No one with the name of Tillis should marry so far beneath her. Besides, she had scorned his own advances. She'd been so young and pretty, and all he'd wanted to do was kiss her. Couldn't an uncle fall in love with a niece? Well, that didn't matter now. Filled with rage because she was in love with a stupid, worthless ranch hand, he'd promptly sent her away.

And he wasn't upset about her death, for that had meant he inherited the ranch. On that inheritance he had built his fortune.

That was a long time ago. Mary Beth was dead, and now Buck Hanner was dead too. He had married Buck Hanner's pretty little lady. For some reason things just seemed to work in his favor. It made life most pleasant.

Harmony began to entertain more now that she was happier and more settled. She was totally convinced she had found her niche and had rid her heart and mind of Buck Hanner. She wanted friends. She wanted to play the role of a wealthy woman. The trip to St. Louis had been good for her, and her decision to become Wade's wife in all respects had proven to be a good one. He didn't bring out the passion she'd known with Buck, but such passion was dangerous. Wade was her husband, and she enjoyed being a woman. It was time to look to the future.

She entertained two and three times a week in their handsome home on a hill overlooking Cripple Creek, serving the finest foods and often hiring musicians to play for her guests. She felt that it was time some refinement came to Cripple Creek. In fact, she intended to talk to Wade about building another theater, and perhaps bringing in some kind of industry to keep the town going once the mines were played out.

It was at one of her many parties, as she strolled in her garden with one of her guests, that she spotted Hank Fisher standing at the fence, watching her with those sorrowful eyes of his. She scowled at him, then excused herself to go and talk to him. The woman she'd just left watched, aware that Hank Fisher had been the one to bring Harmony Jones down from the mountain, and that Harmony had been a bitter, scheming woman ever since. In a few moments she hurried off to join several ladies who still loved to gossip about what had happened between Harmony Jones and Buck Hanner on the mountain.

Harmony was almost grateful to leave the woman. Most women bored her, for they knew nothing of business and generally had no interest in doing anything but dressing up and socializing. Nonetheless, she played the role required of a woman in her position in society. Now here was Hank again. She had thought she had gotten rid of him, of his piercing, knowing eyes. Only Hank knew what had happened on the mountain, and to her knowledge he had never told anyone that she'd lost a baby up there. She had that much to thank him for, but she didn't like seeing him. He reminded her of that winter on the mountain.

"What do you want?" she asked, trying to be pleasant.

He swallowed, his hands shaking. "I . . . I seen him, Miss Harmony."

Her heart leaped almost painfully. "Saw whom?" she asked cautiously.

"Buck. I seen him . . . in Colorado Springs."

She paled visibly and grasped the fence. "Don't lie to me!" she hissed.

"You know I wouldn't. I was on a stage comin' back from orderin' supplies out of Colorado Springs for my shop. I didn't have a chance to say nothin' to him, 'cause the stage took off. I'd just happened to look out the window, and I seen him ride by on a black horse.

His hair was longer, and he was thinner, but I could swear it was Buck."

She strove for control. "How can you be sure?" she asked, her voice shaky. "I've seen . . . lots of men who . . . reminded me of him."

"Maybe so, ma'am. But this one, well, if Buck has a twin, he's it."

Her eyes turned cold, in spite of her flushed cheeks and the perspiration on her forehead. She pressed a handkerchief to her brow. "It's warm today," she muttered casually, as though unaffected by the news. Then she took a deep breath and pressed the handkerchief to her neck. "You're probably mistaken, Hank. Buck would never dare show his face in this territory again. I would have him hanged for stealing my gold. It is a hanging offense, you know."

"But I'm sure it was him, ma'am."

She shrugged, her outward calm hiding the rage burning in her soul. "Then I'll have it checked out. I would appreciate it, Hank, if you told no one about this, not even my husband. If Buck Hanner is found and arrested, I want it to be done on my say-so. I want him to know I was the only one who had a hand in it, that I alone want to see him with a noose around his neck."

Hank's eyes saddened even more. "You don't mean that, Miss Harmony."

"Don't I?" she snapped. "You watch and see!"

"But what if he had a good reason?"

"Reason!" Her eyes spit fire. "There is no reason good enough to warrant leaving the woman you love pregnant and unmarried and stranded on a mountain! And to take her gold on top of it! That man destroyed me, and I shall destroy him! I've done it to others!"

His eyes teared. "Seems to me you've done it to yourself, ma'am, if you'll pardon the remark. You ain't nothin' like the little girl I met that day I come when Buck was wounded."

"Of course I'm not!" she sneered. "I'm smarter now, wiser! I've learned my lessons well, Hank, and I would appreciate it if you'd stop looking at me the way you do and talking about that day. It's none of your business what kind of woman I am. I have every right to hate Buck Hanner, just as I would hate a rattler! I appreciate your not mentioning I lost a child by Buck, but having that knowledge gives you no right to come sneaking around and upsetting me all the time. I wish you hadn't told me this. I'm sure your imagination was running away with you. Buck knows the law. To come back here would mean he'd be arrested, probably hanged. But I'll check out what you said. I'll send men to Colorado Springs."

She turned to leave.

"Miss Harmony?"

Still pale and perspiring, she looked back, but her eyes were cold and impatient. "What is it?"

"If . . . if your men find him, won't you at least give them orders to take it easy on him . . . till he gets here and tells his side?"

She smiled wickedly. "I think dead or alive will do." As she tossed her head and walked off, Hank wiped his brow.

For three days after she'd received the news about Buck Hanner Harmony seemed overly busy. She

410

needed to be occupied, to keep her reawakened memories of Buck Hanner from overtaking her common sense. Secretly, she sent a telegram to the sheriff of Colorado Springs giving him a description of Buck Hanner and requesting that he be arrested and brought to Cripple Creek on a charge of stealing gold. She paid the telegrapher to keep quiet about the message, and she instructed him to say nothing to her husband about it.

Wade thought she seemed nervous as a cat. Suddenly she was interested in going with him every day to make the round of their businesses, and she was talking too much, jabbering away about unimportant matters, although sometimes she seemed pensive and far away. She was pale and jittery, and he noticed that she ate very little. At night she took him with surprising wantonness, as though determined to prove, perhaps to herself, that he was the only man in her life now. It mattered little to him whether she loved him, for his feelings for her were purely physical. And although her abandon made the nights quite exciting, he sensed there was something she was not telling him.

There was. Harmony was preparing herself. If Hank was right, she must be ready for the day she would face Buck Hanner. She wanted to be venomous, to show him she didn't care for him any longer, to flaunt her marriage to Wade Tillis, and to watch, smiling, as he was hung. She would testify to what had happened on the mountain, not caring what people thought, so long as Buck Hanner hung. In her mind, she practiced what she would say, how she would act.

Never had her soul been so filled with a burning desire for vengeance. Indeed, she had trouble hiding

411

her feelings from her husband, so she threw herself into playing the good wife. Revenge would be hers, and it would be sweet.

Three weeks passed, however, with no word of anyone sighting a man who fit the description of Buck Hanner. There was a report that someone who looked like him had been in Colorado Springs at approximately the same time Hank had said he'd seen him. Harmony began to relax. Perhaps Hank had merely seen a man who resembled Buck. Perhaps he wanted Buck to come back so badly that he'd allowed his eyes to play tricks on him. After all, he'd only gotten a glimpse of the man, and it had been well over two years since Buck had left.

She gave up the search, for the moment, but she told the authorities in Colorado Springs to continue to keep an eye open. Surely if Buck Hanner meant to reenter Cripple Creek, he'd have done so by now or he'd have retreated. If he had any sense at all he'd stay away. Perhaps if he had been in the area, he'd heard about her marriage to Wade Tillis and it had cut him so deeply he'd left. Perhaps he'd hoped to find Harmony Jones still free and still in love with him. She couldn't imagine how he could ever think that was possible, but she felt that it was very unlikely Hank had seen Buck Hanner.

At the time rumors of a possible miners' strike circulated, and shortly thereafter involvement in negotiations and in a struggle to keep the mine open took Harmony's mind off the unnerving news that Buck Hanner might have come back. She and Wade could not afford a strike, for the mine was beginning to be played out. They had to keep it going awhile longer, so Harmony convinced Wade to give in to most of the miners' demands. She did not want to see a vicious clash between mineowners and workers, for she'd been told what had occurred in '94, when over a hundred strikebreakers had been hauled in by train from Denver. A small war had broken out then. Such an event could damage property and cost them more than it was worth.

As much trouble as it was, the strike was of short duration, and it provided a welcome diversion for Harmony. Soon the small processing plant that had been built at the site of Harmony's mine was running again, doing in minutes what it had once taken Harmony hours of painful picking away at rocks to do. Chunks of ore were deposited into crushers, then totally smashed beneath half-ton stamping machines, after which the crushed ore was passed through fine screens and on into vanners, that automatically separated out most of the lead and some of the silver. The remaining mixture of gold and silver was dumped into amalgamating pans and was cooked for several hours with mercury and other chemicals; then it was deposited into settling tanks. There were other much bigger mills in and around Cripple Creek, but Harmony and Wade had had theirs built right at the site of the mine so the ore-laden rocks didn't have to be transported to Cripple Creek for processing.

Harmony had not been back up the mountain to see the mill. She had said the trip was too long and the mill did not interest her, but she knew deep inside that it would be devastating to see the ugly mill built into the side of her mountain. She tried not to think of the mountain as belonging to her and to Buck, but she couldn't help doing so, although she now kept her feelings about it so deeply buried that she didn't even recognize them anymore. She simply had no interest in the mill, she told herself. She was only interested in what it produced. By this time, the mine was just about spent, but she was not worried. They would hire men to do some more exploring. And if no more gold was discovered, her other moneymaking ventures insured that she did not really need the mine any longer. Nonetheless, it was difficult for her to picture the mill at the site of the mine, and to realize the output such an operation could attain, compared to her first crude panning. How things had changed since that winter she'd lived there alone and had panned and separated her own gold. It had only been a little over two years since she'd come down from there with news of her strike, but now everything was all done automatically, except chipping the gold ore out of the vein. It was too bad machines couldn't do that, too. Then there would be no bothersome strikes.

But this one was not really bothersome. It was almost welcome. She smiled at the thought of Buck Hanner coming back, possibly going to the site of the mine first. What a surprise he would get! Thinking of his reaction almost made her laugh out loud. Indeed, she did chuckle as she put down her cup of coffee.

"Something funny?" Wade asked, biting off a piece of bread and gazing across the breakfast table at her.

She smiled seductively. "Sort of."

"Want to share it?"

She looked at her coffee and shrugged. "No." She met his eyes again. "You going to the mine?"

"I don't think I need to now. Sage went back with the final settlement. Besides, that mine will be closed completely within another six months, and we still haven't found a sign of a new vein. I'm glad we invested wisely."

"So am I," she answered with a smile, totally unaware that most of what she thought she owned was now in Wade Tillis' hands. "It's strange how fast a mine can play out. You hit a vein and think it will just run on and on."

"Some last longer than others, but they all play out eventually." He winked. "But we'll keep the town going, Harmony Tillis, won't we?"

She tossed her head and her long, blond hair swung back over her shoulders. "Of course we will."

He chuckled lightly and rose from the table. "I'll be back tonight."

"I'll be waiting," she answered with a suggestive look.

Wade Tillis smiled his crooked smile and his laugh had an almost evil ring that pleased Harmony. He was wonderful, because he was powerful and untrustworthy and didn't care if she loved him or not. Life was so easy this way—no feelings, no worries over how he responded to her, no pressure to trust someone explicitly.

"Maybe we'll go to Denver next week," he told her. "We could have some fun, and look into more investments at the same time."

"Whatever you say."

He frowned and bent down to kiss her lightly. "I do so like you when you're still high on revenge," he told her. "I wish I could find someone else you could do in. You're even more beautiful when the venom is flowing."

She laughed lightly. "Find me Buck Hanner, and I'll be the most beautiful woman who ever lived."

Wade laughed loudly as he put on his hat and descended the steps of the veranda. Although it was nearing the end of September, it was warm and beautiful, nice enough to eat outside. Wade got into his rig, whipped the shiny black horse into motion, and was off for town. Harmony stood and watched him ride away while a servant took away the breakfast dishes. She descended the steps then, turning to the right and walking to a flower garden that had become her favorite spot. Its loveliness did not fit the kind of woman she had become; its beauty and softness provided a stark contrast to the bitterness of the woman who walked among the colorful array of blossoms. But the garden brought peace to her troubled soul, its sweetness momentarily softening her hardness, its fragrance reminding her of the kind of woman she might have been had she not been abandoned and abused.

She stooped to pick a rose, then held it to her nostrils, sniffing its delicate scent.

"Harmony." The voice was soft.

She turned and suddenly went white. Buck Hanner stepped from behind a thick shrub, his sky-blue eyes studying her with a mixture of love and anger.

Chapter Twenty

"Harmony . . . Tillis, I believe it is now," Buck added, stepping closer, running his eyes over her as though to take inventory.

She stepped back, unable to do anything but stare. Then she grasped a trellis of ivy for support. He was more handsome than ever, but thinner, honed harder and, she suspected, stronger. She could not know what had made him so. His thick, sandy hair was a little longer, falling gracefully around his neck; and he wore a white, open shirt with loose flowing sleeves, tight pants, and high boots. Harmony thought he looked the way she imagined a man of the sea would.

Her hatred of him rose to the surface, buoyed by hurt, humiliation, and emotional devastation. Her green eyes blazed, and he knew her well enough to know exactly what she was feeling.

"What in God's name are you doing here!" she managed to choke out.

He looked around the garden, then back at her. "I might ask the same thing of you."

Why did he look so handsome, so sure? "I am Mrs. Wade Tillis," she hissed, stepping back again. "That's why I'm here!"

She saw anger and jealousy flash in his eyes, and she enjoyed seeing his response. He took a prerolled cigarette from the pocket of his shirt and lit it. "You love him?"

Her whole body was now wet with nervous perspiration. This was not the way she had planned to meet him. She was not prepared. She wasn't even dressed! She still wore her gown and robe. She turned away. "That is no longer any of your business."

"It is," he said coldly. "Because I plan to kill your husband, Mrs. Tillis."

She whirled, her eyes wide. "Kill him? Because he married me and gave me some respectability after you ran out on me? Do you know what people thought? Everyone knew!" Her breathing quickened. "You . . . you bastard! How dare you say that to me! You knew I trusted you! And now you dare to come back here and tell me you want to kill my husband!" She turned away again. "My God, I wish I had a gun in my hands right now!" she declared. "I'd shoot you myself!" Striving for control, she took a deep breath and stood quietly for a moment before turning to face him again. So far he had said nothing more. He was confusing her. Why had he come at all? "Do you know I've had men looking for you, to bring you back here so you could be hung for stealing my gold? You're taking a risk in coming here, Mister Buck Hanner! Wade and I will have you hunted down, and when you're hanged, I'll celebrate!"

He watched her, his face sad. "You never answered

418

my original question. I asked whether you love Wade Tillis."

She glared at him, love raging in her soul but hate darting from her narrowed eyes. "I said it was none of your business! You get off my property, Buck Hanner! And you'd better ride hard, because men will be coming for you! I can't imagine why you came here, unless it was to laugh at me. But you'll not be laughing long! Now get out of here! I'm going to get dressed."

She started to storm past him, but he grabbed her arm, squeezing it hard. "Answer my question, Harmony Jones!" he growled. He threw down his cigarette. "You'll not leave this garden until you do!"

The touch of his hand on her arm brought forth waves of warmth and desire, responses she'd thought long dead, even though his grip hurt her arm. She turned green eyes up to his blue ones. Close! So close and so handsome. Yet it had all become so ugly. She could have loved him with such utter devotion, but she was hard now, perhaps beyond sweetening.

"Of course I don't love him!" she sneered. "I married him because all decent women get married! I married him because I was lonely! He wanted my body, and I wanted his money! But most of all I wanted to hurt you! I wanted that more than I've ever wanted anything."

He felt her tremble, and wondered if she would fall if he let go of her. But he hung on to her arm, forcing back an urge to slap her. He knew Harmony too well. This was an act, an attempt to hurt him and thereby mask her own hurt.

"Did you really believe I'd run out on you?" he asked, searching her eyes.

419

She looked away, on fire from his closeness, wishing he could hold her again and tell her none of it had happened. She'd been so sure she would hate him when she saw him again. She wanted to hate him, needed to hate him.

"Of course I believed it," she answered quietly. "Why shouldn't I? Everyone else I ever cared about left me. That's what's so nice about being married to Wade. Neither of us loves the other, so no one gets hurt." She looked directly at him, her green eyes colder than he'd ever seen them. "Wade told me about you, about how you go around using women to get ahead, about why you really wanted to marry Mary Beth—for her money! For her ranch! He told me what a drifter you are. I should have seen it, but I had to learn the hard way!"

"And you believed what he told you," Buck said almost sadly. "After all we did together, all my vows of love and devotion, all our talks, our friendship. My God, Harmony, is it that hard for you to believe someone could really love you?"

His words cut her like a knife, wedging into her determination to be cold and hard and cruel, weakening her resolution not to let the love she'd once felt for this man cloud reality. She swallowed and tried to wrench herself away, but he continued to hold her arm, and she felt tears coming.

"No one has ever really loved me!" she choked out. "You promised to come back . . . and I waited . . . and waited! Now, after all the hell I went through, you show up! How can you be so cruel! Do you know what it was like . . . all that waiting . . . the hurt . . . the horror of realizing you weren't coming?"

"Of course I know," he said gently. "I was going through my own hell, Harmony."

She tossed her head, glaring at him again, tears on her cheeks. "Your hell?" she hissed. "I lost a baby up there, Buck Hanner!" Her body jerked as she choked back a sob, and Buck's eyes widened, a look of terrible sorrow appearing in their blue depths. "I was all alone." She was crying now. "All alone up there! I lay all night in horrible pain—bleeding—losing the life you planted in me! If Hank hadn't come along the next morning . . . I might have died!" She hung her head and wept. "It was the most horrible thing I ever went through! I screamed and screamed for you, but you weren't there. Nobody was there! I've never been so frightened. Then Hank came, and he . . . buried it for me. I don't even know . . . what it was!"

Bitter sobs escaped her, and suddenly his arms were around her and he was holding her tightly, so tightly, just as he used to do. For a moment she let him hold her. She wept against his chest and forgot she was supposed to hate him.

"My God, Harmony, I didn't know," he said quietly, kissing her hair.

She pushed away from him then. "Of course you didn't know! You had already left me! Thank God Hank was kind enough not to tell anyone. But my reputation had already suffered from our being up there together. When I came back to town I could feel everyone's eyes on me! I knew what they thought!" She stopped and sniffed, wiping at her eyes. "Finally, to stop the gossiping, I married Wade. At least he stays around!"

Buck sighed deeply and shook his head. "I'm

goddamned sorry about the baby, Harmony—sorry you had to go through that. I suffered too, and it was worse because I couldn't tell you what happened, couldn't explain. Don't you even want to know where I've been?"

She wiped at her eyes again. "What difference does it make now?"

He began to unbutton his shirt. "A lot of difference. It's your husband's fault I never came back, Harmony, and I don't doubt he figured I'd never survive my ordeal. He made a tidy profit on me, and he figured he was rid of me so he could move in on your fortune. I'm not the one who's made a fool of you, Harmony. Wade Tillis has done that."

She frowned as he removed the shirt. "What are you doing? What are you talking about?" she asked, pushing a piece of blond hair behind her ear.

He held the shirt in his hand and turned around, and she gasped at ugly scars on his back, some still pink. It would be many years before they faded, but it was obvious they would never really go away.

"There are more on my legs," he told her. "I earned these stripes trying to escape to get back to you," he added. "I hope that satisfies your vengeful little heart."

He turned to face her, pulling his shirt back on while she stared at him in surprise. "What happened to you!" she whispered.

His eyes showed a trace of anger then. "You mean you actually want to know now?"

"Buck, I—" She didn't know what to say. Could she have been wrong? Was it possible he really had loved her? "What happened?"

He buttoned the shirt. "Your kind husband had me

422

waylaid," he answered, his voice beginning to harden with hatred. "I left a message with the assayer to have someone go and tell you I'd be a little longer. Your gold was worth a lot. I knew it was a hell of a strike, and I didn't trust the only man in town who could hire men to mine it—Wade Tillis. So I decided to take the samples to Colorado Springs, to a man I knew and trusted. I wanted to get the best and most honest men for the job. When I was asleep in my hotel room in Colorado Springs, several men attacked me. They put something over my mouth and nose, something that knocked me out. But before I went under I saw one face I recognized, Harmony. He was a Tillis man, the big one they call Buffalo."

Her eyes widened. She saw Buffalo nearly every day, spoke to him often, had even fed him at her house. "Are you . . . sure?"

He rolled his eyes. "Who can mistake that mug?" He tucked in his shirt as she turned around and half collapsed, sitting down in the grass. Buck came to stand over her. "I was shanghaied, Harmony. When I came to I was in a filthy boxcar, locked in with other prisoners and cattle. We all sat in our own filth, tied and gagged and fed only bread and water. During that ride I slipped in and out of consciousness, and before I knew it I was on a boat, being hauled down to New Orleans, where I was put on a ship—a huge one that was putting out to sea. The ship sailed to China, with several captives like me on it. Most of the others didn't make it through the filth and the rotten food and the whippings. But I did! I made it because I was determined not to satisfy Wade Tillis by dying! And I made it because I thought about you, my poor

Harmony, alone on that mountain. I spent months in that dark hold, then I was forced to work on a merchant ship heading for San Francisco. I tried to escape once. How I lived through the beating they gave me for that I'll never know. I just— I pictured your face . . . pictured lying in your arms. I held that picture in my mind while their damned whip ate into my flesh!"

"Stop it!" she screamed, her hands over her face.

"You have to know, Harmony! You have to know the kind of man you've married, what he did to us! He sold me, Harmony, like a slave! Most men who are forced into that kind of labor never survive! But I beat the odds, Harmony! I beat Wade Tillis at his own game! I lived, and the second time the ship put into San Francisco, I escaped. It took me a long time to be strong enough to make the trip back here, but I'm strong now—strong enough to kill Wade Tillis!"

She looked up at him quickly, tears on her face. "It can't be true! What about your money? All of your money was withdrawn from the bank, as though you'd taken it and run off."

"Harmony, don't be such a fool! Wade Tillis owns the bank! The manager there will do anything Wade says. My God, how else do you think I got these scars on my back? How could I make up such a thing?"

She stretched out on the grass then, weeping, her humiliation and devastation knowing no bounds. How could any man use someone the way Wade Tillis had used her? She'd known he was evil, but she hadn't truly understood how bad a person could be until now. She churned inwardly at the thought of having given her body to the very man who had caused such horrible things to happen to the man she loved. She'd even traveled Europe with Wade. She'd fallen for his game, the stupid child that she was. She realized that at this very moment Wade Tillis was probably scheming to make her entire fortune his, to rid himself of her so he could go on to someone else, leaving her with nothing. It all made so much sense. There was no easier way to get a woman's money than by marriage. She'd known money was the basis for their marriage, but she had thought he'd intended to share and enjoy their wealth. Now she realized Wade Tillis had probably intended to steal everything from her. And Buck! Poor Buck! If only she hadn't been so mixed up about trust and love. She'd been too willing to believe Buck Hanner had abandoned her, and while he'd been suffering, she'd been sharing the bed of his mortal enemy.

She felt a hand on her shoulder then. "I'm leaving now, Harmony."

She sat up and placed her arms around his neck. "Oh, God, Buck, what have I done!"

He sighed and kissed her hair. He loved her, but it was different now. He had a man to kill, and it would be awhile before he could sort out his feelings, before he could hold Harmony Jones again and love her the way he wanted. She would have some thinking to do too, some healing. This was not the time to speak of love.

"I'm sorry, Harmony, but I have to go now." He gently pulled away. "And I'm sorry I have to make you a widow. But I must. The hate in my heart is too great."

She grasped his shirt. "You can't just go into town and kill him!" she begged. "You'll hang!"

"Not if I handle it right." He grasped her wrists and

425

pulled them away.

"Buck, they'll kill you!"

"Not before I kill Wade Tillis."

As he stood up, she scrambled to her feet, her hair tousled, her face soaked with tears.

"But Buck, what . . . what about us?"

Blue eyes looked her over. "What about us? We both have a lot of healing to do, Harmony. Maybe someday we can find what we had once"—he nodded toward Pike's Peak—"up there. I love you just as much as I did then, but there are a few things in the way of that love right now."

He walked farther down the path, toward a black horse. "Buck!" she called out. She ran toward him. "Buck, I still love you. I've always loved you. I tried so hard to forget, to hate you; but deep inside—"

He turned, wrapping her in his arms when she was close enough and kissing her hungrily. As his lips burned into her own with fiery savageness, his crushing embrace took her breath away. Suddenly he released her and pushed her away. "Not now, Harmony. Not this way, and not for a long time. Too much has happened. I'm damned sorry for all of it, for the way people have used you. I never did, and I never will, especially not now. Someday there'll be a right time, a right place for us again."

He hurried to the horse then, mounting up and riding off without another word.

She watched him go, gently touching her bruised lips, then doubling over from the near pain of the passion he had reawakened in her. Buck! Buck was here! He'd touched her, kissed her, held her. He still

426

loved her. What had happened hadn't been his fault after all! Her desire for revenge was gone now. She fell to her knees and wept. What had she become? A money-hungry and power-driven woman with no heart and no feelings. Buck Hanner had brought feeling back to her, in one great surge that actually hurt physically. Everything was so clear now. If only she had trusted a little more, if only she hadn't been so quick to believe the worst . . . Hank was the only one who'd continued to believe Buck Hanner had not left her. Poor Hank. She'd been so mean to him. She'd been mean to a lot of people. She had let her abandonment in childhood destroy her capacity for happiness and love.

What if Buck couldn't love her the same way he once had? After all, she had married Wade Tillis. Maybe it would never be the way it was for them. Maybe Buck would be hung for killing Tillis, and that would be the end of it—both men dead, the love of her life gone, no chance to make things right. Buck! She'd seen him, talked to him, touched him! She had thought he was gone from her life forever, and now here he was, back in Cripple Creek. He'd suffered terrible things just to get back to her; then he'd found her married to the very man who had put him through torment. She knew without anyone telling her that he had left out a great deal, that he'd suffered things he'd not even told her about. He was so much thinner and harder. In the moments he had been with her, she'd sensed a great change in him. His easygoing attitude was gone, his teasing nature, his happiness. There had been no handsome smile. He had become harder, just as she had. Could either of them ever again be the way they

427

were on the mountain? Would that winter, those tender moments, be only a memory?

She stumbled through the garden to the house, the servants staring at her as she made her way blindly up the stairs. In her room, she threw herself on the bed and wept. A maid entered cautiously.

"Are you all right, ma'am?" she asked.

"Yes. Go away!" Harmony muttered. The woman left, quietly closing the door. Harmony did not come out of the room the rest of the day. She wondered how much more hurt she must endure in her life. How many more times would she be used? How many lessons did it take for her to understand that someone was making a fool of her? When would she ever learn who could and who could not be trusted? Why did she allow her childhood abandonment to haunt her? That was what it all came down to. That was what had made her do such foolish things. That was why, when she'd found a man who really loved her and would never desert her, she'd thrown him away when she'd felt betrayed.

Throughout the day she drifted from fits of crying into sleep, visions of Buck filling her dreams. She knew again the warmth of his arms, the glory of sharing his bed, the sweetness of his kiss, the passion his blue eyes awakened in her. But every time she opened her eyes she realized she was lying in a bed she'd shared with Wade Tillis while totally ignorant of how the man had deceived her, of what he had done to Buck.

She waited for what she thought would be news of Wade's death, but that evening she heard him enter the house and ask the maid what was to be served for supper. He was alive! Did that mean? . . . Hurriedly, she washed her face and combed her hair. Then she put on a fresh nightgown and a robe, and hurried downstairs, to her husband's study. He stood near the fireplace, lighting a cigar. She watched him carefully.

"Did you have a good day?" she asked.

Tillis shrugged. "The usual." He puffed the cigar and looked her over as she closed the study door. "You're still in a robe!" he commented.

She sighed. "I didn't feel well today. I was going to come into town, but I changed my mind."

He watched her suspiciously. "One of the maids said you came running into the house this morning looking very upset. Did some gardener bother you or something? I'll have him disciplined."

She looked into his dark eyes. What a clever man he was, making her think he cared. "No. It was nothing like that."

"Well, you look terrible. Here, I'll pour you a drink." He turned his back, and she casually walked to his desk, where he kept a handgun. Apparently Buck had not yet made his appearance. Perhaps she could save him the trouble and keep him from hanging by killing her husband herself. She had nothing left now anyway. Wade poured two drinks and turned, paling slightly when he saw her holding the gun on him. The expression in his dark eyes changed from friendliness to visciousness.

"Well, well," he commented, the cigar still in his teeth. "To what do I owe this loving homecoming?"

"I know what you did to Buck Hanner!" she hissed.

His eyebrows arched, and he carefully set down the drinks. Taking the cigar from his mouth, he set it in an ashtray, then stepped a little closer.

"You stay back!" Harmony warned.

He folded his arms, appearing casual and unconcerned. "Would you mind explaining yourself?" he asked.

"I saw him! I saw Buck this morning, and he told me everything!" she said boldly. "He's going to kill you! Only I've decided to save him the trouble!"

She pointed the gun at Wade, her hands shaking, and he suddenly lunged. The gun went off and she screamed as he tackled her, knocking her to the floor. He ripped the gun from her hand and backhanded her with the barrel, badly cutting and bruising her right jaw.

For a moment everything was a blur, as pain pierced her jaw and neck. Then she heard someone enter the room.

"Get out!" Wade growled. "Get the hell out of here! This is between me and my wife! And keep your mouth shut!"

"Yes, sir," a woman's meek voice replied. The door closed again, and Wade jerked Harmony up, shoving her into a chair.

"Is that the truth? You saw him?" he roared.

She put her head in her hands. "How could you do it? I never knew you were that horrible."

He grasped her wrists. "How many seconds did it take for him to get under your nightgown, wife of mine?" he snarled.

Harmony just stared at him. "You're an ugly, brutal man, Wade Tillis," she said quietly, her words slightly slurred because of her injured jaw. "It was my money, wasn't it? Not just fun and sharing, only money."

"Of course it was the money, you little fool." He let go of her wrists suddenly and straightened, glaring at her. "When those men I sent to scare you off the claim were unsuccessful, I had to think of another approach."

Men? . . . What he'd said suddenly hit her full force. The men who'd tried to rape her . . . if Buck hadn't come along . . . "My God!" she whispered. "You sent them?"

He walked over and picked up the gun from the floor, where he had thrown it. He shoved it into his belt. "Of course I sent them. But again, Buck Hanner spoiled my plans, so I fixed it so the son of a bitch couldn't get in my way again."

He straightened his well-tailored jacket, and Harmony watched him, hating herself more than Wade Tillis. "Is there anything left in my name?"

He smoothed back his hair. "Very little. Of course, that wouldn't have mattered if you had stayed happily married to me. But that probably won't be possible now." He grinned. "I had a hell of a good time while it lasted, though. And you'll have to admit I was good to you, Harmony."

She glared at him, her green eyes fiery. "You betrayed me, in the worst way! You took from me the only man I really loved, a man who loved me. You destroyed my only chance for happiness. Your greed and jealousy nearly killed Buck Hanner, and now he's coming for you, Wade Tillis. I hope he kills you!"

"Well, he won't." Tillis picked up one of the drinks he'd poured and slugged it down. "How in hell he survived, I can't imagine. No man survives a slave ship."

"Buck survived, and he's coming after you."

"Shut up!" He set the empty glass down and came to

431

stand in front of her. "I'm going back into town, dear wife, and I'm going to have our attorney draw up some papers. I imagine there's no sense in putting it off now. I'm divorcing you, and you might as well know that you'll have almost nothing left once I'm through with you. You've served your purpose. I'd have waited longer if things remained as they were. Now I have no choice."

She looked up at him. "Do what you will. I don't care anymore. Nothing matters."

"You can have the mine. It's pretty much spent anyway. I'm pulling my men off it. If you want to keep on mining it, you'll have to find your own crew, but you won't make enough from the mine to pay them, not now. It's worthless."

She slowly rose and walked on unsteady legs to the window from which she could see Pike's Peak in the distance.

"Maybe not," she said pensively. "But it's still mine. I can go there if I want to. I can be alone there."

He laughed, lightly, wickedly. "Go ahead. Women like you always end up alone anyway. Go up there and die for all I care. Die at your precious mine! You came to me once declaring it was yours and you intended to mine it. Well, Mrs. Tillis, I have reaped the benefits of your little claim after all. You may have it back now, with my best wishes." He bowed low in mocking respect. "And I suggest that you start packing your things." He walked to the door then. "Oh . . . don't expect your ex-lover to come running back to your arms. He's as good as dead, you know. If he comes after me, he's putting a noose around his own neck."

432

Wade walked out then, and Harmony stared at Pike's Peak awhile longer. Yes, she still had something. She had her claim, she had memories of the winter she'd spent there with Buck Hanner. As she turned and walked out of the study, she heard Wade's carriage pull away. She knew she had made things harder for Buck, for she'd told Wade Tillis he was in the area. She didn't want to know what was going to happen. She'd hear . . . in time. She'd probably lost Buck for good anyway. It was all different now.

A maid rushed up to her then, taking her arm. "Ma'am, your face! You need a doctor."

"It'll be all right," Harmony muttered. "Just help me to my room, Mary." She looked at the woman. "And send Luke into town, will you? Something . . . something terrible is going to happen. It concerns my husband. I'll wait in my room until I learn what has occurred."

The woman frowned. "Did Mister Tillis do this to you?"

"Yes. But it doesn't matter. I suppose I deserve it— for my stupidity. He's divorcing me." Suddenly Harmony felt lighter and she managed a weak smile. "I imagine I'll have nothing but my claim left. That was all I had when I first came here. Isn't that funny?"

Mary only shook her head. Harmony Tillis was talking strangely. "He can't do these things to you, ma'am." She led her mistress to the bed.

"It doesn't matter, Mary. Nothing matters anymore." Harmony closed her eyes. "I think perhaps I'll go into the mountains again soon. They're always the same, you know. They never change. They're always

433

there . . . so dependable . . . so strong and sure." She thought of Buck. She'd probably never see him again. She'd done this to him—all of it. How could love lead to such horrors? "Strong . . . and dependable," she said, "like some people." She pretended Buck was holding her, and she soon slept.

Chapter Twenty-one

Wade Tillis did not expect Buck Hanner to boldly enter the town. He expected to be attacked from some dark alley so he kept his bodyguards with him. He hoped that he would find Buck Hanner first so he could kill him before Hanner could say anything. Then he would take his body to the authorities, saying he'd shot a gold thief, and no one would hold Wade responsible. After all, the gold that had been stolen belonged to Wade's wife. He was bound to want Buck Hanner hanged. If he shot Hanner instead, before the man could tell his side of the story, what would it matter?

But Buck Hanner was not that careless. He'd planned well. Two days after his visit to Harmony, he appeared, dressed in his familiar cowboy garb. He walked boldly down the main street, and he was not alone. Hank, his faithful friend, was with him, and so were several other prominent men from the town, including Jack Leads and the sheriff himself. These men had long been fed up with Wade Tillis' questionable tactics, and Buck had visited each one of them to

435

explain what had happened and to reveal his scars. They knew the truth, and soon the whole town would know. Buck would get his revenge in the best way; he'd make sure everyone knew what Wade Tillis had done.

"Hanner's coming right down the street, boss," one of Tillis' men said excitedly as he ran into the Mother Lode.

Wade looked up from the papers he was signing. He paled slightly. "Right out in the open?" he asked.

"Yes, sir! And he's got quite a few men with him."

Buffalo rubbed at his jaw. "I knew we should have killed him," he muttered.

"Who'd have thought he'd survive that stinking ship!" Tillis barked. "No man lives through that."

"Buck Hanner did," said the man standing behind Tillis.

"Shut up!"

Already the saloon was emptying out, but people were gathering on the street, eager to see what was about to happen.

"You men stick close!" Wade ordered, rising from the table. "I own half of this town! We'll see who wins this one!" He removed his jacket and adjusted his vest. "Let's go out and greet Mr. Buck Hanner," he growled.

As they exited from the saloon, Buck was approaching. Tillis slowly descended the steps to the muddy street, his eyes on Hanner, who looked at him with frightening hatred in his steady gaze. Buck was thinner, and he wore no gun. Did he expect to fight with fists? Wade wondered. If so, he didn't have a chance. Surely he was too weak from being on that ship. He grinned.

"Well, well," Tillis said. "If it isn't the man who cheated Harmony Jones a couple of years ago. You looking to get yourself hanged, Hanner?"

"You're the one who'll hang." Buck sneered.

"For what? For marrying the girl you swindled?" Tillis smiled. He enjoyed seeing the flicker of jealousy in Buck's eyes. "She's awfully pretty, Buck. I can't imagine why you left her." He looked around at the crowd. "You men all know what this man did. He should hang!" he shouted.

A few voices and fists went up, but the men with Buck stepped closer to him, assuming a protective stance.

"You're the swindler, Tillis!" Buck shot back. "And I've come to even things up. I've done my share of suffering, but I survived—for Harmony, and to come back here and kill you with my bare hands!"

A rumbling went through the crowd. "Harmony is my wife now!" Tillis shouted. "I did right by that girl. You only used her and then rode off with her gold!"

When Buck began to unbutton his shirt, Tillis frowned. Was he preparing to fight?

"It's your word against mine!" he declared, nervous now. "Everybody knows you left here with Harmony's gold. If you want to make up some lies about where you've been, go ahead! But everybody here knows me! Everybody—"

He stopped short when Buck turned around, displaying his back. A low rumble went through the crowd, and even Tillis grimaced at the sight of it. Then Buck put his shirt back on, his eyes roaming the crowd as he did so.

"I took Harmony's gold to Colorado Springs, where I could find some good men to mine her claim!" he shouted. "Wade Tillis had me shanghaied. I've been working as a slave on a ship that sails between China and San Francisco. On the last trip I finally managed to escape. I failed to get away another time and I was severely whipped. That's where these scars came from!"

The murmurings of the crowd grew louder, and Hank grinned. The scars had convinced them. What better proof could Buck have of captivity than the scars?

"You're a liar!" Wade roared.

"Am I? When I was in my hotel room in Colorado Springs I was attacked, and something was held over my face to knock me out. But I saw one face before I went under. It belonged to that big pig who protects your yellow ass—Buffalo!"

The crowd was growing restless now, as Buck stepped closer to Tillis, saying "You planned the whole thing! I left a message for Harmony with the assayer, telling her I'd be gone longer than I thought, but she never got that message! Then you moved in on her, Tillis! You convinced her I'd taken off, and you moved in—not because you love her, but because you wanted that mine!" Buck's teeth clenched; then he hissed, "And you wanted Harmony Jones's body. You're lower than the ground under a snake's belly! You should have had me killed, Tillis! You've just been beat at your own game!"

Buck lit into the man then, and an excited roar broke from the crowd. Some of Tillis' men started to grab Buck, but other men pulled them back, some holding guns on them.

"This is betwen Buck and Tillis," Hank told Tillis' bodyguards. Hanner's story made sense to the crowd.

They felt he must be telling the truth. After all, what man would leave a pretty young thing like Harmony Jones? Despite the change in her, everyone still liked her. They felt sorry for her, knowing her bitterness came from losing Buck. She had loved Hanner, and many had thought Buck had loved her. One man stood in the crowd watching, holding his guitar. He was already thinking up words for the last verse of the ballad he'd made up about Buck Hanner and Harmony Jones.

Meanwhile Buck had rammed Tillis, knocking the man onto his rear. Grabbing Tillis' shirt he landed punches on his face until Tillis locked his fists together and brought them up into Buck's throat. The blow momentarily cut off Buck's air and he reeled backward, gasping for breath. As he did so, Tillis kicked him in the side, then started to kick him in the head, but Buck grabbed his foot and jerked, causing Tillis to fall backward.

Buck got to his feet, feeling weak and dizzy. He wasn't really strong enough for this, but he couldn't bear putting it off any longer. The thought of what this man had done to Harmony, and to the love he and Harmony had once shared, made Buck so furious he kept going, somehow finding strength. He had a terrible need for revenge, and it gave him an advantage over Tillis, who was taller and, at the moment, probably stronger, considering what Buck had been through.

Buck reached down and jerked Tillis up by the vest, landing a foot into the man's privates, then bringing a hard fist up into Tillis' nose when he bent over. Tillis flopped backward and rolled over onto his knees, breathing deeply, while Buck stood over him, panting, fists clenched.

"Get back up, Tillis!" he growled. "You haven't suffered enough yet! When I'm through with you, no one will recognize you! Get up so they can ride you out of town on a rail! You can't hide now, Tillis! You can't cover up what you've done! I didn't die, Tillis! That's where you went wrong! Buffalo was right. You should have killed me! I heard him say so that night they dragged me from my hotel room to be sold into slavery, to live in the hold of a ship with filth and rats, to eat wormy bread and drink slop!"

His eyes were wild. "Get up!" he screamed. "Tell all these people here how you kept me from your niece once because you wanted her yourself! Tell them, Tillis! Tell them about Mary Beth, the girl I was to marry until you said I wasn't good enough for her. Then when Harmony Jones came along, you decided to kill two birds with one stone, didn't you? You'd get rid of me and you'd take my girl—and her gold! You're the one who should hang, Tillis! You're the one who took the gold I had with me, and then sold me like a common slave, expecting me to die! Well, I didn't die, Tillis!"

Buck roared the words, hatred in his voice, Tillis finally recovered somewhat. He stumbled to his feet, his face bleeding, his shirt torn. "He's . . . lying!" he yelled to the crowd.

"It all makes too much sense, Tillis!" Buck shot back. "It's too late! They've seen my back!"

Tillis glowered at him, then lunged. Both men went down again, rolling in the mud, punching and kicking; and the crowd cheered wildly for Buck Hanner, the hero who had returned to Cripple Creek to reclaim his girl. This fight was providing them with excitement, and with more and more of the mines played out, the town needed some. They were all tired of Wade Tillis' control of the community. Apparently, even the sheriff had decided to quit taking bribes and to stand up for what was right, for he watched the fight carefully and then went to stand behind Buck.

For several minutes Wade and Buck slugged it out, each man holding his own for a while, both enduring far more than anyone thought they could endure. Wade had expected his men to jump in and pull Buck off. When they hadn't he'd realized that Buck Hanner had made sure he had some support before doing this. Was there a better way to keep from being killed than to face a man down in the middle of the street and get everything out in the open?

The two men tumbled and rolled and punched, the crowd backing away, those nearest to them often picking up one or the other and throwing him back into the fight. For several more minutes the punches flew, the swings getting slower and weaker, each man now bloody.

Finally Tillis landed on his back, seemingly unconscious. Men picked him up, but he slumped back down. Buck stood over him, covered with blood, his bleeding, swollen fists still clenched. He wiped at his mouth, then looked around at the crowd.

"This man . . . had me shanghaied," he repeated in panting gasps. "Then he convinced . . . Harmony Jones . . . that I'd left her . . . and stolen her gold. You all know . . . what a nice girl Harmony was . . . an innocent! Anybody . . . says anything bad about her

441

. . . they'll get what this man got!"

When Buck turned to stumble away, Tillis moaned and got to his knees. He looked up at Buffalo, and in his unreasoning fury he suddenly pulled Buffalo's gun from its holster and aimed at Buck. Someone yelled a warning just before the gun went off, and Buck whirled. The bullet grazed his neck, knocking him down. In the next moment someone shoved a gun into Buck's hand.

"Shoot him!" a voice said. "He's got it coming!"

Buck looked down at the gun, then over at Tillis, who had slumped to the ground again. He held out the handgun and aimed it; then he slowly lowered it. "Shooting's too good for him," he muttered. "All of you know . . . what he deserves."

The crowd was already in a frenzy; many of the men had grudges against Wade Tillis. They pushed Tillis' bodyguards out of the way and began dragging the man toward a feed store, where a support beam for a pulley stuck out from the upper level. Already a rope was being thrown over the post. The sheriff made no move to stop the crowd. It would have been impossible, even if he'd wanted to prevent them from hanging Tillis. But he didn't particularly care to.

Buck was lifted then, and carried toward the doctor's quarters, while several of Tillis' men hurriedly ran to their rooms above the Mother Lode and began to pack their things, afraid of the ugly crowd that was stringing up their boss at that very moment. They'd be lucky to get away with their own lives.

Buck moaned Harmony's name as he was laid on a cot.

"Ain't it somethin' what that little gal done to this

town?" one man muttered. "Thing's has been hoppin' ever since that little thing come in here chewin' out Wade Tillis and declarin' she was gonna go mine that claim. She sure is somethin'. Look what she's brought these men to."

"You've heard of the power of a woman," another man replied.

Buck felt a cool cloth being pressed to his bloodied lips.

"In this case, the power of a little girl," someone else joked.

"Well, whatever the case, Buck ain't in no shape to go to her now. Somebody'd better get up the hill and let the little lady know what's happened. It's gonna be hard on her, however she looks at it. One was the man she loved, the other was her husband. Now that her husband's dead, I reckon the little lady is right wealthy. Everything he owned will go to her now."

"Good," the doctor answered. "She deserves it. Now help me get this man's shirt off, and the rest of you get going."

Harmony sat up in bed as Luke entered, his face drawn. He frowned at the sight of her swollen, discolored jaw. "Ma'am, you should see a doctor."

"I don't need one," she answered slowly, hardly opening her mouth. "Has it . . . happened?"

He nodded.

Her eyes teared, and he knew immediately who she truly loved. "Buck? He's . . . dead?"

He shook his head. "No, ma'am. It's your husband that's dead. Buck Hanner told the whole town what he

443

did, and then he beat your husband pretty good, only Buck took a pommeling himself. Then your husband, he grabbed somebody else's gun and tried to shoot Buck. Buck wasn't armed and when a man handed him a gun, he wouldn't shoot back. He told the crowd . . . they knew what Wade Tillis really deserved. I'm afraid the crowd was pretty ugly by then, ma'am. You know what they do to a man who steals someone else's gold or tricks people out of what belongs to them."

She closed her eyes, tears slipping down her cheeks. She nodded. In spite of what he'd done to her, she could not help but feel remorse over the fate of the man who had been her husband, the man who had shared her bed. There had been some good times in the marriage, a few tender moments, but not many, though she now knew Wade Tillis had only been putting on an act. She pressed her handkerchief to her mouth. "Buck?"

"He's in a bad way, ma'am. He'll be laid up at the doc's for a while."

"I see," Harmony said. "I'd like to be alone now, Luke."

The man nodded and turned to leave. "I'm sorry, ma'am," he said.

Sorry. A lot of people were sorry, none more sorry than she. Harmony was aware that she probably would own all of Wade Tillis' property now, but that didn't seem to matter. The ache in her heart would be with her for a long time. She loved Buck Hanner and she always would, but there was so much between them now. She needed time. They both needed time.

* * *

444

It was mid-October before Buck Hanner could leave the doctor's office on his own two feet. In his weakened condition the beating had taken quite a toll, and he'd been further depleted by the loss of blood from his neck wound. No one had seen Harmony Jones Tillis. She had not come to town. She had not attended her husband's funeral. She had not visited Buck Hanner. Her lawyer had gone to the house on the hill, but he'd told no one what had transpired there.

Buck did not ask for her. He knew that wouldn't be right, not now. How could she visit the man who had brought about her husband's hanging, despite the way Wade Tillis had treated her, and himself. He only hoped that in time they could again find what they'd had on the mountain. He still loved her, wanted her. He still dreamed of the ranch, Harmony at his side, her belly swollen with his child. His heart ached at the thought of the lost baby, and at the knowledge of what she'd suffered alone. They had both been through so much. They needed time before they could face each other again.

October was unusually hot, and fire watches were posted on the surrounding hills and mountains. It had been a dry summer. Buck saddled his horse, thinking perhaps he should just go away for a while. But he'd not go without seeing Harmony once more, no matter what anyone thought. As he headed out of town, several people watched, noticing he took the narrow road that led up to the Tillis mansion. Soon the town buzzed with excitement.

Buck had felt eyes on his back, and he was glad to get away from them. When he reached the house Wade Tillis and Harmony had occupied, he studied the sprawling veranda and the lovely gardens. Harmony Jones had accomplished a great deal since coming here. It seemed ironic that such an innocent could get involved in such a mess. He dismounted and tied his horse to a post; then he mounted the steps. His heart pounded with apprehension. What would she say? Perhaps she wouldn't talk to him. He knocked on the door, and a maid answered. She reddened slightly as she looked at the handsome man who stood before her, sensing who he was.

"Is Mrs. Tillis in?" he asked.

"I'm sorry, sir. She's gone."

His heart raced with with disappointment. "Gone? Gone where?"

The woman stepped through the doorway and pointed to Pike's Peak. "To the mountain, sir."

Buck frowned. "The mountain? Alone?"

"Yes, sir. She refused to take a guide, said she could find her own way and that she didn't want to be bothered."

Buck frowned, concerned. "When? When did she go?"

"Just a few days ago, sir. We tried to stop her, but she was determined. She can be quite stubborn, you know."

He looked up at the Peak. "How well I know," he muttered.

"Sir?"

He looked down at her.

"She's been real upset . . . since her husband's death, you know," the woman stated. "He hurt her pretty badly before that—hit her, I'm afraid—injured her jaw badly. She was real sad when she left, said something

446

about not caring about the money and the property—said it didn't matter if she died up there. I think you should go after her, sir."

To her surprise his eyes teared. "You didn't have to tell me to go," he said quietly. "Do you have some supplies around here, an extra horse perhaps, that I could pack some things on? It would save me some time, and I'd prefer the people in town don't know I'm going. Can you keep it quiet?"

The girl smiled. "Of course. Come with me. You can tell me what you'll need." She led him inside. "I like Miss Harmony," the girl was saying. "She was always good to me. Some people thought she was uppity and all, but I know she was just hurting way down inside. She was always kind of like a little girl—a scared little girl, you know?"

Buck's heart ached fiercely. "I know," he answered. "That's all she's ever been."

Harmony stretched, wondering if there was some way she could avoid going back to Cripple Creek. Her attorney could take care of the liquidation of her properties, and he could put the money into an account in her name. But she would not sell this place where she had known the only happiness she'd probably ever have. She was glad she had come here, proud that she had found the mine by herself. She had found strength here, in the little cabin that still stood on the site of the now-useless mine. The stamping mill was quiet now, but many things had changed. It hurt her to see that so many trees had been stripped away so the mill could be built. That spoiled the view she'd once had from the cabin. But the creek was still there, and the cabin had been used off and on so it was still intact. The window had been replaced. When she'd noticed that, she'd remembered the grizzly—and she'd remembered Buck Hanner's warm, reassuring arms. He had shot the grizzly, and they had celebrated—with whiskey. Then he had made a woman of her.

How she missed him! She knew now she had always missed him . . . and this place. It belonged to them, to a memory, to love. Here on the mountain it didn't matter what happened in the world below. This was a special world, and it was still beautiful, in spite of the mill. There were the green pines, the bubbling creek, and the lofty peak with its multicolored rock formations, a blue sky and puffy clouds above it.

She quickly dressed and went out, to be greeted by a sunny morning and the sound of singing birds. She picked up her rifle, realizing it was the same one Buck had taught her to fire when he'd first brought her up here. Her eyes teared, and she gently ran her fingers over the stock. Buck. He'd been so good to her, so patient. When things had gotten bad, he'd always been there to help. He'd been sweet and tender and good, but at the same time strong and sure and unafraid. When the breeze blew she caught a scent of pine, and it made her think of Buck's rugged, fresh scent. With Buck Hanner, only with Buck Hanner, she'd been a real woman. She'd known love and desire and passion. She'd been loved by a real man. She'd felt his power, she'd succumbed to that wonderful urge to submit to his strong but gentle hands. She had known the wonderful security of strong arms, the joy of giving and receiving and being one.

She buttoned her sweater and walked down to the creek, rifle in hand, remembering all the things Buck had taught her about survival. She had enough supplies for a week, perhaps two weeks. She wished now she'd brought more. She never wanted to leave this place. Here she could feel close to Buck. She could find the real Harmony Jones again. Here there were beautiful memories. There was peace. She no longer cared for wealth or power, and oddly enough, all her hurt was gone. She didn't even want to avenge herself on her parents. Here no one bothered her. There was no one to care whether she was rich or poor, to discuss her past or her future, and she didn't care. In fact, she thought, it might be pleasant to die up here.

She walked to the place where the creeks met and watched the splashing trout. She thought about vengeance, how it only hurt people. She felt responsible for Jimmie's death, and for Wade's, as well as for Buck's injuries. She had hurt people; she would have hurt her parents if she'd found them. She was glad now that she had not.

This was a good place for thinking, for sorting things out. It seemed odd that she could have been through so much and still be only twenty years old. She felt much older. Her life had been a tormented one ever since she'd been left on the docks of St. Louis, even before that, for her parents had never treated her well. It seemed that people had always used and abused her—all but one. Buck Hanner. Buck, she realized, had been the only truly caring person in her life, the only one she could depend on. But she'd spoiled that by being so quick to seek vengeance, by marrying Wade Tillis without knowing the real truth about Buck. She'd been so ready to believe Buck would leave her as everyone else she'd cared for had.

Perhaps it could never be the way it once was for them, but here she could be with him, in mind and heart and memory. This place was his . . . and hers. Here he had shot the grizzly, had taught her survival. Here he had nursed her after the grizzly attack, and she had nursed him after he'd been shot. She had actually taken a bullet out of him. That seemed to have happened such a long time ago, in another world, to another Harmony.

At least he had kissed her in the garden. Bruising as his kiss had been, surely it meant something. Someday, somehow, they would be together again. A rabbit bobbed up and perched on a rock nearby. She quietly raised the rifle and took aim. He'd make a good meal. She fired, hating to kill the innocent little animal but remembering that survival came first here. Buck would understand.

She stood up and walked over to the rabbit, picking it up and carrying it back up the hill to the cabin to skin it out. That done, she built a fire outside to roast the carcass, careful to clear away the pine needles and to encircle the fire with rocks, for everything was tinder dry. When the rabbit was roasting over the flames, she walked to the cabin steps and looked down at the maze of peaks and valleys, the miles and miles of rugged country that was Colorado.

She'd never go back to St. Louis. Maybe she'd never go back to Cripple Creek. This was a good place, her place. She was free here, free of prying eyes and whispers, of commitments, of decisions about money; free of servants and others who depended on her. And now, suddenly, she was refreshingly free of the thirst for vengeance. She felt she was a woman at last, the kind of woman Buck had wanted her to be in the first place. Now the thought of a sprawling ranch in some peaceful valley, with babies at her side, didn't sound so bad. What more could a woman want than a good man and life in her belly? She glanced at the little grave nearby, hardly noticeable except to her own eyes.

"I love you," she whispered. She looked out over the vast mountains then. "And I love you, Buck Hanner!" she shouted loudly, her eyes tearing. "I love you!"

Only the wind replied.

She slept peacefully, in spite of the lightning that pierced the night—there was no rain, only lightning and occasional thunder—and she awoke to a hungry stomach. She rose to put on some coffee, quickly dressing first. She had some rabbit left. She would eat it for breakfast.

She put the pot on the stove, then frowned when she heard strange popping noises in the distance. She went to the window, and high on a distant ridge she saw smoke.

"Oh, no!" she muttered. She studied if for a while. The wind was blowing in that direction, away from her mountain and the cabin. Perhaps there was no danger. She looked around the little cabin. She could not bear it if this place burned. She ran outside to get a better look at what was going on. The smoke was no closer. She watched the smoke for a long time; then she felt eyes on her. She turned to see the coyote, its yellow gaze fixed on her.

"Amber?" she said cautiously. The animal just stood there at the corner of the cabin. "Amber, is it really you?"

It watched her, not moving when she went back up the steps to get some of the rabbit and bring it out. She waved it at the coyote and it came a little closer, then took it from her and backed away a few feet. Her eyes teared. She'd always wondered what had happened to the animal, if the men had shot it. "Oh, Amber!" she said softly. It felt so good to see something from that special time, something alive that was a part of her stay on the mountain. The animal quickly ate the meat; then it sat down and just looked at her. "Amber," she said with affection. "At least you didn't desert me. You remembered."

When the wind changed slightly, the breeze picked up, and Amber got up and stood, whining and sniffing the air. A few birds flew overhead, calling out loudly, and some small animals skittered past. Now Harmony could smell smoke.

She turned to see fire and smoke coming downward. There was a loud explosive sound, and the wind carried a ball of fire right over to the next ridge. She watched in wonder as that ridge was suddenly ablaze. Amber whined again and darted off.

"Amber, wait!" she called. She was panic-stricken. Would the fire come to her ridge after all? The wind seemed to be rising and it was coming from all directions now. Light smoke drifted over the cabin, high in the sky. She looked around for the coyote, but he was gone. Suddenly the animal was the most important thing in the world to her. She turned and ran around the side of the cabin, calling for him. But he made no appearance. What if he ran into the forest and got lost? What if he got caught in the fire? No! Amber!

She ran farther into the trees. There was no fire near her, but she could hear it crackling and popping, feel heat on the wind, smell smoke. "Amber!" she called again. "Come this way! Come with me!" She ran deeper into the woods. "Please, God, make him come back!" she whimpered. Why did it matter so much that she find one wild coyote? Yet she felt that if something happened to Amber, she would have lost everything. He suddenly represented all that was Harmony Jones, the Harmony Jones she wanted to be. If Amber died, it seemed to her that Buck would die too, that he would never come back into her life. She kept calling to the coyote, until she realized she'd fled far from the cabin. The wind whipped around her in a sucking motion, pulling her hair up with it. It was terribly hot.

She looked back, but the path behind her was engulfed in flames. The cabin! Was that on fire? No! This was her special place! Nothing must happen to it. She turned to look upward again for Amber, but there was no sign of the animal. She ran back down the path. She must find the cabin! She must find it, and save some of her things—the rifle Buck had taught her to shoot with, her horse and gear. She ran blindly through thick smoke, screaming as burning branches began falling nearby. The cabin! Amber! No! This was her place, her special place! She ran and stumbled, beginning to choke on the black smoke now. How could a fire move so quickly? There were explosive sounds all around her now, as huge pines suddenly burst, like bombs, into flame. Her face was quickly blackened by smoke, and salty tears made white streaks through the smudges.

Amber! Poor Amber! Why had he run off? How would he survive? She was confused and afraid, but somehow she reached the cabin. Little flames licked at the roof.

"No! No!" she screamed. "Please don't burn!"

But in minutes the entire roof was ablaze. The rifle! She had to save that much! She ran inside, thick smoke greeting her when she opened the door. Fumbling through the smoke, she reached the rifle in the corner. It was hot, but she grasped it and made her way back to the door on her hands and knees. A piece of roofing fell in front of her and she screamed, quickly shoving it aside and scrambling for the door. She literally fell down the steps, the rifle rolling with her. Through tears of panic and sorrow, she untied her rearing horse and led him to the creek, where she fell to her knees and watched the cabin burn. For some reason she thought of the bed inside, the homemade bed with the rawhide strips for support, the bed she had shared with Buck Hanner. In it she had become a woman and had known true love.

She sat watching and crying, her body bruised and blackened. The horse reared unexpectedly, and when she lost her grip on the reins, the frightened animal bounded away.

She was alone, and all around her fire raged. She could feel its heat, but she no longer cared what happened to her. She hoped a tree would fall on her and kill her instantly. Amber was gone, her means of getting off the mountain was gone, and her little cabin was crumbling. Nearby the stamping mill was ablaze. To Harmony, the fire was an omen signifying that everything was over for her. She might as well die right here in the place she loved. She lay down on the ground beside the creek and closed her eyes.

How long she lay there, she wasn't sure. She'd drifted from time to time for she was exhausted. Then she heard her name spoken softly.

"Harmony." Someone turned her over and splashed cool water on her face. "Harmony, don't die on me!"

She opened her eyes to see sky-blue ones looking down at her, broad shoulders hovering over her. "Harmony, we've got to get to safety!"

She stared at him. Perhaps she had died, and was in heaven. "Buck?"

"It's all right. Everything will be all right now, Harmony. We'll go away together and start over. We can do it."

Tears spilled over her blackened face. Then she reached up, and in the next moment familiar, strong arms were around her, embracing her tightly. "Come with me, Harmony. Hurry."

"Buck, the cabin—"

"It's too late. Come on."

He kept a powerful arm around her and quickly untied his own skittish mount, holding the reins tightly as he hurried with her along the creek, keeping to the water and leading his horse. "I know a place where we'll be safe," he was saying.

It didn't matter. Buck was here. Of course he knew a place that was safe. Buck Hanner always knew what to do. Flaming branches fell around them, but she wasn't afraid. She stumbled on blindly beside him, as he led her to the place where the waters met and pushed her into a little cove. The rocks formed an arch there, and the water rushed through it. Beneath the rocks it was cooler, and she was sheltered from falling debris. He let go of her then.

"I'm taking my horse to an archway of rock not far from here," he told her. "You stay put."

"No!" she screamed. "Don't go away again!"

He touched her face. "It's all right, Shortcake. I'll be right back." As he left her, she screamed his name, but her voice was lost to the rushing waters and the roaring flames. Several minutes later he was back, just as he had promised. He knelt in the little cove and pulled her close, and she embraced him gratefully.

"Buck, our cabin! We have to have the cabin!"

"We don't have to have anything but each other," he told her, kissing her golden hair. "We've never needed anything more, Harmony. Not the money or anything else."

"Buck!" She looked up at his handsome face. "You're really here!"

He searched her eyes. "Here to stay, if you want me."

Tears streamed down her cheeks, and she could taste their salt. "Want you? I've always wanted you, even when I thought I hated you! I . . . I came up here because in this place I could feel close to you. I was going to stay here forever . . . and never go back! I thought you didn't want me anymore."

He smiled that familiar, handsome smile. "Why do you think I went through all that hell to get back here? There were times when it would have been much easier to die, Harmony." He lightly kissed her mouth. "I was so scared when I saw the fire this morning. It was heading right for your area. I about broke my neck to get here in time."

456

"Buck, I didn't know! It was so easy for me to think you'd left me—"

He put a finger to her lips. "It's all over, Harmony. We've both been through hell. But it didn't change our love. That's all that matters."

She sobbed. "But how can you love me now, after what I did?"

"I understand you better than you realize, Short-cake. You've just got to learn there comes a time when you trust someone or you don't." He kissed her eyes. "My God, Harmony, I could never have survived without being able to picture your face and remember you in my arms. I needed the memory of that winter up here on the mountain."

"Oh, Buck!" She wept against his chest. How wonderful it was to be able to lean on him again, to feel his arms around her. He still loved her! He was here! Whenever she'd really needed him, he'd come.

"How about the ranch, Harmony? Will you go with me, marry me, have my babies?"

"You know I will," she replied quickly. "I'd go with you to hell and back. Just don't ever go away without me again—not ever!"

"I won't. I promise." He kissed her hair again. "God, I was so afraid I'd get here too late."

She snuggled against him, both of them sitting in the welcome coolness of the water. "I was going to lie down and die," she told him. "I just didn't care anymore."

He squeezed her tightly. "You shouldn't have felt that way, Harmony, but it's over now. We'll go back and get a wagon, and load up your personal belongings, and then we'll leave Cripple Creek. We'll go someplace new, start a ranch."

"But first we'll be married," she said, raising her face to look into his eyes and assure herself that he was really with her.

Their eyes held, and passion swept through her, the old, wonderful, passion that only Buck Hanner could elicit from her. "First we'll be married," he answered. "I'll make it all up to you, Harmony. I'm so sorry about the baby."

"It was probably better," she answered. "But I knew, Buck. I knew when I lost it how much I'd love a baby. I want more. I'm not afraid to have children now."

He smiled that provocative smile. "Good. Because you might be pregnant quite often, little girl. It will take me a long time to get enough of you, if I ever do."

His lips touched hers, and the fire he brought to her veins seemed hotter than the fire that raged around them. She pressed herself against him as he leaned against a rock, his strong arms enveloping her and assuring her of love and protection. No. Buck Hanner would not leave her. Not Buck. And they would not leave this place, not truly. It would be with them forever, in their hearts and memories. No matter what happened to this mountain, it would always belong to them. The cabin was not gone. It was still standing, in their mind. They would remember it and those days on the mountain where they had learned to love.

She was lost in him now, oblivious to the light whining sound outside the arch. Amber pawed at the water, smelling her scent and knowing Harmony was inside. But she was with someone and seemed very occupied. A rabbit flashed by, and the coyote rushed off into the now smoldering woods. After all, he had a family to feed.

SWEET MEDICINE'S PROPHECY
by Karen A. Bale

#1: SUNDANCER'S PASSION (1778, $3.95)

Stalking Horse was the strongest and most desirable of the tribe, and Sun Dancer surrounded him with her spell-binding radiance. But the innocence of their love gave way to passion—and passion, to betrayal. Would their relationship ever survive the ultimate sin?

#2: LITTLE FLOWER'S DESIRE (1779, $3.95)

Taken captive by savage Crows, Little Flower fell in love with the enemy, handsome brave Young Eagle. Though their hearts spoke what they could not say, they could only dream of what could never be. . . .

#3: WINTER'S LOVE SONG (1780, $3.95)

The dark, willowy Anaeva had always desired just one man: the half-breed Trenton Hawkins. But Trenton belonged to two worlds—and was torn between two women. She had never failed on the fields of war; now she was determined to win on the battleground of love!

#4: SAVAGE FURY (1768, $3.95)

Aeneva's rage knew no bounds when her handsome mate Trent commanded her to tend their tepee as he rode into danger. But under cover of night, she stole away to be with Trent and share whatever perils fate dealt them.

THE BESTSELLING ECSTASY SERIES
by Janelle Taylor

SAVAGE ECSTASY (824, $3.50)

It was like lightning striking, the first time the Indian brave Gray Eagle looked into the eyes of the beautiful young settler Alisha. And from the moment he saw her, he knew that he must possess her — and make her his slave!

DEFIANT ECSTASY (931, $3.50)

When Gray Eagle returned to Fort Pierre's gate with his hundred warriors behind him, Alisha's heart skipped a beat: Would Gray Eagle destroy her — or make his destiny her own?

FORBIDDEN ECSTASY (1014, $3.50)

Gray Eagle had promised Alisha his heart forever — nothing could keep him from her. But when Alisha woke to find her red-skinned lover gone, she felt abandoned and alone. Lost between two worlds, desperate and fearful of betrayal, Alisha, hungered for the return of her FORBIDDEN ECSTASY.

BRAZEN ECSTASY (1133, $3.50)

When Alisha is swept down a raging river and out of her savage brave's life, Gray Eagle must rescue his love again. But Alisha has no memory of him at all. And as she fights to recall a past love, another white slave woman in their camp is fighting for Gray Eagle.

TENDER ECSTACY (1212, $3.75)

Bright Arrow is committed to kill every white he sees — until he sets his eyes on ravishing Rebecca. And fate demands that he capture her, torment . . . and soar with her to the dizzying heights of TENDER ECSTASY.

STOLEN ECSTASY (1621, $3.95)

In this long-awaited sixth volume of the SAVAGE ECSTASY series, lovely Rebecca Kenny defies all for her true love, Bright Arrow. She fights with all her passion to be his lover — never his slave. Share in Rebecca and Bright Arrow's savage pleasure as they entwine in moments of STOLEN ECSTASY.

Available wherever paperbacks are sold, or order direct from the Publisher. Send cover price plus 50¢ per copy for mailing and handling to Zebra Books, Dept. 1889, 475 Park Avenue South, New York, N.Y. 10016. Residents of New York, New Jersey and Pennsylvania must include sales tax. DO NOT SEND CASH.

CAPTIVATING ROMANCE
by Penelope Neri

CRIMSON ANGEL (1783, $3.95)

No man had any right to fluster lovely Heather simply because he was so impossibly handsome! But before she could slap the arrogant captain for his impudence, she was a captive of his powerful embrace, his one and only *Crimson Angel*.

PASSION'S BETRAYAL (1568, $3.95)

Sensuous Promise O'Rourke had two choices: to spend her life behind bars—or endure one night in the prison of her captor's embrace. She soon found herself fettered by the chains of love, forever a victim of *Passion's Betrayal*.

HEARTS ENCHANTED (1432, $3.75)

Lord Brian Fitzwarren vowed that somehow he would claim the irresistible beauty as his own. Maegan instinctively knew that from that moment their paths would forever be entwined, their lives entangled, their *Hearts Enchanted*.

BELOVED SCOUNDREL (1799, $3.95)

Instead of a street urchin, the enraged captain found curvaceous Christianne in his arms. The golden-haired beauty fought off her captor with all her strength—until her blows become caresses, her struggles an embrace, and her muttered oaths moans of pleasure.

Available wherever paperbacks are sold, or order direct from the Publisher. Send cover price plus 50¢ per copy for mailing and handling to Zebra Books, Dept. 1889, 475 Park Avenue South, New York, N.Y. 10016. Residents of New York, New Jersey and Pennsylvania must include sales tax. DO NOT SEND CASH.

MORE SEARING ROMANCE
by Elaine Barbieri

MYSTERIES
By Mary Roberts Rinehart

THE CIRCULAR STAIRCASE   (1723, $3.50)
Rachel Innes became convinced that her summer house was haunted, and the explosion of a revolver along with a body at the bottom of the circular staircase ensured she would have many sleepless nights. She had acquired a taste for sleuthing and her niece and nephew were prime suspects in the murder.

THE HAUNTED LADY   (1685, $3.50)
When wealthy Eliza Fairbanks claimed to have found bats in her bedroom and arsenic on her strawberries, Miss Pinkerton was promptly assigned the case. But apparently someone else was watching too. For the old lady's worries were over, but so was her life.

THE SWIMMING POOL   (1686, $3.50)
With a deadline to meet on her detective story, Lois had no patience with her sister's strange behavior. Except the mystery Lois was writing was not nearly as deadly as the mystery about to unfold. For ravishing, willful Judith was about to disappear from her locked bedroom, and a woman's body would be found in the crystal blue depths of the Swimming Pool.

LOST ECSTASY   (1791, $3.50)
When Tom was arrested for a not-so-ordinary murder, Kay's life turned upside down. She was willing to put her own life in danger to help Tom prove himself, and to save him from those out to silence him or those after revenge.

MISS PINKERTON   (1847, $3.50)
Old Miss Juliet had endured quite a shock when her nephew committed suicide and her nurse, Hilda Adams, was determined to keep an eye on her. But the old lady wasn't as frail as she looked, and Hilda wasn't sure if she had murder or suicide on her hands.

Available wherever paperbacks are sold, or order direct from the Publisher. Send cover price plus 50¢ per copy for mailing and handling to Zebra Books, Dept. 1889, 475 Park Avenue South, New York, N.Y. 10016. Residents of New York, New Jersey and Pennsylvania must include sales tax. DO NOT SEND CASH.